THE
BANDIT QUEENS

ABOUT THE AUTHOR

PARINI SHROFF received her MFA from the University of Texas at Austin, where she studied under Elizabeth McCracken, Alexander Chee, and Cristina García. She is a practicing attorney and currently lives in the Bay Area. *The Bandit Queens* is her debut novel.

THE
BANDIT
QUEENS

PARINI SHROFF

ALLEN&UNWIN

First published in 2023 in the United States by Ballantine Books, an imprint of Random House, a division of Penguin Random House LLC, New York.

Published in hardback and trade paperback in Great Britain in 2023 by Allen & Unwin, an imprint of Atlantic Books Ltd.

10 9 8 7 6 5 4

A CIP catalogue record for this book is available from the British Library.

Hardback ISBN: 978 1 83895 714 8
Trade paperback ISBN: 978 1 83895 715 5
E-book ISBN: 978 1 83895 716 2

Book design by Susan Turner

Printed in Great Britain

Allen & Unwin, an imprint of Atlantic Books Ltd
Ormond House, 26–27 Boswell Street
London WC1N 3JZ

www.atlantic-books.co.uk

To Arthur, my navigator: Nevada-1-2-1-Papa-Papa

ONE

The women were arguing. The loan officer was due to arrive in a few hours, and they were still missing two hundred rupees. Rather, Farah and her two hundred rupees were missing. The other four women of their loan group had convened, as they did every Tuesday, to aggregate their respective funds.

"Where is she?" Geeta asked.

No one answered. Instead, the women pieced their respective Farah sightings into a jigsaw of gossip that, to Geeta's ears at least, failed to align. Saloni—a woman whose capacity for food was exceeded only by her capacity for venom—goaded most of the conversation.

"This isn't the first time," Priya said.

"And you know it won't be the last," Saloni finished.

When Preity mentioned she was fairly certain she'd seen Farah buying hashish, Geeta felt it best to nudge them to more prosaic matters. "Varunbhai is not going to like this."

"Well, now we know where her money's going," Priya said.

"Some devout Muslim." Saloni sniffed, the gesture dainty for a woman of her size. Lately she'd been attempting to rebrand her weight as evidence of her community status. Compounded with her preternatural talent for bullying, this guise worked on the women. But Geeta had known Saloni and her family since childhood—when she ruled the playground rather than their loan group—and could accurately attribute her heft to genetics betraying her in her thirtieth year rather than any posh mark of affluence. Ironic, considering Saloni had spent her first nineteen years perpetually malnourished, thin as paper, and just as prone to cut. She'd married well, curving into a stunning woman who'd reclaimed her slim figure after her firstborn, but hadn't managed the same after the second.

Geeta listened to their rumors, observed how the women contributed and piled on, with clinical interest. This must've been the way they'd whispered about her after Ramesh left—a fallen woman "mixed with dirt"—then shushing each other when she approached, their lips peeling into sympathetic smiles as sincere as political promises. But now, five years after her husband's disappearance, Geeta found herself within the fold rather than shunned, thanks to Farah's absence. It was a dubious honor.

Her fingers toyed with her ear. When she used to wear earrings, she would often check to make sure the backs were secure. The sharp but benign prick of the stud against her thumb had been reassuring. The habit lingered even after Ramesh vanished and she'd stopped wearing jewelry altogether—no nose ring, no bangles, no earrings.

Tired of the gossip, she interrupted the women's musings on Farah's defection: "If each of us puts in another fifty, we can still give Varunbhai the full amount."

That got their attention. The room quieted. Geeta heard the feeble hum of her fan stirring the air. The flywheel's tight circles oscillated like a tiny hula hoop. The blades were ornamental; the heat remained thick and unforgiving. The fan hung from a strong cord Ramesh had tied in their old house. It'd been early in their marriage, so when he'd stumbled on the ladder, it had been okay to laugh—he'd even joined her. Rage hadn't found Ramesh until their second year together, after her parents passed away. When she'd been forced to move into this smaller home, she'd tied the cord herself.

A lizard darted up the wall in a diagonal before hiding in the lintel's shadow. Geeta's mother used to tell her not to be afraid, that they brought good luck. She itched to see it plop from the dark pocket onto one of the women—preferably Saloni who was terrified of all animals except, inexplicably, spiders. The other two—sisters Priya and Preity—were neither kind nor cruel, but they deferred to their leader. Geeta could sympathize, having herself once served under Saloni.

"No way," Saloni said. "It's Farah's problem."

Geeta stared at the dark wall, willing the lizard to be a good sport. Nothing. "It's *our* problem," she snapped. "If we default, Varunbhai won't give us another loan next year." The women were somber; everyone knew the center extended loans to groups, not individuals.

Then began a communal metamorphosis from fishwives to martyrs: the women spilled their excuses onto each other, all pushy contestants in a competition with no judge to rule as to who was the most aggrieved party.

"I have to buy my kids' schoolbooks. They keep getting more expensive." Saloni's lips compressed. "But it's such a gift to be a mother."

"We just bought another buffalo. My kids guzzle so much milk. I keep telling them 'if you're thirsty, drink water!'" Preity coughed. "But still, they bring me joy."

"My boy needs medicine for his ear infection. He cries *all the time*." Priya hurried to add, "But there's no better blessing than a son."

"Joys of motherhood," they murmured.

"Such a privilege, na?"

Preity and Priya were twins, formerly identical. The scars across Preity's face and neck shimmered like heat when she toggled her head in agreement.

"What about you, Geetaben?" Saloni asked. Her upper arms were plump and wide, straining against her sari blouse's sleeves, but they then abruptly transitioned to the trim elbows and forearms of her youth. The two halves could've easily belonged to separate people.

"Well, I don't have the joys of motherhood," Geeta said after the women were emptied of excuses. Her voice was patient, but her smile was feral. "But I do have the joys of sleep and money."

No one laughed. The women looked at the ceiling, the fan, each other, the door, anywhere but at her. Geeta had long ago released the idea that one needed eye contact in order to feel seen. She'd grown accustomed to their discomfort around her; people didn't like being reminded that what you'd lost, they took for granted—though Geeta no longer felt like Ramesh had robbed her of anything by leaving. There were times she wanted to tell the women that they could keep their blood-sucking husbands, that she harbored no envy, coveted no part of their messy, small lives. It was true she no longer had friends, but she did have freedom.

Another lizard skittered along the wall. While Geeta appreciated luck as much as anyone, she had no use for two lizards. It was said that if you happened across two lizards mating, you'd meet an old friend. If you saw them quarreling, you'd pick a fight with a friend instead.

"I'll pay," she told the women, as she reached for the grass broom she kept in the corner. "I don't have children, I don't have a husband and I don't have a buffalo." She tickled the ceiling corner with the *jhadu*'s stiff bristles. When that failed to cajole the lizards, she thumped the wall twice.

Someone gasped at the loud sound. Priya scooted behind Saloni's larger frame as though Geeta were a threat. Which many assumed she was: a *churel* who, depending on the gossiper, gobbled children, rendered women barren or men impotent. That a woman had to have perished in order to return as a *churel* did little to staunch the village's rumors.

Saloni blotted her upper lip with the back of her wrist. Fresh sweat bloomed quickly. She glared and Geeta could easily recall her at fourteen—slender and haughty as she held court, hip jutting against a bicycle while the boys sighed.

The lizard finally dropped from above—alas, missing Saloni's disdainful face—and scrambled for its bearings. With the broom, Geeta slapped the floor, herding it toward the open entrance.

"Right," Saloni said. "So we agree: Geetaben will cover it. You'll settle it with Farahben later, correct." It was not a question.

Given Saloni's stamp of oppressive approval, the others did not even pretend to mew or protest. Saloni's social weight was as robust as her physical. Her father-in-law was the head of the *panchayat*, the village council. Five years ago, when the government demanded their village observe the reservation system and elect a woman to fill one of the five council seats, Saloni was the obvious choice. In fact, these pre-loan meetings were usually conducted at Saloni's house, but this week Geeta's empty home had been selected for reasons no one had bothered explaining to her.

The twins stared at Geeta, wary, as though she were the death goddess Kali and her broom a sickle. She knew they were thinking of Ramesh, what had allegedly become of him at her hands. And just like that, she was no longer a part of the pack; they avoided her gaze and her touch as they handed her their money on their way out. Saloni alone met her eyes, and though Geeta recognized the scorn as easily as she would her own face, at least it was some manner of acknowledgment. A response, however negative, to the space Geeta occupied in this world, in their village, in their community.

She slammed the door shut after the three of them. "No, no," she muttered effusively to no one. "Thank *you*."

———

Farah visited that evening, wilted and scared, bearing a gourd as a gift. Her left eye was swollen shut, a tight pistil amidst a purple bloom. Geeta made it a point not to stare as Farah thrust the long green vegetable toward her.

"What's this?"

Farah waggled the vegetable until Geeta took it. "You can't show up to someone's house empty-handed, everyone knows that. Saloniben came by my place. She said you covered for me. Thank you. She said I should work out an interest rate with you for—"

"Saloni's a bitch." Farah blinked at the language. "I only have one question," Geeta said, leaning against her doorframe. She thumped one end of the gourd against her palm like a nightstick. That she should invite her guest inside was not lost on her.

Farah fidgeted. "I'll pay you as soon—"

"Navratri just ended, so I know you had plenty of new dress orders." Farah's bent head nodded. "And I think we both know who did that to your face."

"I don't hear a question, Geetaben." Farah's hands cupped her opposite elbows, the movement further rounding her already stooped back.

"What're you going to do when he takes the money again?"

She closed her eyes. "I don't know."

"What's he doing with it?"

"Karembhai." Farah sighed.

Geeta knew Karem; so had her husband. Karem sold his dead wife's spectacularly ugly costume jewelry out of a small shop. That business was hardly thriving, but his bootleg liquor sales fed his litter of children. "If some of the other women complained to their husbands, maybe they could confront your husband."

"No!" Farah's thick eyebrows rose and her good eye stretched open in fear, making its swollen sister appear smaller. The image was so disturbing, Geeta focused on Farah's collarbone instead.

"No, please," Farah repeated. "He'd be so angry. And anyway, I doubt you could convince the other women—I'm not exactly their favorite."

This bit of news surprised Geeta, who'd assumed she was the only outsider in their loan group. She sighed. "Can you hide some of your money away from home? Or just lie about what you're making?"

"I thought of that last week, after I missed those other payments." Farah swallowed and Geeta watched the walnut of her throat retreat and return. She pointed to her split lip. "But he found out." She shuffled forward. "May I come in?"

Geeta asked, "Why?" even as she stepped aside. Farah removed her sandals, and Geeta noticed her shoulder blades protruding from her thin blouse like nascent wings.

Geeta did not offer her a place to sit, or a glass of water. A guest was to be treated like God, but Farah was not her guest; and while Geeta went to the temple about three times a year, she wasn't the serial supplicant her mother had been.

The two women stood barefoot in the middle of Geeta's single-roomed home. Farah moved closer and Geeta, alarmed, took a step back. It upset her, that intimate liberty, as though she were this woman's confidante. They were not friends—covering the payment had been a necessity, not a kindness. And yet Farah had latched on to the gesture with the desperation of a neglected dog.

Geeta suddenly wanted to tell her to retain some pride. To withhold parts of herself because there were plenty of people like her husband waiting to pilfer what they could. It was unlike Geeta, not only to intrude in others' affairs, but also to offer advice. Advice was a cousin of caring; apathy was Geeta's mantra.

But then Farah said: "Y-you must remember how hard it is. Rameshbhai went to Karem all the time before . . ." and any desire to counsel the woman vanished. Farah trailed off due to some sense of belated tact, but the damage was already done, and stopping short was just lazy. Various endings to her abandoned sentence whipped around the room like detached lizard tails, all echoes of the gossip that had consumed their village on the heels of Ramesh's disappearance. *Before she'd sprinkled crushed glass in his food, before she'd used her fangs to desiccate him into a husk, before she'd chopped up his body and fed it to the dogs.*

"Yes," Geeta finally said. "Before." It was past time for Farah to leave, and Geeta itched to shut the door on Farah's swollen, judgmental eye and her presumptuous camaraderie.

But she pressed on. "I need your help—a favor."

It was a bold move, enough to surprise Geeta, which in turn cadged a bit of begrudging respect from her as well. "Piling on, are we? Well, I don't have any more money for you."

"No, I mean, I think I know how to stop him."

"Good," Geeta said. "You do that. Then you can pay me back."
She herded her unwanted guest toward the door as she had the lizard
earlier, all but thumping a broom at Farah's chapped heels.

"No, wait." Farah sidestepped deeper into the room. Geeta sighed.
"You stopped Ramesh. He drank and he hit you, I know he did. I saw.
We all did."

"You all did," Geeta repeated. "But nobody did anything about
it."

Farah's head lowered, diffident once more. "It was a family
matter."

Geeta nodded her agreement. "Yes, and so is this. Good luck, Farahben." The respectful suffix of "sister" was not required as Geeta
was elder. However, she took comfort in the distance it created. She
reached for her door handle.

"Just teach me!" Farah burst out, more hyper than Geeta had ever
seen her. Her good eye was manic with possibility. "I can stop Samir,
too. I just need to know how you did it, how you got away with it."

"And by stop him, you mean you want to—"

"Kill him!" Farah said, her voice far too loud. She chopped one
hand on the opposite's palm with a meaty thunk. "Get rid of him.
Take him out. Give him a dog's death." She clicked her tongue as her
thumb sliced across her throat.

Geeta gaped at her. "Have *you* been buying from Karem?"

"Of course not!" Farah took deep umbrage, as though *that* prospect was morally repugnant. She was breathing heavily, too fast and
nearly hiccuping. She fanned her face.

"Calm down," Geeta instructed.

Farah nodded while hyperventilating, and began muttering with
one long breath. *"Kabaddi, kabaddi, kabaddi . . ."*

Geeta stared. "The fuck're you doing?"

Farah's breathing steadied. "It helps me breathe deeper. You know?
Like the game?" She shrugged. "Whenever I get stressed or scared, it
soothes me. It's, like, my mantra."

"Your mantra is *'kabaddi.'*"

"I know it's a little odd, but—"

"No, *you're* a little odd. *That's* super weird."

Geeta inhaled. This meeting—which should've been a brief *ThankyouGeetaben–WhateverFarah* one-off—had derailed into insanity. That Geeta had even allowed it to get this far spoke of an unusual loss of control—was she really so starved for company that she'd indulged Farah's madness? She smoothed wayward strands of hair against her crown and spoke calmly, "You have no idea what you're saying, Farah. You're not the Bandit Queen that you can run around killing men as you please. Go home and think of something else."

"I *have* thought about this!" Farah said, her hands clenched into fists, the thumbs tucked in like little turtles. A child on the verge of a tantrum after being dismissed by the adults as adorable but untethered to reality. "If I don't get rid of him, I'll lose the loan and the business. Or, Ya'Allah, I could end up like poor Runiben." She shuddered. Even Geeta instinctively gulped at the mention of the unfortunate woman who'd once been a part of their loan group.

"He's the father of your children; think of what this would do to them."

"I'm doing this *for* my children, not *to* them. You don't know the things he's capable of. He—" She exhaled. "I think if it were just me, I could handle it. But I can't be everywhere at once, and there's three of them, and sometimes I—" She blinked. "Not that I'm complaining."

"Of course not."

"No, obviously, *obviously* I love the—"

And here Geeta chimed in, too: "Joys of motherhood."

Farah closed her eyes as though receiving a benediction. "So rewarding. But, Geetaben, everyone is better off without him. Me, the kids. Our loan group. Please," she begged, pressing her palms together. "Remove my nose ring." Though it was a figure of speech Geeta hadn't heard for many years, she understood Farah's plea: *Make a widow out of me.*

Geeta crossed her arms over her chest. "Two men disappearing in one village won't go unnoticed. What would you tell the police?"

Farah bobbed up and down, practically airborne with hope. Her enthusiasm was pathetic. "We'll leave the body for them to find. It'll look like an accident. Besides, Ramesh was what, five years ago now?"

"An accident? Where are your brains? What, he tripped and fell onto a knife a couple of times? He shot himself with a gun he doesn't own?"

"Okay fine, I don't have *all* the details sorted yet. That's where you come in! We'll do what you did, only we'll make it look like an accident."

"'We'?" Geeta held her hands up, palms out. She stepped back. "I'm not with you."

"Yes, yes you are." An odd calm spread over Farah's bruised features. Her shoulders relaxed and her voice lowered. Dignity uncurled her spine and seemed to elongate her limbs; the transformation unnerved Geeta. "The others will expect you to keep covering for me if Samir keeps stealing from me. Think about it. You're the only one without a family to take care of. But if we end up losing the loan, you're the only one without a family to take care of *you*." Farah crept closer. "So it is 'we.'"

Her logic was immaculate; she had only spoken the truth. But Farah's sudden, clever bravery inspired Geeta's resentment. "Keep your filmy dialogues to yourself and get the hell out of my house."

Then Farah slumped, exhausted, and Geeta recognized her once again. "Please, Geetaben."

"No."

Farah left as she'd arrived: head lowered, back falcate as though the evening air presented too much of a burden. Watching her leave, Geeta felt an unexpected urge to call her back. Not to capitulate to her batty plan, but to make tea and talk about the terrifying loneliness and loathing that accompanied the black eyes and broken ribs. Then Geeta remembered that Farah was walking home to her family. And the urge cured itself.

TWO

While Geeta regarded herself as a self-made woman, she was not, in fact, a self-made widow. Contrary to neighborhood chatter, she did not "remove her own nose ring" by killing Ramesh. She never had any desire to destroy him, just *parts* of him. The part that drowned himself in drink, the part that was quick to fury but slow to forgive, the part that blamed her for their childlessness, though it could've just as easily been him. But little was monochromatic in marriage and even in abuse, because there were other parts, too, parts she'd loved, parts that, when she wasn't vigilant, still drew drops of unwilling tenderness from her.

But missing Ramesh now was more habit than compulsion; the memories she had felt like someone else's—all soft focus and cinematic. Like when his parents first came to inspect her suitability, and he'd saved her skin by properly roasting a papadam for her. How, for the first year of their marriage, he'd slept with one hand on her shoulder, her hip, her stomach. The time he'd tried to teach her how to whistle with her fingers. The way he'd laughed, his eyes folding at the corners as she failed, spittle shining on her chin and hands.

But there were other things Ramesh had taught Geeta, too: how not to interrupt him, how not to oversalt his food, how to correctly apologize in the event she failed at the aforementioned (*You're right, I'm wrong, I'm sorry*), how to be slapped and not cry out. How to feed them on half a typical budget because he'd siphon their money to Karem and still demand a proper dinner.

She no longer needed such lessons. In the time after Ramesh left, Geeta blamed first herself, then Karem. She associated him with the smell of her husband's bootleg alcohol: sweet yet repulsive, cloying as it enveloped the bed, the house, her. She wondered whether Farah ever felt suffocated by the stench. Did she, too, learn to breathe through her mouth? There was that pesky urge again, the desire to share and listen, to compare survivor notes with Farah.

If she was this lonely, Geeta berated herself, she should get a damn dog.

Ramesh hadn't possessed the decency to leave after a huge row; no, he absconded after a cloudless Tuesday evening—she didn't interrupt him once, the *undhiyu* was not salty, he peppered her jawline with kisses before bed and she'd fallen asleep smiling. Like a goddamn idiot. His final blow: sneaking away and leaving only his debts and her dusty womb, so that everyone took turns whispering as to which terrible vice of hers had driven him away. That is, until Ramesh didn't send for the rest of his belongings, or lay claim to their house. Even his elder brother, who lived in a bungalow a few cities away and took care of their parents, was unable to contact him. Then the whispers shifted toward foul play. Ramesh was clearly dead, there was no other explanation.

The police descended with their questions and unsubtle hints that they could be paid to focus on another case. Upon realizing Geeta had little to either her married or maiden name, they scampered away. The village, however, remained unconvinced of her clean chit, and gave her the wide berth bestowed to any social pariah. There were rumors she was a *churel* of old folklore: a witch roaming on reversed feet, targeting men for revenge, her twisted footprints ensuring they ran toward her rather than away.

To the village, she became a disease, her name a slur. She was, as the idiom went, "mixed with dirt." To now say, with the acclimation five years afforded, that it had not been humiliating would be a lie. Once, early on, when she was still naïve enough to believe not everything had changed with Ramesh's defection, she'd paid a visit to her favorite second aunt, a spinster. After Geeta knocked on the green door, its paint flaking to piebald, a shower of rotting potato peels, tomato offal and eggshells, among other wet waste, tumbled over her. Geeta looked up to see her Deepa-aunty, her wrinkles and loathing framed by the second-story window, holding an empty pail and instructing Geeta to leave and take her shame with her.

She complied, while the neighbors tittered, her hair matted with tea dregs. On the walk home, for courage, she thought of the Bandit Queen, and the stories Geeta had compiled of her life from the radio and newspapers, though the accounts often contradicted each other. Born in 1963 as simply Phoolan Mallah, a Dalit girl in a small village, she'd been eleven when she vehemently protested her cousin's theft of her family's land. The cousin beat her unconscious with a brick. In order to send her away and out of trouble, her parents married her to a thirty-three-year-old man. He'd beaten and raped her, but when she ran away, the village sent her right back to him and his abusive second wife. When she was sixteen, the same diabolical cousin arranged for her to be thrown in jail for the first (but not last) time. She spent three days being beaten and raped in jail at her cousin's behest. Soon after, she ran to or was kidnapped by—accounts varied—a gang of armed robbers known as dacoits. If Phoolan could not only survive but escape and exact savage revenge on her tormentors, then surely Geeta could walk home while people stared at the rancid rinds hanging from her neck.

Eventually, she taught herself to enjoy the perks of ostracism, as she imagined Phoolan would've done. The upsides of being a childless *churel*-cum-murderess: raucous kids never played *kabaddi* near her house (*She'll gobble you like a peeled banana!*), vendors rarely haggled with her (*She can bankrupt you with one blink!*), some of Ramesh's creditors even left her alone (*She'll curse your wife with nothing but stillborns!*). Then the microfinancers came around, offering low-interest loans. City people were hell-bent on helping them—women only, please—acquire independence and income.

Hell yes, Geeta had thought, and signed her name. She'd first eaten her father's salt, then her husband's; it was time to eat her own. After Ramesh left, money's importance had suddenly rivaled oxygen's. With the first cash installment, she walked three hours to Kohra and bought beads and thread in bulk. She scavenged a wobbly desk and pinned a grainy photograph of the Bandit Queen above her workspace to remind her that if she was indeed "mixed with dirt," then at least she was in fine company.

At first, sales were nil. Superstitious brides, it turned out, weren't keen on wearing black magic wedding necklaces cursed by a self-made widow. But after two short-lived weddings where the brides were sent back to their natal homes, the village's superstitions swung in her favor. If one did not petition a Geeta's Designs *mangalsutra*, one's marriage would last about as long as the bridal henna did.

She wasn't respected here, but she was feared, and fear had been very kind to Geeta. Things were good, *freedom* was good, but Geeta had witnessed that survival was contingent upon two hard rules: 1) take on only one loan, and 2) spend it on the work. It was an easy trap to sign for multiple microloans and then buy a house or a television set. Poor, myopic Runi had taken on three loans for her tobacco-leaf-rolling business but had spent it on her son's education instead. Then the money and her son were gone and, just like that, so was Runi.

Farah's unwelcome visit had delayed Geeta's planned errands. The sky darkened under twilight's thumb as she closed her front door, but Geeta still needed vegetables and some grain to be ground. Her empty jute bag scratched the exposed strip of skin between where her sari blouse ended and her petticoat began. Purple and white onion sheddings lined the bag's bottom. As she walked, she shook it upside down and the crispy skin trailed behind her, joining festival decorations that were now rubbish—tinsel, broken *dandiya* sticks in various colors, bright wrappers—on the dirt.

The festival of Navratri had ended in late September; for nine dance-filled nights, the village had celebrated various goddesses. Although she never attended any of the *garba* dance parties, Geeta's favorite story was of the goddess Durga's triumph over Mahishasura, a power-drunk demon with the head of a buffalo. He'd been granted a boon that he could not be killed by any man, god or animal. Various gods tried to defeat Mahishasura to no avail. Desperate, they combined their powers to create Durga. She set off on her tiger and confronted Mahishasura, who arrogantly offered to marry her instead. After fifteen days of fighting, Durga beheaded him. It tickled Geeta: never send a god to do a goddess's job.

She passed the local school. It'd been orange when she'd attended, but the sun had since blanched it into a pale yellow. Tobacco stains the color of rust streaked the walls; kids and men often held spitting contests behind the building. Government slogans, for a clean India or encouraging only two children per family, were stenciled in neat bubble letters on walls. Others were less official: sloppy red warnings against love jihad or Bihari migrant workers stealing jobs. In a village with two Muslim families and zero migrant workers, Geeta found these warnings absurd.

Now a few children played *kabaddi* in the dirt yard, which made Geeta think of Farah yet again. One team's raider sucked in a deep breath before invading the other half of the makeshift court as he chanted, *"Kabaddi, kabaddi, kabaddi."* The raider was meant to tag the other team's defenders and make it back home without being tackled, all in a single breath. Geeta was already late, but still paused as a dispute arose.

"You inhaled!" a girl shouted to the raider. She and the other defenders were in a W formation, holding hands. In a village this cramped, Geeta should've known the girl and her mother, but couldn't place either of their names. If she herself had been a mother, impelled into the bullshit rotation of teacher conferences and game-day events, she'd have memorized which offspring belonged to which woman.

"Did not!"

"Did too!" The girl broke the chain and pushed the raider, who fell back into the dust. She was taller than the other kids and, in her mien, Geeta saw an incipient Saloni. Which was why, when Geeta should have been buying groceries, she yelled through the gate:

"Oi!"

The girl swiveled her head. "What?"

The other players nervously divided their gazes between the *churel* and the bully.

"Leave him alone."

"Or what? You'll boil my bones into soup? I'd love to see you try."

Geeta's brow arched. She was accustomed to children's deferential terror, not their sass. Before leaving, she muttered the names of a few fruits in Sanskrit, which sounded ominous enough to elicit some gasps, though not from the bully.

Away from the school, the evening was unusually quiet. Not one of the four Amin children, who often escaped the hot confines of their shanty to play *kabaddi* or make deliveries for pocket change, was anywhere to be found. Geeta passed their home, a cube of tin. Three bricks and a large stone weighed the roof down. A rumor she'd heard last week returned to her: the Amins were building a four-bedroom house.

Geeta respected the widowed Mrs. Amin. She, like Geeta, was one of those women who was About the Work. Mrs. Amin's husband had been a farmer; when the rains failed, he'd succumbed to loan sharks to buy seeds and fertilizer. But the rains failed again that year, and the next. One morning he poured pesticides in the chai his wife prepared, mistakenly believing the government would grant her a compensatory sum. She received only his debts. So Mrs. Amin, after removing her nose ring, used her microloan to start selling homemade sweets, and now she couldn't cook or fry fast enough. She'd even pulled her eldest daughter out of school to help meet the demand.

Geeta would've preferred to be in Mrs. Amin's microloan group, with other women who moved their hands rather than their mouths. Women unlike Saloni, who'd only joined the microloan because she couldn't bear not being the nucleus of anything—even a labor circle. It was this same cocktail of anxiety and arrogance that'd prompted Saloni to turn on Geeta when Geeta's family arranged her engagement with Ramesh's.

Geeta would've bet five months of loan payments that Saloni had never actually wanted Ramesh. Wanting to be wanted was simply her nature. But Ramesh—not even particularly handsome what with his pocked skin and crowded teeth—hadn't wanted her. He'd married Geeta and after he vanished, Saloni hadn't offered a single word or food item of support, instead ensuring that the rumors kept churning. *It'd've been so easy for Geeta to just slip some rat poison in his tea, na? What else could it be, just the two of them in that house. And I know for a fact she's a perfect liar—she used to cheat from my exams, you know.*

All that venom from a girl who'd practically been her sister for the first nineteen years of their lives. Two halves of a gram seed, they'd shared food and clothes and secrets, they'd cheated from each other's papers and lied beautifully in unison about the same. As Geeta's father had said dryly, *Nakal ko bhi akal ki zarurat hai. Even to copy, you need some brains.* Saloni had preferred Geeta's small home and tired parents to her own small home and tired parents, but this did not parlay Geeta into the alpha. Beautiful Saloni (whose comeliness masked the true viciousness in her humor) was far more suited for the politics of childhood; it was her caprice alone that determined which girl they'd be ostracizing to tears that week, which boys were cute, which film hero was in and which song was out. Geeta was happy to follow, content in her safe, undemanding beta role. Until her wedding to Ramesh was announced. Then, quick as a shot, Saloni changed the rules, pointing the barrel of her weaponized popularity at her oldest friend's stunned head.

Geeta sidestepped a sitting cow, whose jaw circled in a desultory rhythm. Its tail echoed similar circles, but did little to dissuade the flies communing on her rump. By the time Geeta reached the shops, it was too late. Gates of corrugated metal in various colors covered the entrances, sealed with padlocks near the ground. *Fucking Farah*, she thought as she turned back.

But voices paused her feet. Geeta closed her eyes to hear better. Two men were talking inside the last store of the strip, Karem's shop. Geeta inched closer, instinct keeping her tread light. The entrance yawned wide. Despite a twilight breeze, an anxious heat prickled her underarms.

She held her breath as she listened to Karem. It took a moment, but she eventually recognized the second voice, low and burnt: Farah's husband. Samir had the throat of a smoker.

"No more 'til you pay your tab," Karem said. Even from outside, his impatience was audible. She pressed her back against the neighboring shop of sundries. "This isn't your sister's wedding where everyone can just drink for free. I have kids to feed, too."

Geeta could not see either of them, but she imagined Karem, his thick hair, narrow forehead, the small hoop in his right ear. And Samir, his scalp fuzzy like a baby bird's. "I gave you a hundred yesterday!"

"*Bey yaar*, but you owe five hundred."

"I'll get it to you soon. Just help me out tonight, na?"

"No."

Samir cursed and a cracking sound made Geeta jump, her sandal tripping over the store's padlock. A hand—Geeta guessed Samir's—had slammed atop a table. Everything from her jaw to her anus clenched as she waited to see if she'd been heard.

"I'll get you the money soon," Samir said, calmer now.

"Yeah, right."

"I mean it, I will. My wife has a friend who's been helping her, she'll help me, too."

A thread of sweat wove a thin course down Geeta's spine.

"Why would she do that?"

"Because if she doesn't, I'll make her regret it."

"Whatever," Karem said. "Just pay your tab and you can have the *daru*."

"Make sure you have something decent ready for me. Your *tharra* could turn a horse cross-eyed."

Geeta left then, her heart flapping as she tugged her earlobe. She walked in the littered alley behind the shops. It was not the most direct way home, but it provided cover. If Samir left Karem's, he'd spot her immediately. That thought made her run, her empty bag bouncing against her like a numb limb. Geeta was not accustomed to running; with each step Samir's threats slalomed in her head. Would he just beat and rob her, or kill her? Would he rape her? When shock gave way to anger somewhere around the Amin shanty, she changed her physical and mental path.

That drunk *chutiya* thought her hard work, her life of carefully preserved solitude, was an open treasure chest for his convenience. The Bandit Queen wouldn't stand for it; she'd killed the various men who'd brutalized her, starting with her first husband. After she joined the gang, she returned to his village and beat him and his second wife, who'd harassed and humiliated Phoolan. Then she dragged him outside and either stabbed him or broke his hands and legs, Geeta had heard differing stories. Phoolan left his body with a note warning older men not to wed young girls. (That last bit might've been untrue, as Phoolan Mallah was illiterate and knew only how to sign her name, but it made for excellent lore, so no matter.) The point was: if the Bandit Queen caught wind of burgeoning betrayal, she wouldn't wait to be wronged. A gram of prevention was worth a kilogram of revenge.

By the time Geeta reached Farah's house, her throat was dry and she needed a cool bath. Still, she was certain she'd beaten Samir there and pounded on the door. While waiting, she cupped her knees with her hands and panted. Crickets chirred. Her pulse thrummed to the beat of, irritatingly enough: *kabaddi, kabaddi, kabaddi.*

"Geetaben?"

She had to suck in two gulps of air before she could manage to say: "I'm in."

THREE

It was after ten when Geeta heard someone approach. Solar lantern in hand, she opened the door before Farah could knock. Without the lantern, it was as dark inside as it was outside. The scheduled power cuts ("power holidays" they called them, as if it were a rollicking party to grope in the dark and knock your knees on furniture) were increasingly longer and less scheduled. They'd all grown up with kerosene lamps and candles, but after many fires, NGOs came into their town with a rush of concern and gifts, like lanterns and the larger solar lights installed in the more trafficked portions of the village.

Farah stood in the dark, her thin elbow at a right angle, hand still lifted. "Oh, hi!" she chirped, as though they'd bumped into each other at the market. She had, Geeta noticed, a rather uncharming habit of finding amusement in everything, even premeditated murder.

Farah rubbed her hands together and a clean rasping sound filled Geeta's home. "So what's the plan?"

Which was exactly the question that had been squatting on Geeta's head for the past few hours. Farah was counting on Geeta's one-for-one score in the murder department, and Geeta had long ago stopped protesting her innocence. Telling someone the truth was asking them to believe her, and she was done asking for anything from this village. Because Geeta saw no reason to reveal the truth now—how hard could it *actually* be?—her voice was fairly confident when she said: "It should be done at night. It should look like he expired in his sleep. No blood—too messy."

Farah moved to sit on the floor in front of Geeta, who sat on her cot. "Well, how did you do it before? To Ramesh?"

"None of your damn business."

"Fine." Farah sighed. "So are you gonna come over to my place now or . . . ?"

Geeta narrowed her eyes. "I said I'd help you, I didn't say I'd do it for you."

"But you're smarter than me. You'll do it right, I know you will. I'd just mess it up."

Geeta scoffed. "If you used this much butter on your food, you wouldn't be so scrawny."

"*Arre, yaar,* it's not like that. I'm just saying you've already killed one, another won't make a difference."

"Your *chut* husband, your murder."

Farah again winced at Geeta's language but followed her and her lantern out into the night. They avoided the open water channels, walking along the sides of their village's common pathways, where garbage aggregated. Farah covered her nose and mouth with the free end of her sari. Her voice muffled and miserable, she asked, "What are we doing here?"

Geeta doubled over, her head closer to the ground as she squinted. "Looking for a plastic bag."

"Why?"

Geeta modulated her voice as though it should've been obvious: "Tie his hands and feet while he's sleeping and then put the bag on his head. Smother him. He dies. You remove your nose ring; I keep my money. Everyone is happy."

"Smart."

It was almost sweet, the way Farah looked at her. Like Geeta's ideas were gold, like she could do no wrong. Despite herself, such adoration filled her with the desire to prove Farah's faith was well placed and to perform as best she could. Geeta imagined this was what having a child would've been like.

"I know."

"So, ah, is that how you did it?"

Geeta stiffened. She rolled her shoulders back to make her height more imposing. "If you want my help, you'll stop chewing on my brains with your questions. What I did is none of your damn business."

Farah looked chastised. She sucked her teeth, complaining, "*Bey yaar,* fine. What do I tell people? After, I mean?"

"Heart attack, he drank himself to death, anything you like. Just don't let them do an autopsy."

"Okay." Farah drew out the word slowly. "But if you smothered Ramesh, why didn't you just use a pillow? A plastic bag seems like a lot more work, you know?"

Geeta blinked. Dammit. That thought had not occurred to her. She covered her ignorance with ire. "I didn't say I smothered Ramesh."

Farah threw her hands up. "What? Then why are we here? Why not just do what we know works?"

"Oi! 'Even to copy, you need some brains.' Do you want my help or not?"

"What I want," Farah sulked, "is your *experience,* not your *experiment.*"

"Forget it. Why should I break my head over your drama?"

"No! Sorry, okay?" She tugged on her earlobes in an earnest apology. "Let's keep looking, na?"

They walked along the more trafficked areas, where the lines of compost and trash thickened. Geeta toed aside torn packets of *mukhwas* and wafers. A few meters away were the public toilets the government had recently installed. There were two, designated by helpful yellow and blue cartoons of a card deck's king and queen. Though she used the squat toilets daily, it'd never occurred to Geeta before now just how silly the drawings were.

Geeta's home didn't have a pit latrine like many others did, but she still saw men take to the fields. Despite all the recent clamoring about open defecation and sanitation issues, it didn't bother her; she'd grown up doing the same, they all had. Even those who had pit latrines declined to use them—after all, someone would eventually have to empty them and caste Hindus were quite touchy about polluting themselves by handling their own waste. Some tried to force such work onto local Dalits, an oppression that was technically illegal, though authorities rarely came around these parts to enforce the law.

But for women, the new installations, public and private alike, were wholly welcome. While men could take to the fields at their whim (Geeta had heard that in the West where there were clean facilities galore, men still *su-su*'d anywhere for the hell of it—nature of the beast and all), the women and girls could only make their deposits either at sunrise or sunset—otherwise they were inviting harassment. So they held it. Better to brave the scorpion than the horny farmer.

Around Geeta and Farah, the crickets' song swelled. It was difficult to hear Farah as she ambled along another line of rubbish, her attempts half-hearted. After picking up and immediately dropping a bag of chips with carpenter ants inside, she asked, her voice carefully casual, "How come Ramesh's body was never found?"

Acrid smoke filled the night air; the heat amplified the odor. Throughout the village, trash was being burned. "You're beginning to sound like one of those gossipy bitches from the loan group."

Farah cringed, but no longer from the stench. "Why do you curse so much?"

"Because you talk so much."

"It's not right for a woman to swear. And it doesn't suit you." After a few moments, she asked, "You and Ramesh—were you a love match or arranged?"

"Why are you asking?"

"No need to be so suspicious. We're on the same side." Farah sighed.

"You won't talk about the end, so I thought maybe the beginning is less painful for you. Samir and I were a love match. My parents didn't approve, but we eloped and I moved here." Her smile was dreamy.

"Maybe you should've listened to your parents."

Farah's smile sank.

Unwelcome memories of Ramesh crashed into Geeta: the heat of his arm against her side as she'd burned the papadam. The gentle way he'd nudged her aside to fix her error. "Mine was arranged."

"Oh." Farah sniffed. She wiped her nose on the back of her hand. The movement pulled up her nostrils, and Geeta saw the underwire of her nose ring. "Sorry."

"Don't be. At least I can blame my parents. Your situation is your fault."

"I guess." Farah held up a pink bag. Red letters covered one side. "What about this one?" She put it over her head. A rip at the seam allowed her nose to poke straight through.

Geeta growled her disgust, smacking her forehead. "I swear, you can't even count on the trash in India."

Someone else spoke: "What's going on?"

Geeta immediately recognized Saloni's voice. Of course she'd turn up here, her radar for rumors—and therefore power—had always been finely tuned. Geeta turned with a deep breath, giving her back to Farah, who worked to yank the bag from her head. "Oh, *hi* there," Geeta greeted with faux charm. "Ram Ram."

Farah's breathing fluttered. Geeta nearly groaned as she heard a whimpering, *"Kabaddi, kabaddi, kabaddi."*

"Ram Ram." Saloni stood a few meters away, her own solar lantern in hand. "Well?"

"Kabaddi, kabaddi, kabaddi . . ."

"Not now, Farah!" Geeta seethed.

Saloni squinted in the night. "What—is she saying *kabaddi*? Are you *playing*?"

"Uh . . ." Geeta started, but every conceivable excuse fell from her like clipped hair.

Farah, mantra apparently having worked, was calm when she said, "We were just looking for Geeta's bag. She thought she dropped it here."

Saloni nodded toward the torn, pink bag still in Farah's hand. "That thing?"

Geeta cleared her throat. She grabbed the bag from Farah and pressed it to her chest. "Yes. It has, er, sentimental value."

Saloni rolled her eyes. "As weird as ever, I see. You know, just because your name's mixed with dirt, doesn't mean you have to, like, *literally* mix with dirt."

Geeta's heart thumped in anger; being dubbed weird at thirty-five years of age should hardly sting, but it figured that Saloni wouldn't let an opportunity slide, not when she could twist the blade instead. She thrived on spite, always had. Geeta's voice was accusatory when she demanded, "What are *you* doing out this late?"

Saloni shifted her weight onto her other foot. "Not that it's any of your business, but my son left his workbook at the school, so naturally I'm the one walking in the dark to get it." She blinked. "But I'm happy to do it. It's a small price to pay."

"Because it's so rewarding," Farah said, nodding.

"Joys of motherhood," Saloni added on automation, her eyes dragging heavenward. "I'm blessed. It's exhausting, though. I sometimes think, 'Saloni, how do you manage to raise those kids and run a business?'"

Farah gushed eagerly, "Yes, you're practically a divinity."

"Good god," Geeta muttered.

"Stop." Saloni flicked away the praise but then agreed solemnly. "Yes, I suppose I am. But it's worth it. I always say, 'Until you've brought forth the gift of life, you're not complete.'"

Geeta guffawed.

When Saloni opened her viper mouth, Geeta braced for a bite, but instead Saloni narrowed her eyes at Farah. "I didn't know you two were friends."

"Like sisters," Geeta said. "That's why I call her *ben*."

Saloni's brow folded like an accordion. "You call every woman *ben*."

"Not every woman, Saloni."

Saloni glowered at the pointed lack of suffix. The wind carried a small biscuit wrapper across her toes and she kicked it off. "If I were you, Farah, I'd spend less time pawing through trash and more time figuring out how you're going to pay back this week's loan. And Gee-taben of course."

Farah hung her head and Saloni, clearly feeling her work was done, left. Until now, Geeta had been too occupied with her own pariah status to notice Farah's. She crushed the plastic bag, imagining it was Saloni's fat head.

Farah turned, hand over heart, eyes and voice hopeful. "You think of me as a sister?"

Geeta groaned. "We should just kill *her* instead," she muttered. "Nosy bitch. 'Saloni, how do you manage to raise those kids *and* run a business?' I dunno, could it be your rich husband?"

"What's the scene there anyway?"

"What do you mean?"

"You two hate each other."

"So? No one actually likes Saloni, they just pretend to because they're scared of her."

"I'm not scared of her."

"Well, you've got a bigger bully to deal with."

"Oh, you're not so bad once you—"

"Not *me*," Geeta snapped. "Your husband."

"Oh. Right, right." Farah cleared her throat. "But what I meant was, like, there's regular hate, right? Which is really just dislike. Kinda like how you don't like . . . well, anyone. But that dislike disappears when you're not looking at them, 'cause you got other things going on. But you and Saloni hate-hate each other."

"What's your point?"

"Well, in my experience, that kind of hate comes with a good story."

"And?"

"And . . . I like good stories?"

"I'm not here to entertain you, Farah. We're here for one reason only."

Farah sighed. "I'm not your enemy, Geetaben, you don't have to treat me like one. You're doing me a huge favor—the biggest—and I'm just trying to make it easier. Friendship can make things easier, you know."

"Saloni and I were friends," Geeta admitted. "A long time back."

Farah's face turned supportive, encouraging Geeta to delve. "What happened? Was it a boy? It's usually a boy."

"I didn't tell you so we could gossip, Farah. I told you to correct you: friendship doesn't necessarily make anything easier."

"I said it *can*. It didn't work out with Saloni, I get it. But what—you're just never going to have another friend again? That's bogus."

"Oh, fuck off, yeah? When were you ever interested in friendship before you needed me?"

"I—"

"After Ramesh, you lot couldn't be bothered to look at me, much less talk to me. And that's fine. But don't stand there banging a *bhajan* about the importance of sisterhood." Geeta let the bag fall to the dirt. "Forget it. Let's go."

Farah did not move. "But what about the plan?"

"Saloni saw us. It'll be too suspicious if he dies tonight. She's a nosy bitch, but not a stupid bitch."

Farah released a one-note noise of admonishment. "The cursing!"

"Tell me she's *not* a nosy bitch." When Farah opened her mouth, Geeta added, "And remember lying is a worse sin than cursing."

Farah's jaw clicked shut.

FOUR

*W*as it a boy? It's usually a boy.

Farah's perspicacity and Geeta's ordinariness were not welcome realizations.

Yes, it was a boy. If you could call Ramesh—mustache at fifteen, when his family moved from a neighboring village, full beard in by twenty-two—a boy. Ramesh, like Geeta, was neither particularly good-looking nor gregarious. Had he been, his attention would've raised her suspicions. Had he been, he'd likely have been smitten with Saloni instead. But while all the boys were wild about what filled Saloni's undergarments, their parents only cared about what filled her dowry, which was zero rupees and zero paise. (In an early school lesson, their economics teacher explained the custom of dowry. Saloni tried to correct him: the groom's family pays to take the bride, after all, they're gaining a whole entire person to help the household. The teacher laughed: no, the groom is *paid* to take the bride because she's a liability, another mouth to feed. And, naturally, you can't buy a person, that's slavery. But, Saloni snapped back, if you sell one, that's tradition? She was made to sit in rooster position for the remainder of the econ class.)

Saloni had grown up a severe brand of poor. Geeta's family was ordinary poor: vegetables with rice or *chapatis*. In Saloni's family, they rotated the days half of them wouldn't eat, always favoring the boys. She was only sent to school due to the state's Midday Meal Scheme, which offered a free lunch. Most afternoons, they went to Geeta's home. Once, Geeta's father brought from work rejected apples that would soon rot; they already suffered from dark spots that Geeta's mother intended to carve. When she returned from the kitchen with a knife, however, Saloni had already eaten her apple, core and seeds and stem and all.

Geeta's parents said nothing, but as they finished their apples, and Saloni saw the discarded, evidently inedible bits, her fair skin flushed. That night, Geeta's parents insisted Saloni stay for dinner before walking home. In their nearly two decades of friendship, Saloni never invited Geeta to her home, and Geeta never asked.

In other parts of the world, Saloni's nadir of poverty would have subjected her to bullying. But nearly everyone in their village practiced mild asceticism—most possessed simple clothes and two pairs of shoes. Chocolate and cake were rare; on Diwali, they passed around homemade sweets. Besides, while Saloni's feet may have been bare, her other coffers were full: she was sharp and funny and high caste and, above all, beautiful. So, so beautiful with green-gold eyes that had bewildered her parents, high cheekbones and heart-shaped lips atop a delicately pointed chin. A beautiful child who spawned into a beautiful adolescent, Saloni wasted no time with acne or awkwardness. Like waves under the moon, their classmates bent to her will. Such was her social currency; everyone wanted to be near her, felt promoted by her presence.

But being both penniless and impudent naturally led to very few offers of marriage. Saloni's older sisters were wed to men in far villages, older men who'd lost their first wives and didn't demand dowries—much like the premenarchal Phoolan had been given to that thirty-three-year-old pervert.

It was neither a secret nor a surprise that Saloni's dominant aspiration in life was money. Not bungalow-car-big-city money—Saloni was ambitious but not greedy; she steeped her dreams in practicality. She wanted the normal-not-abject poverty the rest of the village didn't think to appreciate. They sighed about the rising cost of rice, but could still buy and eat the damn rice. The kind of money that allowed for declining a food based on taste or mood; the kind of comfort where it didn't occur to her to ask the price of a staple.

Every morning her father walked to the lorries, where he and seven other men spent the day filling a truck with rocks in exchange for twenty rupees. Her eventual husband—she said during hot nights when they'd sleep on Geeta's terrace with the stars sprinkled above them—needn't have Ambani-level wealth with crores of rupees, but he needed to have (or have ready access to) a leg up. Saloni realized back while Geeta was still struggling with basic sums from the third row of their shared school bench, that a head start made all the difference. You could be smart—like her father, like her—and still have no means to get even half a step further in life. You could be smart and still break your back for coins that disappeared directly into your children's bellies as they scratched their plates.

And so, Saloni committed her early teens to scheming. The gifts the boys gave—the cheap knickknacks that crumbled in her rucksack or the erasers shaped like fruit that erased nothing, including her hunger—were useless. No, what she required was a bit of money to secure a dowry and therefore a boy. You've got to spend money to make money, she told Geeta, whose opinion differed.

"All the boys love you, but you'll know 'the one' when he's willing to tell his parents not to take a dowry. At least *one* will stand up for you. I'm certain. You just have to ask."

Saloni laughed and bumped Geeta's shoulder with her own. "Don't be naïve, Geeta."

"You don't think any of them want you more than they want a bit of money?"

"Maybe," she said. "But not enough to stand up to their mummy-daddy."

Geeta twirled her earring stud within its piercing. "I just don't believe that's true."

"Because you love me," Saloni said. "You see me in a way no one else does." She poked out her tongue. "And because you're a duffer."

Saloni's attempts to cure her penury more often than not involved a reluctant Geeta. Like when they'd tried selling test papers and discovered one needed correct answers in order to ensure repeat business. Or when Saloni struck a deal with a frippery vendor to turn his hideous goods en vogue, and by the time they posed for the class photo, one would've assumed the shoddy butterfly clips glued to all the girls' heads were an element of their regulation uniform.

Hair clips turned into jewelry to impress the other girls, which turned into lipstick and rouge to impress the boys and, with that hormonal tide turn, Saloni realized she'd overlooked half of the available market: boys. Thus began the short-lived matchmaking era, which ended in Saloni dope-slapping boys, shouting, "I'm a matchmaker, moron, not a *whore*."

There was also the fake raffle, the eyeliner that gave the gift of pink eye, the public phone service that was just Saloni's cheap mobile and gave everyone the idea to purchase their own cheap mobiles, and the communal tiffin trial, which was shockingly successful among the older women. That is, until they realized they could arrange it themselves and cut her out.

Geeta couldn't assemble the linearity of these schemes—what age, what year (they'd been deeply unconcerned about time in those days). But she knew that they must've been around nineteen when Geeta's parents informed her that a boy and his parents would be visiting to meet Geeta. She was getting married, she told Saloni, and her excitement and terror mingled into a soup of nausea. If he was truly repugnant, or some thirty-three-year-old relic, she would be able to say no; she knew that because she knew her gentle, indulgent parents. She was their only child and they gave her all they could, including an education.

When she recognized Ramesh crossing her parents' threshold (right foot first as he was, she'd soon find, didactically superstitious) she was neither pleasantly nor unpleasantly surprised. She was just surprised. She'd seen him around; he caned chairs and fixed other broken items. But here he was, in her living room, taking a biscuit from her proffered tray and vying for eye contact. It was an attempt to reassure or relax her. But tradition and values—*sanskaar*—were not to be ignored. She refused to look at him because his parents were looking at *her*. Just as they watched her pour the tea and would, in half an hour, inspect how she prepared the papadam.

Geeta's own parents were betrothed after her mother did not burn the papadam. Her paternal grandparents had heard whispers of a girl of suitable caste and color, and called upon Geeta's mother's home to verify these qualifications. Once seated, they partook of the usual tea and biscuits, but the visit's real motive was, of course, the papadam performance.

While Geeta's father sat, his plate full, a bolster pillow uncomfortably lodged above the small of his back, her mother was outside, partaking in neither the chai she'd prepared nor the biscuits she'd selected that morning. His parents stood, watching as Geeta's mother, perched on two bricks, rotated and flipped the disc over the clay *chulha* stove, taking care to sacrifice her fingertips before the papadam. The ends curled and yellowed like a love letter set ablaze. Once they saw that she did not singe a single seed or grain, the matter was settled. They nodded above her bent head: she was patient enough to serve as a daughter-in-law.

Decades later it was Geeta's turn. She was handed a raw papadam and nudged toward the *sigri* stove. Ramesh entered the kitchen to see about some more biscuits, his parents having already consumed an entire package. He found Geeta there, her long braid heavy as a bell rope. She wore her mother's nicest sari, the small of her back revealed to him like a secret. She sensed his eyes, of course, and while they didn't exactly send her wild with desire, they unnerved her enough to burn the papadam. Before she could throw it away, he was there. After disposing the ruined disc, he plucked a new one from the tin and began roasting it, his parents still in the other room.

He worked methodically, like she might have, had his eyes not ruined her earlier attempt. But now that his gaze was focused and they were alone, she was free to observe, to discover whether the face before her was appealing or frightening or, worse yet, induced nothing. He flipped and rotated, the corners crinkling and bubbling but never charring. Then he set the papadam on the plate, closed the flame and left the kitchen.

So Geeta was betrothed after the papadam did not burn.

Ramesh's kindness excited her. The story they'd crafted in that kitchen was different, and that excited her as well. Until then, Geeta did not realize she shared a universal, impossible desire with every other woman: to be unique. Ramesh had seen her braid, the thick coil neatly tapering to a slice of forbidden skin and knew, simply knew, with the kind of steadfast, stubborn humility that sends modern women sighing behind clandestine romance novels, that he wanted her.

It never occurred to Geeta that Ramesh and Saloni might not get on. But as the wedding date neared, she became territory to be staked and claimed by their dueling flags. If Saloni liked her in red, Ramesh preferred orange. If Saloni suggested marigolds, Ramesh insisted upon roses. Saloni thought a bridal *nath* was essential; Ramesh thought it too provincial.

"Never in my life have I seen a man with so many wedding opinions," Saloni grumbled.

"It's sweet he's so involved, though, right? He, like, *cares*."

Geeta was a bride while Saloni was still plotting to secure her own future. A fact Geeta forgot, but Ramesh did not.

"This isn't your wedding, *Saloni*," Ramesh said.

"I know that, *Ramesh*. But I also know Geeta. Orange doesn't suit her. She's dusky so the red works better."

"Do you see what I mean?" Ramesh demanded of Geeta, who watched with dread as Saloni's green eyes narrowed; she now knew they'd discussed her privately. "Do you see how she talks to you? Stop putting her down, Saloni."

"She doesn't even *like* orange!"

"*I* like orange! Plus, she's not supposed to design her own dress—
it's bad luck!"

"No one cares, Ramesh! Just like no one cares about black cats or
if you cut your nails after sunset. It's all backwards bullshit."

"See how she talks to me?"

"How about this one?" Geeta said, lifting a random silk. "It's red
and orange, kind of, depending on the light."

They ignored her.

When they were alone, Geeta asked Ramesh: "Did something
happen between you two?"

"Did she say it did?"

"No, I just— Why don't you like her?"

"I just hate how she talks to you. Like you're lesser. You're not,
Geeta. Without you as a friend, she'd be nothing. And she has the
nerve to say you're ugly in orange."

"Did she? I thought—"

"She did. Remember? She said you were too dark to pull off such
a pretty color. It makes me sick, really."

"I— That's just how Saloni is; it's just her way. She's blunt, yes.
But she means well."

"See how you make excuses for her? She doesn't deserve you
defending her, that's all I'm saying. Friends should be nice to you."

"She's been through a lot."

"And you haven't?"

"Not like her, Ramesh. You don't know. You didn't grow up here."

He bristled. "I'm sorry for wanting more for you. I'm sorry that I
can't stand by while someone abuses you and you just take it."

"Abuses me?" Geeta laughed. "Saloni doesn't *abuse* me!"

"Just because she doesn't hit you doesn't mean it's not abuse. You
can abuse someone with the things you say or don't say or . . ." He
waved his hand, losing steam.

"She doesn't—"

"She does. Because she's jealous." And here Ramesh averted his eyes at the perfect time, looking humble and honest and as though he genuinely regretted telling her this, as though his imminent confession weren't self-inflating and presumptuous and ridiculous. "I see her looking at me. She . . . she *wants* me, Geeta."

Of course she didn't believe him. Saloni was hers. They weren't just on the same team, they were the same player. Their victories doubled, their losses halved; loyalty was as given as gravity. Even failing their friendship, there was the undeniable truth that Saloni was stunning. There were film stars who'd claw her face if they knew she was roaming about, potential competition. If Geeta and Ramesh were ordinary mango people, Saloni was a goddamn custard apple.

Geeta did not, however, make the mistake of scoffing. Nor did she say the humorous proverb that leapt to her mind, the one about an ugly guy nabbing a gorgeous girl: *grapes in the hand of a monkey.* She simply told Ramesh, her diplomacy and tenderness ruling, "Saloni wouldn't do that to me."

Still, she sensed what life would be like if she didn't unearth and destroy the root of their animosity. Torn between her best friend and her husband, she'd never know peace. She needed them both to be happy. One would give her children, but the other would help her raise them. One would make her cry, and the other would comfort her. So she asked Saloni, "Did something happen between you two?"

"Did he say it did?"

Perhaps preservation glued blinders onto Geeta. She did not even think to investigate their mirrored answers. It endangered the plans she'd made, the ideal she'd fabricated in the kitchen when Ramesh roasted the papadam. Instead, Geeta played her part and asked her friend exactly what she'd asked her fiancé: "Why don't you like him?"

"I didn't say that I didn't . . ."

The prevarication was so weak, Geeta didn't even need to press for it to crumble. She stared at Saloni until Saloni sighed. "I just don't, okay? He hogs all your time and barely lets you see me."

"Well, what would you prefer? I don't get married so I can spend all my time with you?"

"What? No, of course not. Get married. Just not to him."

"Why?" When there was no answer, Geeta had the terrible, sticky feeling that perhaps Ramesh had been correct. "Why? Are you . . . jealous?"

"What! Come on, look at me. Of course I'm not jealous."

That stung. *Like you're lesser. Like you're ugly. Friends should be nice.* Geeta continued, "Saloni. Do you . . . *want* him?"

Saloni displayed none of the diplomacy and tenderness Geeta had with Ramesh. She laughed. And Geeta felt herself pulled from Saloni's team to Ramesh's. While earlier Geeta had had the same reaction—Saloni was a goddess and Ramesh a mere mortal—to see Saloni underscore this admittedly true fact with her lovely, cruel laugh suddenly raised another question: how did Saloni see *her*?

"Nice," Geeta said. "Very nice."

Saloni coughed. "No, Geeta, come on. I just don't see him like *that*."

"Because he's not good enough."

Saloni shrugged. "He's not."

Geeta's hurt quickly cloaked itself in rage. "Because what—you're beautiful? That'll fade, you know. One day you'll be old, grey and wrinkled. Maybe bald! Maybe fat! And nothing will change the fact that you can't afford to get married anyway. So it doesn't matter that he's not good enough for you because he wouldn't have you anyway. He wants *me*."

Saloni blinked. "I meant," she said quietly, "that he's not good enough for *you*."

Maybe that was true, maybe it was not. But it was too late. She'd already laughed. Everything after, in Geeta's eyes, was a deliberate walk back, crafted and constructed, not genuine.

"You were right," Geeta cried later while Ramesh stroked her arm. "She's not my friend. Maybe she never was."

"You were wrong about her."

"Yes."

His hand stilled. "Say it."

Geeta looked at him through lashes spiked with tears. "I just did."

"Say it again. You owe me an apology. You made me feel like I was crazy, when all this time Saloni's been the problem between us."

"I'm sorry, I shouldn't have made you feel like you were crazy."

His fingers were soft against her skin, which rose with goosebumps despite his and the sun's warmth. "Tell me. Say 'You're right, I'm wrong, I'm sorry.'"

Because they were just words, because it was easier than fighting, because she'd already lost so much that day, she said, "You're right. I'm wrong. I'm sorry."

FIVE

The next evening Farah bounced up the two cement steps to Geeta's door with a proud smile. The village temples were playing their evening *bhajan*s, the nasal song of the *shehnai* floating over the thumping drums. Farah sailed in past Geeta before she'd even finished opening the door.

"I took care of it," she said, sitting on Geeta's bed rather than the floor.

Geeta raised her brows at this liberty, but her curiosity superseded her offense. "How?"

"I put all his sleeping tablets in his last *daru* bottle." She dusted her hands. Her black eye had darkened to violet. Above it, her *bindi,* small and maroon, was off-center. "He should be dying any moment now."

Relief warmed Geeta. "I'm impressed. What kind of sleeping tablets do you even get around here? Do you have the packet?"

Farah handed her a ravaged square the size of a playing card, each bubbled unit crushed and emptied. Geeta squinted at the writing across the torn foil. She looked down at Farah, who was reclining on Geeta's cot like a *maharani* on a divan.

"This is Fincar, it's for hair growth. He won't be dead, but he might be better-looking."

Farah shot up. "What?" She snatched the packet and stared. "He said the doctor prescribed them! That he needed them! I've been paying ten rupees a day for his *hair*?" She crushed the packet in her fist. "Ya'Allah, I could *kill* him!"

"No shit." Geeta shook her head. "How did you not know? Didn't you check?"

Farah's face twisted in desperation, further uncentering her *bindi*. It was unclear whether she was on the verge of tears or rage. Finally, Farah wailed: "I can't read!" She hurled the packet as hard as she could. Despite her zeal, the empty packet had no heft and it fluttered to Geeta's floor with a languid ease that rebooted Farah's despondency. She thumped Geeta's pillow like it was at fault. "Now he's gonna wonder where all the tablets went!"

"Why did you bother, then?" Geeta yelled. "Why not just wait?"

"Wait for what? India's most perfect plastic bag? Meanwhile, he'll steal more of my money. We're just sifting dust here, Geetaben. And every time I ask you what you did to Rameshbhai, you bark at me," Farah said, forming a claw with one hand. "Is this like a murder-mentor teaching moment or something? Because I don't think I've learned anything."

"Okay, enough," Geeta said. "We'll think of something else."

"Like what?"

"Well, the poison was a good idea. Easy. Clean."

"My idea was good?" Farah's lips stretched into a smile. Her cut began bleeding again. "Ow." Geeta gave her a handkerchief. Farah dabbed before licking her lower lip to test the wound.

"Yes," Geeta said in a rare moment of generosity. Then she caught herself and pointed to the medicine on the floor. "Though your execution requires improvement."

"So what now?"

Geeta considered that for a moment. "What does he like to drink?"

Farah looked at Geeta as though she were daft. *"Daru,"* she said slowly. "That's kinda the whole problem here."

"No, idiot, I mean what else. Milk?"

"Hates it."

"Juice?"

Farah shook her head. "He says it's too sugary. Diabetes is a growing epidemic, you know."

"Liver's about to fall out of his ass and he's worried about diabetes." Geeta paced as she mused. "I guess there's no other way around it: we'll have to buy him some more booze."

Farah released a strangled cry. "Whose side are you on?"

Geeta continued, speaking as though to herself, "It'd be cheaper to poison his food, I guess, but even then, it's better if he's drunk. Then he won't notice or care about the taste."

"Good thinking. So," Farah said, her voice innocent, "did that work before? On Ramesh?"

"Nice try. Let's go to Karem's."

"Ah," Farah said, drawing out the sound. "You can handle that alone, right? You don't, like, *need* me there."

The implication that she needed anyone bristled. "Of course I don't, but—"

"It's just— I can't be seen buying *daru*. What will people think?"

Geeta scowled. "But I can?"

"But I'm a *mother* and *Muslim,* and well, people . . . I mean, Geetaben, come on. People already think, *you know,* about you and plus, you don't even care about gossip—which I've always thought is so cool of you, by the way—so what's the big deal?"

"Fine," she said. It was silly of her to assume the company. Hadn't Geeta been the one to insist there was no "we" and that necessity— not friendship—had only temporarily tied their necks together? Besides which, Geeta reasoned, it wouldn't do to be caught in public with Farah yet again on the eve of Samir's death. It could raise suspicion. "I'll get some and meet you back here."

"Oo," Farah said. "Could you drop it by the house, actually? It'll be easier for me, what with the kids and everything."

Geeta heard her teeth grind. This woman was a connoisseur of piling on.

"Geetaben, you're the best! Oh, but what do we poison him *with*?"

That one Geeta was already prepared for. "Something easy and cheap, like rat poison."

"Okay, I'll buy some!"

Geeta sighed. "We can't buy it *here*. A few questions and you'd be found out. We gotta get it from the city."

Farah toggled her head in slow appreciation. She tapped her temple. "You're clever, Geetaben. Like, proper clever."

"I know."

"So . . . not to rush you, but you should get going, na? Before Karem closes for the day?"

Geeta stared at her. "How is it that *your* husband is ruining *my* life?"

Farah left, buoyed by such satisfaction that Geeta had the prickly feeling she'd been tuned like a resistant instrument. It was possible that Farah's dottiness was a convenient act. "Forget it," Geeta told herself as she put on her sandals. "Just get the booze and be done with all this fuckery."

She navigated the same route as the evening before. Children played cricket in the schoolyard, a stack of rocks as their improvised wicket. No sign of the tyrannical mini-Saloni this time.

The chai stand near the corner had only three customers. At this time of day, most men, temple time being over, were smoking hookah and playing cards near the *panchayat*'s office. Two men sat on plastic chairs, reading newspapers while sipping from small glasses. The third was a barefoot Dalit man, sandals tucked into his waistband as he squatted a prophylactic distance from the other two. He blew on his tea, which had been served to him, as it was to all Dalit patrons, in a disposable plastic cup.

When Geeta approached Karem's shop, she pulled in a deep
breath before entering. Rather than being shocked, Karem seemed
pleased to see her, which Geeta found odd. No one was ever happy to
see her, not even her clients, who considered her wares good luck.

"Geetaben! What can I do for you?"

Plastic boxes of costume jewelry lined the display case in a dusty
rainbow. It was clear they hadn't been moved in many years. Even
through the glass, Geeta could spot the asymmetrical, shoddy work-
manship. She deliberated over the proper process of bootleg ordering,
whether a clandestine passcode or phrase was required.

Geeta held up a finger. "One alcohol please."

Karem gaped. Doubt clouded his face. "*You* want hooch?"

"Yes."

"You got a guest or something?"

"No," she said quickly. "It's for me only. I enjoy . . . inebriation."

He smiled. "All right, then. What kind?"

"Kind? Uh . . ."

"I got *desi daru* and my *tharra*."

"Er . . . what's the *tharra* like today?"

"'Like today'?" he echoed, confusion and amusement tugging his
eyebrows. "Same as every day, I guess. Rough, but it does the job."

"I see." She nodded with what she hoped was casual authority.
"And the *desi daru*?"

From behind the counter, Karem extracted a squat bottle of
clear liquid. A mixture of Hindi and English lettering crowded the
label. The only images Geeta initially recognized were a drawing of
a palm tree and the ubiquitous symbol reassuring Indians that something was purely vegetarian: a green dot housed in a green square.
As her focus sharpened, she saw it was made in Bareilly, a city in a
northern state of Uttar Pradesh, which was famous for the Taj Mahal,
handicrafts and escalating drug abuse. The Bandit Queen had also
hailed from UP.

"It's locally sourced rum," Karem said, presenting the bottle like
a sommelier. "No English-Vinglish stuff. All Indian-made."

"Where do you get it?"

"Kohra."

"Oh," she said. "I'm going there tomorrow. How much?"

"Sixty-five. It might be cheaper there, though."

"And how much is the *tharra*?"

"Twenty." He grinned. "It's even more locally sourced."

"*Tharra*, then."

"Okay, but go easy, Geetaben. This stuff could turn a horse cross-eyed." Karem chuckled at his recycled joke, which he had no way of knowing she'd already overheard Samir say. When Karem failed to elicit a similar laugh from her, he turned uncomfortable, transitioning into a cough. With none of the tenderness he'd reserved for the bottle, he dumped a baggie of clear liquid on the counter. Smaller than a milk packet, its top had been twisted in a knot. It was difficult to believe such a tiny thing could be so powerful.

"That's it?"

"That's plenty to get you there." He bounced the packet between his palms. The moonshine plashed pleasantly. "Twice even."

"Two packets."

"What? Why?"

"Do you want my money or not?" Geeta snapped. "If you'd cautioned Ramesh like this, I'd still have feeling in these two fingers." She lifted her left hand, which he'd broken their fourth summer together and which hadn't healed properly. The injury had extended her reach, but as that wasn't a talent Geeta found particularly useful in beadwork (perhaps if she were a pianist), her gratitude was limited.

Karem said nothing for a moment. "I didn't know. Until later, I mean."

She released a scoff of disbelief.

"I swear to you," he said, pinching the skin covering his Adam's apple, the semiotic for a vow. "I didn't. How could I? I never saw you—and you obviously never came here."

"Everyone knew."

"All the women did! But I didn't know until Ramesh was gone and *everyone* was talking. I can promise you that, Geetaben."

She no longer wished to discuss this. She regretted throwing her injuries in his face. Not to spare him, never that, but because she was not a victim and he was not anyone to pander to. She was suddenly furious at her own folly. "Keep your promises to yourself and give me two packets."

Karem obeyed one of her directives and produced another packet. "I really am sorry."

"Fuck you."

"At least he got his. Blind is pretty clear karma."

She stilled. "What?"

Karem squinted at her. He wore the careful, frozen mien of someone who'd stepped on a twig in a lion's den. "What?"

"What did you say about being blind?"

"Nothing. What? You said blind."

"No," Geeta said slowly. "You did. Just now."

"It was a compliment. Like, he must've been blind. Obviously. To leave a woman like you."

He was lying. Poorly, too, which was somewhat endearing: a criminal incapable of a fib. Like a baby in a three-piece suit. But Geeta had what she'd come for and much fatter problems than Karem's half-assed riddles. Tomorrow she'd have to walk the three hours to Kohra to find cheap poison. She placed four ten-rupee notes on the counter.

Karem shook his head. "No, no need."

Geeta stared at him for so long, he had no choice but to reluctantly return her hostile gaze. "No," she told him. "I don't want you thinking you're off the hook. Ever."

SIX

When Geeta returned home, she left her sandals by the door and rinsed her dusty feet in the compact cubicle she used for bathing. Her water buckets were low, but she'd replenish them tomorrow. Feet damp and restless, she milled about with an unusual ennui. Typically, she was quite content at home; she'd learned she was a woman who fared well alone. But now she wandered from her worktable to her kitchen alcove, where she set down the two *tharra* packets. She toyed with one's knot, but did not open the bag. Outside the back door was an old clay stove, which she still often used, cow pies being far less expensive fuel than gas.

Against the wall to her right, where the ever-present lizard was currently resting, its throat puffing—that was where she wanted her refrigerator to stand. Geeta had been saving up for one since she'd joined the loan group. It would be so convenient to cook a few days' worth of meals at once and store them. She would often look up from her work and be pulled under a wave of hunger so strong, it left her dizzy. By that time, there was no question of cooking, just scarfing biscuits until she no longer felt faint.

And she'd finally be able to buy and keep perishables, the juices and pickles that families could finish in one go, but a single woman could not. Her bread wouldn't mold as quickly; her milk would survive independent of the season; she might even try eggs. A refrigerator would change everything—including how others saw her. Her mother had frequently said: *Elephant goes to the bazaar; thousands of dogs bark.* Though Geeta was accustomed to the village's stale contempt, she worried about the renewed attention, the envy and the spite and the fresh whispers. Even as she told herself that she didn't care, that she'd manage, imagining the sneers filled her stomach with stones.

Well. There would be no sneering and no refrigerator unless she got back to work. Geeta left the kitchen and stood at her worktable. Jars of black beads lined her station like soldiers awaiting orders. An organized desk was a source of comfort to her. She should put on some music and begin sketching a wedding *mangalsutra*. If that project didn't suit her mood, she could begin converting another necklace into a bracelet. That was the trend with modern brides—a marital bracelet was far easier to pair with jeans than a traditional, looping necklace. This suited Geeta just fine as it doubled her work and income: craft a necklace before the ceremony, a bracelet afterward.

Geeta unlocked her metal armoire. On the top shelf sat a maroon jewelry box and a small lockbox where she kept gold wire and beads for necklaces. She ignored the combination lockbox and took down the jewelry box. Age had blackened the corners, but the felt remained soft. When Geeta opened the lid, she released the faint smell of saffron. Inside was her own wedding necklace and, in a false bottom below that, her savings: 19,012 rupees.

In her second year of marriage, Geeta's parents passed away, her mother first, her father a few months after. Fate's thin kindness meant that they'd seen her happy, not cowed. Her father, though many things (funny, kind, doting), hadn't possessed a head for money, a secret that only saw daylight upon his death, when he could no longer hide the true condition of his finances. They'd apparently lost Geeta's family home to the bank long ago. New loans taken to pay old loans to pay other loans; Ramesh had shaken his head at the state of it—*an absolute mess, Geeta*—the callous censure of her dead father barely penetrating through Geeta's grief. Her parents had been fortunate, Ramesh told her, that his family had eschewed dowries as archaic, but now they'd have to sell Geeta's wedding jewelry (it was, after all, *her* side's debt). She supposed that was fair but wished Ramesh had kept it a private matter. He criticized her father's mistakes to the village, bemoaning that he'd received no thanks for not demanding a dowry. Geeta's maiden name died with her father, and perhaps that was for the best, as Ramesh ensured it was synonymous with shame.

Then Ramesh disappeared, bequeathing her with even more debt, and only Geeta's *mangalsutra* had survived her efforts to keep afloat. She'd been tempted many times to sell it. It was likely worth twenty thousand rupees, and she could buy a refrigerator immediately, with funds to spare. But she didn't want the refrigerator that way, linked forever to Ramesh. She ate no one's salt but her own.

Geeta toyed with her wedding necklace, chosen by Ramesh, testing its tensile strength.

Perhaps it was pathetic to have kept it, and by extension to have wasted any time missing Ramesh, but he was all she'd known for a while. At first the new solitude had scared her. Friendship might've eased the transition but, much like a refrigerator, that was a luxury she lacked, and so she managed without.

Eventually, through discovering her talents for jewelry making, salient truths emerged: There was a Geeta before Ramesh's hands had found her, and that Geeta was still alive, and even if no one else was interested in knowing her, Geeta was. She found extra salt pleased her palate. She made it a point not to apologize. She liked music and danced to her old radio to jump-start her mornings (though after stumbling upon an interesting bit about orcas, she'd been tuning into Gyan Vani's nature program of late). Biscuits and tomato Lay's were a perfectly acceptable dinner some nights. And (this might've been the magic of converting an impossibility into the illusion of choice) she wouldn't have done well with babies, primarily because she just didn't like them very much. Her grapes, whether sour or fair, were *her* grapes.

Conditioning, not actual desire, had informed her that she wanted children; and Ramesh—cruel as he'd been about the matter—had at least released her from its constraints.

Geeta dumped the necklace back in the box. She identified with the Bandit Queen's disappointing revelation about marriage: the necklace men tied to them, it was no prettier than the rope tying a goat to a tree, depriving it of freedom.

But freedom, Geeta had once heard or read somewhere, is what a person does with what's been done to her. Geeta used hers to start a business. It would never be a big business, that was a given, but it existed solely because of her talent and vision, which made her, according to the loan officer, an *entrepreneur*.

All the French words in the world, however, didn't cure the fact that she was only as successful as the men around her allowed her to be. As Samir was proving, a man didn't even need to be *your* man to oppress you. The microfinancers were keen on converting *abla nari*s into *Nari Shakti*. It was an admirable goal but also kind of futile, because the microfinancers came and went, and the women were left to do what they'd always done: abide. Whether you dubbed a *nari* "helpless" or "powerful," she was still a woman.

Geeta returned to the *tharra* packets. Not one drop of alcohol had ever passed her lips. But she did wonder what all the fuss was about. Ramesh had chosen this over her. For the joys in this bag, Samir was willing to harm her.

In threatening her purse and pride, Samir had reminded her of her vulnerability. So when a fist thumped on her door, Geeta jumped and let the *tharra* fall onto the counter with a benign plop.

It was not Farah or Samir, but Karem who stood on the dirt before her front steps. He had returned to the ground after knocking, rather than remaining on the stairs. It was a nod to her space that Geeta appreciated. Not that she showed it:

"What?"

"I—I have to go to Kohra tomorrow morning for, ah, inventory purposes."

"Meaning booze."

He sighed. "Yes. Do you want to come?"

"Why would I?"

"'Cause you mentioned you were going, and it's a free trip—I'm getting a ride on a truck."

Geeta clamped down her instinct to rebuff him and considered the offer on its face. It was clear he was attempting amends, which didn't interest her, but a trip would save her time, perhaps enough to survey some refrigerators.

She still hadn't answered and his smile turned nervous and crooked. "It'll be fun."

"Fun?"

"Okay, Geetaben, it won't be fun. It'll be strictly business. Just come, na? Save yourself a day of walking in the sun. Even an *adarsh nari* needs rest."

"I'm hardly an ideal woman."

Karem looked at her door, which she'd opened only enough to accommodate her body. "Are you alone?" He must have immediately realized those words—irrespective of intent and tone—when spoken by a man to a woman were inherently threatening. He fumbled and took a step back. "Not— I didn't mean . . . I just asked in case you had company, you know, because that'd explain the moonshine."

"I told you it's for me."

He squinted at her and for a moment she thought he was going to press. Then his face relaxed and he said, "Have you tried it yet?"

"No."

"Well, let me know what you think. It's better cold, of course." He pocketed his hands into his brown slacks. "We leave at eight-thirty, so don't go too crazy."

"I won't."

"Good night, Geetaben."

"Whatever."

———

She met Karem by his shop because it was closer to the highway than her home. As they walked toward the paved road, she was surprised to find that it was her, not Karem, who could not tolerate the silence between them. She asked, "Will your kids be okay with you gone?"

"School," he said. "God knows they don't learn anything, but at least it's free babysitting."

"How old are they now?"

"Eleven, nine, six and five. Nope, wait—*seven* and five."

Geeta was too stunned to make a crack about his clearly being an attentive father. "Wow."

"I know, I know, 'family planning' and all. 'Us two, our two.' But Sarita and I wanted a girl so we kept at it. Finally got her."

Geeta did some math. "I remember your wife passed away in . . ."

"Five years ago. Around the time Ramesh . . ."

"Disappeared."

"Right."

"That must be hard. Doing it alone."

Karem shrugged. "It's hard with someone, too. That's marriage."

A flamboyant Tata truck with mud flaps reading HONK OK PLEASE slowed toward them. Its flat nose was mainly red, with smatterings of yellow and blue and every color in between crowding onto the vehicle. While it was loud, it was also beautiful. After greeting his friend, Karem hopped in the back bed, which was lined with bales of hay. He offered a hand to Geeta, who ignored it and, gathering her sari skirts in a fist, scrabbled onto the hay, righting herself with a great deal of satisfaction but only half her dignity.

A tethered buffalo groaned at their arrival before burying his head in a steel bucket filled with grass clippings. They sat with their backs against opposite sides of the truck, facing each other. Karem's wrists rested on his bent knees and Geeta arranged herself cross-legged, her right knee cracking, jute bag in her lap.

Karem gestured toward his head. "You have . . ."

"What?"

"Straw."

"Oh." She patted her crown until she found the offender.

They headed south, past the outskirts of the village, where the local Dalits lived in closer quarters. The thatched roofs of the huts were too squat to be seen past the trees surrounding the area, but some taller homes, mud and cement, were visible. Geeta recognized the hanging tree. While not actually called that, she'd heard the story as a child and since then, she always thought of it as such—though never aloud.

One early morning, long before Geeta was born, two lower-caste girls—thirteen and twelve—were found lynched by their *dupattas*, their pants pooled around their ankles, dew dripping from their fingertips. The cops came and the girls' illiterate parents signed a report authorizing the police to investigate the rape and murder. But what they actually signed—what the cops had been instructed to draft in advance—was a false confession stating the parents had discovered that their daughters were promiscuous, so they'd hung them to preserve their family's honor. Off they went to jail, the entire family ruined by dawn.

Geeta looked away from the hanging tree. Whether it was a true story or a myth, she knew the village *panchayat* had recently been hearing complaints of an unknown man in a balaclava assaulting Dalit girls at dawn, when they left their beds to relieve themselves in the fields; he first choked, then groped them. The five members of the *panchayat* were elected by the villagers in a direct democracy meant to allow the village to self-govern. Here, however, the *panchayat* could only extend its sympathies to the families; justice was elusive because there was no way to identify or catch the culprit.

Fields, some green, some brown, some gold, blurred on either side of the road. Once, their truck braked hard to let a seemingly endless mass of buffalos cross. Karem held fast, swaying sideways before righting. Geeta did not manage to steady herself in time and flopped onto the straw. Karem had the decency to pretend not to notice. They were paused near an active construction site with a large pile of bricks. A queue of girls walked, each carrying a brick or two on her head to add to the cairn. Around them, herds of goats and cows grazed, their red-turbaned shepherds wielding long sticks. At times, Geeta forgot how verdant this land was.

After what felt like forty minutes but was more likely twenty, they stopped at a neighboring village and Karem's friend came to the back to dump stacks of sugarcane around them and the unflappable buffalo. The engine rumbled and they were off again. Karem extracted a long cane from a stack and offered it to her. When she shook her head in refusal, he gnawed on one end, extracting the juice and spitting the desiccated fibers onto the road.

Unbidden, Geeta tried to imagine him drunk—giggly or slurring or violent or amorous. The last of the list startled her and she turned, squinting into the sun because she couldn't look at him as he picked a stray cane filament from his tongue. And it was the sun, obviously, that heated her cheeks. Hers wasn't the kind of skin that blushed, unlike Saloni's, and it was perhaps the only time in the annals of Indian history that a woman felt gratitude for a dusky complexion.

When they arrived in Kohra, Geeta turned to Karem, intending to pick a meeting point in a few hours. But he had other ideas.

"Let's go."

"What? No. I have my own errands."

"This'll be quick. We'll do your errands right after."

"It'll save time if I just go alone."

"What time needs saving? That guy's not coming back for us until five-thirty."

When she opened her mouth to protest, he sighed. "Geetaben, if you want to be alone, that's fine. But first let me show you something. Then you can do whatever you'd like." He pinched the skin of his throat. "Promise."

She capitulated with a sigh. "Fine. Let's get this over with."

They walked toward residences rather than the bazaar nearby, which unsettled Geeta, and stopped before a large two-story home with an intricate parapet delineating the terrace. Children played near a low gate that blocked a short, flower-lined pathway to bright blue double doors. She heard dogs barking but saw none.

As they opened the gate latch, a man in his midforties came outside to greet Karem with widespread arms. A swing with rusted hinges but polished chains sat on the porch, flanked by large plants. "Karembhai!" The two embraced while Geeta lingered behind. Over Karem's shoulder, she saw the pale, blank island of the man's crown. They were about the same height, but the older man bore a stomach that was testing the limits of his polo shirt.

"Geetaben, this is Bada-Bhai."

Bada-Bhai pressed his palms together in a namaste, which Geeta returned. "Your elder sister?"

"No, just a friend," Karem said, while Geeta felt every one of her wrinkles and grey hairs. "She's come to Kohra for business only."

"Does she also have a first-class secret *tharra* recipe?" Bada-Bhai joked, leading them inside. As they shed their shoes, she noticed the lemon and green chilies strung near the doorway. Ramesh had had her keep a similar decoration under their bed to ward off the *buri nazar*—evil eye. As though he weren't its very incarnate. "If it's as good as yours, Karembhai, I may have to switch suppliers."

"No, no." Karem laughed as Bada-Bhai shepherded them into a sitting room with three sofas and a television. A woman in long sleeves and house slippers approached with a tray of water glasses. After Geeta drained hers and returned it to the tray, she noticed the tribal tattoos of the Rabari decorating the woman's hands. Geeta tried to establish eye contact so she could mention that her village housed Rabari herders every winter—was the woman from Rajasthan or Kutch? But her gaze was fixed on the floor, and Geeta realized with growing unease that something was amiss. It was peculiar that any member, let alone a woman, of a nomadic tribe would have a city job as a helper.

Karem took a glass of water. "Geetaben makes jewelry."

"Oh, like Sarita-*bhabhi*."

Geeta's scalp itched at the slight, piled atop the recent one about her age. To say her jewelry was like Sarita's was a conflation of art and carpentry. But Karem's poor wife was dead, this duffer a stranger, and it was a pedantic waste of breath and ego to correct him.

Karem shook his head. "High-end jewelry, I mean, not a hobby. She has her own business: Geeta's Designs. I wanted to show her your shop. Depending on how the microloans fare, she's looking to expand Geeta's Designs beyond the village."

Which was news to Geeta's Designs.

"*Shabash!* If Kohra's not careful, your little town will soon exceed ours."

It was a compliment, surely, albeit a condescending one, but hard reservation lined its edges, and Geeta felt as though they'd been warned rather than flattered. Bada-Bhai clapped his hands.

"Karem has the best *tharra* I've ever tasted. I'm not sure what he does with those sugarcanes, but his could be actual rum."

"Oh," Karem said, dismissing the praise with a wave. "Hardly. Bada-Bhai here took a chance on me a few years back, after Sarita expired. I didn't have any contacts or seed money. But he said there was a market for my *tharra* recipe and the next thing you know, we're a hit!"

Bada-Bhai clapped Karem's back. "He makes it sound like I sold *gobar* to a cowherd—try *not* selling moonshine in this state! It's impossible. Speaking of, do you have something for me?"

Karem nodded. "*Ji.*" He offered his jute bag to Bada-Bhai, who peered at the contents before summoning a man Geeta hadn't noticed waiting in the corner. The man took Karem's bag and gave Bada-Bhai an envelope before leaving the room.

"Can't forget this," Bada-Bhai said, fishing in his pocket for a one-rupee coin, which he slid into the envelope. "For luck."

It was considered auspicious to add one rupee to any gifted amount, though Geeta never attributed the practice to business, just birthdays and weddings.

"Count it."

Karem pocketed it instead. "I trust you."

"Where there is business, there is always room for doubt."

Karem smiled. "But where there is friendship, there is none."

Geeta, still curious about the Rabari woman, asked to use the toilet. She was pointed in a direction near the open mouth of the kitchen, where she overheard snatches of an argument.

"—entirely inappropriate, Lakha, *entirely,* for a servant's son to eat the—"

"But he's not the son of a servant, is he?"

As Geeta hurried past, she saw a well-dressed woman her own age slap the Rabari woman.

Burning with vicarious indignation for Lakha, Geeta grew distracted and found herself outside. A chain-link fence cordoned a dirt patch of nothing. It was as ugly as the front yard was lovely. There was no outhouse, so Geeta turned to walk back inside. She'd forgotten herself; in larger places like Kohra, indoor plumbing was ubiquitous. Dogs barked, the cacophony so proximate that Geeta startled.

She hadn't noticed the four dogs chained to the fence. Their leashes were short enough to ensure their paws didn't comfortably rest on the dirt. Rather than tied under the tree in the far corner, they were clustered in the sun and Geeta didn't see any water vessel in the barren yard. She was about to go inside and remind Bada-Bhai that it was meant to rocket up to forty-one degrees that afternoon when she noticed the smallest dog curving and straightening his spine in a strange dance that resembled yoga's *marjariasana* and *bitilasana* poses. She thought perhaps he was just stretching, but then his jaw opened to release gagging noises that sounded more human than canine. He was going to vomit, she realized a moment before liquid spewed into the dirt. His compatriots attempted to avoid the waste, but they were tied to the same link on the fence, and it was impossible.

Geeta stepped toward the house, then stilled. The Bandit Queen didn't wait for help, she *was* help. Geeta approached the dogs tentatively; the last thing she needed was rabies. While she wasn't afraid of animals per se, like Saloni, neither did she coo over them like you saw in the films where rich people in mansions had fluffy dogs named Tuffy who ate better than the help. But it was clear these four dogs had been adopted from the street and Geeta didn't know if they'd come out biting and attacking. Her breathing was too quick and she felt dizzy under the sun. With some reluctance, she whispered under her breath as she examined the dogs' restraints. *"Kabaddi, kabaddi, kabaddi."*

The leashes were attached to the fence by a simple carabiner clip. She pressed the spring-loaded portion and ran away in case the dogs gave chase. *"Kabaddi, kabaddi, kabaddi."* Damned if it didn't help immediately. By chanting, she forced herself to expel more air than she ordinarily would have before her next inhale, thereby deepening her breaths.

Farah would never shut up if she knew.

Geeta's head cleared and she looked back to witness the dogs' reactions. Though the grip around their throats slackened, allowing them to properly stand on the ground, they didn't roam and explore their new freedom. They remained stationary, surveying her. Then one took a few steps toward the shade, leash trailing, and another dog followed suit. The sick dog flopped onto his side, his brown torso rising and falling, his tail a limp, dirty rope. He needed water, if not medical aid.

Geeta walked along the fence's perimeter until she found the gate. There was no lock. The dogs watched her as she tested the latch, flipping it up twice before returning it home. Then she retraced her steps inside, her *su-su* needs forgotten, but the sitting room was empty. She followed voices to a bedroom that had been repurposed into a workstation. Geeta loitered outside the doorway, craning her neck to peek. Tubes and pots, both clay and steel, sat on various surfaces as men moved between tables. Karem and Bada-Bhai stood near the wall across from her. They watched as a man poured half of Karem's *tharra* into a clay pot. The other half was set aside.

"What's the need for all this, Bada-Bhai? I thought you liked my recipe as is?"

Bada-Bhai laughed. Karem did not. "Of course I like your recipe— if there's one complaint, it's that it's too good."

"I don't understand."

"We must cut it with something. That's just good business. We double our profits." Bada-Bhai clapped Karem's shoulder. "That's how we're able to pay you so much."

"What is that?" Karem pointed to a clear liquid a worker poured into the pot. "Another *tharra*?"

Bada-Bhai was quiet.

"Ethanol?" After a beat, Karem did not ask, but said, his voice flat, "Methanol."

"It's good business. Don't concern yourself."

"You could kill people."

Bada-Bhai narrowed his eyes. His smile was tight beneath his mustache. "You've managed to make room for doubt after all, it seems." He shrugged. "No one's died. We test it."

Geeta filled the doorway and asked, "On the dogs?"

Karem swiveled toward her, a question in his eyes. Geeta angled her head. "There are dogs tied up out back."

Bada-Bhai sighed, as though much aggrieved. "The dogs try the moonshine and after two days, we know it's good to sell."

"If they live," Geeta said.

He shrugged. "Most do."

Karem looked as though he'd just been told his father was a eunuch. "Th-that's cruel."

"What else? Are *you* going to volunteer to drink it?" Bada-Bhai smirked at Geeta as he would to an ally and informed her, "He doesn't drink. Ironic, na?"

Karem grimaced. "A natural reaction, I think, given the line of work."

"Do *you* drink?" Geeta asked.

Bada-Bhai sniffed and tugged down the hem of his maroon shirt.

"I indulge from time to time. There's no crime in it." He paused. "Well, no sin anyway."

"Then maybe *you* should drink the poison you're shoving down those poor dogs' throats." Geeta bared her teeth into a smile. "Since you like to indulge."

"Listen, *budi*," Bada-Bhai said, one finger erect toward her. "Keep your lecture to yourself. They're just street dogs. If I had children tasting it, then yeah, sure, you could call me a monster."

There was no time to smart from the insult: "old woman." "That's the best defense you have? That you don't tie up and poison children? And to think, they nominated Gandhi for a Nobel instead of you."

"Hey! I took those dogs in. They were homeless and diseased. I gave them shots and paid to deworm and de-sperm them or whatever. They get food and water—"

"And poison."

"Oi! I don't need grief from a bored old housewife who makes *do kaudi ka* jewelry. Karem, you wanna handle her?"

"It's not two-bit," Geeta snapped.

"And she's not a bored housewife."

Geeta tried not to let it bother her that he did not dispute the old part. Bada-Bhai released a grunt of irritation. By advancing toward Karem, who instinctively stepped back, he herded them out of the room. "This is my business and as long as you want to keep getting paid, you'll keep your nose out of it."

"Free the dogs," Geeta said.

"No."

"Untie them or I'll call the police."

"Geetaben." The caution came from Karem, whose sudden shift in loyalties dismayed her.

"What?"

He gestured to the makeshift lab. "We can't call the police. I'll get arrested. You might, too."

"Oh."

"Listen to the man," Bada-Bhai said, smug. "He has brains at least."

"We're not calling the police," Karem said. "But we're done here. That was the last batch I'll sell you."

Bada-Bhai shrugged. "Fine. But don't expect to sell to anyone else in Kohra. I'll make sure everyone knows your stuff is lethal. That's why, with a heavy heart, I had to terminate business with you . . ." He put his hand over his chest and looked to the ceiling. "Because I couldn't in good conscience risk my loyal clients' lives with something as seedy as methanol. But luckily for them, I found new, clean *tharra*."

"Which you'll just keep putting methanol in."

"Naturally. But who are they going to believe? Some Podunk *ghogha* farmer thrashing sugarcane or a proper businessman?" Bada-Bhai looked at Karem's clenched jaw and shook his head. "Big mistake, Karem. How are you going to feed those kids now? Make sure to tell them that the reason they're hungry is because their idiot daddy chose a bunch of stray dogs over them."

"He's not an idiot," Geeta said.

"He is if he thinks anyone else would've done anything different. This is business, Karem. Which you and Mother Teresa over here know nothing about."

Geeta blinked. How old did this *chutiya* think she was?

"No," Karem said. "The business was supplying a demand. Not poisoning people over a few rupees."

"A few rupees!" Bada-Bhai laughed. "This is how I know you're a villager—you just have no idea, do you, boy?"

"Come on, Geetaben," Karem said. "Let's go."

"Fine," she said. "But." She held up her pinky finger, the semiotic for *su-su*, or a "number one" deposit.

"Again?" Karem asked.

"No, no," Bada-Bhai said. "My mother has similar problems." He told Karem, "It comes with the age."

Geeta gritted her teeth. "I'll meet you outside."

Bada-Bhai was at her heels the entire way. In the hallway, Geeta recognized the woman who'd slapped Lakha. "Chintu," she called Bada-Bhai. "I can't tolerate her much longer, I *won't*."

His voice was dismissive as he said, "You'll have to, and you know why. I can't talk, I'm busy right now."

As they reached the bathroom, Geeta spun and nearly bumped his belly.

"Are you joining me?" she asked snidely.

He appeared appalled, which was doubly insulting. "Of course not."

"A little privacy then?"

He refused.

"What do you think I'm going to get up to?" She gestured to herself: harmless, apparently old, armed only with a sari and jute bag.

He hesitated, but then seemed to concur with her self-deprecation with a roll of his eyes.

"Sir?" a young boy called.

Bada-Bhai walked down the hallway to rest his hands on the boy's shoulder. "Papa," he corrected, his voice gentle, leading his son toward the kitchen.

Geeta closed the bathroom door and retraced her steps to the backyard, where she ran straight to the latch. She pushed open the gate and whispered to the dogs, "Go! Get! *Hutt!*"

Three of them listened, bolting. The sick one limped, eager to please, and accomplished a sloppy circle. "This way," she hissed at him. "Follow my voice." He veered toward her in a promising turn, but then bopped his nose on the fence and promptly fell onto his side.

"Oh, for fuck's sake." She didn't have time for this. Even if she plopped the whelp outside the fence's boundary, he wouldn't get very far. They'd find him immediately. Geeta petted him twice, allowing him to sniff her hand with his black nose. Then she scooped up his thin brown body. He had a long torso, but his legs were stubby. His crowning feature were his ears, foxlike with pink innards and far too big for his tiny face. His fur was dirty, his tail a nasty rope. She felt his warm skin give between each rib. As she placed him in her empty bag, he whimpered, tongue lolling. He offered no resistance to her foreign touch, curling into himself with a defeat that triggered Geeta's simultaneous sympathy and rage.

Back in the house, she checked the hallway and quietly locked herself in the toilet. *"Kabaddi, kabaddi, kabaddi."* Her heart barely had time to settle before Bada-Bhai came pounding.

"Ben?" he called. "Oi, *ben*! What happened? Did you fall?"

She seethed into the mirror above the pink sink. Good god, did she really look frail enough to be on the hip-shattering watch list? Sure, she had a few wrinkles congregating near her eyes, didn't everyone who'd wasted their youth smiling? She was well into her thirties, so she'd earned her few wisps of grey, but she was still overwhelmingly black of head. And, she thought with relished spite, at least she still *had* hair.

Her home had one mirror and she rarely bothered with its warped surface; there was little need for vanity. She no longer wore *bindi*s or jewelry. She knew how her clothes looked on her: serviceable. She could even do her hair blindly. Comb, comb, comb, roll in a bun, tie. It was apparent now that the look wasn't exactly doing her any favors, scraping the hair from her forehead and temples with a severity that mimicked schoolmarm caricatures, but who the hell cared about her appearance anyhow? It wasn't as though she *wanted* people looking at her—it was far safer to be invisible. And yet . . . how old did Karem think she was?

At that uninvited curiosity, Geeta flushed the toilet and opened the door, hoping Bada-Bhai wouldn't notice the new bulge in her previously empty bag.

"Finally," he grumbled. "Would you care to take your leave now?"

The dog, whose warmth seeped through the bag to Geeta's midriff, mewled. It wasn't particularly loud, but the house was silent.

"What was that?"

She flattened a palm against her abdomen. "Indigestion," she explained. "It comes with the age."

SEVEN

Karem waited for her outside the gate, his demeanor glum as he toed a rock. "Everything okay, Geetaben?"

"Yeah," Geeta said. "But we should get going."

"Yes, you had errands, correct? Where to?"

She looked behind them. How long before Bada-Bhai or his men wandered into the backyard? She pulled on Karem's forearm. Her touch seemed to surprise him; he looked down at their skin. "Um . . . we should probably run."

"What?"

A yawp of outrage rose from the house.

"Like, now. Run."

They scurried to the end of the street, neither of them remotely spry, and turned the corner into the busy bazaar. Geeta wove through rather than around the most crowded portions, hoping to lose anyone in pursuit. She worried the jostling was further harming the dog, but she didn't dare slow down. Karem kept pace behind her; he likely thought her mad. Lackadaisical vendors sat cross-legged on tarps, swatting flies with desultory flicks of handkerchiefs tied to sticks. The more aggressive peddlers stood, thrusting everything from shoes to bouquets of fennel seeds into passing faces. The end of the bazaar deposited them on a street lined with brick-and-mortar establishments. By tacit agreement, they stopped running.

"What—?" Karem gasped before bending over, hands cupping his kneecaps. "Just—what was that about?"

"I released the dogs. I had to."

"You *what?*" But he wasn't angry. Geeta knew anger; Karem was bewildered.

They inched back as a truck, its windshield smothered in marigold garlands, wove through the market toward the temple on the other end. Mounted on the vehicle's roof were two horns and some political banners. The horns squawked, but Geeta's heart was pounding too loudly to hear.

After a moment, Karem straightened and said, "Well, good."

"You're not mad? What if Bada-Bhai comes after you?"

Karem shrugged. "He already took away his business. That's plenty. Hit me right in the belly."

Geeta swallowed. It occurred to her then that she and Farah had been planning on letting Samir's tab die with him. They'd planned on essentially robbing Karem and, until this moment, it'd seemed a victimless crime. "You'll find another."

"Not here, I won't."

Geeta's fear of retaliation returned. Now she'd have two men gunning for her blood. "Is Bada-Bhai really that big of a don?"

Karem laughed through his nose. "He's not a don at all, he just wants to be. He gave himself that name to seem tough, but he's mostly just stuck between his wife and . . ." He coughed and quieted.

"Lakha? The Rabari woman?"

Karem nodded. "You're observant. Took me a few trips to figure out she's his son's mother."

"Bastard?"

"Yup, but his only son, so Bada-Bhai would never disclaim him. Plus, Bada-Bhai's . . . I wouldn't call it love, but he's a bit, I don't know, *obsessed* with her. Hard to say which pisses his wife off more."

Geeta had far more questions, but instead she asked, "If he's not dangerous, why can't you find another vendor here?"

"This place is too small. He's the only game in Kohra. I'll have to start from square one somewhere else. Make contacts, let them sample the *tharra*, build a reputation. Until then . . ." He shrugged.

"We can get you help. The loan officer can—"

"Geetaben," he said, "you know the loans are only for women. Besides which, I doubt they'll be queuing up to fund a liquor business in a dry state."

"You're just doing what other states do. A random map line decides if you're a criminal or not? Nonsense." When he squinted at her, she asked, "What?"

"Nothing," he said. "Your support is surprising, is all. Given what happened with Ramesh."

"Well." Geeta paused. After what she'd said to him in his shop last night, she had to be damn sure any retraction was sincere. She decided that she didn't know who he'd been before, but the man she was with now, the one who'd refused to poison people for profit, deserved a second chance. "Ramesh made choices."

"Yes," Karem agreed. "That he did."

Their eye contact flustered her. Geeta pulled on her earlobe, her arm brushing her bag. The dog whimpered from within. Karem blinked. "Is that—"

"Oh!" She'd forgotten. Guilt softened her touch as she extracted the dog. His fox ears were the only perky part of him. His mottled tail sagged; his own vomit had dried on his fur. "This one was sick. He couldn't run. I don't think he can even see."

Karem petted him. "Let's get him some water."

"What about a doctor?"

"For dogs? Kohra isn't exactly Bombay."

They found a public tap. The dog sniffed before drinking, his black nostrils fluttering. He drank for a good two minutes before stopping to pant.

"He looks a little better," Karem said.

Geeta assessed the dog in her arms with doubt; he trembled from the exertion of lapping. The fur around his paws was white but dirty. The remainder of him was light brown save a dark stripe wrapping his long torso like a belt and one black ear. "You think?"

"Not really, no."

"Do you think he could die?"

"If he keeps the water and some food down, I think it'll be a good sign."

"What do dogs eat?" The Gyan Vani radio segment talked about the wild; they didn't offer tips on domesticating strays. Geeta set him down, but he cried out so she held him again. His warmth and weight, minimal though it was, was reassuring against her midsection. She felt maternal and needed; the feeling was not wholly repugnant.

"Street dogs? Anything that's not tied down."

After they exited a sundry kiosk with a fat packet of Parle-G biscuits, Karem asked, "What are your errands?"

Geeta coughed. She'd come here to poison one man but punished another for doing the same to a dog. It was different, she knew that in her bones, but couldn't articulate how or why.

"I need some beads and wire. And some jump rings and chain ends, oh and clasps."

"I'll just pretend I know what those are. Lead the way."

As they walked, they were a peculiar sight and people stared at the filthy dog she cradled like a baby. She was not, she wanted to tell them, one of those film idiots with more money than sense, and this was clearly not any pampered Tuffy with paws too pristine to touch the earth.

Her usual supply store was tucked between a passport-photo shop and a line of Muslim tailors. An iron spiral staircase led to the second floor, where the shopkeepers lived. On the uneven curb, two men were drinking tea, their sandals off. One discussed seeking a suitor for his daughter: "And that asshole says to me, 'My son's a graduate, you'll have to give a car and ten lakh rupees.' I say to him: 'Have you seen your son? Twenty-three and balder than an acorn! Even a two-wheeler and one lakh is too much.'"

The men laughed as Geeta and Karem passed them to enter. "Dowries," she said. "Barbaric." When he was quiet, only nodding his agreement, she asked, "Did you take one? For Sarita?"

"Technically, maybe? Her parents gave us the shop as a wedding present. It was in her name, but it was still for us."

"That's not—"

"Namaste, Geetaben," the owner greeted, before his face seized in aversion. "What is that thing?"

"A puppy."

"I don't think I want a dog in here."

"Look at him: he's too weak to walk, much less break anything."

When the owner said nothing, Geeta knew she'd won. He was a slender man with delicate hands and a mustache that reminded her of a meerkat. She listed the amount of thread and black and gold beads she required.

"That's double from last time, isn't it? Things must be going well!"

Normally she would have chatted with him. In Kohra, she was neither a witch nor a widow, just a businesswoman. But now she only gave a noncommittal murmur. It didn't feel right boasting of her success when, not an hour prior, she'd cost Karem his entire livelihood.

"You'll get that refrigerator in no time."

Geeta wanted to stuff his meerkat mouth with beads. But then, it was her own damn fault, confiding in him. Despite her panic, Karem didn't appear interested, instead roaming the narrow shop with polite interest. Still, once they were outside, she offered context.

"I'm thinking of buying a fridge—if I save enough." She shrugged. "It's stupid."

"No, it's not. It's great. Be proud of your accomplishments. They didn't come easily."

"They didn't," she repeated. Then again, more firmly. "They really didn't."

"Geetaben—"

She interrupted with more aggression than she intended. "Why do you call me *ben*?"

"I—uh—I dunno, never really thought about it. Why does any-one? Respect, I suppose. Why?"

"How old do you think I am?"

"Er—" He squinted at her. "My age?" At her thunderous expression, he corrected: "Younger, much younger! Meaning, it's not like you're an aunty-type or anything."

But given her peers and their progeny, that was precisely what she was. She told him as much.

"Okay," he amended. "Well, you're not *my* aunty." He assumed a countenance of faux outrage, meant to loosen the tension Geeta had knotted. "And by the way, I'm only thirty-nine myself."

"It's not your fault," she soothed. "You have, like, a lakh of children. They age you, you know."

"Ah, yes, thank you. Though, if you think four is a lakh, then you might not be that great of a businesswoman, Geeta . . ." He smiled. "*. . . ben.*"

She scowled playfully. "Ass."

They passed a temple, divested sandals and sneakers crowding the staired entrance. The gold paint on the statues winked down at her.

Karem asked, "Did you and Ramesh not want children?"

It was mighty nice of him, Geeta thought, to not just assume (as the rest did) that she couldn't have them. Still, it was easier to discuss such matters with busy hands. So Geeta offered the dog another biscuit and answered, "I thought I did, but it didn't happen."

Despite Karem's prior diplomacy, Geeta braced herself: people thought the saddest thing was a childless woman. Anyone could sympathize with that scenario—a woman who couldn't be, in their view, a woman. It was easier to throw pity than to wrap their minds around a woman who preferred it that way. But to Geeta, the actual saddest thing, the real waste, was a woman with children she didn't want.

"You thought? Meaning you don't?"

She hesitated; a childless woman was unfortunate, a happily child-less woman was unnatural. She finally said, "I don't think I do."

"Good for you, then. Doing what suits *you* rather than everyone else."

"But still," Geeta said. "'Parenthood is a privilege,' right? With all the 'joy and rewards'?"

Karem snorted. "What? No. I mean, okay, well, yes sometimes, but it's also just thankless work. I love my kids, I can't imagine not having them, but I also completely *can* imagine not having them." He laughed. "It's strange. But you have to really be sure you want them to make it worth it. Otherwise, don't do it."

"Well, it's moot anyhow."

"I dunno." He shrugged. "I was the youngest of twelve. My mother was having children well into her forties."

"Your father couldn't leave her alone, eh?"

"Well, no televisions back then, right?"

Geeta laughed. "I don't have that problem."

"You could," Karem said. "If you wanted that problem."

And Geeta, ridiculously, grew warm.

"What about you? Any siblings?"

"Nope," she said, grabbing the prosaic turn of conversation. "Just me." Though Saloni had been like a sister. "I think my mother was pregnant once when I was six, but then she wasn't." Geeta shrugged. "We didn't really talk about it."

Just now, in once again oversharing with Karem, it struck her that her mother had probably endured miscarriages before Geeta as well, but outside the papadam story, it'd never occurred to her to imagine her mother's premotherhood life. Even after her mother had passed, Geeta's thoughts of her were caged by her own lifespan. Extrapolating those rules, all of Geeta's childless life would evaporate upon her childless death. Perhaps *that* was a reason to have children: to be remembered.

And yet, the Bandit Queen hadn't had any children, and she was remembered. While serving her prison term for killing twenty-two men in one day, she'd been rushed to the hospital for an emergency hysterectomy, where the doctor apparently joked, "We don't want Phoolan Devi breeding more Phoolan Devis." It didn't escape Geeta that the "we" he meant was not civilians, not officers, but men.

Karem nodded. "No one does. Sarita went through it, too. I think most people don't want to risk saying the wrong thing, so they say nothing instead. Not sure that's any better."

"I'm sorry," she told him. It seemed, to her at least, that Karem never said the wrong thing. Or perhaps he did, from time to time, but his sincerity salvaged it, saved him from being trite or callous or, worse, placating.

"Me, too."

It would be offensive to allow him to believe they shared this particular grief. "I didn't— I mean, I haven't. Had one, I mean."

His nod was slow and gentle. "Good. That's good."

Geeta focused on the puppy in her arms. They'd been wandering the streets, neither of them following, neither of them leading.

"He's kept the biscuits down. Does that mean he's okay?"

"I think it means he's going home with you."

"Excuse me?"

"Well," Karem said, stroking the tangled fur behind the dog's ears. "He trusts you. With some rest and food, he'll make a good pet."

"I don't need a pet."

Karem was cheerful. "Oh, sure you do. You live alone."

"And that's how I like it."

"He's the perfect company for you anyhow."

"How do you figure." Geeta wasn't curious, she only said it because there was a proud punch line waiting behind Karem's smug smile, and she was feeling generous.

"Handsome, but mute."

Her face remained stoic. "Hilarious."

"What'll you name him?"

"Nothing."

"'Nothing, no-thing,'" Karem tried it out like a new food. *"Kuch nahin, kuch-nay."* He shook his head, apologetic. "I don't think it suits him. Also, the poor guy probably already suffers from low self-esteem as it is."

She glared at him. "Do your kids tell you you're funny? Is that why you're like this?"

He gave her a goofy shrug. "I *am* funny."

"Listen, I'm not keeping him. I didn't want him to die, that doesn't mean I'm taking him in."

Karem shrugged. "We'll see." He squinted at the sky. "We got another hour or so before we're getting picked up. What were your other errands?"

She'd forgotten all about the rat poison. "Er—ah—I'll be quick and then meet you?"

"I'll go with you."

"Ah, no, please. It's a . . . woman thing."

Rather than recoiling, his expression was earnest. "If you need to buy sanitary napkins, Geeta, there's no shame in it. There's a chemist to the left."

Geeta prevaricated. She didn't purchase pads, no one from their village did; they were prohibitively exorbitant. Even Geeta, who had few other expenses, couldn't reconcile paying six rupees per napkin. She, like every other woman she knew, used and washed old cloths and handkerchiefs. Was she now going to have to buy napkins in front of Karem just to excuse her strange behavior?

No. Even if her pride could stand it, her pocket could not.

"The shop is—"

"No!"

"They wrap them so no one can see, if that's what you're worried about."

"It's fine—"

"But—"

She shouted, "I don't need napkins!"

He took a step back, blinking his surprise. "Okay. Ohhh," he drew the sound out like a siren and Geeta dreaded whatever ersatz epiphany awaited. "Is *that* why you said it was moot now? Because the . . . *seasons* have stopped coming?"

She protected her belly from his gaze with the dog. Her tone frosty, she said, "The seasons are fine, thank you very much."

Geeta handed him the dog, who growled until Karem scratched behind his ears. Only when the puppy settled into Karem did she enter the store. But the chemist carried no rat poison; she bought some Pudin Hara tablets she did not need and left.

"Ohhh," Karem said in that same infuriating manner when he saw her purchase. "But diarrhea isn't a woman problem, it's an everyone problem."

"I do not," Geeta seethed, "have diarrhea."

"Then . . ."

"It's just in case, okay? What're you, a cop?"

"Nope," he said, still in enragingly good cheer. "Just nosy." They passed an appliance store, with a frozen, toothy film star beaming his approval at the customers' choice of vendor. "We must," he said, grabbing her hand. Suddenly she was a passenger, carried through the door and into air-conditioned silence.

Unlike the bead shop, here Karem did not browse or wander. He marched toward the far wall, where refrigerator models loomed over the washing machines and cooktops. An associate in a short-sleeved collared shirt met them by a stout LG fridge. Painted purple flowers bloomed across its door. The young associate looked nervous but did not comment on the dog.

"Good afternoon, sir," he greeted. The two pens in his blue breast pocket were unprotected. "May I help you?"

"Just looking," Geeta said. From the mournful way the salesman appraised them—Karem in dusty slacks, her in a weathered sari—she knew the fellow worked on commission.

"Do you deliver?" Karem asked.

"Yes, sir."

Karem offered the rough distance and area of their village.

"Yes, there too we can deliver."

Geeta asked, "For free?"

"That depends on which refrigerator, ma'am."

"This one." She touched a steel door.

The associate tried to smile, but he was likely new to this work because he looked closer to laughter. His eyebrows soared. "Ah, your wife has good taste, sir—"

"Oh, he's not—"

"But that's a new Samsung, fifty-five thousand rupees"—Geeta snatched her hand back as if the door had turned into a man—"so yes, it qualifies for free shipping, but . . ." He gestured to them, then realized his discourtesy and dropped his arm.

"Yeah," Geeta said.

"But! The domestic models are ah, of course, less costly."

"Of course," Karem said.

"Like this one?" Geeta asked, pointing to the awful purple flowers.

Karem laughed and spoke to the associate. "Still think she's got good taste?"

All of a sudden, everything about Karem infuriated her: his ease, his confidence, his jest. She felt dowdy; clearly, Karem thought fancying her was so absurd that there was no risk of her misunderstanding his intentions. That he should think it was a joke—flirting, playacting at married and happy, complete with the jovial deprecation of a domestic life shared—was insulting. It was a mockery, but she didn't feel complicit. The prank was on *her*, not this novice salesboy whose pens were beginning to leak onto his pocket seam. The sharp blue dots were still small but would swell.

So she snapped, "Of course I don't. After all, look who I 'married.'"

At Karem's surprise, she bared her teeth into a smile. His forehead pleated. To see his confidence hiccup was satisfying in the same way scarfing four kulfi bars was: wonderful until the sugar sick rolled in. The associate divided a look between them, unsure of where to place his loyalties. He filled the air with jabber: "Perhaps, ah, a mini fridge would be better? If you don't need much storage? Are there children, sir?"

In her fantasies, her refrigerator had been taller than her, like the steel-door type. The purple flowered one was ugly and shorter, but at least it was still clearly a refrigerator, unlike the stumpy box the sales-boy now approached. He had to squat to open its door. The item felt like a concession rather than a victory.

"This is Samsung, nine-thousand-five rupees, sir. But this other one is only seven thousand rupees, domestic model, sir."

Karem spoke quietly. "I should be clear. She's not my wife, I'm just a friend. She'll be buying a fridge of her own choosing with money she's earned on her own."

The salesboy nodded, as though this were interesting rather than acutely awkward. He left them alone, chasing after a phantom phone call, and Geeta found she wished she could do the same. She exited the store, Karem at her heels, and once they were outside, the heat soothed the goosebumps on her arms.

"Sorry," he said, hands returning to his pockets after passing Geeta the dog. "It was fun pretending, and I got carried away. I didn't mean to let him assume I could afford it."

There were times in one's life, Geeta knew, where one was con-fronted with one's own assholery. After his terrible day—brought about largely by her own actions—she hadn't even been able to allow him a small flight of fancy. Sometimes she could be the worst fucking version of herself. Usually, with no one around to suffer the conse-quences, it went unnoticed. But when she was allowed near people . . . well, she could sabotage like it was a well-paying job.

"No, no," she said with such uncharacteristic intensity that she felt Karem believing her. "*I'm* sorry. I didn't realize how expensive it would be," she lied. "I took my disappointment out on you."

He smiled for peace, and she offered it back. "Okay, so maybe it takes a bit longer, but it's still going to happen."

Détente in place, they continued walking. Karem, not Geeta, real-ized it was time to turn back to meet the truck. While they waited near the highway, the fantastic weight of her failure found her and settled. This day—Karem, the dog, shopping—had all been a diversion from the life and duties that awaited her, namely a solution to the Samir problem. As Karem had phrased it: *It was fun pretending, and I got carried away*. Though she appreciated the anonymity of Kohra, she wasn't built for the city and usually suffered a mild anxiety until she neared home. But today, she found the inverse true. It was like bunking school; consequences were suspended until it was time to come home and face the gavel.

Perhaps Karem felt similarly because he sighed. "Was a nice day."

She observed him from across the truck bed. The sun was leaving them, staining the sky a confection pink. "Even with Bada-Bhai?" *And my brattiness?* she wondered.

He shrugged at her doubt. "I dunno. I just feel like everything's going to turn out okay, can't tell you how or why, but I like it. It can't last, so I'll just go with it."

"Why wouldn't it last?"

"Most feelings don't last."

"That's sad."

His half smile was quizzical. "Is it? I always thought it was reassuring. Like, knowing it's all temporary lowers the stakes. You can let yourself go to the limits of it all, because it will pass."

"So love doesn't stay? What about your kids?"

"Love can stay. But that's because it's not a feeling."

She already disagreed with him but asked anyway, "What is it, then?"

"It's a commitment."

"Like an obligation?"

"No, not in a bad way. I just mean it's a choice you renew every day."

Geeta thought about the orcas on her radio program. And Lakha, stuck in Bada-Bhai's awful house for her illegitimate son's sake. "I don't know. I don't think you *choose* to love your kids. I think you just sort of . . . do? Like, you're compelled to. It's biology or nature or whatever."

"Yeah, sure, parental love is primitive, but the love that commits to the sacrifices, that puts their happiness and needs over mine, that does it daily on repeat—that's a choice." He squinted in the way

Geeta now knew he did while thinking. Words came faster to him when he closed his eyes. "It's a choice I make. It's important, for me at least, to recognize that, because when you don't, resentment creeps in."

"Are you lonely?" A dumb question that highlighted her own state.

But, eyes still closed, he only said, "At times, very."

"It's harder for you than others, isn't it? It's all on you. There's no help."

"Oh, they take care of each other. My eldest is like a second parent. He even reminds me to eat."

"That's nice."

"Not really," Karem said. "It's not a childhood."

Geeta again felt inadequate; she was no good at comforting people, that was a muscle she'd long allowed to atrophy. Once, with Saloni, she had been. *Because you love me. You see me in a way no one else does. And because you're a duffer.*

If Karem was to be believed, she and Saloni had chosen each other, chosen to love each other—until they hadn't. (It was odd, how her thoughts these days returned to Saloni like a homing pigeon.)

Had Geeta chosen to love Ramesh? She supposed she had. What if he'd stayed? Would she have continued to choose to love him? Would she have forgiven him his fists and slurs, and renewed her commitment to sacrificing slivers of herself for his needs: food, sex, venting, validation?

It was not a road worth traveling. She and Karem disembarked the truck, the sherbet sunset turning to ash, and said their goodbyes.

Karem gestured to the dog. "Think of a good name for him."

"A name?" She looked down at her arms. So accustomed was she to his weight and warmth, she'd forgotten she was holding him. "I'm not really an animal lover."

"That's okay. They do most of the loving anyway."

She hadn't yet decided what she'd say to Farah, how she'd explain her failure; she assumed she had some time. But when Geeta walked to her house, there was Farah sitting on the step, folded into herself:

chin stacked on arms stacked on knees. When she saw Geeta, she stood, unfurling like a slow cloud. Stubborn light lingered through the dusk. And as Geeta registered Farah's fresh bruising, the swollen lip and cut cheekbone, it occurred to her that her dereliction, her bunking class for a day, had consequences well beyond herself.

EIGHT

here have you been?"

Geeta set the dog near her bed and turned to Farah. The bare overhead bulb was unkind to them both. Farah was wrecked and Geeta was disheveled, her hair frizzy, her face oily. Both she and the dog would have greatly benefited from a bath. Farah held yet another gourd. Geeta accepted it.

"What the hell happened to your face?"

"Where have you *been*? Is that hay in your hair?"

"Did Samir do this?" It was a foolish question, but she needed time.

"Where have you been all day? And why do you have a mutt?"

"I was in Kohra."

Farah's shoulders relaxed. "Oh, right. Of course. Sorry. So then, you got the stuff!"

"Partly."

"Meaning?"

"I have the *daru* in the kitchen, take it. But I couldn't manage the rat poison."

"Geetaben! That's, like, the most important part!"

At Farah's ire, the dog lifted his head to growl his disapproval, lips bared as his caret ears canted back. He sniffed the air above him, dark nose wiggling. Farah startled at the sound. Geeta watched her body tense; she seemed as uncomfortable around dogs as Saloni had been as a child. He rose to his fours, which Geeta would have taken as a sign of improvement, except he then ran his snout straight into one of the cot legs and crumpled, sniffing the floor. His soiled tail curled around himself in a weak fence.

Farah's frown was skeptical. "What's wrong with it?"

"He's blind."

"Oh. So how come you didn't get the poison?"

"That Karem fool wouldn't leave me alone and I couldn't very well buy it in front of him."

"Karembhai? Why were you with him?"

"He had a ride to town."

"Couldn't you have ditched him for, like, two minutes to buy it?"

Geeta's spine prickled. She was defensive because she felt guilty, parading around town with Karem like a carefree teenager while Samir was making Farah's backbone and ribs one. He'd come for her and her money next, she reminded herself. "Don't you think I would've if I could've? What, you think I *liked* hanging out with him all day, following me around like a dog? No, it was . . . annoying."

"Okay, okay."

"I mean it," Geeta pressed, her mouth running even though she knew it was more credible to leave well enough alone. Even girls in the fifth standard knew protesting more only exacerbated matters. "Very annoying."

"Geetaben," Farah said, rolling her eyes. "You don't have to prove anything to me, okay? I may be illiterate, but I'm not a moron. I know no *chakkar* is going on between you and"—Here Farah started laughing, and Geeta found that she was insulted, incredibly so, as she had been in the appliance shop—"Karembhai."

"And just why the hell not?"

"The man's no saint. I mean, he's plenty handsome, very much a pigeon fancier."

"A what?"

"You know," Farah said with a sly turn of her hand. "With the *lay-deez*. Great head of hair—Samir goes on about it all the time, he's so jealous it's pathetic, and I'm like: 'What did you expect? Your father was bald as a marble, na?' Not that I actually *say* that, can you imagine?—sorry, ahem, right. Anyway, Karembhai goes to town to get his . . . needs handled. But you're—you're not like that, Geetaben, you're about business, not mixing in the dirt. Aboveboard, you know? *Sidhi-sadhi*." At Geeta's clear displeasure, Farah sighed. "I'm *complimenting* you."

"It's fine," Geeta said abruptly, more to herself than Farah. The flash of hurt she'd experienced upon hearing of Karem's exploits was only because, above all else, she hated feeling like a fool. She decided not to care whether the rumor mill found her to be a viable prospect for Karem, because really, it made no difference. Cradling an ego, she told herself, was as useless as throwing water into the sea. "We can't wait any longer. We need to improvise the poison."

"How?"

"Give me a minute." Geeta sat on her mattress, worrying her earlobe in thought. She let the dog lick the fingers of her free hand while Farah paced. Each time he sensed Farah's passing, his lips curled, his snarl reverberating.

"Shouldn't it be outside?"

"He can't see."

"So it's just gonna live with you?"

"I didn't say that. But he'll sleep here tonight."

"I don't think it likes me."

"He's just protective. If you pet him, it might help."

Farah's disgust was evident. "Is that even safe? It might have fleas. Or rabies." She squinted at the dog. "Hey, maybe that could work! It could, like, *bite* Samir and then—"

"That's it!" Geeta snapped her fingers and moved toward the door. "Come on."

"Wait, don't we need it?" Farah asked, pointing to the dog.

"He doesn't have rabies, Farah. And look at him—he can't even find his own face, much less bite anyone. Let's go."

"Where are we going?"

"The school."

"What, why? Listen, I don't think now is the time to teach me to read."

When Geeta said nothing, Farah gave up and they walked in silence: Farah shuffling to keep pace and Geeta wielding her lantern. A few minutes later, they stood in front of the formerly white gate that enclosed the school. The paint had chipped on some bars more than others, revealing the dark iron underneath, and the result was zebraic. Beyond the gate was a long, one-story building, skinny white beams framing each brown door. A billboard atop read MODERN SCHOOL, with (ENGLISH MEDIUM) spelled below, but Geeta recalled every lesson inside being conducted in Gujarati, even English class.

Farah rubbed her palms together. "Let me handle this." One foot on a rung, she heaved herself up with a grunt and straddled the top. As she maneuvered her sari around her knees to get to the other side, Geeta pushed the unlocked gate open.

"Ooh," Farah said as she swung in an arc along with the door, sari pleats bundled between her legs.

They walked down the line of classrooms. Various bulletin boards were on the walls, posting students' marks.

Geeta's lantern cast a puddle of light in front of them. Like a bright moon, it was strongest in the center, surrounded by a dim, pallid ring. It reminded Geeta of *su-su,* but that comparison could have been due to the uric smell.

As they moved from door to door, Farah asked, "What're we looking for?"

"Shut up," Geeta hissed.

Farah looked over both shoulders and lowered her voice. "Oh, right, 'cause we don't want to get caught."

"No. Because you're annoying."

"Oh. Sorry." Farah's eyes were sunken and bruised in the tepid light. She looked like a baby panda.

They found a door with an unlocked bolt. Opening it, Geeta traced her lantern through the dank classroom corners. Brown water damage, ubiquitous and benign in the daylight, loomed with new menace. She signaled to Farah, and they stood over an extinguished mosquito-repellent coil. The grey incense spiral had been reduced to a nub, fallen ash circling the stand.

"What?"

"We need another coil."

"Why?" Farah stared at Geeta. "I think you're overtired. Let's go."

"They're poisonous if you eat them."

"O-kay." Farah blinked. "Ohhh-kay!" She clapped her hands. Her smile was not minacious, it was almost sweet, but with her bruised face and the jaundiced light, Farah looked contradictory, a zygote on the precipice of monsterhood. Her fresh injuries had distracted Geeta from those that were healing. Her erstwhile black eye had faded to the color of diluted turmeric, rimming her eye like an unwashed glass. "This is a great idea!" She stopped applauding, her hands on her hips. "Is *that* how you did it?"

"Didn't I tell you that's none of your business?"

"I'm asking because I want to know if it works. So we don't lose another day."

"I'm aware of the stakes, Farah. It's *my* goddamn money. If you're so eager, why don't you just sew Samir's lips shut like one of your fancy dresses? That way he'll stop drinking you poor."

Farah took no offense. She shrugged. "We're poor regardless, Geetaben."

Geeta's sigh filled the classroom. "I know." Closing her eyes, she said, "Just help me find a fresh coil."

They located a series of drawers below the windows. Most held rulers, pencils, workbooks with weak spines. Farah squatted and yanked at a stuck drawer, her teeth bared in effort. Her acorn biceps hardened beneath her skin as she jerked. When nothing budged, Geeta handed her a wooden ruler. Farah shook her head. "You do it."

"Why?"

Farah massaged the meat of her palms with her thumbs. "It hurts. My hands are my livelihood!"

"And how do you think I make my money?" Geeta snapped. "Disco dancing?"

"You put beads on string. Monkeys can do that. I do fine crafts-manship," Farah said.

Geeta rolled her eyes. "You're a *tailor*."

Farah elevated her palms like an Islamic prayer. "Art, Geetaben," she said in English. *"Art."*

Geeta glared at her. "I've never understood Samir more than I do right now."

"He may hit me, but he'd never touch my hands. *He* knows their value."

It would have been satisfying to abandon her right then. To volley her ingratitude straight back into her already pummeled face. But they were stuck together, like wet pages of a book Farah couldn't even read. So instead Geeta snapped, her voice as nasty as she could manage: "I guess it's just too bad you're not as good a mother as you are an *artist*." Farah's face folded, but Geeta had no desire to stop. "Oh, everyone knows he beats them, too. You know, when he has to spare your hands because they're so 'valuable.'"

"I *am* a good mother. I'm doing all this to protect them."

Geeta forced a nonchalant shrug. "It seems to me that a good mother would've never let it get this far."

"And what do you know about mothering? Hm?"

"So much, thanks to you! One helpless baby." She gestured to Farah and ticked a finger. "Check. One exhausted woman who must constantly wipe helpless baby's ass. Check."

"Not the same thing at all. Not that you would know."

"And I'm glad I don't. More trouble than it's worth."

Farah gasped. "That's not true. The joys are—"

"Rewarding. Yeah, yeah. Just move."

Geeta hipchecked Farah aside. After jamming a ruler into the crevice, she invested her fury into a sharp downward yank. Wood splintered from both the ruler and the drawer. Inside sat matches and a stack of green coils.

Geeta returned the ruler to another drawer while Farah selected a coil. They said nothing as they left the school, but once past the gate, Farah attempted peace.

She pinched both earlobes in the apology semiotic. "Geetaben—"

"Don't," Geeta said. "I don't want to hear it. We're not friends. We were never friends. I say plenty about Saloni, but at least she's an honest snake. You have honey on your tongue and a knife in your pocket."

"No! I—"

"I don't have to defend my work to you. I eat no one's salt but my own. And until you and your drunk *chut* of a husband started harassing me, I was fine. You begged me to save you because you can't save yourself. You can't seem to do much of anything."

Farah began crying, but it was quiet and earnest rather than her usual overblown, onion-cutting tears. "Please forgive me." She sniffed. "I didn't mean any of it. You *are* my friend, Geetaben." She launched herself at Geeta, the impact forcing her to take a step back. The hug was fierce, Farah's reedy arms surprisingly strong, and Geeta could smell the coconut oil on Farah's hair, the regret and fear emanating from her skin. Geeta was not accustomed to hugs; she did not return the embrace, but neither did she pull away. She patted Farah's shoulder twice before extricating herself.

Farah gathered the skin of her throat with her thumb and forefinger in a vow. "I swear, I won't ruin it this time. I promise, Geetaben. You can count on me."

NINE

The dog, obviously, was just a ruse. Even he seemed to realize this, snuffing trash and humping tires on the way to Karem's door, as though he smelled her intent and was bent on procrastination. If so, his perspicacity impressed Geeta, because she herself wasn't clear on what she was seeking. Exasperated, she called him over and carried him the remainder of the way. He smelled like unwashed feet and stale sweat. His odor had worsened since the truck ride from Kohra.

"Tomorrow's bath day, Bandit." The name had been more of an inevitability than a decision. He squirmed as they arrived, climbing up her chest, attempting eye contact. His cold nose found her chin. She maneuvered around his smelly face to knock. Maybe Bandit knew what she refused to admit, that she was chasing trouble.

After the row with Farah, Geeta hadn't wanted to be alone. When she'd first pushed open her front door, Bandit bounded toward her, pink tongue lolling. She cooed over his seemingly restored vision, rubbing his fox ears. She'd forgotten about him and it was pleasant to have companionship without the onus of speaking.

In the kitchen, she prepared lentils and rice in a *khichdi* that neither of them touched. It had been her favorite comfort food as a child. Whenever her stomach had pained, her mother made it, but Geeta always added dollops of spicy mango pickle that, her mother chided, defeated the purpose. But her parents stored loads of *achaar*— carrot, gooseberry, green chili—in the pantry for her and Saloni, a gesture of love so minor that its absence shouldn't have stung her eyes, though it did.

Bandit's body, warm and pulsing, proved a panacea for Farah's lackadaisical cruelty. Geeta had steeled herself against the typical rubbish: that she could turn children cross-eyed and render men lame. But Farah had struck what Geeta had neglected to protect: her pride in her work.

Geeta rubbed Bandit's belly, his hind legs extending in wanton hedonism, until he fell asleep on her lap. Her affection, it seemed, was addictive; he awoke each time she stilled her hand. Until she resumed petting him, he glared at her with such focus, it was a marvel he'd been blind only a few hours prior. She muttered that he was already spoiled, but obediently stroked his coat, detangling as she went.

It was satisfying, the unabashed love he'd shown her so quickly for so little in exchange, but after a few minutes, her restlessness proved no match for him. Her mirror revealed the dog hair liberally peppering her sari. Sluicing it off was futile, so she changed into a black one. Though it was plain enough, the bijou blue embroidery announced she was trying too hard. So she changed again into a maroon one that announced she had the aesthetic sense of the gourd on her counter. After shaking out the original sari as best she could, she changed back. As she tamed her brows and hair, Bandit observed her titivations knowingly.

"I liked you better blind," she informed him.

Now Karem, and thankfully not one of his kids, opened the door. "Geeta! Everything okay?"

"Yeah, sorry, but it's Bandit. Here." She thrust Farah's gourd at him. "For you."

"Er—thank you. Bandit?"

Geeta lifted her arms to indicate the pungent dog.

"Nice name. That was fast."

She scowled at his smile. "I don't want to hear it."

"What's the problem?"

"Well, I made him some *khichdi,* but he won't eat it."

"Are you sure you're not just a bad cook?" He laughed. "I'm kidding, come on in."

She looked past him but did not cross the threshold. "I don't want to disturb."

"Not at all. My youngest two are sleeping, but we can talk out back?"

She left her sandals outside. "Sure."

He rubbed the soft space between Bandit's eyes, and they closed in pleasure. "Hey! He can see me!" When had he removed his small earring? Like her, he wore no jewelry, and she saw the divot in his lobe.

She was soon busy ogling his home without appearing as though she were ogling. Really, all there was to the house could be observed at once. The space near the front door was also the common area, where makeshift toys littered the thin rug and the cement floor. A stack of steel plates and utensils were housed in a far nook. On either side of her were two bedroom doors, closed now. She imagined the younger two slept in one, while the older boys had their own room. Then Geeta noticed the charpoy leaning against the common room wall, legs sticking out like an insect's. Like many people, Karem likely slept on his terrace beneath the stars.

Thinking about Karem in bed was not the smartest idea. But then, neither was a surprise nocturnal appearance at his home.

"Papa?" A boy in shorts and a torn red shirt that read NIKE emerged from one of the rooms.

"Shh, it's okay. Go back to sleep."

The boy rubbed his eye. "I'm thirsty."

"You are not." Karem turned to Geeta. "This is Raees."

"Hey, you're the lady from the playground."

She placed him after a moment. "*Kabaddi* kid?"

"Yeah."

"Did you win?"

His smile turned alert. He was missing two bottom teeth. "Yeah. She said she wasn't scared of you, but she was lying, 'cause everyone knows that you can make sweets taste like *gobar* if you get mad at someone."

"I—er—how old are you, Raees?"

"Seven. It was my birthday last week."

Which, Geeta realized now, was why Karem had corrected his kids' ages on the way to Kohra. "Many belated happy returns."

"Thank you. Wanna see my balloons?"

"Let's not bother Geeta with that. She can see them some other time. And you need sleep."

"What's that?"

"This is Bandit."

"Does he bite?"

"Not that I know of. He's very gentle. Just let him smell you first." She set Bandit down and Raees joined him, plopping cross-legged on the floor. Bandit rolled onto his back, front paws bent, his exposed belly both an invitation and demand.

"What kind of dog is he?"

"That's a good question. I don't know. I think he's a lot of different things. I bet that's what makes him so cute."

"Is he the one you fed your husband to?"

"Raees!" Karem's voice was appalled. "Apologize at once. I'm so sorry, Geeta."

"It's all right," she said. That one stung more than the sweets comment. She'd forgotten herself. Forgotten that children were scared of her. Forgotten that she preferred it that way. "It's not his fault he hears things."

"Well, he didn't hear it here." Karem didn't lift his gaze from his son. "Apologize."

"I'm sorry, Geeta-aunty."

"It's okay, Raees. No, I didn't feed my husband to Bandit."

"So then what happened to him?"

"Another good question. Can you keep a secret?"

When Raees issued a somber nod, she bent at the waist and curled a finger. The boy floated closer. "I don't know what happened to my husband."

"That's not a secret!"

"It's not?"

"No, a secret is like when you break your father's watch but then you say your sister did it 'cause she never gets in trouble for anything." Raees clapped a hand over his mouth. "Sorry, Papa."

Karem shook his head. Farah was right; his hair was very thick. Grey heavily decorated his crown and temples. "I'll forget I heard that, but off to bed."

But Raees was adroit in the art of dithering. He showered their guest with attention, avoiding his father's unamused eyes completely. "Geeta-aunty, can I *please* show you my birthday balloons? Papa brought them all the way from Kohra."

Geeta, too, ignored Karem. "I'd love to see them."

Raees slipped inside his room. Karem stage-whispered, "Don't wake your sister."

"He's a nice boy."

Karem smiled. "He's got a crush."

She patted her bun demurely. "Oh, well, I wouldn't call it—"

"He's really taken to Bandit."

"Yes." Her hand fell. "The dog."

Raees returned holding five strings. The speckled balloons still hovered near the low ceiling, but they were beginning to sag. The pastel skins puckered, no longer taut. For some awful, horrible, inopportune reason, Geeta thought of her breasts and how this was what she had to look forward to.

She offered the proud boy her soft applause. "Lovely!"

"Bed," Karem said.

Raees made an unsuccessful plea for water, and then padded to his room, head hanging comically low, balloons in tow.

She followed Karem through the house and outside to the small, unfenced dirt patch that was his backyard. A bicycle with a broken kickstand was on the ground. In the far corner, a buffalo slept, tied near the clay stove and a jumble of tins and jars.

"Sorry about all that."

"Don't be." For a brief while, she hadn't spared a thought to her problems. Or Farah. Their tiff suddenly mattered little to her. When Farah once again bungled things tonight, she'd land on Geeta's door-step and Geeta would grant her both forgiveness and a new plan to eliminate Samir.

"So did you poison him or what?"

Geeta balked. "What?"

"Bandit? Your cooking, remember? It was a joke."

"Oh, yeah." She forced a laugh that came out a wheeze. "I mean, no. No, he wouldn't eat the *khichdi*."

It was a very strict truth. She surmised that Bandit had eaten so many Parle-G biscuits that the rice and lentils held little interest. Geeta set him down and Karem squatted to inspect the pup. Arms bereft, Geeta didn't know what to do. She tugged her ear and stared down at the back of Karem's dark head.

"He seems very happy. I wouldn't worry about it. Has he *tutti*-ed?"

"What?" she sputtered.

His question didn't scandalize her, it was that he used that benign but infantile word.

He sighed in self-deprecation. Bandit hopped near his ankles, demanding attention. "Sorry. Habit. In this house I forget how to talk to adults. I may remind you to go *su-su* next."

Bandit jumped at Karem's shins, higher and higher.

"Bandit! No! Off!" Geeta rapped his snout. He whimpered but settled and as a reward, Geeta scratched his rear, which she'd noticed he enjoyed. "Oof. Did he hurt you?"

Karem laughed. "No, he's the size of your gourd. Ugly thing," he said, squinting. "So ugly he's cute."

"Oi! Show some respect. This dog is a hero. He's a survivor of abuse."

Karem continued to chuckle. "Well, so are you, and you manage to look great."

Geeta scoffed before she could stop herself. Not because she didn't believe him—which she did not, to be clear—but because it was so wildly audacious: presenting a smooth line while addressing her marked history. It was preferable, she found, mentioning Ramesh as a footnote rather than the thesis. Once again she admired how Karem managed it—always saying things she liked hearing, rarely offending even someone as prickly as she was.

In return, she offered him a scarce gift: the truth. "That was nice. Thank you."

"You're welcome."

Then he touched her, his palm on her cheek.

It had been eons since someone had touched her with purpose rather than by chance. Even before she and Ramesh, more by time than agenda, became strangers, she didn't feel touched. They'd devolved into a perfunctory dance. Enough time passed and touch became a hollow parody of itself. It was, however, a basic human need. Now, she found she could not bear to be touched, all the while craving it with a dipsomaniacal desperation that drove alcoholics to eat their vomit or addicts to snort or smoke dead scorpions. Geeta's raw brain yelped even as she leaned into Karem's hand like a heliotrope toward the sun.

And it wasn't that she went wild with desire or that arousal skewered her abdomen. It was worse than merely being confronted with her own sexuality after five years of dormancy. Geeta discovered a few awful things under Karem's light, unsuspecting palm. That she'd spent years assuming she was no longer a creature of want. That despite this first fact, she'd been starving for touch that entire time. That despite the first two facts, there was absolutely nothing to be done, not in a speck of a village where her name was mixed with dirt.

Which was why she stunned no one more than herself when she unglued his hand from her cheek and kissed him.

He tasted of tobacco, but it was fresh enough to not be unpleasant. His kiss was open-mouthed and intimate, but tidy. Nothing about his technique was as tentative as hers was, his was not a mouth that had taken long hiatuses from kissing. She was surprised by how quickly she adjusted and emulated his style.

Karem nuzzled the space between her neck and ear. "He's a fool. A blind fool."

The kissing was excellent, but Geeta was not so swept up that she didn't think to ask, "Who?"

"Ramesh."

She canted back. "Why are you thinking about Ramesh?"

"I'm not. Well, earlier, but not now—"

She was being prickly again, ruining things for herself before they began. They'd mentioned Ramesh before in the abstract and now Karem was giving her another compliment. It was what normal people did, she reproached herself, people who weren't busy squashing their libidos. "Never mind. It's okay," she said, and returned to his mouth.

She didn't care that the excitement she felt was a direct result of his experience, dalliances with the *lay-deez* Farah had mentioned earlier tonight. It was precisely why she'd come here. She supposed she could admit that now, what with Karem's tongue against hers. She was possessive of nothing other than her own pleasure.

Geeta often wondered how Phoolan Mallah had tolerated having lovers after being subjected to such systemic sexual abuse. She'd run away from a bad childhood and worse husband to join a gang whose leader, an upper-caste man, immediately planned to rape her. Vikram Mallah, a man of her same caste, killed the leader and became her lover and husband. She joined his dacoit of mixed-caste men. But even among thieves, caste polarized. The upper castes turned on

Vikram, slaughtering him. Then they trapped the seventeen-year-old Phoolan in their village, alternating between beating and raping and parading her, naked and leashed, through neighboring villages, where they encouraged the locals to use her.

After three weeks, she escaped with the help of men from her own caste, one of whom became her lover. They created a new gang— comprised solely of their own Mallah caste—and on Valentine's Day, she returned to that village, and stained it red with the blood of twenty-two upper-caste men. After her revenge resulted in an interminable imprisonment, Ummed Singh helped secure her release, and she married him.

Geeta had assumed that each time Phoolan embarked on a new relationship, it was a purely strategic move, seeking protection rather than love. Each new man shielded her from the past's consequences. Such circumstances could hardly spell choice. In a world where her vagina was a liability, was there even room for petty things like love? But maybe Phoolan had managed to separate Vikram from those before him, and exercise trust. Perhaps it wasn't about power after all, but companionship.

Geeta had thought she'd frozen herself, but all the while, time had chipped away at her. She was not now what she'd been then, but enough remained to thaw. Enough to realize why and how Phoolan had managed.

Still, discretion was essential to her survival. While widower Karem was expected to service himself outside the village, Geeta was afforded no such berth for humanity. If people discovered that she was a woman rather than a virago, shit would shower on her head. The women's gossip would worsen, and men would issue lascivious invitations. Seeking his understanding, Geeta managed to choke out her request between heady kisses, "No one can know."

His mouth stilled. "What?"

"I just meant . . . you know, the village is so small and you . . ."

His hands were gentle but firm as he removed her from his orbit. "I, what?"

It was difficult to face him in light of what they'd shared. Geeta wished to resume kissing so they didn't have to suffer the intimacy of eye contact. She moved for another embrace, but he deflected.

"Listen, no one minds your indiscretions, they're natural because you're a man, but for me . . ."

"My indiscretions?"

"You know, what you do in Kohra . . ." She gave a vague wave of her hand. "And wherever."

"What do I do in Kohra?"

"You know."

"Work?"

"Sure. And *chakkar chal* or whatnot." She added, "Look, I'm not judging. That's my whole point. You and I get it. *They* don't. That's why—"

"No one can know."

She went limp with relief. "Yes."

He nodded, rubbing his stubbled jaw. His gaze shifted to a spot behind her. "Do you not know how insulting you are, Geetaben, or do you just not care?"

The distance of his formality was crushing. She scrabbled for understanding so she could resume control. If she knew where she stood, she could protect herself. She blinked, trying to adapt, but she had no idea how they'd landed here.

"I should go," she said, hoping he'd contradict her.

"Yes."

It was a long, mortifying walk through Karem's house to the front door. Geeta burned while Bandit trailed behind her, so content and oblivious that she wanted to cry out her jealousy. Though Karem had accused her of being insulting, she felt terribly insulted. And rejected. Not to mention stupid. She could never face him again. Which was feasible, she reasoned as the door closed behind her, because before her whole killing club with Farah began, she'd barely seen him around the village.

Maybe it wasn't Farah, Geeta thought as she held Bandit for

comfort. Maybe it was her. She couldn't keep or maintain any relationship. She was impossible to be around, to get on with. Such was her toxicity that she was awful even when she thought she was being agreeable. She'd driven away everyone from Saloni to Ramesh, only to sit around her barren home, puzzled over her solitude. Even Karem—patient, abiding Karem—whose unflappable good humor could withstand four exhausting children, had a limit to her bile.

She should have had a child after all, at least then there'd be someone forced to stay. Bandit would wise up one of these days and run away; she gave him tacit permission by keeping him unleashed. He was free, never a goat tied to a tree, never a bride with a *mangalsutra*. She was so engrossed in self-pity that she didn't realize she was crying until Bandit licked her face.

"Well," Geeta said as she nuzzled his sour body. "Fuck."

TEN

The following morning, while she nursed her humiliation hangover, temple *bhajan*s screeched outside and Bandit finally ate the stale *khichdi*. She eyed him warily, afraid he'd get sick, but he chased the lizard in hale cheer, paws scrabbling around her unused desk. In addition to all her other failures, she'd also been neglecting her business.

Matters, she assessed as she flopped back on her bed, were not ideal.

She'd awoken with a dull headache from crying herself to sleep like some love-starved teenager, but at least her shame was private. She couldn't look at her reflection, her swollen eyes and lips neatly summarizing the duality of the previous night. She examined the events under the day's new light: she'd shared a kiss and an argument. It was nothing to cringe over. She'd endured grosser mortifications than rejection. It would've been far worse if she'd flung her lips at him and he'd batted her away immediately. Still, the mere prospect of facing Karem made her want to hide under her bed with Bandit, who was romping around with such unapologetic joy that Geeta found it a bit rude.

"You," she told Bandit, "need a bath."

Outside, he dodged her like he sensed her agenda. By the end of it, they were both dripping and Geeta had used two days' worth of water. All of her tubs were empty, but Bandit's dingy paws were white again and his odor benign. He flung a welter of droplets at her as she wrung out her nightdress. It was before ten, but already very warm. She couldn't locate a single cloud. Bandit panted, clean tail wagging. It curled up in an attractive question mark, the fur already fluffing.

"Well, look at you. Who'd have thought you'd be such a handsome devil?"

She changed and hung the wash on her clothesline. When there was still no Farah wailing over some fresh misstep, Geeta grew anxious. Either Farah had changed her mind about the entire plan, or she'd actually managed it. Each theory lent a bit of relief and a bit of terror. Unless, Geeta thought with a start, Samir had caught Farah mid-attempt and punished her.

Bandit succumbed to a happy nap in a sun-warmed corner, nose buried in his clean paws, his luxurious tail alongside him. She couldn't concentrate at her desk, so Geeta decided to investigate under the guise of fetching more water; all important matters were discussed over the pump. Saloni had a private hand pump in her courtyard, but even she habitually drew from the communal well, lest she miss any valuable scuttlebutt.

As insurance, Geeta took a circuitous route that passed Farah's house. A bucket in each hand, Geeta saw the mourners from meters away. A few were already in white, some cried, others comforted, some shared urgent whispers. As she approached, she did not see Farah but she did see her children, huddled in a nucleus of grief. Farah's eldest daughter carried her baby brother, her nonexistent hip jutting to create a shelf for his small body. Her two younger sisters were crying, but she remained dry-eyed, her face a blank slate, and this was how Geeta recognized her from the playground. She wore the same vacant expression now as she had when she'd shoved Karem's son.

After Geeta absorbed the tableau, their island of the recently fatherless, she hurried away. The empty buckets jangled against her calves, and she dropped them. She barely made it to a neem tree in time, vomiting over its dry roots, one palm against the trunk. Hinged at the waist, she stared at her sick, her breathing ragged. Vinegar and bile coated her mouth.

By the time she straightened, she'd accepted two salient truths: they were murderers, and if she herself felt this shocked, Farah must be demented. There was no way Geeta could join those mourners, feign horror at the news, face the children she'd robbed of a father.

Geeta collected her buckets with clumsy hands and stumbled home, inner ears and throat burning.

Bandit immediately sensed her distress and licked her face in comfort. She allowed it for a moment, but then pressed him away to pace, trying in vain to properly breathe—*"Kabaddi, kabaddi, kabaddi"*—until she felt dizzy when pivoting within the confines of her cell. She should get accustomed to it, she thought with climbing hysteria, this was her future. She'd been so preoccupied with finding a way for Farah to remove her nose ring that Geeta hadn't realized how much of her own future she'd put in Farah's inept hands. Farah was neither thorough nor cautious; she'd probably left a hundred clues that pointed back to them.

The day dragged, consuming Geeta in a maw of anxiety. Her condition was contagious; Bandit roamed underfoot, needy and dissatisfied. She flicked on the radio, tried to listen to the hyena segment of the Gyan Vani program but was too distracted. There was only one person in the world Geeta wished to see, only one who could understand her plight. The irony did not escape her; the woman she'd shooed like a pesky mosquito, she now craved like a cold drink.

Farah came that evening, bearing her usual gourd. She wore a white *salwar-kameez* and no jewelry. A white scarf covered her crown, but her dark hair was visible through the diaphanous cloth. She was smiling. Once inside, she pushed the scarf down to her shoulders and twirled. "Grieving widow is a good look for me, don't ya think?" She shimmied in a dance, singing an impromptu song: "I got no nose ring,

I got no nose ring." Her spirits were high enough to tolerate Bandit.
She bent to scratch his neck. "Hello, doggy woggy." Bandit did not
growl, but neither did he fall into her touch with his typical shameless
solicitation. "Hey, it can see!"

When Farah registered Geeta's stricken face, her blithe manner
changed. "What is it? Is your stomach paining? Sit down, Geetaben."
She took Geeta's hand and led her to her own bed.

"We're screwed," Geeta said. "We're really screwed." She let her
hands catch her head, one heel pressed against each temple. With
everyone else thinking of her as a murderess for so long, she, too, had
forgotten that she wasn't. There was no way they'd get away with this;
two village women were no match for actual authorities with resources.

Farah kneeled, and her cold fingers tugged Geeta's wrists, prying
them away from her face. Geeta resisted, but Farah won. She seized
Geeta's gaze and held fast. The cuts on her cheekbone and lip still
bore seams of dried blood, but her eye was now chartreuse. Farah was
on the mend. "No, we're not. Everything went perfectly. It's over."

Farah stood, her mourning clothes whispering. She paced, much
like Geeta had most of this horrid day, but Farah's mind had flown to
more prosaic matters. "They took the body today."

"Who?"

She waved a hand. "Some Dom. It just looks like alcohol poisoning since Samir puked before he died, but I'm going to cremate him
as soon as possible, just in case."

Geeta blinked. It had not occurred to her before, but now she
said, "But you're Muslim."

Farah shrugged. "So what? You think that drunk was a strict Muslim? Trust me, if he doesn't get into Jannah, it won't be on that tech-
nicality. Besides, he deserves to burn."

Geeta herself wasn't a religious enthusiast. She made temple
rounds on the big-ticket holidays and festivals, but there was no *puja*
corner in her home and, more important, no guests to judge her for
not having said corner. Her mother, however, had believed. Or maybe

it was only habit that led her to light ghee-soaked cotton every day and recite god's myriad of names on her *japamala*, one name for each bead.

But now, worry pricked Geeta. Not at aggravating whatever higher power waited to smite her, but fear of overstepping. For thinking she was more than she was. Not only had they played God, now they were tampering with last rites? The latter somehow seemed worse than the former, which was, with some light moral gymnastics, justifiable given Samir's threats, vices and abuse.

"But what will people think—"

"We can't risk the body being dug up if people get suspicious later." Farah picked lint from her top. "You see it all the time on that *C.I.D.* show, where they realize the spouse is up to some *dhokhebaazi* and they're all, 'Oh no, the evidence is gone!' But there's a twist! The victim's Muslim so they're able to catch the spouse after all by digging it up—"

"Exhuming," Geeta offered on autopilot.

"Yeah, that. Whatever. And anyway, he's got no family left and there're, what, like, three Muslims in this village? I doubt Karem is gonna holler at me for messing up Samir's burial— Oh!" She snapped her fingers. "I can always say there was a paperwork mix-up, or that the Dom messed up. See, this is the easy part, Geetaben. You did the hard part already."

"We shouldn't have done it."

Geeta noticed grey hairs near Farah's temple and realized that she may not have been as young as Geeta'd assumed.

"We had to." Farah's brows drew together. "Listen, it's done now. 'What's the use of crying when birds ate the whole farm?'"

"But your children," Geeta said. "They're—"

"Sad now, but they'll be happier for it. We all will be." She patted Geeta's head. "Don't forget: now that he's gone, we both get to keep our money."

"It's not about the money," Geeta said. The back of her neck pleated as she looked up at Farah, blazing in white like a deity. Geeta was not crying, but her eyes watered. "What good is money if we spend our lives in jail?"

Looming above Geeta, Farah gave her an odd look. Strange and quizzical. "Of course it's about the money, Geetaben; it was always about the money. Get some rest and you'll see that." She let herself out, stepping over Bandit, while Geeta remained frozen on her bed.

———

The authorities arrived soon enough, faster than Geeta'd expected, slower than she'd hoped. The anticipation was gnawing and persistent, like hundreds of mosquitos after a monsoon rain. Farah, she'd heard through water pump gossip, had declined a medical report but requested that Samir be "returned" within twenty-four hours for his burial, per Islamic ritual. However, the Dalit corpse handler, somehow both outcaste and lower caste and thereby the only one who'd go near the pollution of a dead body, had apparently confused Samir with a Hindu man (despite the circumcision) and Samir was ultimately buried in an urn under three clumps of dirt that a brave Farah, sans nose ring, had lovingly tossed.

The cop arrived in the middle of the weekly loan meeting, his presence sparking the women's tittered curiosity. He waited, respectfully, outside Saloni's packed house, where they now held their meetings. Before poor Runi's death, she'd hosted them on her porch. Even with the swing in the center, Saloni's front porch was spacious with good acoustics, conducive to large gatherings.

The loan officer, Varun, perched on the thick parapet lining Saloni's porch, collection box to his side, while the women sat cross-legged in a sloppy circle. Varun began the meeting and everyone quieted.

Geeta crushed her group's money in her hands, then remembered herself and smoothed the bills. She tried not to look at Farah, still clad in her mourning whites, or the cop, but her eyes sought them time and time again. Fear tethered her like a yoke. Certainly the officer could smell her guilt from her copious sweat alone.

That all six of the smaller loan groups were gathered together again signaled one week, just one week since Farah's timid shuffle and swollen eye had come begging. To Geeta, it felt more like months. Back then, Farah's imploring had been morbid, yet somehow sweet. *That* Farah, Geeta had not seen lately. The Farah now sitting in the circle, subdued but confident, had a healing face and a perfectly centered *bindi*. Geeta looked down; she was wringing the money again. How was it that Farah—arguably the more culpable between the two of them—exhibited no fear of reprisal?

After taking attendance, Varun called each of the leaders to approach with their group's weekly repayment. Mrs. Amin went first, teasing Varun as she always did about extending bigger loans. "That's up to hats bigger than mine," he laughed. They called him Varunbhai out of respect, despite the fact he was younger than most of them. He hailed from Delhi, and he often fumbled for the correct word in Gujarati. He had a good sense of humor, joining the laughter when the women giggled at his pronunciation. Saloni in particular had taken to him, her eyelashes batting like a turbine whenever he neared. What Geeta noticed most about him were his city shoes. While nearly everyone here wore open-toed sandals or sneakers, Varun wore black dress shoes that arrived polished and left dusty.

Most of the women sat with their groups, knees stacked atop another's to accommodate all thirty women. Geeta's group was dispersed: Farah sat across from her while Saloni (predictably) had nabbed the spot closest to Varun. Twins Preity and Priya sat near Saloni. When the sisters were sixteen, Priya's spurned suitor tossed acid on the wrong sister. Preity's face had healed with the help of an NGO devoted to such attacks, but the burns puckered dark islands across her face and neck, and one ear suffered enough damage to preclude earrings. Two years later, the man married Preity with her parents' consent. Who else would have her?

Geeta had no idea how (or even why) they all lived in the same house: Preity, her husband and attacker, her unmarred sister and her brother-in-law. Surprisingly, it seemed Darshan was a doting husband—word was that Preity had complete control of his balls and wallet.

Half of the women had brought their children, each bribed into silence with a different trinket. Geeta watched a small boy shake a miniature bronze bell with tremendous effort. The barren bell ignored him, its clapper long gone, its shell rusting. The dimples of his knuckles were endearing. They reminded her of Raees's. So mild and so unwelcome was the thought that Geeta didn't hear her name being called.

She blinked and looked at Saloni, who laid a bug-eyed, slack-jawed glare on her. "The rest of us have things to do today, Geetaben. Give poor Varunbhai his money."

The twins tittered and Geeta handed him her group's abused money while the cop looked on. Her hands were so very moist; she wiped them on her sari, but fresh sweat cropped immediately.

"Sorry," she whispered to Varun. She heard Saloni snort behind her.

Varun, gracious as always, thanked her. He counted the damp bills with crisp economy before organizing them in his tin and marking notes in his ledger. She'd once prided herself on being that efficient. Now, thanks to Farah and this nosy cop, she was a sweaty, shambolic disaster.

After Varun had all six payments, he led them in the same pledge they parroted every week. When the microloans first began, he'd distributed slips of paper with the oath in Gujarati, but by now the women had it memorized. As they began, an idle thought struck Geeta: Farah hadn't been able to read hers. " 'We are here to help our own and fellow sisters.' "

During the second line, " 'We will pay our loan installments on time,' " Saloni made a point of staring down Farah. Geeta watched her meet Saloni's censure with a serene smile.

Saloni averted her eyes on the next oath: " 'We will help sisters of our center in a time of crisis.' " Geeta perspired through her sari blouse. It was a hot, breezeless day, and all the women had dark islands under their arms; even Varun's pressed shirt was wilting.

The meeting ended. Geeta was keen to go home and hide. The women crowded the narrow entrance, hundreds of toes inching into sandals. Everyone stared at the officer in his khaki uniform, a curious sight in their jejune village. They left in pairs and sets, baldly speculating about the cop despite his standing within earshot. Geeta ducked behind Preity and Priya, walking closely as though part of their clique.

Preity stage-whispered, "Sunil Shetty."

"No, no," Priya said. "He looks like Ajay Devgn."

"Well, that's just insulting."

Geeta's laugh was too loud. "I know, right? So where shall we shop?"

Preity turned to look at Geeta in confusion. "Huh? What are you—"

The officer stepped between Geeta and the twins. "You," he demanded. "Stop."

ELEVEN

Geeta stopped. As did her heart.

"Farahben?" he asked, and Geeta panted inelegantly. The sun eclipsed behind the officer's head. The twins left.

"That's me," Farah said from the porch. She took her time locating and donning her sandals. Meanwhile, Geeta aged a decade. The cop greeted Farah, his notebook sandwiched between his pressed palms. "Namaskar." Farah brought a cupped hand near her forehead. "Salaam."

He looked at Geeta and then his notepad. "And you are?"

"Geeta." Her damp palms met in a greeting. "Ram Ram."

"*Jai Shree Krishna,*" he said. "You loaned Farahben and her husband money, yes?"

"Well, just Farah," Geeta said, toying with her ear. "For our loan, the group's."

The officer nodded. "I see." He made a note that Geeta knew would spell her doom. Then he ignored her. "I have some questions for you, Farahben. Can we speak in private?"

They walked away, leaving Geeta and her limp lungs. She looked around, her heart hyper and alone. Children were playing; people done with chores were drinking tea and reading papers, playing cards and smoking hookah. Though restless, she walked slowly, stalling. She passed a woman snapping neem twigs for teeth cleaning into a basket.

Near her home, two boys hovered over a dead dog. They were young but their proximity, not their curiosity, should have struck Geeta as odd, since no one here would touch a carcass; they'd summon a Dom—a subcaste of the Dalits—from the southern part of the village to drag away animals for tanning, or carry humans to their funeral pyres. But none of her thoughts were this organized. The dead dog hijacked her attention, which had previously been obsessing over what the cop was asking Farah. For a terrible moment, Geeta thought the body belonged to Bandit. But then the happy rascal bounded over, tail swishing as he barked. Relief sagged her shoulders. Her brain resumed. Geeta realized the barefoot boys weren't inspecting the dog, but preparing to remove the carcass, signaling they *were* Doms. But they were quite young to be working.

Bandit raced to Geeta's feet, yipping and jumping. Before Geeta could pet him, a woman approached to shoo him. She clapped her sandals together. *"Hutt! Hutt!"* She wore a sari, with the free end covering her head. Bandit did not heed her and she again smacked her *chappals*. Despite her nose ring, her wrists were bare.

"It's okay!" Geeta said. "That's my dog."

The woman nodded once, slowly, while surveying Bandit. Her confusion was understandable; people didn't voluntarily adopt extra mouths to feed. Animals were fed in exchange for utility. "Better that one than that one, I guess," the woman said, pointing to the street dog on its side. Flies swarmed.

"Are you looking for someone?" Geeta asked. "I live right there, so I know everyone."

"No, just here on business." She still held her sandals.

"Oh, you work around here?"

She looked amused. "Not always, but I come when I'm called."

Bandit wandered to survey his fallen compatriot, weaving around the boys' legs and impeding their work.

Geeta called, "Bandit! Leave them alone!"

The younger child petted the dog.

"Oi!" the woman reprimanded the boy sharply. "No!"

"It's okay. He won't bite."

"No. They're my sons." Which meant she was also a Dom, which meant she didn't want to pollute Geeta's things, dog included. "Yadav, I said no!"

During Geeta's school days, the teacher always sat the Dalit students in the back, and they took their Midday Meal separately. Many parents were irritated by the *panchayat*'s ruling on Dalit integration, but the council insisted on complying with the law. Technically it was also illegal to ban Dalits from the wells and temples, but that segregation the council strictly followed. There'd been a girl in the third standard, a quiet girl with two braids whom Geeta would've considered part of their friend group; they all played together after their separate lunches and whenever she required water, one of the girls poured it for her since everyone knew she wasn't permitted to touch the pump.

It never occurred to any of them that she was clever.

One day, the girl—Geeta couldn't recall her name now, adding to her own guilt—received the highest marks on a math exam. This angered an upper-caste boy so much that he insisted she'd cheated, a theory the teacher readily investigated, seeing as how everyone knew "Harijans" didn't have it in them to be sharp (such was their nature). The only hiccup was that there was zero evidence of her cheating, or even being able to since the school was short on textbooks and the girl, along with two other Dalit students, wasn't given one. But this did not deter the boy, who started a ragging chant that they all—Geeta included—echoed. It must've been something about her being smelly, because Geeta recalled everyone pinching their noses.

That girl's achievement mattered little; she—as Geeta herself would feel later in life—was only as successful as those around her allowed her to be. At playtime, it was understood that anyone who gave the cheating *chuhra* water would be next in line for the boy's wrath. So, she waited near the pump in the heat, children blithely passing to drink their fill, until class resumed. Things slid back to normal after a few days but, by the fifth standard, the girl had dropped out.

Years later, Geeta knew that she hadn't joined the chant out of any acute hate, but neither had she possessed enough compassion to abstain. Bystanders shoulder their own blame, and Geeta was now shamefully puzzled as to why a tiny act of bravery had been so beyond her.

"They can play," Geeta said to the woman, guilt tearing her chest like Bandit pawing at dirt. If she were honest, she felt more remorse over how they'd treated that clever girl than the fact that she'd helped kill Samir; one hadn't deserved it. "He really likes children."

The woman looked at Geeta as she told her son, "It's okay, Yadav." She was likely about a decade older than Geeta, but her eyes already bore the blue rings that heralded cataracts. While not fat, she was a curvaceous woman, which her sari could not disguise.

"So you . . ." Geeta trailed off, looking between the boys and their mother. "I just assumed. Never seen a woman . . . you know."

The business of corpses—collecting, preparing, burning—was reserved for Dalit men, specifically Doms. The villagers didn't encounter many Dom women because they were usually housebound. Many Dalit families confined their daughters in *purdah*, where it was easier to shield them from upper-caste men's concupiscences. Easier perhaps, but not completely effective; Geeta recalled the recent cases brought before the village *panchayat*—those poor girls assaulted at dawn while relieving themselves. Historically, Dom women tended to night soil, but here the villagers either went out in the fields or used their new plumbing, so there was little reason for the women to wander across the tacit line. Bigger areas like cities still forced the need for manual scavengers, which Geeta didn't think about too often. But now, talking to this woman, Geeta felt ashamed of wanting things like refrigerators.

"Yeah, I'm the only one I've ever seen, too." The woman did not appear offended. "After my husband died, I took over the business.

Had to. They'll take over after me," she said, nodding toward her kids. "Yadav, ay-ya, what are you doing? It's a dog, not your firstborn—just grab the ankles, na?"

Geeta did not bother masking her admiration. "What's your name?"

"Khushi."

"Geeta."

"Geetaben, that your house over there?" When Geeta nodded, Khushi's lined face broke into a huge smile. Her teeth were straight, except for one missing bicuspid, but tinged with red; it was clear she was a fan of *paan*. "My house is way bigger than *that*! When you said you had a pet dog, I thought, you know, madam with a *bada-bada* house."

Geeta was all too happy to have the joke be on her. "Well, it's just me. So what's the need for a big-big place?"

"No babies?"

"No babies."

Khushi calculated Geeta's lack of jewelry, her barren nose piercing. "Widow?"

"Something like that."

"How'd it happen?"

"He was just . . . gone."

Khushi nodded. "Mine died in the earthquake."

"That's awful."

She shrugged. "Not really. The life of a widow is more peaceful than the life of a married woman. And I got the business and the fire, not that his parents didn't rain shit on my head over it, ay-ya. Do you work?"

A tenacious part of Geeta's ego was eager to display herself as a kindred spirit also About the Work. "I do. I have a small jewelry business, I make *mangalsutra*s. So keep me in mind when your sons marry."

It had been a joke, but Khushi just nodded. She looked at her boys, who were finished playing with Bandit and now each held two of the dog's legs. They stood patiently, awaiting their mother's instruction. Geeta saw that they'd tucked their sandals into the waistbands of their shorts. When they left this part of the village, and reentered the south where no upper castes were present, they could wear their shoes again. "We'll be going."

Though Geeta couldn't pinpoint how, she was worried she'd somehow offended Khushi. Had she unintentionally drawn attention to their social disparities? "Oh. Right. It was nice meeting you. I'll see you around?"

"I hope not." Khushi grinned again. She jerked her chin toward a jouncing Bandit. "It'd be a shame to lose that one."

"Excellent point." Geeta gave a final wave before unlocking her door.

Once inside, she refilled Bandit's water bowl. He tried to keep his eyes trained on Geeta, but he had a habit of blinking each time he lapped, and the result was more flirty than vigilant. He was so keen to be near her that she couldn't help but smile.

"Not sick of me yet, eh? Well, at least someone isn't."

Okay, so Karem loathed her. A week ago, she'd loathed him. Now balance had been restored. She'd lost nothing. If she wanted to agonize over something, it should be that she'd killed a man. Or that she'd starve if she didn't resume working.

She unlocked her armoire with a key and then aligned the lockbox's combination (it was silly, but she'd used the same password since she was ten: 2809, Saloni's birthday) to remove some gold wire. The most costly part of any wedding necklace—the gold pendant *thali*—was thankfully never in her care. Upon delivering the chain to the family, she'd connect it to their chosen *thali*. Even with the various locks, keeping that amount of solid gold in her home would have been too stressful.

Geeta forced herself to follow a design she'd sketched earlier, but her mind wandered to the interrogation Farah was currently undergoing. What if, Geeta thought, Farah blamed the entire thing on her?

Anxiety held her captive, her shaking hands unable to mate the beads and wire. She looked up from her hands, impatient with herself, and saw the pinned photograph of Phoolan.

"You," she said, "killed plenty of shit men and didn't fall apart." She turned to scold her morose reflection. "So get it together."

One bead at a time. Geeta hoped to lose herself in the work as she frequently did. To look up and find it was dark, or that she'd skipped a meal or desperately needed to *su-su*. Instead, she awaited Farah's return, though they had no plans to meet. As she worked, each rustle from Bandit had her leaping toward the door. Then she'd slink back to her desk, sheepish. When exactly had Farah become someone she *wanted* to see?

Geeta switched on the radio. The nature segment on Gyan Vani's channel was about bonobos in Africa. Bonobo females had to leave home before puberty and find another sect to join. Meanwhile, males remained under their mothers' aegis for life, counting on them to procure food and mates. Geeta snorted at the radio; evolution had limits, it seemed. But unlike apes, which were the other closest relative to humans, female bonobos, though not kin, forged alliances to obtain food and ward off male harassers. Two females in estrus once fought an overly aggressive male, and bit his penis in half in the process.

This reminded Geeta of the story of the Bandit Queen once castrating a man. It'd been after Vikram's murder and her three-week captivity and torture. Dressed as a male cop, she was doing reconnaissance in a village while plotting revenge on her rapists. The man she was spying on, ever the good host, "offered" her one of the many young Dalit girls he'd already assaulted. After the cut, she'd allegedly tied it around his neck. She let him live—the Bandit Queen said she'd never killed without reason. Geeta tried to rationalize: didn't she and Farah, too, have ample reason?

When Farah finally arrived, Geeta's rush of relief pained her pride. "What did the cop want?" she asked.

"Just a few questions about Samir's body." Farah smiled. She still wore all white. "He asked if I wanted to sue the corpse handler! Can you imagine? I swear, the way this country white-knuckles caste . . . it's a disgrace. Those poor guys can't catch one damn break. Y'know, back in my village, our mosque had a big conversion drive for Dalits: 'Convert to Islam, there's no caste in the Qur'an!' And these Bhangis were like, 'Okay, we're not allowed inside the temples, so why not?' And after they converted, the Muslims had the cheek to say, 'No, no, you can't pollute our mosque, we'll build another for you Bhangis.' Can you imagine a bigger sin?"

Geeta's jaw slackened at Farah's oblivious irony, but no words came out. Yes, she wanted to say, she could indeed imagine a bigger sin.

"Allah will get them, that's for sure."

"And possibly us," Geeta snapped. "Are you sure you didn't give anything away? He's not suspicious?"

Farah went to pour water and found there was none. She sat at Geeta's desk. It was a trespass she couldn't be bothered to correct. "You need to calm down, Geetaben. You were very jumpy with that cop. If you're not careful, you'll look guilty."

"We *are* guilty!" Geeta's voice rose. "Which is why we—*you*—need to be careful." She shook her head, turning away from Farah. "I'm not going to jail for you."

"No one is going to jail," Farah said, her voice hardening. "Everything is fine. The cop doesn't suspect a thing."

"That you know of. You didn't leave behind any evidence, did you?"

"No, I covered all the tracks. Would you stop being so hyper?"

"Can you blame me? You're not the most capable person, Farah. I mean, you tried to poison him with hair-growth pills."

Farah's lips twisted in offense. "I got the job done, didn't I? So back off."

But Geeta was too stressed to listen. "Are you sure nothing could be tied to you?" she pressed. "Because I'm not taking the fall for this.

You're the one who *actually* murdered him, so if the police were to come sniffing around, they'd be far more interested in you than me, right? You have way more motive than I do."

"Have you gone mad?" Farah demanded. "Or is this a poor joke? It was *your* idea."

"Right," Geeta said. Oddly enough, she'd reassured herself with her rambled musings, but now Farah appeared agitated. "No, I know that. I just meant that, *if* we were to get caught, *hypothetically*, you're more guilty since you, *technically*, did the, you know . . . killing part."

Farah pulled her hand down the side of her face, temporarily distorting her features. Then, as Geeta stared in dark awe, Farah visibly calmed herself, inhaling and nodding. She massaged her temples for some time, chanting quietly, *"Kabaddi, kabaddi, kabaddi."* When she spoke again, her voice was pleasant. "I'm not going down for this alone. I'm not going to rot in jail while my orphan children starve on the streets. So don't you dare threaten me."

Geeta blinked. "Wait. I'm not—"

"What? Guilty? Neither am I." Farah crossed the room to float her face near Geeta's. "Samir was nothing but a sister-fucking son of a pig. He wasn't even worth this conversation. He died a dog's death, covered in his vomit, shit and piss, and that's more dignity than that *chutiya* deserved. They don't get to make all the choices, Geeta. We get to make some, too. And I've come too far to let you ruin this for me." She held Geeta's forearms and gave her a hard shake. "Understand me?"

Fear, dark and oily, numbed the tips of Geeta's fingers. Farah's epithets stung her cheeks like wind. From behind a veil of dazed horror, Geeta wondered if that's how she looked when she cursed.

Farah shook her again. "We did this together. Get that through your head. And if we are caught, *hypothetically*, if you try any *dhokhebaazi*, you'll go to jail longer than me. You're a serial killer. Ramesh, remember?"

She squeezed Geeta's skin, which gave easily beneath the

pressure, and Geeta could feel Farah's finger pads against her bones. Pain flared. Suddenly, it was eight years ago and she'd burned a *chapati* and Ramesh was looming over her, his breath hot on her neck.

Farah pressed, "You see why double-crossing me would be a very bad idea, Geeta?"

And then Geeta finally, stupidly realized that she was being threatened. Though their conversation had been a misunderstanding, Geeta now understood more than ever that Farah was only a simpering idiot when it suited her. To guarantee her safety, she'd played on Geeta's ego perfectly and pulled her into this mess.

Farah waited for an answer, brows lifted. Self-preservation jumpstarted Geeta's desultory brain. Farah believing Geeta was an experienced murderer was the only ammunition remaining in Geeta's depleted arsenal. It would do no good to admit the truth about Ramesh because this woman was not her ally.

There was nothing to do but grit her teeth and say, "Yes."

Farah's mien and grip immediately relaxed. Geeta's upper arms ached where Farah's fingers had burrowed. "Good." As her brows relaxed, the yellow center of the bruise surrounding her eye expanded, a leonine mane. It would soon be gone entirely. Geeta could not recall Farah's face before this week, before the bruising and the cuts.

When Farah released her and returned to the desk, Geeta shook her numb hands, flicking them as though to remove excess water. The fan chuntered above their heads. "This is pretty," Farah said, toying with the unfinished *mangalsutra* chain while looking at the picture of Phoolan Devi.

"I know a thing or two about the Bandit Queen myself," Farah said casually. "Do you know what her first lover told her? Vikram something. He said, 'If you are going to kill, kill twenty, not just one. For if you kill twenty, your fame will spread; if you kill only one, they will hang you as a murderess.'"

Delayed anger pulled at Geeta's gut: that this ungrateful, brainless bitch thought she could out-alpha her was laughable. Still, she needed time to think of her next move; she needed Farah gone, so Geeta simply waited. Farah grinned and lifted one shoulder in an "oh well," as though she'd spilled a bit of milk.

"I know you admire her, Geetaben. What's not to? A woman abused and cheated, crushed and humiliated, raped and discarded, that's nothing new here. But she got revenge each time. Every single time. None of them knew what she was capable of. You know why? I mean, just my theory, of course; what do I know, I'm an illiterate widow. But *I* think that she was capable of anything because everything had already happened to her. She'd been beaten up and raped and betrayed so many times by so many. She was fearless because she'd already suffered what the rest of us live in fear of.

"I can understand that, I think. On a smaller scale of course. But here's where it might sting a bit, Geetaben: you're no Bandit Queen. No Phoolan Devi. You're Phoolan Mallah. Before she ran away from home, before she got Vikram and the gang and the name. You're her before she had any power. A paper tiger. And that's fine; not everyone can be a Devi. We need some acolytes, too, na?"

When Farah moved for the door, Geeta's shoulders relaxed. Then Farah turned. "We're friends. Right, Geetaben? And you'd never betray a *friend*, would you?" Her voice was suddenly imploring and meek. Geeta knew a brief flash of fear.

She nodded. "Sure."

Farah's smile was beatific. "I thought so." Concern gathered her eyebrows together. "Eat something. You're wasting away these days."

TWELVE

The following week, Farah paid her share of the loan. It was Tuesday again, and the women met at Saloni's home. Bandit was banished outside after Saloni and Farah each expressed their displeasure. Preity, however, had rubbed his ears with enthusiasm, laughing when he licked her scars. Geeta felt a silly spark of jealousy seeing Bandit take so eagerly to the woman. After the collection, Farah presented the other four women with samosas, made fresh that morning, as a thank-you for their patience with her.

"I figured it'd be a nice treat before we all fast tomorrow." Farah lowered her gaze and touched her unadorned nose. "I mean," she corrected herself sadly. "Before *you* all fast."

Geeta watched the performance with self-deprecating irony—how had she fallen for *this?*—but the twins rushed to encompass her in their sympathy. Though Farah was Muslim and Karva Chauth was a Hindu festival, all the married women fasted together, from sunrise until the full moon rose, for their husbands' long lives.

"I'm okay, I'm okay," Farah said, fanning her shimmering eyes. "Don't worry about me!"

Farah's recent widow status had deepened everyone's well of

understanding. Suddenly, there'd never been a question of Farah mooching or defaulting; *all* the women could vouch for Farah's *superb* character, they'd *always* known she'd come through. In fact, hadn't *all* of them volunteered to cover Farah's portion of the loan repayment? They'd ultimately given Geeta that honor as she was their group's leader, but any one of them would have been *delighted* to do so.

"Potatoes with extra peas for you," Farah said to Geeta, handing her a plastic container. The tiffin boxes she had distributed to the other women were metal. "Your favorite. You've really been losing weight, Geetaben," she announced loudly. Saloni made a plosive sound of derision. "I hope you're not falling ill."

Preity used her free hand as a plate as she bit into a samosa. "Tasty!"

"Like, so tasty," Priya gushed. "But we should be bringing *you* food. After what you've been through . . ."

Saloni did not open her tiffin box.

Farah made herself demure. "Oh," she said. "It's been difficult, of course, but we're managing. I don't like to speak ill of the dead, but . . ."

The women leaned toward her, the scent of promising gossip stronger than the fried food.

Farah sighed, as though begrudgingly relinquishing a treasure. "Samir was a drinker."

"No!" Preity gasped.

"O Ram," Priya moaned.

"Yes, it's true. He was a drinker, and that's not all." Farah paused and closed her eyes, summoning courage. "He struck me. Often."

"No!"

"O Ram!"

"Excuse me," Geeta said. "Are we all just going to pretend that that's news? That we all didn't see her busted face last week? I have eggplants less black than her eye was."

Except for Saloni, who looked at Geeta with more bemusement

than annoyance, the women ignored her. After pulling in a brave breath, Farah added, "And I'm ashamed to say, he hit the kids, too."

"No!"

"O Ram!"

"Oh brother," Geeta muttered.

Perhaps it should've been a relief that she wasn't the only sucker in the group. Ramesh had manipulated her plenty, kept her in a suspended state of believing she didn't deserve him. Her pride could admit that because she'd been so very young and so very in love. But to be played by a seeming dolt like Farah stung, and Geeta required a plan to remind Farah of their hierarchy.

This past week had been odd in its mildness. Geeta had risen and worked with her usual diligence. She'd eaten with her usual appetite. Apparently, all you had to do was get used to something, then it was like it couldn't have happened any other way. While it was true humans were impressive in their capacity to adapt, Geeta felt it should have taken her longer to grow accustomed to being a murderess. Even three weeks would have been more respectable. But—and this was shameful to admit, though more for its immaturity than moral repugnancy—what truly troubled Geeta about the week before was how she'd left things with Karem.

The initial humiliation that left her promising to never lay eyes on him again dissipated, replaced by the urge to reconcile. She required a friend now more than ever and, while she would confess nothing to Karem, his company would have been a balm.

So, earlier that day, before this meeting, she'd capitulated. After tucking her pride in the back of her closet and grabbing the slightly softening bottle gourd, she walked to his store. Music played from the shops, all of which boasted of sales that were not really sales. Most households were preparing for tomorrow's festival, buying henna cones, clay pots, sieves decorated in tinsel, new *thali* plates. Karva Chauth celebrations were a recent trend and women were dedicated to ensuring that everything was in its proper place on their prayer plates: the rice, the vermillion, the water cup, the *diya* and incense. Why anyone would voluntarily add another fast to the already endless list of fasts was beyond Geeta. But apparently movies could make anything popular and romantic.

The participants also check-listed the sixteen adornments of married women: the *solah shringar*. From *bindi*s to anklets, armbands to kohl. Gold noosed around their neck, arms, waist, ankles and feet, wrists and fingers, ears, and of course, nose. For her own wedding day, Geeta had chosen a *haathful* piece, four rings linked to a bracelet by delicate gold chains. Saloni had been adamant that the *aarsi,* a fat thumb ring with a mirror on it (so that a veiled bride could catch a glimpse of her groom), suited Geeta better. Ramesh had sided with Geeta, though his loyalty had sounded like anything but (*It's not meant for your build; your fingers are too stubby*). In any event, after her father died, Ramesh had sold all of her *solah shringar,* except her wedding necklace, that stalwart rope tying her to the tree.

Karem's shop was empty, the plastic boxes of his wife's atrocities as dusty as usual.

"More *tharra?*" Karem asked without looking up from his ledger.

"Ah, no."

"Then?"

"I—I wanted to see how you were doing after . . ."

"After you came into my house uninvited to shame and insult me?"

Had she done that? Geeta felt dazed. Her words tripped. "No, I meant after Bada-Bhai and the business stuff."

"I'm fine."

"Really?"

"No, Geeta, not really. I have children depending on me and nothing to give them. They're my top priority. I don't have time to make you feel better about the shitty way you treat people."

She'd felt so ashamed that she stammered an apology and fled, still carrying the gourd.

Now, during this ridiculous loan meeting, she'd been thinking about the savings in her armoire. It was the height of foolishness, but she was tempted to give it to Karem. Not to bribe his forgiveness, but the universe's. Amends were in order. She'd stolen a life but could help five others'. He'd never take it if she offered, but he didn't have to know its source. She could delay the refrigerator a while longer; after all, she'd made it this far. Such goodwill wouldn't buy her into the heaven she only faintly believed in, but it might ease her nights. An idiom her mother'd often said returned to her: *After eating nine hundred mice, the cat goes to Hajj.*

Farah was still talking. ". . . trying to be strong for them. I don't want to focus on the negative, you know, I just want to remember the good times with Samir—"

"Like when he was asleep?" muttered Geeta.

"—and move forward and provide for my children. Which it's a privilege to do."

"Yes, so rewarding."

"Joys of motherhood."

"You're brave," Preity said, shaking her head. The movement swung her hair, revealing the tiny nub that remained of her ear.

Priya said, "Like, *so* brave." Geeta had noticed a while back that Priya, perhaps in solidarity, had also stopped wearing earrings.

"*She's* brave?" Geeta gaped, gesturing to Preity with a wild hand. "What about *you?*"

Preity blinked. "What about me?"

"Seriously? Has everyone gone mad?"

Farah coughed. "Geetaben, aren't you gonna eat?"

"I've lost my appetite."

"But I made them especially for you!" Farah looked crestfallen. "I wanted to thank you for all your help."

Preity wrapped an arm around Farah's crumpled shoulders. "Rude."

Priya glared. "Like, *so* rude."

"For fuck's sake," Geeta snapped. "Here." She yanked off the plastic lid and selected a fried pyramid. Making elaborate eye contact with the twins, she bit into one tip. Though the dough was dry and adhered to the back of her throat, she emitted loud noises of enjoyment. As she concentrated on swallowing, she looked down at the now open samosa. Turmeric and masala dyed the potatoes yellow, but the peas retained their bright green skins. One pea in particular, however, appeared faded, a shabby sibling of the others. Geeta squinted and recognized the small jewel of a mosquito coil nestled into her samosa with the loving concentration of a dressmaker's hand.

She choked and immediately looked at Farah. Farah was ready, her smile impish, her brown eyes clear and healed and waiting. She winked so quickly Geeta couldn't be sure she hadn't just imagined it. Geeta coughed and Saloni thumped her back, continuing, Geeta noticed, long after she stopped hacking.

"You can," she wheezed. "You can stop hitting me now."

"It's okay," Saloni assured her pleasantly. "I don't mind it."

———

After the meeting, Geeta cut open the samosas and found mosquito-coil pieces in all four. First Samir, now Farah. Talk about "dropping from the sky only to get stuck in a date tree." Geeta stood in her kitchen nook, staring at the deconstructed samosas, trying to digest the new turn of events. She'd heard or read somewhere that people didn't panic in emergencies so much as they froze, their brains unable to draw from a comparable previous experience, so they were simply glued to an awful moment, spinning their wheels in amber.

What she desired was to return to anger. Fury was fuel, at least temporarily, before despair chased it away. She found, however, that she couldn't summon any. Exhaustion held her immobile. She didn't feel each of her years so much as she felt each of the lonely ones. *Do something*, she instructed herself, *do one productive thing and hope it will lead to another.*

So she burned her trash, in case Bandit poked around and ate the samosa remains. As the smoke plumed, Geeta regarded Bandit, who was investigating the carcass of a busted cricket ball. His pudgy haunches waggled in the air as he tripped over his own paw in excitement. His tail was an extravagant stole, wasted on a dog his size, but pleasing all the same. He was a harmless whelp who was more obsessed with cadging physical affection than serving any master. And yet— Farah was wary of him and his bite. Bandit was the one weakness of Farah's that Geeta knew of. Given that she was currently burning poison meant for her, perhaps it would behoove her to make use of it.

"Bandit!" she called. He responded promptly, tail flicking like a feather duster as he trotted. She'd discovered early on that he'd been trained with English commands. Whatever his previous name, Bandit could come, stop, sit, and stay.

Inside her home, she shucked her pillow and wrapped its case around her arm. She tapped Bandit's face; he shied away but returned. His ears drew back when she rapped his snout again, but his mood remained buoyant. With his front paws, he tried to stay her arm and lick her nose. She fended him off to hit his face again. Finally irritated, he sulked away from her, mopey tail dragging across her floor.

"Bandit! Come."

When he complied, she hit him again. Before she could blink, his jaw was around her pillow-cased wrist. The points of his small teeth poked her through the thin material, but he was careful to only warn, not injure.

"Good boy! That's attack, Bandit. Attack. Do you understand? *Attack*." She shook him loose and repeated the exercise until dusk darkened her window. As rewards, she gave him Parle-G biscuits and belly rubs. Finally, she removed the abused pillowcase and set it on the kitchen floor. She stood on the other side of her home, near her desk.

"Attack!" she said, pointing. "Bandit, attack!"

Bandit came to her, stout legs waddling.

"No, Bandit," she said. "Over there. See where I'm pointing? Over *there*. Licking is not attacking, Bandit. Attack!" He snuffed her hand for an unearned biscuit. "No, no treat. Bad dog. Very bad!"

After many failed attempts, Bandit eventually obeyed, hurling himself toward the pillowcase. His ears canted back in aggression. He growled. Geeta clapped her approval. As soon as Bandit shook out the case, he found the entry and wormed his butt inside, wiggling into the makeshift bed. He then fell asleep.

She looked at him, self-swaddled and content. "I'm gonna die."

THIRTEEN

Geeta regarded the familiar door, limbs heavy with dread as she took a reluctant step forward. Her hands tightened, punishing the soft gourd she'd brought as a peace offering. The irony pressed heavily on her skull. After years spent voluntarily sequestered, for the second time in one day she was going around knocking, begging for scraps of company in exchange for unwanted gourds. She'd brought Bandit along, though he'd likely be no more welcome than she'd be. She hoped she didn't look as pathetic as she felt. She would probably be turned away, with more hurtful words at her back to boot, but she had few options left. Her pride was important to her, true, but no more than her heartbeat. She was outmatched; she needed help.

"Stay," she instructed Bandit, who heeded, his tail swishing. She approached the door and rang the bell, which pealed eight notes of tinny music.

The door opened. Geeta heard children playing inside.

"What're you doing here?"

"I need you," Geeta blurted, thrusting the gourd forward like a bouquet.

"I think meeting twice in one day is our limit, Geetaben."

"Believe me," Geeta said. "I wouldn't come here if it weren't an emergency."

Saloni sighed. "Fine, but make it quick." She assessed the calabash and rolled her eyes. "I swear, there's probably only one gourd in this entire village, and it just makes the rounds." She exited, a solar lantern hanging from her wrist. After closing her double doors, she settled onto the swing, eyes widening when Geeta sat next to her rather than on the parapet. Saloni made a giant production of shuffling over to accommodate Geeta. The swing skittered, adjusting to their weight.

Saloni wore a long house dress, floral with short sleeves. Her upper arms were plump and fair. She waxed regularly, and her skin was smooth.

"So?" she prompted when Geeta sat tugging her earlobe rather than speaking.

"Farah is trying to kill me." Why had she burned the evidence? Then she could simply show Saloni the samosas instead of sounding like a lunatic. She hurried to say, "I know it sounds crazy and totally unbelievable, but if you just hear me out, you'll—"

"Go on," Saloni said, her voice so calm, it further agitated Geeta.

"Y-you don't think it sounds, you know, *gando*?"

"Oh, it's a hundred percent batshit. But so is Farah. So keep going."

But this information was too distracting. Geeta shook her head as though to clear it. "Wait. You think Farah is . . . ?" She twirled a finger near her temple.

Saloni snorted. "That woman has serious snake eyes. Like Dipti, from school? Remember, she kept telling everyone that her real father was Anil Kapoor?"

"Yeah, but we were just kids."

"No, see, *this* is why the *gando*s always flock to you, Geeta, 'cause you use reason where there is none. What made Dipti batshit wasn't that she was lying, it was that she actually believed it."

"She did?"

"*Yes*. So are you going to finish the story or what? I don't have all night. Karva Chauth is tomorrow, you know."

Geeta began, taking pains to be honest about her culpability in Samir's demise, but omitting the Karem portions. "And then, today, she put mosquito coils in my samosas." She looked at Saloni's impassive face in the weak porch light.

"That's kind of lazy, isn't it? Doing it the same way to you as she did to him?"

"I think it was more a kind of, you know, *message*."

"A message? We're talking about Farah. She may be batshit, but she's also an idiot. She can't string two sentences together without falling over her feet. She's hardly some don sending you a 'message.'"

"Why aren't you more surprised?"

"I am. I mean, I can't believe you're actually a real murderer." Saloni's voice held no censure, just awe. For her tone, she could have swapped the word "murderer" with "prime minister."

Still, Geeta bristled. It was the truth, but hearing it from Saloni's smug lips was unwelcome.

"Well, so are you."

Her brows arched. "Excuse me?"

"Oh, wow. You forgot about Runi already?"

Anger and guilt competed across Saloni's face. Her lips pulled in, souring her beauty in a way Geeta recognized immediately. It was odd realizing that sixteen years later, they were the same people they'd always been. Saloni's green eyes went dark, but that could have been a trick of the weak bulb mounted near the lintel. That the power was still available this late was unusual.

Saloni's lips pursed. "*I* didn't murder anyone. Runi hung herself."

"And *why* did Runi hang herself?"

"She couldn't repay her loans."

"Saloni, you tell yourself whatever you need to. But I remember the things you said to her. As if it wasn't enough to humiliate her, you even brought people with you. And the very next day? We found Runi's body."

"I didn't know she'd do that," Saloni said, eyes flaring. "How could I have known? The *panchayat* just wanted her to stop borrowing from every bank that offered! She was *ruining* herself. We were concerned."

"Concerned?" Geeta shook her head in disgust. "You don't even care about the loans! Your pottery is a *hobby*. What's-his-face makes loads of money—"

Saloni clenched her fists. "Saurabh. You don't know anything about it. The council said I *had* to take people with me to talk some sense into her. I didn't know she'd decide to—"

"Oh, very nice. She 'decided.' Some choice you gave her. You were mean for mean's sake because you're a bully. You always have been."

"*I'm* a bully?"

"Obviously. Why else would I be here? I need a bully to save me from a bully. I need you to take down Farah like you did Runi, before she kills me."

"I didn't 'take down' Runi! You don't know what the hell you're talking about, so just shut up."

"Maybe you didn't kick the chair from under her but I didn't poison Samir myself either. We can't wash ourselves clean with technicalities."

"What a lousy detective you'd make. Runi killed herself because her son stole all her loan money for heroin, dumbass; so you can leave the heavens and join us mortals now."

Geeta balked. "What?"

"She thought he was going to school, but he wasn't. And then *he* borrowed money, but not from a bank, if you know what I mean. They were going to kill Runi and her boy if she didn't pay up. So excuse me for trying to scare some sense into her. That boy took advantage of her left and right, but she gave him every bit of her until it killed her." Saloni's head tilted back. She looked at the ceiling, where the swing chains were secured.

Geeta's posture sagged, unsure of any new argument or even why she'd devolved into accusations in the first place when she was there seeking help. Saloni had a way of milking poison from her in a Pavlovian manner. And if Saloni could shed her guilt, why couldn't Geeta? Runi had been far more blameless than Samir.

"I didn't know," Geeta said. "Sorry."

Saloni shook her head once, her voice tight as she said, "Forget it."

Mosquitos formed halos overhead. After the summer swelter, October evenings were comfortable, and it would be many weeks still before winter nights necessitated shawls and balaclavas. With one foot, Geeta pushed the floor away, setting the swing into motion. Saloni lifted her feet so as to not impede. It was, Geeta, recognized, a tentative truce. They rocked in silence. The contrived breeze disturbed the mosquitos and the grey hair near their temples.

Geeta's parents' home had a swing, or at least used to. She missed the place too much to visit, taking longer routes to avoid its frontispiece. "Hey," she suddenly asked. "Do you know if anyone lives in my parents' old place?"

Saloni nodded. "The Handa brothers bought it."

Geeta's nose wrinkled. "The Handa brothers? Didn't they used to eat each other's boogers?"

"I think they still do."

Geeta laughed. "Any ideas about Farah?"

Saloni tapped her soft chin. "If you produce Ramesh, then it's proof you didn't kill him. And if you aren't a killer, no one would believe you helped Farah."

Geeta glared at her as they glided forward. "That's the best you have? 'Produce Ramesh'? No one's seen the guy in five years and I'll just 'produce' him? Sure. And after that, I'll just 'produce' five lakh rupees. Or I'll 'produce' a cure for cancer. Or a Mercedes. Or—" She cut herself off. "Wait. How do you know he's alive? I mean, *I* assume he's alive. I've always assumed, but you and the entire town gossip about how I—"

"Fed him to the dogs?" Saloni's smile was sanguine. "I've also heard that you didn't kill Ramesh, you just drained the life out of him and now he's the old, senile guy in the next village who lets pigeons eat out of his mouth."

Geeta remained unamused. "And?"

"Geeta, you can't even kill a lizard. Only an idiot would think you could've killed a man." She cocked her head. "Though I guess now you actually *have* . . ."

"Then why all the rumors?"

She shrugged. "Eh, it's a small village. Not everyone has a TV; people make their own entertainment."

"So people don't think I killed him?"

"Oh no, most of them definitely think you're a murdering *churel*. I just know you."

"Well, thanks so much for being on my side."

All humor evaporated from Saloni's expression. "That you can say that to me with a straight face proves how clueless you are. About Runi, about Ramesh, about everything."

Their brittle treaty was close to snapping. Even as Geeta told herself to let it go, she said, "It's been how many years, and you're as bitchy to me now as you were when I got him and you didn't."

"Oh my god, do you actually still think it's about me wanting *Ramesh*? First-class detective work, yet again."

"Isn't it? Come on, Saloni. The minute I married him, you cut me out of your life completely."

"*I* cut *you* out?" Saloni scoffed. "You made all the choices, not me. A stupid *boy* came along and you believed him over me." Saloni shook her head and halted the swing by planting her foot. The sides jerked before stilling, the chains jangling. "I knew he was trouble from the beginning, I just knew it."

"Why didn't you say anything?"

Saloni's laugh was mocking. "I did! You just were too stupid to listen. God, you should've heard yourself going on about him and that moronic papad story. One moment does not make a person, Geeta. He was kind to you for one lousy moment, it didn't make him kind, did it? Maybe I was awful to Runi for one moment, but it doesn't make me awful."

"You've been awful to me for plenty of moments."

"You deserved it. You're a traitor." Above them, the light expired. Saloni set the solar lantern between them.

"*I'm* the traitor?" Geeta sputtered. "When he . . . changed . . . when he started hitting me, where were you? My parents were dead; my father left all those debts. I was humiliated and terrified and I had nowhere to go. I was so alone because you wouldn't talk to me. You wouldn't even look at me. It was inexcusable."

Saloni sat up straighter. Shoulders back, chin out. Geeta would have recognized the battle pose even if she hadn't known Saloni their entire lives. "Excuse? Who says I need an excuse? I—"

"You should've reached out, Saloni. You had a family, a husband, friends. I had no one. I was all alone. I've *been* all alone."

"How would anyone know you didn't want it that way? Acting like you're better than everyone all the time!"

"Oi! I think you're getting us mixed up."

"Like that's possible," she said with a haughty sniff.

"Right. Because you're twice my size."

Saloni looked like she might rip the skin right off her. Instead, she pointed an imperious finger into the night. "Get the hell out of my house."

"I'm not in your crummy house. You didn't even have enough manners to let me in."

A phlegmy gurgle of disgust left Saloni's throat. "You always were so pedantic. Get out!"

"Oh, I'm going." Geeta hadn't removed her shoes, so she quickly cleared the four steps to the dirt. Bandit barked, alarmed by their raised voices.

"You brought that filthy mutt to my home?" Saloni screeched.

"Oh, please. My dog's cleaner than your kids."

Saloni planted her hands on her wide hips. She threw Geeta a saccharine smile. "A perfect pair, a couple of bitches."

"Idiot. It's a *boy* dog."

"Why are you still here even?"

"Too bad it's not Karva Chauth every day; you might lose some weight!"

"Oi, *gadhedi*! *You* try having two kids and staying thin." Saloni closed her eyes and put a hand over her chest. "Not that the joys of motherhood aren't—"

"Rewarding. Everyone fuckin' knows."

"Not you."

Geeta's eyes narrowed into slits. Their rage had turned the air sulfuric. "Oh, I hate you."

"I hate you right back double. And I really, really hope Farah finishes you off tonight."

"Me, too! I'd rather be dead than have to look at your fat face again."

"Same!"

Geeta growled. "Bandit!" she pointed. "Attack!"

Saloni gasped but had no reason to fear. Bandit was otherwise occupied gnawing on his private bits.

Geeta fumed all the way home. First Karem, then Saloni. Fantastic. Another successful interaction on her part. What temporary insanity had let her think she could count on *Saloni* of all people? Fear had made her weak and she'd desperately galloped to Saloni like an abandoned dog trying to find home.

Poor Bandit was ill prepared for the tempest incarnate stomping around her house as she cursed Saloni with verboten invectives even she'd never dared utter before: pig fucker, onion butthole, a fried ball of pubes, vile offspring of viler semen, a lizard dick, a lizard's pube, a lizard's ass sweat. Only when she ran out of lizard parts did she collapse onto her mattress, spent.

Bandit, ever the quick learner, refused to emerge from under her bed.

"Fine," she huffed. "What do I care? You're as useless as she is."

FOURTEEN

The following afternoon, Saloni sent her son to fetch Geeta. Though they'd never met, Geeta had seen him playing around the village and had recognized his eyes. They were hazel rather than Saloni's green, but held the same shape, with thick lashes that could easily be mistaken for kohl. They were wasted on a child, much like Bandit's glamorous tail was wasted on a street dog. Geeta stared at the kid; it was odd, Saloni's progeny walking this world, a stranger to Geeta. In an alternate universe, this boy would have grown up calling her Geetamasi. In that same alternate universe, she'd've had a hand in rearing him. But in this universe, they were no one to each other.

She'd wasted much of the late morning angling her chin before the armoire mirror, vying for maximum daylight to hunt and pluck the wiry chin hairs that had suddenly cropped up in the last year or so. Her tweezing hand was vicious as she fume-monologued all the criticisms she should've spat at Saloni: that Saloni could've used her social cachet for good, like defending Geeta and Runi, but she used her powers for evil instead; that she was selfish and ruthless; that she was no friend to women. Geeta had been revising this to "no *ally*" while uprooting a dark hair with a victorious flick when the knock came.

"What?" she snapped at the boy after opening her door.

Wary, he took a step back. "Please don't make my bowels boil and fall outta my butt!"

She would've rolled her eyes, but she hadn't heard that one before. She could appreciate imagination. "Fine. Your bowels will remain as is."

"Thanks." He closed his eyes in brief relief. "Mummy says come quick."

"I don't care what your mummy says."

"Why're you so cranky?"

Bandit barked and the boy's round face perked. "Hey, is that a puppy? I love puppies, but we can't have one 'cause Mummy is allergic."

Geeta snorted. "The only thing your mother is allergic to is brains."

The boy craned to peek inside her home. "D'ya have any snacks?"

Appalling. Would that she *had* helped raise this heathen in short pants. "No, I do not have any snacks, you rude boy. You have your mother's manners. Go home." She slammed the door.

He knocked again. "Please come, Aunty. She'll be angry if I don't come back with you."

Geeta paused in shutting the door again. "Will she hit you?"

The boy looked at her strangely. "No."

"Pity."

"She said if you refused, I should tell you . . ." As he strained to remember, his eyes and lips bunched toward his nose, as though try-ing to overcome a prolonged constipation. The boy's body relaxed in defeat. "I dunno. Something about Farah-aunty and samosas and—"

"Let's go."

They shared about three peaceful steps before the boy started again, his voice helium high with hope: "Does Farah-aunty have samosas? I love samosas."

Geeta muttered, "Well, I'd stay away from hers."

"Why?" But he paused for neither an answer nor air. "My mother never keeps snacks around the house. She's always on some diet or the other. My father says it's why she's so cranky. Hey! Like you. Are you dieting, too?"

"No."

"Then what's your excuse?"

"Let's play a game."

"Okay!" He stopped near the Amin home. "Ram Ram!" he greeted Mrs. Amin. Outside their shanty lay a bedsheet of desiccated chilis, the skins bright but shriveled. Mrs. Amin nodded, then squatted to sift the peppers. "It's not the quiet game, is it? Adults always wanna play the quiet game with me."

"I can't imagine why."

"I love all kinds of snacks, but sweets are my favorite."

"How unusual."

He gave her a peculiar sideways look. "Not really. You must not know many children."

"I do not."

"That's okay," he said graciously.

The town's bustle held a different timbre today on account of the festival. Many women were fasting and therefore exempt from the usual chores, so younger, unmarried girls were outside. Geeta and her ward turned onto a lane and a girl passed them, two steel pots balanced on her head, cushioned by a sequined round pad. Behind her, two teenagers carried the opposite ends of a thick stick, buckets of water hanging from the log.

Men decorated houses for the night's festivities, some on bamboo ladders to reach second-story balconies. Marigold garlands and gold tinsel framed doorways and windows. Nearly every house had an auspicious Hindu swastika painted with four red dots. Vegetable carts rolled alongside snack vendors, calling out wares.

"Ooh! Ooh! Let's get *pakoras*!" Saloni's son looked at her plain clothes. "You're not fasting today, right? 'Cause you don't got no husband—or you *did*, but then you went all crazy and fed him to the—"

"Dogs?"

His brow furrowed. "I heard it was leopards. You fed him to your
dog? The one at your house?"

Geeta sighed.

"Hey, how'd you become a *churel*? I think it'd be cool to turn people into cockroaches, or cover them in boils or make them eat worms."

"That would be pretty cool."

"What'd he do to get you so mad, anyway?"

"Asked too many annoying questions."

His nod was sympathetic. "I totally get it; I have a sister. So you're
not fasting?"

"No."

"Great! Mummy won't let us bring *pakora*s inside, but we'll just eat
quickly."

"Do you have money?"

His brow creased. "Well, not exactly."

"Then?"

"Couldn't *you* give me money?"

She was getting pretty sick of people asking her that.

"Well on your way to becoming a man, I see."

He shuffled his weight. "So . . . *pakora*s?"

Geeta thought for a moment. "I'll buy the *pakora*s if you give my
dog a bath."

"Deal."

They shook hands and Geeta purchased the fritters. The boy did
not wait and *ho-ha*'d around the hot food. Steam floated across his
face.

"You have your mother's appetite, eh?"

"Yeah," he said, his mouth chockablock full, gracing Geeta with
an unobstructed view of a half-masticated *pakora*. "But I'm never
gonna get fat like her."

"Things change. You don't remember, but before your sister was
born, your mother used to be thin." At his slack jaw, she said, "It's
true. Back in school, if she turned sideways, she disappeared."

"You knew my mother? When she was a kid?"

"Of course. We were born and raised here. Like you."

"Wait," he said, his steps halting. "So *you* were a kid once? Were you a *churel* then, too? A mini *churel*?"

"Yes and no and no."

"What was Mummy like back then?"

"Bossy."

He rolled his eyes. "So the same then. Hey, how come you've never been to our house?"

"I have. I come for the loan meetings every week."

"I mean to visit Mummy."

"We don't have that kind of relationship."

"Maybe you would if you visited."

They approached his home, where Saloni was hosting a henna circle. Women chatted, waiting their turn with the two artists Saloni had hired. Preity was on the swing, an artist painting her hand, which rested on a throw pillow. She waved her free arm at Geeta and greeted, "Ram Ram!", which Geeta found strange since they weren't friends. Farah was not present; it would have been inauspicious to have a widow casting a pall over women fasting to ward off that very misfortune.

But no one seemed to find it odd that Geeta was joining the festivities for the first time. Even though she'd been expressly summoned, part of her had expected to be banished; similar to Mrs. Amin, who'd been widowed by the time her daughter wed and was banned by the other guests (*Inauspicious, na? Why invite the evil eye?*). The woman ran a business, she alone fed her kids and paid for her daughter's dowry and the wedding to which she'd been denied entry. It was, Geeta felt, just another example of women living within the spaces that others defined. She was reminded of Farah's words: *They don't get to make all the choices. We get to make some, too.*

It was stirring, but it just wasn't true.

"Go get your mummy." The boy moved to obey, but Geeta stopped him. "What's your name?"

"Arhaan."

"Arhaan, you have some crumbs. Right here." She pointed to her lower lip.

His tongue darted. "Thanks, Geeta-aunty."

Perhaps the heathen wasn't totally beyond redemption.

Saloni appeared in the double doorway. Now sun-soaked and teeming with chattering women, it was hard to believe this was the same porch upon which they'd bickered hours prior. It was made even harder by the fact that Saloni seemed chuffed to see Geeta.

"Finally!" she crowed, grabbing Geeta's upper arm and leading her inside. Excitement transformed her face and Geeta saw that her former friend was still lovely. "I've been thinking about last night."

"Me, too," Geeta said, spying her opening. "You," she proclaimed with what she hoped was haughty but dignified censure, "are no frie—I mean, shit, are no *ally* to women. You—"

"Oh," Saloni said, eyes slitting, "if you want to *go*, we will *go*. I woke up with plenty to say to you, too. But not in the middle of my party. And not when I'm trying to help you, you ingrate. You haven't changed a bit. Still watering your weeds and pulling your flowers. And you wanna talk about *allies*. Fool."

"Did you call me here just to abuse me?"

"No. That's a bonus." Saloni smiled. "I called because I know how we can find Ramesh."

Geeta felt a ringing in her ears, as though they'd been boxed. Her "What?" came out more aggressively than intended.

"Shh!" Saloni hissed, checking that none of her guests had overheard. "Not here!"

"Where is he?" Geeta demanded after being led to the kitchen, which was, Saloni said wryly, the emptiest place today of all days. Despite her preoccupation, Geeta noticed the tall blue refrigerator in the corner.

"So I don't know where, *technically*, but—"

When Geeta sighed, Saloni continued a bit louder, "*But* I know how we can find him."

"How?"

"Okay, so you know how Preity's husband used to be in a *teen patti* game in Kohra, but since he's lousy at cards, he kept hemorrhaging money, and Preity cut him off?"

Geeta blinked. "No. Why would I know any of that?"

Saloni huffed. "Whatever. He did and she did. I swear, she has him by his pubic hairs ever since he got high at the Raval wedding with you'll-never-guess-who."

"Ramesh?"

Saloni threw Geeta a look of superb disgust. "No. Why would Ramesh randomly show up at the Raval wedding to get high with Darshan? Use your brains a little. No, he got high with Priya's *son*, Sonny. I mean, how inappropriate can you get? The kid's sixteen and his *nephew*. He hallucinated something about the *punditji* saying he'd spend his next *thousand* lives as a black widow spider—but not a female, a *male*, which is really the one time you don't wanna be a—"

"Sonny did?"

"*No*, you duffer. Darshan. On account of his shit karma because of, well, you know, the whole"—Saloni pantomimed splashing something on her face—"acid debacle. So ever since then, Darshan's been atoning and *prayashchit*ing and licking Preity's soles like you wouldn't be-*lieve*. Especially since after they got high, some *chakkar* happened with one of the Amin girls and the twins were *pissed*. But I wasn't surprised—she's always all over him."

Geeta cringed. "All over *Darshan*?"

"No, Geeta! *Che!* Sonny, obviously."

"Oh. But what does—"

"I'm getting there. *God*. There's a natural build to these things, Geeta. You never could appreciate a good story. So anyway, Darshan has his whole black-widow-cannibalism epiphany, or whatever you wanna call it, and he's obeying Preity's every whim. So Preity decides she would very much like to play *teen patti* herself. Why cards? I dunno. She's always been a gambling fanatic. Priya can't bluff to save her life, but *Preity* could tell you the sky is green and you'd check."

"What—"

"I'm *getting* there. God. So the game in Kohra is *supposed* to be all men, but Darshan does some *hera pheri* and gets Preity in, and, long story short—"

"Really? This is short?"

Saloni glared. "*Long story short*: you'll never believe who's a regular in the game!"

"Ramesh!"

"What? No. How would that—why would—just no, Geeta. No." Her disgust dissolved into a grin. "Varun!"

"Who the hell is Varun?" Geeta stopped. "Wait. Our loan officer?"

"The one and only." Saloni sighed. "He's quite a handsome young man. He flirts with me from time to time, I'm sure you've seen it. Not that I'd ever, you know, but it's nice to know that I can still—"

"What the bloody hell does any of this have to do with Ramesh?"

"Well, that part doesn't. It's just interesting, na? But, so Preity wins some good money—she says she made this cute joke about for once *taking* money from Varun instead of *giving* it. Okay, you're not laughing, but she tells it better than I do. I'll get her to tell you— Where *is* she anyway?"

"Saloni, I swear to Ram, this bogus story is longer than Draupadi's sari."

"Yes, yes. I *said* I was getting there. I don't know why you're so impatient, it's not like you have anywhere to be. Where was I? So Preity decides she wants to splurge and spend her winnings on a fountain. Why a fountain? I dunno. They're far more trouble than they're worth, which I've *told* Preity a hundred times. If you ask me, she doesn't even *want*-want it. She just wants to see him twist. And that's fair. So Darshan goes along with it because of the whole—"

This time they made the splashing motion in unison, Geeta hurrying Saloni along. "Debacle," Geeta said. "I got it."

"And who do they see at the store? Guess!"

For a terrible moment, Geeta thought she and Karem had been

caught and her heart whumped against her ribs. The prospect both thrilled and mortified her: it would jostle the village into thinking she was more than a dowdy witch. But vanity aside, the news would further mix her with the dirt. A Muslim man *chakkar*ing with a Hindu woman—the village could punish them for that as well. Then she realized even if anyone had seen them together in Kohra, nothing untoward had happened until Karem's backyard; she and her seedy secrets were safe. Meanwhile, Saloni was still waiting for her to answer.

"Sonny?" she ventured tentatively.

Saloni blinked. "*That's* your guess? Why would I waste time telling you a story about *Sonny* of all people? You stink at this, Geeta."

Preity rushed into the kitchen. The thin scarf she'd tossed over both shoulders fell from one. Hands still wet with henna, she raised her arm to try to return it. She failed and Saloni fixed the *dupatta*, tying the ends behind Preity's back.

Preity blew on her palms. "Did you ask her yet?"

"Ask me what?"

"I was just about to."

"Ask me what?"

"I thought you would've by now."

"*Arre, yaar,* I was *just* about to."

"Ask me *what!*"

"Ramesh," Saloni said, beaming. "*Ramesh* was at the store."

It was absurd, and yet Geeta's biggest grouse with the story was: "But why was Ramesh buying a fountain?"

Saloni slapped her own forehead. "Who cares? This is your ticket out!"

Preity smiled. "Isn't it such a relief, Geetaben? You didn't kill him!"

Geeta squinted at her. "You know I knew that already, right?"

Preity nudged Saloni with her elbow. "What about the other part?"

Saloni exhaled. "Okay, so Preity's happy to say she saw him and clear your name—"

"Amazing! Thank you. That would solve—"

"However," Saloni interrupted, "she requires a small favor first."

"Which is?"

Preity, impatient and flushed, rounded on Geeta. "Help me like you did Farahben. Help me remove my nose ring."

Geeta choked on air. "What?" she wheezed. "*What?* You *told* her?"

Saloni moved her hands defensively. "I had to!"

Preity's daughter ran to them, one of her braids sagging.

"Careful of Mama's *mehndi,* Pihu."

"Mama, I'm hungry."

"Ask Arhaan. He always has snacks hidden around."

Saloni looked around her kitchen, as though a culprit might spring out. "He does?"

"You eat, too, Mama."

"Mama can't, Pihu. Mama's fasting for Papa's long life, remember? Run along." She turned to Geeta. "Well? You gonna kill him or what?"

"First of all, that's not a 'small favor.' Secondly, you two need to work on your extortion skills because you already told me where to find Ramesh. Kohra. Why would I need you to vouch for me when I can find him myself?"

"Wait. Is this extortion? On *C.I.D.,* it's blackmail."

"No, I think it'd be blackmail if I, like, threatened to say she *did* kill Ramesh."

"So this is like reverse blackmail."

"Isn't that bribery? 'Cause it's, like, offering a good thing, not threatening a bad thing."

"Hm. Okay. Extortion, then." Saloni gestured to Geeta with a gracious flick of her wrist. "You were correct."

"Thank you?"

"But you're also wrong," Preity said, smiling. Her scars puckered around her lips. The skin looked both loose and tight. "Because we *saw* him in Kohra, but that's not where he's staying."

Geeta waved her hands. "Let's back up. Why do you even *want* to get rid of Darshan? Saloni just spent half an hour telling me you have him dancing on your finger. You have the best husband of anyone, the way I hear it. I'm surprised *he's* not fasting for *you*."

"The best husband?" Preity's smile died, her eyes hardening. "Look at my face, Geetaben."

But Geeta found she couldn't. Abashed, her eyes fixed upon Saloni's immaculate floor. "I—yeah, sorry," she stammered. "I thought— I don't know, I thought you all had, sorta, made peace with it. Or something. Somehow."

"No, Geetaben, I haven't 'made peace with it.' Maybe in my next life, but in this one I wanna see that *chutiya* die." She paused. "And suffer, if possible. But mostly die."

"I—okay, look, you have every right to your anger. But I still—"

"My name is fucking Preity. *Preity* of all things! Do you know what it's like introducing myself to people?"

"Do *you* know what you're asking here?" Geeta hissed. "In order for me to prove I haven't killed anyone, I have to kill someone?"

Priya joined them. "Ram Ram! Oof, what did I miss? Will she do it?" She looked at her sister's palms. "Ooh, very pretty, Preity."

"Oh, come on!" Geeta bellowed at Saloni. "*Her?* Is there anyone you *didn't* tell?"

Saloni's shoulders bunched toward her ears. "They're kind of a package deal."

Preity implored Geeta: "Every day I see my sister and know exactly how I would've looked if it hadn't been for the bastard I have to sleep next to every night." Priya swallowed. She, too, stared at Saloni's kitchen floor. "Whose children I have to raise." Preity coughed. "Not that it's not a privilege," she belatedly added.

Saloni toggled her head in agreement. "Rewarding."

"Like, *so* rewarding."

"But I want him gone."

"And have you thought about your life afterward? Farah's Muslim, she can remarry. You can't. You can't even wear colors. You'll have to shave your head. Everyone will think you're bad luck. No more parties or weddings—not even your own children's!"

Preity rolled her eyes. "Who even shaves their head anymore? This isn't 1921, Geetaben. You're being dramatic."

"Like, *so* dramatic," Priya said.

"Oh," Geeta said. "You're right. Forgive me. I forgot that we live in London, that you'll just wear lipstick and dance two weeks after removing your nose ring."

Saloni said, "She'll mourn for an appropriate time and then resume her life. Just like Farah."

Priya pulled a face. "My sister can do a better job pretending than *Farah*. She's a great bluffer."

"You didn't buy that Farah was mourning?" Geeta asked. Fresh panic roiled through her. If these fools didn't believe Farah, did anyone in the village?

Saloni snorted. "Oh, please. I've seen that girl cry more convincingly over a broken sandal. But after it's done, we'll continue inviting Preity to events and functions. Others will follow and the men won't even notice. Anyone who gossips or gives her trouble will have to answer to us. Plus, she's already suffered plenty—no one's gonna fault her for wearing red to her daughter's wedding."

Preity pouted at Geeta. "Be a friend, *yaar*."

"We're not friends! You guys are nasty to me all the time."

"That's not true. You're the one who's always such a snob, refusing invites."

Incredulity pitched Geeta's voice higher. "What invites?"

Preity raised a painted hand. "I invited you over for Navratri."

"And you never came to our Holi party." Priya shrugged. "After a while we just stopped trying. It was clear you didn't like us."

Geeta had assumed the invites were a perfunctory social convention at best, and a trap designed to humiliate her at worst. Memories of her walking back home from Deepa-aunty's house, alone and covered in garbage, kept her in hiding long after Ramesh had disappeared. It was the same reason she'd refused to believe Arhaan today when he'd insisted his mother wanted Geeta at the party. Had she imprisoned *herself,* all the while nursing a sad anger and tricking herself into thinking she preferred it that way?

Priya clucked her tongue. "*Arre,* just do it, na?"

"'Just do it?' Oi, Nike, this isn't any small thing." Geeta looked to the ceiling. "I just wanted to make my *mangalsutra*s in peace. Samir was— It was a mistake, not a new career path."

Priya giggled. She nudged Preity's shoulder with her own in jest. "It's not a bad idea, actually. *Mangalsutra*s for the wedding; murder for the marriage."

Preity matched it with her own infantile giggle, bumping her twin back. "Repeat business."

Saloni sighed at their private joke. "I told you," she whispered to Geeta. "Package deal."

Geeta glared at Priya. "What about you? You want in on this, too?"

Priya held out her bare palms to ward Geeta off. "I am fine. I mean, Zubin snores, but you learn to live with it."

FIFTEEN

How, Geeta wondered on the walk home, did these things keep piling up? Also, in other disturbing news, was *everyone* a better Bandit Queen than she was? Why was she the only chump saddled with qualms and compunctions over this new village pastime? Her sandals punished the dirt, anger propelling her at a speed too fast for comfort.

While none of the women appeared to be concerned by the optics of two dead husbands in as many weeks in one village, Geeta guessed the police would feel differently. The women, Geeta decided, were myopic little bitches. Not to mention shameless criminals. It would've been no use trying to reason with them, trying to explain how this was an entirely different situation than the Samir fiasco. If Geeta hadn't acted, who knew what he'd have done to her? While Darshan had behaved unforgivably toward Preity, he was not an imminent threat to Geeta or anyone. But here she was, coerced into yet another half-cocked murder plot.

"Just don't do it the same way," Priya had advised in Saloni's kitchen. "And you'll be fine." Geeta thanked her for the insight.

They had insisted she stay and get her hands decorated. When she'd protested, Saloni forcibly sat her on the swing. "I'm paying them anyhow, why not? It's not like you're a widow."

The henna artists asked for her husband's initials so they could hide them into their design. While Geeta stammered, Saloni's answer was smooth: "G.P.K." Geeta's maiden initials.

Which was how she was now walking home with useless painted hands, trying to avoid smearing the paste. She'd forgotten how wet *mehndi* immobilized you. How the moment you could no longer use your hands, your nose itched or you required the toilet.

Geeta had left as soon as the artists finished. They'd pestered her to wait until it dried so they could dab her palms with lemon-soaked cotton balls. "The darker the henna, the stronger the love."

Gross.

For Indians, superstitions were so embedded within blessings and religion, it was difficult to divorce silliness from tradition. Ramesh had been full of expectations—and therefore disappointments—for their wedding day. It didn't rain, there was no knife to stab into the earth, candles sputtered and, at some point, milk had boiled over. With the fit he'd pitched, you'd've thought someone had set fire to his hair.

Geeta had never fasted for Ramesh; the Karva Chauth festival only gained popularity after he'd left. It was primarily a North Indian custom, but she knew bits and pieces of the rituals from films. A silly hullabaloo, she scoffed, to wish long lives upon the men who short-ened theirs.

It wasn't, Geeta mused while walking, so much that women loved their husbands and couldn't live without them. It was that the outside world made life without them utter shit; you needed a man in the house in order to be left in peace. They didn't really do much, but their simple pulse was a form of protection. Like pimps. Maybe those female bonobos were onto something. Smaller in solo stature, might-ier in numbers, they could—

"—because you have to. Otherwise, the *churel* will get you."

"But I don't *want* to."

So preoccupied was Geeta with her internal rant that she nearly missed the two children arguing. She squinted. Dusk disguised their small frames, but their voices carried.

"What does that matter? Go find me some bangles. The moon is almost out."

"Bey yaar!" the boy moaned. "But we're not Hindu! Or married."

The girl set down a steel plate bearing one *ladoo* and a rapidly decaying marigold. She stamped her foot, frustrated with the boy, who was sitting on a cairn of broken bricks. His elbows were stacked on his knees and his forehead burrowed in his arms, so Geeta couldn't see him, but she recognized the girl as Farah's daughter.

"We will be. We're the only Muslims around so you know our parents will make a *rishtaa*."

"But you're, like, a hundred years elder to me."

"A *hundred*? Pay attention in maths class more. Go get the bangles."

"Where am I gonna get bangles?"

"Your father's store."

"No!"

She pushed him then. His head was still down and he didn't see it coming. Unable to brace himself, he went tumbling from the bricks to the dirt.

"Oi!" Geeta called. "Stop that." She was prepared to be gentle with the girl, this now fatherless girl, courtesy of Geeta. But then the little fucker said:

"Mind your own business." Without turning back to the fallen boy, she added, "See? I told you the *churel* would get you."

"You must not have any pictures of elders in your home," Geeta snapped, her palm itching. But slapping the girl would ruin the henna, which Geeta was now partial to. "To be so rude. *Hutt!*"

"Or what? You'll make me childless? Go ahead—I never want kids anyway."

"How 'bout I give you ten, then?"

Her arrogance faltered, but she sniffed. "Whatever."

"I— My condolences about your father."

The girl's face puckered and then broke. Geeta couldn't be sure if she was crying. She abandoned her plate, sprinting down the alley, the twin ends of her scarf flying behind her like streamers.

"Er—you okay?" Geeta turned to the boy. "Raees!"

"Hi, Geeta-aunty." He sounded as weary as his father.

"What's all this about? Come on, I'll walk you home."

"We were playing house. She wanted to do the moon thing."

"But you didn't?"

"No. But I have to."

"Why?"

"Because," Raees said miserably. "She's my girlfriend. And boyfriends have to do what girlfriends tell them. That's the rule."

"She doesn't seem very nice to you."

"Girlfriends don't have to be nice."

"Another rule?"

"Yes."

"I think," she said carefully, "that you may be *too* nice."

"Is that a bad thing?"

She mulled that one over, thinking about the invites she'd ignored because it'd been easier to hide than potentially risk censure. Perhaps the men and children would have still spread tales, but if she'd used the loan group as a way to connect instead of sequester herself, maybe the stories would have dimmed. All this time assuming she was a pariah when perhaps she was a hermit. She heard Saloni's words, spoken with such confidence: *Anyone who gossips or gives her trouble will have to answer to us.*

"No," Geeta decided. "I don't think it is. But you also can't be a doormat. So you must exercise kindness *and* judgment. Not everyone will deserve your kindness. When they show you they're not worthy, believe them."

"But she's right. We're, like, the only Muslim kids here."

"Well, who says you have to marry a Muslim girl?" Caution was warranted here. While she doubted Karem was a stickler for communalism, this was not her child to be indoctrinating.

"I don't?" He looked at her with a sudden, wild awe that left Geeta a bit jealous. To have simple words from a trusted adult crack open the darkness like a walnut . . . she'd likely never feel that again. That was childhood, she supposed.

"Nope. And anyway, if you decide you want to marry a Muslim girl, I'm pretty sure there are loads of them outside the village. Some might even be nice to you."

"I guess. But it's our 'kismet,' she says, because I only have a father and she only has a mother."

She hoped the dark hid her wince.

"Hey, is Bandit with you?"

"No, *beta*, he's at home."

"Can we go see him?"

"Maybe some other time. Your father must be very worried."

"Nah, I'm no baby."

Geeta had planned to leave the boy at his door, but Karem opened it immediately. He blinked at his son. "Oi! Where're your brothers? They're supposed to be watching you!"

"Dunno."

"I thought I'd better walk him home," Geeta said. She smiled at Raees because it was easier than facing his father. "Even though you're no baby."

"Thanks," Karem said.

"Anytime. Good night. Oh, and Eid Mubarak. I didn't wish you earlier."

"Geetaben, wait. Raees, inside."

"Why can't I stay?"

"Now."

Raees went, cowed. Karem shook his head and stepped outside. "New crush, I suppose."

Her temperature spiked. "Huh?"

"Raees."

"Right," she said. Then: "Huh?"

"He likes you. It's cute."

Geeta laughed to avoid answering. She knew herself well enough to know she'd later regret most of what she said now as being too stupid, too self-conscious, not funny or casual enough.

"Listen, I owe you an apology. You came into the store the other day to be nice, and I wasn't. I'd been fasting—you know, Ramadan—and I was cranky. I lashed out at you and I shouldn't have. It took me some time, but I think I understand what you meant . . . that night. You're a woman and it's not the same. It's not fair that it's not, but you were just trying to protect yourself. And you had every right. My meter skyrocketed because I was thinking about my feelings, not yours."

Geeta was not accustomed to men apologizing. Her father had never said sorry to either her or her mother. He hadn't been a tyrant; it simply hadn't been expected of him. "Sorry" was an English word, brought to cover all manners of sin and, with the increased use of English in films, "sorry" (as well as "thanks") was bandied about more often. It was more casual than the literal equivalent, which Indians only dusted off for the really big slights, not bumping into someone or being tardy. Ramesh, for all he impelled her apologies, had certainly never offered one. She wanted to hug Karem, but she tamped down the urge to further embarrass herself.

"Me, too. You don't believe the rumors about me, but I didn't return the favor."

He thrust out his hand. "Friends?"

She held up her painted palms. "But yes, friends."

"Oh, did you go to a party today?"

"Yeah, Saloni's."

"That's great."

"Is it?"

"Sure. People can always use more friends."

"But," she said, "the problem with friends is that they ask favors."

Karem shrugged. "One should always help a friend if they can."

"Even if what they're asking isn't good? I mean, isn't right?"

Karem's lips rolled inward as he thought. "I guess intentions are what matter. Sometimes to do the right thing, you have to do the wrong one first." He held up one finger. "'If you can't get the butter with a straight finger . . .'"

Geeta smiled as he hooked his index finger. "'. . . then use a crooked one.'"

Their truce was a new and precious thing. She said good night before she could poison it. Above her, the moon was fat and swollen, and the way home was easy. As she walked, she rubbed her palms, dried henna flakes leaving a trail behind her. It was true that she had a host of problems currently squatting on her head: Samir's death, Farah's threats, and Preity's demands. But Karem didn't hate her, and that left her a bit lighter.

When Geeta approached her home, Saloni was pacing in front of it. No, not pacing. Marching. Ample elbows at right angles, pumping them as her knees rose considerably higher than Geeta assumed a sari permitted. Saloni spotted Geeta, but continued.

"Hi," Saloni said, pivoting. She was a bit breathless. "Just getting some exercise while I waited. Couple more, hold on."

Geeta'd had more visitors in the past month than she'd had in the five years prior. "What're you doing here? What about your party?"

"Oh, it's done. We ate and then the power was cut and everyone got sleepy. You forgot your gift pot."

"Huh?"

"All my guests get a bunch of, you know, goodies. Like bangles and candies and stuff. You forgot yours."

Geeta then saw the clay pot on her doorstep, next to Bandit's empty water bowl. Saloni marched onward. "Okay, stop. I'm getting dizzy. Did you want to come in?"

Saloni hesitated. "I should head back."

"Right." Geeta felt foolish for opening herself to certain rejection in the first place. But the clay pot had seemed like an excuse and she'd responded in kind. She picked it up. Saloni had painted it red, with yellow swastikas.

"Well"—Saloni blew out her breath, disturbing a stray strand of hair—"some water wouldn't kill me."

As Geeta unlocked her door, Bandit ran down the lane toward them. When Arhaan had summoned her, she'd left Bandit outside, which had been wise considering how long she'd been gone. Though a solar light had been installed in their alley, Geeta could have recognized the outline of his large ears by the abundant moonlight alone. She bent to scratch his striped ear, and he licked her wrist. "Did you have fun today?"

Her body rearing back, Saloni asked, "Is—uh—he coming in?"

"Bandit? He can stay out, but actually . . . let's see." She pushed open the door for Saloni, who went ahead. Bandit aimed to follow, but Geeta stopped him. "Bandit," she said, pointing at Saloni. "Attack!"

"Geeta! No! What—oh, he's—ah, he, er, does that a lot." Saloni actually blushed, turning in embarrassment from Bandit's obscene self-ministrations.

"Yeah, I think he thinks 'attack' means molesting himself."

"And *why* do you keep trying to get your dog to attack me?"

"Practice." Geeta flicked on the light, but it remained dark. She used the lantern to bring Saloni a steel cup of water, which she gulped in one go. "I'm trying to train him. For protection."

"From Farah?"

"Yeah."

They considered Bandit, hind legs spread, thoroughly absorbed with his genitals. "I'd get a backup plan if I were you."

"*You* were my backup plan, *gadhedi*! Only instead of fixing my one problem, you broke my head with more!" Glaring, Geeta refilled the cup, which went down much like the first. "Can I ask—why the exercise?"

Saloni cocked her head and hip. "Oh, come on. Don't make me say it. You were more than happy to last night."

"I'm sorry I called you fat. That was out of line." Geeta brought her a third cup of water. Saloni sipped this time.

She shrugged. "It's fine. Nothing my mother-in-law doesn't say all the time. 'Saloni, you've gotten wider, no?' And I wanna be like 'Mummy*ji*, you've gotten uglier, no?'" She let out an aggravated grunt. "So where've you been?"

"Hmm?"

"You left my place ages ago and you're just now getting home."

"Oh. Some kids were fighting so I broke it up. Told them I'd tell their mothers."

Saloni nodded her approval. "Aunty law. So who were the brats?" She straightened. "It wasn't my Arhaan, was it? No, that boy's too obsessed with finding snacks to fight." She snapped her fingers. "Farah's girl? I swear she's always brawling. Little *mukkabaaz*. She was probably born with her fists up."

"Not surprising. Given her father."

"Well, he can't hit her anymore. *You* did that, Geeta. Now that girl might stop smacking kids long enough to make a friend." Saloni coughed. "And about last night: you were wrong about plenty, understand? Plenty. But I *guess* . . . you were right about my being a little controlling."

"A little? In sixth standard, you made that girl Sonali change her name because it was too close to yours."

"Hey, I helped Radha, okay? She found that Krishna boy and moved to a bungalow in Ahmedabad. *I* did that. And I didn't even get a wedding invite, much less a thank-you."

Geeta rolled her eyes. "You're an emotional guerrilla, yes, but at least you're not like that *mukkabaaz*. You never actually hit anyone, right?"

"No! I can't even manage to spank Arhaan when he acts oversmart. Talk about emotional guerrilla. Big cow eyes."

"Wonder where he gets those from."

"Yeah, yeah. But the boy could've also inherited my grit, na? And hunger wouldn't kill him either. He's soft."

"I thought people always wanted better for their kids."

Saloni traced her cup's rim with her index finger. "No, you're right. We do. But we also want them to learn. Suffering is where you get your fire from. I don't want him to *suffer* suffer, but he should know . . . I dunno . . . lack."

"So do it."

She let out a plosive scoff. "With the mother-in-law from hell on my back? No way, her little *yuvraj* gets whatever he wants, whenever he wants. You know she hired a clown for his birthday? Meanwhile poor Aparna barely got a party. Anyway, what were we talking about?"

"How you and your lackeys are extorting me into killing a man."

"Ah, yes, correct. That's actually why I came over."

"No!" Geeta feigned astonishment. "It wasn't just about delivering a clay pot of rubbish?"

"Hey! Those are some high-quality bangles—"

"Saloni!"

"I know you're worried about the Darshan . . . situation."

"How are you not? When did everyone in this village get so casual about murder?"

"They do a million things worse than murder to us every day all over the world, and no one blinks."

"We're not the *gram panchayat* that we can decide fates like this."

"Aren't we, though? We're not being cruel or arbitrary here. It's a judicious punishment, Geeta, based on their crimes. Karma." Saloni regally stretched her arms toward the heavens, her head tipped back. "We are facilitators of karma."

"Isn't karma for the next life, not this one?"

Saloni's hands fell. "You're always so pedantic."

Geeta was too deep in thought to strike back. "You know, female bonobos band together to protect themselves from males. That's not karma, though, that's just nature, right?"

Saloni blinked. "What? Geeta, quit fucking around. We have to move quickly if we want to keep the twins on your side. Darshan doesn't drink like Samir did, so we need a new way."

"Don't you get it? It's too soon after Samir. We can't kill him *any* way without it looking suspicious."

"The man treats butter like a vegetable. He could easily have a heart attack."

"Okay, so tell Preity to ghee him to death then."

"You know," Saloni said, moving around Geeta's home. She

dragged a finger along the desk, adjusted a jar of black beads. "In Kerala last year, a group of girls made a suicide pact. Their maths teacher gave them failing marks and they were too ashamed to go on. They left a note and poisoned themselves with suicide-tree fruit."

"That's terrible, but—"

Saloni took a draught from her steel cup. "Some people don't buy it. Some people think the girls were murdered to keep them quiet about their maths teacher molesting them. That the note was forged."

Geeta sat on her bed. "O Ram. How awful."

"Isn't it? I mean, four fourteen-year-olds dropping dead of heart attacks. That's what it looked like 'cause the tree's poison is undetectable, you know, even in an autopsy. A simple heart attack. Only suspicious 'cause of the . . . well, volume. And the note, of course. Otherwise just an ordinary, flat, boring old heart attack."

"Saloni, I swear, your stories—"

"You know, Samir's family has owned Farah's house for as long as I can remember. When we were kids, his brother once invited me over to study. Well, 'study.' Pervert tried for *chakkar*ing—don't they all? But anyway, I smacked him around and he got the message. Then we played some games in their backyard, which was lined with a nice hedge. I'd never seen a hedge—well, I'd never seen a proper garden or yard either, you know, since my folks were so poor—but this hedge had these pretty white flowers and fruits that looked like mangoes. Now," she laughed, "you remember back then I'd eat anything, I was always so damn hungry. But he stopped me, told me they were poisonous. 'Pong pong,' he called it. Cute, na? Not many of them here, but they're everywhere in Kerala, where they call them—"

"Suicide trees."

Saloni clicked her tongue and fired a finger gun at Geeta. "Tubelight."

Geeta was too busy cursing herself to continue arguing that they shouldn't murder a man. She thought of all the unnecessary pains she'd taken to help Farah with Samir. Pawing through trash, hitchhiking to Kohra, breaking into a school. When the perfect poison was in Farah's goddamn backyard the entire time. Typically a quick study, she'd really bungled it this time. Her pride smarted louder than her morals.

"I can't believe I was screwing around with *tharra* and mosquito coils when it was *right* there. Unbelievable. God*dam*mit!"

Saloni examined her cuticles. "'A single blow of a blacksmith is equal to a hundred blows of a goldsmith.'"

"But wait." Geeta's brow furrowed. "Farah lives there, she must know about the pong pong. Why wouldn't she just handle it? Why bother coming to me, and risk someone else knowing?"

"You know," Saloni said, "I've been wondering that exact same thing since you told me. Something's black in those lentils. She's either fantastically stupid or smarter than the rest of us combined. Either way, we can't trust her."

"Yeah, I pieced that together when she tried to poison me." Geeta's breathing quickened and she felt light-headed. "I can't do this, Saloni. I really, really can't. Not again. You talk about facilitating karma, but what about mine if I kill Darshan? He's not like Samir; he hasn't threatened me. Or anyone! Lately, I mean. I'll have to find some other way to prove Ramesh is alive." She lowered her head between her knees. *"Kabaddi, kabaddi, kabaddi."*

"What're you doing?"

"It calms me."

"Listen." Saloni sighed. "I'll help you with Darshan. Your karma won't have to bear it alone, okay?"

Geeta looked up with hope. "But why?"

"I'm not saying you were right about Runi. Ram knows you're wrong about most everything—you have bogus instincts, always have. And you're also wrong that I don't feel bad about what happened. It wasn't my fault; she made a choice. But. I'm human. I have regrets. So I'll help you. Like your bonobo or whatever."

"How are you not afraid? What if the police find out? We could go to jail!"

"No one is going to jail, Geeta. Me and Preity and Priya and even Farah aren't afraid because we *know* that."

"*How?*"

"Because we're middle-aged housewives. Who's more invisible than us? We can get away with murder. Literally. Once you realize that, you'll stop whimpering like an incontinent baby raccoon."

That, Geeta felt, was uncalled-for. "Kit," she said absently.

"Eh?" Saloni rummaged through the kitchen and helped herself to some biscuits.

"Baby raccoons are called kits."

"O-kay. And while all your fun nature facts are super fascinating, do you have anything to drink?"

"There's water in the pot."

Saloni grimaced. "No, I mean something more . . . you know."

Surprise lifted Geeta's brows. "You drink?"

"You don't?"

"No. Can we focus? What's your plan?"

"We need to get into Farah's yard. That's the only tricky part. After that, we're set. I'll cook the seed in some dish for him."

"How do we get the seed?"

"Well, I think it'd be suspicious if I visited her; we're definitely *not* friends. But you two have a weird bond now, so tomorrow you'll visit, play nice, tell her you've got no plans to turn her in, that your little freak-out or whatever has passed and you're on the same side. Be convincing. She's not an idiot, but I do think she's lonely. And while you're inside distracting her, I'll get the fruit outside."

"That's a rubbish plan."

"You don't have to be rude, Geeta." Saloni snapped a biscuit in two with her front teeth. "Manners don't cost anything, you know."

The power returned. They blinked as their eyes adjusted. Saloni flicked on the radio and lowered the volume.

"The fruit part is first-class, absolutely. But the other part sounds . . . not great. Like, how are you going to sneak into the back without the *mukkabaaz* noticing?"

"They'll be at school."

"Tomorrow's Sunday, and anyway the *mukkabaaz* stopped going to school so she could help Farah at home."

Even as she said it, Geeta had a solution as to how to distract Farah's daughter, but she was reluctant to pull Raees, and thereby Karem, into their crime, even tangentially. On the radio, a film song ended and an advertisement began. Geeta immediately recognized the Nirma washing detergent jingle.

"The boy the *mukkabaaz* was fighting tonight, he's a good kid. We could have him get her out of the house while you get the pong pong."

Saloni hummed quietly. " 'Washing powder Nirma, washing powder Nirma.' Who?"

While Geeta thought, she absently joined the tune. " 'Turns whites like milk.' Raees. Karem's son."

" 'Even colors glow!' Since when are you friends with children? You hate children."

"I don't *hate* children; I just don't see what the big hoopla is. They're kinda boring, and dumb. But Raees has a good heart. He'll play with the *mukkabaaz* if I ask."

"Okay. That's good. 'Greater whiteness at lower costs.' " Saloni's head danced. "Oh! Maybe they could play in the backyard, and *he* could grab a fruit—"

"No," Geeta said, her voice sharp. "Absolutely not. We're not dragging him into this. 'A pinch of powder, piles of foam.' I mean, what if it was Arhaan?"

"Yeah," said Saloni. "You're right."

They both sang as the song concluded: " 'Washing powder Nirma. Washing powder Nirma.' "

"Do you remember when we used your mom's entire box on your underwear?" Saloni asked.

Geeta laughed. "I wouldn't have had to if she'd warned me about periods." At twelve, Geeta had been traumatized. Saloni'd been zero help. Malnourished and underweight, she didn't get her period until sixteen, so she'd somberly listened to Geeta's story of a massacre in her undergarments, and they both concurred that scrubbing the symptom would cure the malady. Geeta's mother had found them neck-deep in foam, several months' supply of washing powder wasted, the suds encroaching from the washing cubicle into the bedroom.

"She was so pissed." Nostalgia softened Saloni's features.

"I know," Geeta said. "She told me my period cramps would be better or worse depending on how well I behaved that month."

"She told me you could get pregnant if you used a toilet after a boy did."

"No!"

"Yeah."

"Did you believe her?"

"Only for like a day." Saloni paused with a grin. "Or two years."

They laughed. Saloni looked around the room. "You really don't have anything to drink?"

"Saloni!"

"What! It relaxes me. You look like you could use some, too. I'll stop by Karembhai's tomorrow."

"You buy from Karem?" Her initial reaction was happiness that he'd have customers and income for his family. But her invocation of his name was too familiar, and she tried to rectify this by adding the belated suffix, "bhai." But Saloni had already heard, Geeta could tell from the way she tilted her head, filing away the tidbit, though she said nothing.

"Yeah, everyone does. He's the only guy around. Not *tharra* of course; that stuff'll grow hair on your chest. But the hi-fi booze. What I'd *really* like to try is the classy stuff in the films, you know"—Saloni arced a hand in the air like a marquee—"wine." Only in their alpha-bet, "w" was pronounced "v," so she actually said, "Vine." She shrugged. "But you only get vine in the big-big cities."

"When did you start? Drinking, I mean?"

"After I got married. Saurabh likes his whisky and I join him now and again. You've *really* never? Not even a sip?"

"No. Ramesh changed so much when he had the drink in him, I just . . ." Geeta shrugged.

Saloni looked away. "Yeah, that'll do it. Men."

"I liked Arhaan. I don't think you have to worry about him. He seems like a good kid. Chatty and snacky, but really decent."

Saloni's smile was crooked, but pride perked her face. "Yeah?"

"He was shocked we used to know each other."

"I don't talk to them much about my childhood. I should, so they realize how good they have it. But it's just—I don't really like thinking about that time."

Hurt pricked Geeta's chest. It wasn't about her, she reminded herself, Saloni had plenty of hunger worth forgetting. Still, she found herself fishing. "There were some good things, too."

Saloni agreed with a nod. "Sure. But when you picked Ramesh over me, it kinda tainted the memories. You were just on my side until something better came along."

"You stopped being on *my* side."

Saloni's gaze was intense enough to make Geeta look away. "Incorrect. Anyway, I felt stupid. And I hated you for making me feel stupid."

The pain worsened because Saloni's voice, for once, wasn't accusatory. It was so resigned and matter-of-fact that Geeta sought to comfort rather than argue. "You're not stupid, Saloni."

Saloni sniffed, her chin elevated. "I'm aware."

"I mean it, your looks aren't the most interesting thing about you."

She gestured to her zaftig body. "Especially now." She released a heavy sigh. "Poor Saurabh probably thinks I tricked him. I came into the marriage with nothing, just my looks and now they're . . ."

Geeta tilted her head and squinted at her. "Is that what your mother-in-law said? Forget her. You still got some paint in the tube."

Saloni laughed loudly but then caught herself. She dusted her hands of biscuit residue. "Hey. Just because I'm helping you, it doesn't mean we're friends or that I forgive you, okay? I just don't wanna feel guilty if Farah kills you; I don't have the time for that nonsense."

Geeta nodded. "I understand. Thanks."

SIXTEEN

Sunday morning, Geeta was on her way to bait Raees with Bandit when Arhaan arrived to wash him. She didn't need the delay; Saloni had said to be at Farah's around eleven.

"Remember?" Arhaan said, talking over the blaring *bhajans*. He plopped onto her cement step to scratch Bandit's long ears. Bandit rolled onto his back, spread his legs and bent his paws for better belly access. Shameless. "For the *pakoras*?"

"Oh," Geeta said. "Right. Tell you what, he's not that dirty yet. You can bathe Bandit some other time."

"Oh." Arhaan continued petting Bandit, who twitched in excitement and upended his water bowl. Arhaan righted it on her step. "Are you sure? I don't mind. Really."

"I promised another boy that he could play with Bandit today, so—"

"We can play together! Where?"

"Do you know Raees?"

"Raees? Sure, he's a baby, though." Arhaan's hand stilled. Bandit opened his eyes in displeasure and pawed at Arhaan's wrist to solicit more attention. "I can't play with babies."

Geeta shrugged. "Then don't."

"Okay, okay."

She grabbed a spongy gourd and locked her door. She and Arhaan took care to avoid the open water drain that bifurcated most of the village lanes. This water ran clear; the sewage drains, fewer in number and routed differently, collected at the south part of the city, where Khushi and the other Dalits lived. Geeta and Arhaan hugged the left side of the alley, nodding at people they recognized. "Ram Ram," they greeted. To their right, a herder led his goats, his stick perfunctory as they all knew their way to the pond.

Some deity must've been looking out for her because they weren't even halfway to Karem's house before running into Raees, who was kicking a partially deflated ball. It appeared to be some sort of dark red, but was coated with so much dust that it was difficult to be certain.

"Geeta-aunty! Bandit!"

"Hi, Raees, do you still want to play with Bandit? Arhaan here wants to play with you both."

Arhaan issued a reluctant wave.

"Yah!"

"Great, but I need a favor from you both. Okay?"

The two looked at each other. "Okay!" Raees's voice turned heavy with suspicion: "Whydya got a gourd? Are you gonna see my father? 'Cause we had to eat the last one you brought, and I hate gourds."

"Me, too, actually." Geeta smiled. "This is for Farahben. I need to speak to her."

The boys nodded, busy stroking Bandit's tawny fur.

"And while I talk to Farahben, you two will play outside with the *muk*—er—Farahben's daughter."

They jerked up. "What!" Bandit, bereft, put his paw on Arhaan's leg, but the boy was too distraught to heed. "Not *Irem*!"

Bandit changed tactics, imploring Raees, who was also looking at Geeta with a dread that dunked her into guilt.

"But you said . . ."

Arhaan fumed to himself. "But she's so . . . so . . . *angry!*"

"I know, Raees-*beta,* and I meant what I said last night. That's why this is a favor, because I know you don't want to. I'd really appreciate it. And I'd owe you a favor in return."

This perked up his mood. "Really? Me?"

"Yep. I bet you she'll be nicer with Arhaan there. And Bandit."

Such was Irem's reputation that Arhaan didn't question why Raees required protection from her. Instead, he was shrewd. "How long we gotta play with her?"

"An hour. Outside. But not in the backyard."

Raees was about to nod, but Arhaan stood in front of him, arms crossed. He squinted those Saloni eyes at her. "Twenty minutes."

"Forty-five."

"Thirty. *And* we get to play with Bandit until dinnertime. *And* we're even on the *pakora*s."

"Deal." As they shook hands, Geeta muttered, "She's right, you are a little guerrilla."

They walked toward dead Samir's childhood home. It was already eleven and Saloni would be wondering about the delay. Ram knew what she'd think of seeing Arhaan as part of Geeta's ever-expanding squad of motley children. She recalled a time when children feared her rather than bartered with her. "Bandit!" she said, her voice sharp when he wandered to sniff a seated man's food. The man, irritated, twisted his torso and snack away, standing when Bandit continued to beg. "Leave it." Behind her, the boys were chatting. Few topics fostered conversation faster than a common enemy.

"So what's the scene with Irem?"

Raees kicked at a plastic bottle but missed with glum indifference. "She's my girlfriend."

Arhaan was equal parts impressed and dismayed. "You have a girlfriend? Already?"

"Yah."

"And it's *Irem?*"

"Hopefully not for long, though."

"She's so much senior to you."

"I know! That's what I keep telling her. Hey, how old're you?"

"Eleven."

"D'ya want a girlfriend?"

"Definitely. But not Irem."

"Be nice, boys. The girl's father just expired."

"What was her excuse before?" Arhaan whispered to Raees, who giggled. Geeta let it slide. She halted near a mud house, the boys nearly bumping into her, when a tractor backed into the alley. Its huge tires dipped into the drain, splashing water before continuing.

In front of Farah's home, Irem paced in the sun, jouncing a crying baby. Though it was Sunday, she was wearing her school uniform, cerulean *dupatta* pinned to her flat chest. When she recognized Geeta, her eyes saucered.

"Aw, shit! Did you come to tattle on me?" she demanded. "Don't you got anything better to do, like make someone's nose hairs grow into their brains?"

People really needed more hobbies in this village. "I need to talk to your mother, but not about you. And the boys came to play."

"Can't. Gotta watch my brother." Irem gestured to the baby.

It was already too late to find another avenue. Geeta reluctantly extended her arms. "I'll take him. Is your mother inside?"

"Yeah, she's steaming some dresses," Irem said, passing the child.

The baby was denser than Geeta anticipated. Tiny thing, likely less than ten months, but he felt heavy in Geeta's untrained arms.

"Watch his head. *Offo!* What—you never held a baby before?"

"I got it. Go on, you kids have fun."

Arhaan tapped his naked wrist and mouthed, "Thirty." Geeta bit her lip and reared one hand back in a faux threat. She felt the baby shift and quickly held him with both hands.

"Oh and, Irem?" Geeta kept her voice pleasant as she smiled. "I know you think you're a tough brawler, but you so much as look at that dog wrong, and I'll cut you up and feed you to him like I did my husband, got it?"

Irem opened her mouth to share some venom and then closed it.

She gave Geeta a tight nod. Geeta hurried into Farah's courtyard, calling out her name. Her cement home followed the open layout of most in their village. Blue doors stood all around her. Laundry hung overhead. The kitchen was empty, a sack of rice slumped against one corner.

"Irem! Did you get the grain from the mill? I hope you told him not to make it so coarse this time."

"Hello?" Geeta said.

"Geetaben? Is that you?" A flushed Farah emerged from her cooking nook—a stool and a clay *chulha* stove—which was tucked in the triangle beneath the stairs leading up to the terrace. Heat frizzed the hair around her forehead and temples. Sweat studded her upper lip. "What a nice surprise!"

"Do you have a few minutes to chat? Here." Geeta offered both baby and gourd to Farah, but she just kissed his head as though Geeta had asked him to be admired rather than taken. After relieving Geeta of the gourd, Farah fanned her dewy cheeks with her hands. Behind her, the kitchen windows were open, revealing the back space through the iron bars. A tethered buffalo chewed with bored leisure. Lining the green hedges stood a stone wall with sloppy cement. Broken glass decorated the top as a deterrent, but Saloni was threading her arm through the gate to undo the latch.

"Of course. Would you like some tea or water?" Farah made to turn.

"No!" Geeta exclaimed, then calmed herself. "No tea or water, I'm fine. Come sit, you look like you could use a break."

"I could, thanks! Let's go to the back, it's cooler out there. Nice *mehndi*, by the way."

"No! Ah, no, let's just sit here."

"It's actually great that you've come. I was going to drop by later." Farah lowered herself onto a charpoy with a fantastic sigh and gestured for Geeta to sit as well. Geeta chose a plastic chair, dragging it so that she could view part of the garden through the kitchen window.

Farah cradled two walnuts in her hand and lined the grooves to crack them.

"Really?" It was a distracted question as she watched the free end of Saloni's silk sari flutter up and catch on the broken glass. Saloni remained unaware, confidently sauntering into the garden until she was yanked back as though collared. On reflex, Geeta gripped the baby tighter and he cried. Farah set the walnut shards on a nearby dish and took her son back.

"He's colicky," she explained. Then she grinned. "Or maybe he just misses his father, na?"

Geeta's eyes closed as Saloni tried to turn to see what'd trapped her. She looked like Bandit when he attempted to catch his own tail. "Listen, I came to tell you that I thought about what you said and you're right. We're in this together. I was just overwhelmed at first, you know, with the cops showing up, but I'm all sorted now."

Saloni gave a good yank and the silk tore and returned to her. Geeta watched Saloni's mouth form a streak of blue words as she beheld her ripped *pallu*. The baby, as though a helpful accomplice, shrieked, masking Saloni's cursing.

Farah bounced her son on her lap, her expression friendly. "That's wonderful to hear. I knew you'd come around; you're very smart."

"Well, the samosas helped clear my head."

Farah's smile was not one of contrition. "Wasn't that too funny?" She fished out the walnut meat and offered a half to Geeta, who declined. Saloni waved from the yard as though their both being present was a pleasant surprise.

Geeta nodded. "Hilarious," she squeaked as Saloni inspected the tall pong pong bush.

Farah splintered two more walnuts and once again offered some to Geeta. "There's no poison, Geetaben," she teased. "I promise."

Geeta tried to smile. "You know how it is: 'One who has been burnt by milk drinks even the buttermilk very carefully.'"

Farah pealed a laugh. "You always have the best proverbs."

"I try. So we're good?"

"We're excellent. I just have a small favor to ask."

Geeta's teeth gritted. What was it with these women and their "small favors"?

"Last time you had a small favor to ask, someone died."

Farah giggled again. In the yard, Saloni bent her knees and jumped toward a green fruit. The buffalo watched her with mild interest. She missed, instead disturbing two crows. Outraged, they dove toward her face and she ducked. Their caws were louder than the baby.

"Well, it's nothing like that. This is a much easier favor."

Geeta narrowed her eyes at Farah. "You sure about that? 'When someone lies, a crow caws.'"

"Well," Farah sighed. "While I can't say I miss Samir, I do miss his income. We're down to one paycheck. I mean, I'm cooking with *gobar* instead of gas."

"So do I. You have a buffalo, at least it's free. But Farah, you didn't think of this beforehand?"

"Oh, you know me. So spontaneous. Aren't all artists?" She shrugged. "I thought we could make do. Turns out, he didn't have much saved."

"His stealing your money to buy *tharra* wasn't your first clue?"

Farah nodded in acquiescence. "So I figured you could help us out."

As the mother crow shat on Saloni's head, Geeta felt dread chill her toes despite the warm day. "I've already helped you out, Farah. Exceedingly so."

"A little more wouldn't hurt. Let's say, two hundred rupees each week?"

"So another loan?"

Farah let out a short, fat "ha." "Goodness, no. A loan, you pay back. This would be more like a gift. And I'd give you a gift in return, too."

"And what would that be?"

"My silence. About your crimes."

"You little pirate," Geeta seethed. She ignored Saloni's thumbs-up from the yard. Her hair resembled the nest she'd disturbed, white guano dribbling down her crown, and she had scratches on her arms and face. She was sweaty as she showcased the acquired fruit to Geeta like a trophy. "You're just as guilty as I am. More so—you fed him the coil."

"But the way I see it, I think it's more likely that they'll believe you acted alone. I wasn't the brightest student. And I'm certainly not well read. I doubt the police would think I was capable of cooking up such a complicated plan. But *you*, Geetaben." Farah leaned forward and let her baby crawl. "You're super clever. No one would underestimate you."

"Thank you?"

"So it's settled? Two hundred rupees starting next week? Or actually, let's make it this week, why not? I figure the easiest way is just to have you cover my weekly loan repayment with Varunbhai. Less hassle for us both."

Saloni vacated the yard, limping. Geeta said: "I'll think about it."

"What's there to think about? It's an obvious choice."

"Hardly."

"Geetaben, was I unclear? Oh dear. I do hope I wasn't unclear. I'm blackmailing you."

"No, I got that part."

"Okay, good. Sometimes I'm not clear when I speak. Samir always complained about that."

"You were very clear."

Farah grinned. "Thanks, *yaar*."

"I don't think you can call me 'friend' while blackmailing me, Farah."

"No, no, you're still my closest friend! I don't see why a small business matter would get in the way of that."

She wasn't being over-smart; Geeta could see she was earnest. It boggled the mind. Had this always been part of Farah's plan, or had she just sniffed an opportunity and taken it? "I'll be off then."

"Are you sure? I could make some chai."

"With or without the poison?"

"Well," Farah said, crushing two more walnuts. "That's really up to you now, isn't it, Geetaben?"

SEVENTEEN

I don't understand."

"Welcome to the party."

"Why would Farah blackmail you?"

"Why are we going to the twins' house for a poisoned dinner party? Because this village has turned into a lunatic asylum."

"*Bey yaar,* I keep telling you, only Darshan's is poisoned, obviously." As they walked through the village, Saloni raised the dish of spicy vegetable curry she'd prepared with the seed. Deep burgundy swirled across her palms; her henna had taken very well. Geeta's was an unappetizing orange. "She's nervous, okay? We're there for moral support." Saloni threw Geeta a pointed look. "It's what women do. Watch out—*gobar.*"

Geeta dodged the fresh cow pie on the dirt. A stack of dried ones were propped against the building to their right, to be used for fuel. "Isn't Priya there for *im*moral support?"

"Look, it will throw off any suspicions of poison if it looks like we all ate the same meal. Haven't you ever seen an episode of *C.I.D.*?"

It was dinnertime and the streets were fairly empty, though some men in *dhoti*s squatted outside their homes to roll and smoke prandial *beedi*s. The scent of tobacco braided the air. Geeta unwillingly thought of Karem and how he'd tasted of smoke, though she'd never seen him with a cigarette. *Focus,* she scolded herself. Saloni's curry smelled delicious enough to draw a few jokes from the smoking men about sharing.

"Oh, you don't want any of this," Saloni quipped. "Too fattening. It'll kill ya." Everyone except Geeta laughed.

Saloni, it seemed, had no qualms about what she carried. Above them, lines of shining tinsel loped from building to building, leftovers from the festival decorations. They'd been strung perpendicular to the power lines, forming an overhead grid.

Geeta whispered, "But I don't want to be there when he . . . you know."

"You think *I* do? We won't be there for *that*. He won't *die*-die for one or two days after."

"Oh, okay," Geeta deadpanned. "What a relief then."

"Plotting is all well and good, Geeta, but it's hard to actually execute these kinds of things alone."

"Farah managed," Geeta grumbled.

"Oh, and now Farah is the gold standard, is it? Farah, who's fallen in her drunk husband's footsteps to snatch your money?"

Geeta's groan was baleful. "One woman's blackmailing me to kill her husband and the other is blackmailing me *for* killing her husband. God knows which unlucky star I was born under."

"I told you the crazies flock to you."

"Why not you?"

Saloni balanced her dish with one hand so she could flex a bicep. "'If they are one, I am a one and a quarter.'"

"So humble," Geeta snorted. "Let's get this over with. I've had a crap day."

"You're not the only one. Those crows *attacked* me. I was shat on. And that was one of my favorite saris, you know. Farah said it was totally unsalvageable. But she's turning it into matching *kurta*s for the kids."

"You went to *Farah*?" Geeta gaped.

Saloni shrugged. "What? She's the best tailor in the village."

Geeta rubbed her forehead as they approached Preity and Priya's door. Saloni knocked. It still bore Karva Chauth decorations, scarlet bunting lining the doorway. Two unlit *diyas* were on the ground, next to a hill of sandals. The lamps were tear-shaped, the wick resting against the peak. How had she never realized that *diyas* were shaped like vulvas? Geeta shook her depraved head. *Che.* One kiss and suddenly she was some randy—

Preity answered the door, Priya behind her. "He's napping, come quietly!"

As the twins led Saloni through the dim hallway, Geeta lagged behind, peering at their home. The space was very large, though she supposed it'd have to be to accommodate two families. She passed a dining area and common room to join the others in the kitchen, where the women surveyed the meal. The twins had prepared a sizable amount of spicy vegetable curry. Saloni had matched the recipe, but had added cashews and, of course, pong pong.

"All the kids ate with Zubin's parents earlier, so it'll just be the six of us for dinner." Preity extended her hennaed hands in an invitation. Priya gripped one and Saloni the other. Each reached out for Geeta's to form a circle. She did not want to, but her hands rose of their own accord.

Preity exhaled with gravitas. "I just want to say thank you, sisters. You are my strength when I have none."

Priya said, "'We are here to help our own and fellow sisters.'"

The rest of them joined in the loan oath, even Geeta. "'We will help sisters of our center in a time of crisis.'"

When Geeta moved to free her hands, Priya held fast. Preity looked at her. "Saloni just told us that Farah's blackmailing you, Geetaben. It's underhanded."

"Like, *so* underhanded."

"Don't you worry. As soon as Darshan is gone, Ramesh will be here and Farah won't have any leverage."

Priya squeezed Geeta's damp hand. "We're in this together now, Geetaben. Don't be tensed."

"Aren't any of you worried that Farah will figure it out when Darshan also dies? She may blackmail us all!"

Saloni shook her head. "There are more of us than her. If she pushes her luck, we'll get her in line. But one thing at a time."

Preity grinned. "Let's pluck this bastard's mustache!"

Maybe the village hadn't turned into a lunatic asylum after all, Geeta thought, dazed. Maybe they were all normal and *she* was the only lunatic. Was sanity, like beauty, in the eye of the beholder?

After Preity returned from rousing Darshan so he could freshen up, the women set the table. It was a different experience for Geeta, placing water cups next to each identical steel plate. She was accustomed to eating alone at her desk. But most families usually ate cross-legged on the ground. This house, however, had a proper, circular dining table with mismatched chairs. Saloni's did as well, Geeta remembered from her visit, but then again, Saloni also had a refrigerator. The women sat down and waited for the men. Between them, a lazy Susan held a jug of water, papadam and green chili pickle.

"Wait, where does he usually sit?" Geeta asked.

"Here." Priya pointed at one chair while Preity pointed at another, saying, "There."

The women divided looks among each other. Then they all stood and rearranged themselves.

"Is that the cashew one?"

"Yeah, I think I see *kajus*."

"You *think*?"

Priya's husband, Zubin, entered, forestalling the conversation. He was taller than average, the type of man who'd be slender all his life. Zubin aimed to sit next to his wife, but she stopped him, guiding him to another plate.

"Aren't you sick of me yet?" Priya teased, her voice too thin and high. "We can't be apart for one meal? Acting like it's still our honeymoon!"

He looked confused but sat where he was told, to the left of Geeta and before an unpoisoned plate. Saloni was on Geeta's right.

Darshan joined them, drying his washed hands on his pants. He wore two rings on each hand. "You all are in for a treat, my Preity's vegetable curry is legendary. Isn't that right, *jaan?*" Despite the company, he had no reservations about showing affection. He kissed Preity's scarred temple.

"I made it extra spicy today." She moved his chair back. "Sit."

"Wonderful! That's why you're the absolute best, *meri jaan.*"

She tolerated his second kiss with a copacetic smile. Darshan sat, Zubin grunted a greeting at his brother-in-law. Preity did not sit, instead shuttling in and out of the kitchen with a series of freshly cooked *roti*s, distributing them where needed.

"My Preity's *roti*s are first-class, aren't they?" Darshan asked, though no one but Zubin had begun to eat. "Priya's are also good, but one is made stronger when he's fed from his soulmate."

Geeta looked at Saloni. "Is he serious?"

Saloni stomped on her foot.

Geeta explored her *roti* with an index finger. "Yes, Preity, you must teach me how to get them so . . . so buttery."

Zubin looked at her. "Butter," he suggested.

"Right," she laughed. "Why didn't I think of that?"

She looked down at her plate. Dinner smelled enticing—it was times like these she realized that while she prepared food, she was no actual cook—but choking down food at the moment seemed as feasible as sprouting wings and flying to freedom. She tore her *roti* with one hand and pinched a mound of curry. She opened her mouth and froze. With a mewl, she immediately set down her food. She kicked Saloni. Saloni kicked back, harder.

Geeta's shin ached. She bent to massage it, hunching over her plate awkwardly. *"Kaju,"* she mouthed behind her hand, pointing to her plate.

"What?" Saloni mouthed back.

"Ka-ju," Geeta hissed, stabbing at her plate twice with her pointer finger.

"What?" Saloni hissed back.

"Kaju!"

"Bless you, Geetaben," Darshan said. "Please use your handkerchief, we're eating here."

"Sorry."

When Preity returned with two more steaming *roti*s, Saloni established frantic eye contact. Then, as Priya chittered about the local elections, Saloni glared at Darshan's plate and then at Geeta's. Twice. Thrice. Preity cocked her head to the side, confused, and Geeta saw when sudden understanding transformed her features. *Tubelight,* Geeta thought.

"Darshan!" Preity yelped.

"Yes, *jaan?*"

"I need you to get the pickle from the top shelf."

"There's pickle here, na?"

"But I want carrot pickle."

Darshan stood. "Whatever my *jaan* desires, she shall have." With a solicitous bow, he left. Zubin barely raised his head from his food as Priya and Saloni hurriedly swapped plates over the lazy Susan.

Empty-handed and sheepish, Darshan returned. "I can't find any carrot pickle, *jaan.*"

Preity laughed. "Oh, that's right, silly me. I didn't make any. Just sit and eat."

While the others ate, Geeta chewed on a bare *roti* until she abruptly asked, "I'll just use the latrine?"

"Oh, we have a toilet," Preity said. "We got it last year!"

Zubin snorted. "Government said, 'Go on, Clean India, we'll pay for it.' Rubbish. We only got twelve thousand rupees. Damn thing cost three times that."

Priya glared. "Isn't your women's dignity worth a measly thirty-six thousand rupees? Or do you not have a daughter or a wife or a mother?"

"*Arre,* who's saying no but? The toilet's in, na? Crying about dignity all the days and nights."

"Oh, do you want a parade and a thank-you? As if my loan didn't pay for most of it."

"Er— I'll show you the way, Geeta." Saloni stood.

"Are we sure about this?" Geeta whispered when they were alone. "Do you see him? He adores her. 'My Preity this, my Preity that.' Love songs use *jaan* less than that man."

"Geeta!" Saloni said. "Get it together. Should I slap you?"

"What, no, why?"

"'Cause that's what they do in films when a woman is hysterical."

"I am not hysterical! We can't kill a perfectly nice man who loves his wife!"

Saloni's brow arched. "Need I remind you that that 'perfectly nice man' threw *acid* on her? And anyway, it's too late. The poison is in the pudding. Or curry. Whatever, you get it; he's halfway through his plate by now. There's the toilet, be quick. And make sure to act natural when you come back, don't snivel like an—"

"Don't say it."

"Incontinent baby raccoon," Saloni said. "I mean . . . *kit.*"

Geeta scowled, opting not to reveal her lie about having the cashewed plate. Darshan would eat her unpoisoned food and "miraculously survive," a sure sign, she'd convince them, that Ram wanted him on this earth. Meanwhile, she'd somehow hide her now-tainted food and toss it later. She'd done that a few times as a child whenever her mother cooked gourd, which Geeta despised. She'd stopped, however, once the acuity of Saloni's hunger dawned on her.

Geeta did not need to *su-su* so she ignored the cement stall's squat toilet. Instead she loitered in the courtyard and poked her head in a bedroom. She required a cloth or handkerchief to smuggle her contaminated curry before she could return to dinner. A colorful square tapestry hung above the room's *puja* corner, sequins flashing in the light she'd flicked on, but she'd have to untack it and shove it down her petticoat. Plus, it'd leave a glaring blank space on the wall.

Below the tapestry stood a marble socle bearing a statue of a

flute-playing Krishna and an adoring Radha. The bedroom smelled
of the incense her mother used to burn; Geeta saw the familiar sticks
next to a matchbox. Beneath these prayer items lay a red tasseled
cloth. Its absence, Geeta figured, would be less detectable. Still, however agnostic she was, it seemed disrespectful to shovel curry into a
holy cloth. Whatever. She was saving a man's life here; Ram or whichever deity did the karmic accounting would just have to be reasonable.
Never mind that a few weeks prior she'd abetted a murder, this tally
would net her even. Besides, Samir's was anticipatory self-defense.
And, she promised the universe, once this was all over, she'd *prayashchit*
her ass off.

"Sorry, guys," she whispered as she displaced the brass Radha-
Krishna to extract the cloth. "You get it, though, right, Radha?"

"Need something?" Darshan said behind her. She jumped as she
spun. "Did I scare you?" He smiled. Unlike most Indian men Geeta
knew, Darshan had difficulty growing full facial hair. While his beard
was hirsute enough, his mustache hairs were wispy.

"It's fine," she lied. "I—I was just admiring your statue, but we
should get back to dinner."

"And here I was admiring *you.*"

"Huh?"

"It must be lonely living all by yourself, Geetaben. Especially," he
said, standing so close she could smell the onions from his meal, "at
night."

"Uh, it's fine," she said, moving away until the backs of her knees
hit the *puja* ledge. "Some people sleep better alone."

"I wasn't talking about sleep."

"Yeah," she sighed. "I didn't think you were." She tried to sidestep
him. Instead, his arms found her waist. "Oi, *gadheda!* You are married,
Darshan. Mind yourself!"

"Am I not merely human that I should be punished for admiring
physical beauty?"

"Er—they'll be wondering where you are."

"I doubt it," he murmured. "I told them I needed the toilet after eating so much curry. That seemed to make them happy. Kitty party, I guess. Which works out well for us." He nuzzled her neck. Geeta shoved him, but he pinned her arms between their bodies. Her back thumped against the wall. "You have to admit, you're far more attractive than my wife." He lifted his head briefly. "Then again, most women are."

"Whose fault is that?"

"But she's also crazy. Is that my fault?"

Geeta tried to claw his unappealing face. "Probably." He laughed. "Get off."

"Now, now. Come, be a good girl."

Geeta wriggled. "I'm not a girl."

Darshan did not release her. "Exactly. This is a compliment for a woman your age. Are you getting many offers these days, Geeta? I know how you widows have needs."

Geeta managed to worm her hand up to push his mouth away from hers. "The only thing I *need* is you away from me right now. I mean it. I swear to Ram I'll scream."

"That'd be embarrassing for you, Geeta, because then I'd have to tell Preity how you're so starved for a fuck that you invited yourself into my house and snuck into my bedroom to throw yourself at me. You're not even friends with Preity. You're not friends with anyone." He ground his pelvis up and against hers; though his frottage was violent, the rough fabric of his pants soughed against her sari. This close, she could see the blackheads stippling his nose. Her revulsion was as perfect as her anger. "*I* could be your friend, though."

There were, of course, times in Geeta's married life when she hadn't wanted sex, but Ramesh did. Those times, Ramesh usually prevailed. Not by brute force, but by censure—at times silent, at other times not—as though by obstructing access, she was failing. But that was simply a part of marriage—everyone knew the law: it wasn't rape when it was marital.

Never before in her life, however, had she experienced what Darshan was now attempting. Forget two, he had six arms, like some

horny sketch of a deity. And they were everywhere, hunting for whatever flesh she left unprotected. Darshan's initial advances were so
clumsy and utterly lacking in charm that it took a long, foolish moment
for Geeta to realize this was an attack. She was being attacked. His
fingers dug into the space above her navel, where she'd tucked her
sari's pleats. He tried to undo them, his uneven nails scratching her
skin.

Oh, she thought, the rasp of his zipper guiding her from anger to
fear. This was how the Bandit Queen had felt. No, not the Bandit
Queen. Not a divinity or legend. This is how Phoolan had felt when
each and every one of her rapists had pushed himself past her nos.

Geeta opened her mouth to scream, but Darshan's fingers pressed
against her windpipe and she choked. Her fists shoved into his gut, but
he only *oomph*ed and persisted.

"I told you, you don't want to do that. You want to be a good girl."
He didn't let up, his face calm as he increased pressure. It was just
uncomfortable at first, but pain soon followed. She struggled, trying to
dislodge his grip, but he adjusted easily. And because his face didn't so
much as distort or reveal that he even regarded this—her—as an
inconvenience, and because his practiced hands knew that it was less
effort on his part to push on her throat rather than cover her mouth,
Geeta realized he'd done all this before, and would again. Because
fallen women like her, mixed with dirt, were asking for it, as did each
Dalit girl who awoke at dawn, discomfort leading her to the field hem,
checking left and right as she undid her drawstring, bared herself,
squatted, made herself vulnerable.

He was going to kill her, Geeta thought as darkness bled, like a
light dimming. She'd stupidly, weakly spared his life and this was to be
her thanks.

EIGHTEEN

The night Ramesh broke her fingers, they'd shared a nice evening. He'd poured himself plenty of *tharra,* but not enough to curdle from sanguine to mean. She'd already filed it under one of their "good nights." Dinner was, in Ramesh's words, a huge improvement, especially considering her limited skills. He even sang along to the radio while she cleaned, clapping and rocking in an overly exaggerated dance. She giggled as she dried her hands. Part of the sound was genuine enjoyment, the other part was for his sake, contrived to *show* him she enjoyed him. Because she loved the moments—and strove to encourage them—when he was silly for her benefit, like her pleasure was a priority to him. Wasn't that love? When a man was willing to be a fool for you?

His Hindi was clumsy, but who cared? He sang the wrong word. Geeta often wished she could remember which word, which error. As though context mattered.

She'd corrected him with a laugh.

"What, you think you're smarter than me?" he snapped.

"What? No, I—"

"You finished twelfth standard, so what? It's not like you did anything with it. You don't work, you don't do anything. Can't even give me children."

She'd thought they shared an understanding. That they'd tacitly agreed: since it just wasn't happening, and they couldn't afford to investigate whether it was one or both of them, that they'd turn their circumstance into a mutual choice, devoid of recriminations. Even in his deepest inebriation, when he slurred that she'd gained weight or was greying or didn't care about him, on this point he didn't slip and neither did she. But tonight, détente shattered, she blitzed, her diction barbed:

"Who's to say the *kharabi* isn't yours—"

And then her ring and pinky fingers were broken.

Yes, other things happened in the interim. Surely, there was the moment she'd realized what she'd said (flaw, failing, *defect*), the moment he grabbed her, the moment her nerves communicated pain, the moment she'd realized safety was a false assumption, the moment she twisted one way and he another. But none of that survived the sieve of memory. She remembered being cold. Her hand was so very cold, a chill pervaded the remainder of her body.

"God, Geeta, see what you made me do? See how you go too far?"

The pain delayed, then bloomed. It eventually ceased—returning cyclically with the monsoons—but her fingers never healed properly. How could they when there were chores? "It's a painful lesson, for us both," he repeated while observing her struggle with the cooking and cleaning, "but we've learned."

He was correct.

Because wounds from one battle prepare you for another.

In Darshan's bedroom, his hand against her throat, Geeta's arm flailed behind her and encountered a thin bit of salvation. More specifically, a thin bit of the cold brass statue, perhaps Krishna's flute. She told herself to stretch, but obedience required oxygen, which Darshan was currently stealing. That left pinky finger, broken by Ramesh years ago, could reach farther than its counterpart. She strained. The statue toppled on the ledge sideways, toward her. She snatched it and struck Krishna's headpiece against Darshan's temple.

Darshan released her immediately, staggering. She wheezed, drank in the air too fast and coughed. He cradled his head. "You mother-cunting bitch!" He lunged toward her, fist ready, and Geeta greeted him, the statue now in her dominant hand, with another blow. She swung it as she would a cricket bat. Radha was the culprit this time, her brass elbow clipping Darshan's chin. He didn't curse, but he wheeled, dizzy and disoriented, toward the bed, which was decorated with four bolster pillows and a matching spread.

"Darshan," she said to stop him, not because she cared that he was profusely bleeding, but because Preity might not want him staining her pillows.

How was it no one had come to check on either of them? How much time had passed? Hadn't they made a ruckus?

She blindly returned the statue to the socle and took a step forward. "Hey." Her voice was scratchy, foreign to her ears.

Though blood streamed from his forehead into his eyes, he seemed to register her approach because he scampered away sloppily, warding her off with one ringed hand. She halted, but he slipped in his haste and pitched forward, smacking his head on the dresser corner. The sound was loud and thick. He dropped, landing on his side.

"Oh shit!" Geeta cried, hands covering her mouth.

He was inert, resembling some sort of rodent that had failed to properly time its highway passage.

"Darshan. Darshan? Fuck, fuck, fuck."

She then heard the hands pounding on the bedroom doors. Darshan had drawn the bolt when he'd entered, his intent clear and premeditated. For a moment, she was frozen. From a recessed corner of her mind, she had enough detachment to wonder at her reaction. She would've assumed panic, hysterics, fluttering frenzy, but she was slow and congested, any movement of her mind laborious. The knocking continued. Geeta's unsteady hands fumbled with the long bolt. She had to pump a few times to squeak it free. The doors parted. The women nearly stampeded to gain entry.

"What—"

"Oh my God."

"Dhat teri ki!"

Preity bent, fists hitting her thighs with each "No, no, no, no!" she tantrumed as she viewed her husband's body, a corona of blood expanding around his head.

"I can explain," Geeta said, her voice still hoarse. "It was an accident. He—"

"It was supposed to be a heart attack! Natural causes!" Preity seethed. She kept her voice low and Geeta realized that the children were somewhere in the house. Saloni locked the door again. "What about any of *this* looks natural, Geeta!"

Geeta worried her earlobe as she tried to explain. "He . . . I . . ."

"Wait, is he even dead?" Saloni asked. "He could just be . . . out."

"He'd better be dead!" Priya said. "For all this trouble."

"We should check, though, right?"

Everyone nodded. No one moved.

Preity glared at Geeta and pointed at Darshan's body. "Well? Check, dammit!"

The prospect of touching Darshan repulsed her far more than the prospect of touching a corpse. "Why me?" she squeaked.

Priya *tsk*ed her disgust. "It's, like, the least you can do, Geetaben. Considering how royally you've bungled this."

Saloni held out her palms in peace. "I'll do it." To spare her sari, she climbed on the far side of the bed and leaned over in prone position to check his pulse. She closed her eyes and waited a long, long while. Their collective breathing was heavy. The room grew warmer. Geeta felt like she was drowning in her own adrenaline. Her head buzzed as though stuffed with mosquitos. How had she let this happen? *"Kabaddi, kabaddi, kabaddi,"* she whispered to herself, rubbing her hands up and down her opposite arms.

Saloni rolled off the bed.

"Well?" Priya asked.

"Definitely dead."

Preity said, "We're fucked."

"Like, *so* fucked," Priya said.

"I had to! He was—he tried to—" Geeta gestured to her body, her abused neck, Darshan's cadaver, but the words wouldn't leave her throat and she felt dizzy and sick.

"This was not the deal," Preity soft-shrieked. "This was not our deal!"

"Yeah." Priya held her sister's shoulders. "Great job."

"Let's let Geeta tell us what happened." Saloni positioned herself between Geeta and the twins. "Breathe, Geeta. *Bolo.*"

On the floor, Darshan bled near their sari hems as Geeta told them about his hands on her. "I grabbed the statue," she said, point-ing. "I hit him, but he came back. I hit him again and then he tripped. And fell there. I'm sorry." Geeta did not notice when she'd begun cry-ing. It was humiliating to narrate it all for them—like she was announc-ing her appeal and how much she thought of herself. Opening herself to ridicule with the notion that she, looking as she did, could be the object of lust. She felt not only violated but conceited. Shame coursed through her and she couldn't even look at the others.

Saloni touched her shoulder and Geeta launched herself into an embrace Saloni hadn't offered. "Please. You have to believe me, I—"

Preity shook her head. "Of course I believe you. He's a first-class pig. Was." She moved away from her sister to stand over her husband's corpse. She kicked his side with her bare foot. Her toe ring glinted in the overhead light. "Asshole. *Ghelchodiyo.* Of course you couldn't even die easily for me. You couldn't keep it in your pants for *one* more day to just let the poison do its job, you nasty pervert *chutiya.* Goddamn you. I hope worms eat your tiny okra dick in hell and—oh, gross. *Che!*"

"What?"

"He *su-su*'d!"

Geeta closed her eyes. Saloni smelled of sweat and talcum pow-der, but it wasn't unpleasant, rather the opposite. The scent of skin and soap and life was comforting. But soon the urine Preity com-plained of reached Geeta's nostrils. She released a mewl that Saloni understood.

Saloni palmed Geeta's head. "Geeta, he'd finished the food. He was going to die anyway."

Geeta said nothing.

"You didn't do anything wrong. Try to breathe, na?"

"Kabaddi, kabaddi, kabaddi."

"This is inconvenient."

"Like, *so* inconvenient."

Saloni asked, "What're we going to tell people?"

Priya snapped her fingers. "We could just say it's a mystery. That we found him like this. People will think the witch got him." She performed a sad moonwalk. "We just step in his blood, and walk backward so they think it's the *churel*."

They all glared at her, even her twin.

"This," Preity announced, moving her arms in a wide arc around her, "is the real world. Join us?"

"Plus, everyone thinks Geeta's the *churel* anyway." Saloni patted Geeta again. "Sorry, *dost*, but it's true."

Preity exhaled. "How about this? He was drunk. He got up to go *su-su* in the middle of the night and fell and hit his head and died?"

Priya and Saloni both shook their heads, but for different reasons:

"Zubin went drinking with the guys after dinner, but Darshan said no. Zubin will know something's black in the lentils."

Saloni said, "How does that explain the other two wounds from the statue? And an autopsy would show he was sober, na?"

Geeta swiped at her wet cheeks. She felt the need to contribute. "We could tell the truth, but just that you did it."

Preity was outraged. "I'm not saying I did this! The whole point was to keep me out of it! What would my defense even be, Geeta? 'My husband tried to have relations, so I killed him?' Everyone knows you can't . . . rape"—her voice lowered on the word like everyone's did when they said *balatkara*—"your wife unless she's under eighteen. *You're* not married to him, Geeta, *you'd* have a stronger case for . . . you know."

The idea of telling people, strangers, this story over and over again, imploring them each time to believe her, to believe a man wanted *that* from her—no. It was mortifying. Geeta's nausea roiled stronger.

Priya licked her lips. "I could say I did it."

"You?"

"Think about it. We live in the same house. He tried with me years ago, so people would believe it, correct?"

Saloni nodded. "It does seem likely—"

"No! Not you. *She* was supposed to fix it for us. I won't put you through that."

"Let me do this. For you. For us." Priya gripped her sister's hands so tightly Geeta saw the tips blanch of color. "It should've been me. I'm the one who laughed him off. I was the one who was supposed to go to the store that day. He thought it was me, and then your entire life was ruined. Let me do this."

"It wasn't your fault. I never blamed you. Only him."

"Listen to me. This is the best way out. I'll say that after dinner, Zubin and you all left. Then I came in here for incense sticks or whatever, and Darshan trapped me. He tried to force himself on me and I hit him with the—" Priya looked at Geeta, who pointed at the beaming Radha-Krishna.

"Statue."

"Right. Statue. Twice. And then he fell and I ran away to my room."

"What about fingerprints?" Saloni said. "Geeta's will be on it."

"Fingerprints?" Preity snorted. "Don't tell me you watched another *C.I.D.* marathon. We're talking about the Kohra police department. Forget a lab, they've been petitioning for a computer for the past six years."

"It's like I always tell Arhaan: don't do something ninety or ninety-nine percent of the way. Do the full job properly."

Preity rolled her eyes. "Well, fine, then. We'll both touch it. To be safe."

"Not the blood, though!"

"Yes, yes, inspector *saab*, not the blood. I swear, a couple of those *C.I.D.* episodes, and suddenly you think you're Rajani Pandit."

The twins dabbed their fingers up and down the statue in a lazy massage. "Sufficient?" Priya asked Saloni, whose mouth twisted in diligent scrutiny.

"A bit more."

"Bonobos."

They looked at her, the twins still touching the statue. Geeta hadn't realized she'd spoken aloud.

"What'd she say?"

"What's bobobos?"

"I think they're tapioca balls."

Saloni said, "They're these chimpanzees in Africa. She's obsessed with them for some reason."

Priya shook her head. "No, I'm pretty sure they're tapioca balls."

Saloni's brow creased. "What are tapioca balls?"

"Like, bubble tea."

"When have *you* ever had bubble tea?"

Priya sniffed. "*Meri mausi ka chota sala ki saheli* took me when I visited her in Ahmedabad."

Saloni appeared no less dubious. "Your maternal aunt's youngest brother-in-law's college friend?"

"Yes. We're very close."

Preity thunked down the statue like a gavel. "Who the shit cares? Can we get on with it?"

Saloni nodded. "Ladies, we all need alibis. Geeta and I need to be seen in public and we need to make sure Zubin doesn't come home for a while."

Geeta snapped her fingers. "Karem. We'll buy *tharra* from him. Give it to the guys. That way, we're seen *and* they stay out drinking longer."

Saloni tapped her chin. "Okay, that's good. Really good, actually. What about Preity? Priya came into the room for incense sticks, sure, but why didn't Preity see his body when she came to bed?"

"Because I stayed with the kids!" Preity said. "Pihu had a nightmare and I stayed with her. All night. I do that sometimes. That's why Darshan thought it was his chance, because I told him I'd be with them."

Geeta raised a hand. "But why didn't Priya wake Preity up after he attacked her?"

"I dunno," Priya said, shrugging. "Honor. Shame. Embarrassment. Any one of those things they're always trying to make us feel. Oh! *And* I was worried about my sister; I didn't want to hurt her further."

Preity nodded. "You didn't realize he was dead. You didn't see the blood, you just ran and locked yourself in your room."

"Okay, I think that works, actually," said Saloni. "But you have to really sell it with Zubin, okay? When he comes home, he'll be drunk, and you'll tell him immediately. You have to be . . ."

"Hysterical," Geeta said.

"Like, *so* hysterical," Saloni said dryly, and Geeta barked a laugh despite herself. When Priya looked confused and a bit suspicious, Geeta coughed and ticked her fingers with renewed efficiency. "Okay, you two have your stories, Saloni and I will get our alibis, we have no prints, we have—"

Saloni bit her lip. "Wait. Wouldn't it make it easier if Priya's face sold the story more than her words?"

Priya frowned. "Is that some kind of riddle?"

"Hear me out. We came in here and started screaming at Geeta because she looked fine. Too fine."

The twins were skeptical. "Not really. I don't even know where to start. That hair—"

"Forget the hair. Look at the skin, *offo*. *Yahan* dry, *wahan* oily."

Geeta touched her nose. "Okay, I—"

"Lipstick wouldn't hurt."

"Is that a sari or a dishrag?"

"I said okay!"

"Yes, yes, everything you've said is true. And then some," Saloni muttered. "But the point is she *always* looks that bad. I'm talking *unusually* bad."

"Wow," Geeta said. "Wow."

Saloni squeezed her hand. "When this is over, we'll fix you. One disaster at a time, na?"

Before Geeta could comment, Preity spoke. She addressed Saloni but was surveying her twin. "So . . . she needs bruises?"

Saloni nodded. "I really think that would, you know, make it irrefutable."

Priya held up a finger. "Uh, wait a minute—"

Preity considered this. "And what, we just, like, hit her?"

"Okay," Priya said, taking a step back. "Let's all just *slow* down."

Saloni continued, "Nothing crazy, just like a bleeding lip or black eye."

"Ex*cuse* me!"

Geeta nodded. "Like how Farah was after Samir."

Saloni snapped her fingers. "Exactly! Yes. That's totally the look we're going for."

"'The look we're going for?' Okay, Lakmé, all of you back off."

Saloni checked the clock in the corner. "It's really getting late, na? We need to *fatafat* smack her and get on our way."

"No way. No smacking."

"Listen, Priya," Saloni said, hands on her hips. "If your face is fucked, you won't have to act so hard. People won't ask as many questions. Are you such a good actor, Amitabh Bachchan, that you don't need any costume?"

"I—er—"

"Exactly. One or two *thappad*s now will save you tears later."

Saloni was as persuasive as she'd been in her school days, coaxing girls into buying bogus, ugly hair clips or fancying bogus, ugly boys. It was equal parts admirable and intimidating. Geeta recalled then what it was like to have someone in her corner, advocating no less than she would for herself. It had been so long, she'd grown too accustomed to stooping under the burden of solitude. The relief was immediate. She felt taller, as though seeing the world from a greater height.

Priya exhaled her capitulation. "Okay, let's do it."

It was decided it should be Preity. Since the twins were blood, there was a lower likelihood of lingering resentment. Preity moved to pull off her rings.

Saloni stopped her. "What're you doing?"

"The rings will mark—Oh, right, obviously."

Priya stood, eyes closed, body tense. She kept her arms tight near her sides while Preity reared back her arm and struck. It was a soft slap, like the ones the women gave their children for minor offenses. Priya's head didn't so much as move.

"That was . . . not great, Preity."

"And shouldn't it be a punch, not a slap?"

"*Bey yaar,* do I look like Farah's daughter that I'll just smack her around so easily? She's my *sister*."

"What's that *mukkabaaz*'s name, anyway?"

"Miriam."

"No *yaar,* Imani."

"Irem," Geeta said.

"Ohhhh," they said in unison. "Correct."

"Shall we focus?" Geeta asked.

"Get angry!" Saloni suggested.

"*How?*"

Saloni pulled her shoulders back and declared, as though at a campaign rally, "How are you not angry that she's the beautiful sister and you're the ugly one? That for years you've had to have sex with a man who's picturing her?"

The women gasped. Geeta joined: "Or that you two look like before-and-after pictures?"

"Well, now I just wanna hit *you*."

Priya sighed. "Remember when we were kids and you really, really loved Mummy's gold *jhumkas*?"

Preity frowned. "Yeah, of course. What about them?"

"Well, the reason she gave them to me instead of you is because she thought some *chakkar* was happening between you and that Sikh boy, and she never really got over it."

"Why would she think that?"

Priya's smile was sheepish. "Probably because some *chakkar* was happening between *me* and that Sikh boy, and I told her it was you when someone saw us?"

"What!"

"I'm sorry! But you were always her favorite anyway! Me, she'd've *never* forgiven."

Preity punched her sister in the eye with impressive accuracy. Priya reeled. "I loved those earrings! I always thought I'd be married in them!"

"But you couldn't have worn them anyway because of the acid— Ow!"

Preity easily landed another blow. One twin cowered, the other stalked forward. They both nimbly avoided Darshan's body, but it was an inelegant tussle: Preity manacled one of her sister's wrists to keep her within reach while she used her free hand to attack.

"I'll give them back to you!"

"What the fuck good are earrings to me now!"

"Okay," Saloni said after reading her watch. "Last one, Preity. She's already bleeding."

"I dunno! For Pihu, maybe? *Ow!*"

Priya ducked, protecting her face; Preity improvised deftly, grabbing a small slice of available flesh under Priya's arm and twisting hard. Priya yowled.

"Shh!" Saloni said. "The kids!"

"*Bahut ho gaya,*" Geeta said. And to think, she'd once mourned her lack of siblings. "Enough. Last one."

Saloni turned to Geeta while the twins combatted, sari *pallus* fluttering this way and that. "I mean," Saloni said, "she *did* lie, take the earrings and, you know, mix her name with dirt and all."

"Ugh! It all makes sense now! Mummy gave me the silent treatment for *months,* and I thought it was because my exam marks were low! Plus, she had all those 'no one marries *dheeli* girls' talks with me. God! You *randi!*"

"*Really,* this time. Last one, Preity!" Saloni said. When Preity ignored them, Saloni and Geeta intervened. Geeta guided the bleeding twin away while Saloni soothed Preity. "I know, I know, you didn't even like the Sikh boy. If it makes you feel better, everyone knew it was really Priya who was *dheeli*. Always has been."

Preity fumed. "I loved those earrings! *And* my mother!"

Priya was crying. Geeta tried to pry her hands away to assess whether the damage was convincing. She shushed Priya, instructing her to save something for her husband's return. The four women convened near the foot of the bed. From her vantage point, Geeta could see the statue behind Saloni. She closed her eyes and saw Darshan's sneering face, his hands on her as though he not only owned her but was extending her a favor. *I know how you widows have needs.* Her eyelids sprang open as realization washed down her spine. Her rage and adrenaline drained, leaving her weary. All this, she now knew, had been for nothing. She was in a worse soup than before.

"Remember: Geeta and I left right after Zubin did. Preity, go to the kids. Priya, go to your room and wait for Zubin. Everyone set?"

The women nodded. Saloni continued for Geeta's benefit, "After things quiet down with the police, we'll find Ramesh."

Geeta exhaled. Her eyelids felt heavy. "No, no we won't."

"I don't follow."

"We can't find him because they don't know where he is." Geeta looked at Preity, who suddenly found the floor fascinating. "Do you?"

Preity shook her head without looking up.

"Still not following."

"He called me a widow," said Geeta, pointing to Darshan's body. "When he attacked me, he thought I was a widow. Which means you never saw Ramesh."

Preity's face scrunched in guilt. "I needed your help," she said quietly. "When Saloni mentioned . . . I thought it was my chance."

"You won't tell, will you?" Priya whispered. "About Darshan?"

"How can I? I killed him. We're all trapped in the same net."

NINETEEN

I didn't know," Saloni said as they left the twins' house for Karem's store. Just then, another power cut darkened the rows of homes on either side of them. The moonlight was strong and Geeta saw Saloni pinching her throat in a promise. "I swear, I didn't know."

"I believe you."

"Geeta, really, seriously. I didn't—"

"I said I believe you and I do."

"You know, maybe it's actually better that we can't find Ramesh."

"How so?"

"Because we've been on the defense when we should be increasing our offense instead. If we keep allowing Farah to believe that you killed Ramesh, then at least she thinks she's dealing with an actual killer. If you threaten her—convincingly, mind you—she'll back off."

"I'm not threatening Farah. She's a killer, too." Geeta shrugged, resigned. While the events in the twins' house seemed to whirl by, now time was molasses; she felt as though she were watching a film slowed by half. "Whatever happens now, happens. What good is proving my innocence with the Ramesh *tamasha*, when I have nine other sins tied to my neck?"

"What are you babbling about?"

But Geeta wasn't babbling. Odd calm shrouded her. "I've killed not one but two men. If I land in jail, I can't say I don't deserve it."

Saloni stopped in the road. "Listen to me. Darshan killed himself. No, *listen* to me. I'm serious. Sure, you're not supposed to kill, but you're not supposed to rape either, okay? He broke the contract first. Gandhiji had it wrong about some things. When someone threatens your body, you have every right to protect yourself. *Satyagraha* or passive resistance or whatever may be fine for freedom and salt marches, but not when someone's trying to rape you. You don't have to love the assholes oppressing you, and don't let anyone tell you otherwise."

"Why aren't *we* ever the oppressing assholes? Why is everything a reaction for us?"

"Because," Saloni said. "Women were built to endure the rules men make."

"But don't we get to make choices, too?"

"You did, with Darshan. And you're going to stand up for yourself with Farah, you hear me? You're going to tell her that if she doesn't get in line, she'll go the same way as Ramesh and Samir, and who will feed her rude children then?"

"I just want this to be over."

"Soon. You gotta meet crazy with crazy. 'People like that don't understand words, only kicks.'" They were outside Karem's store. "Ready?"

"Geeta!" Karem smiled, only catching himself when he saw Saloni, who observed him with shrewd interest. "Saloniben." He coughed. "How're you?"

"Fine, fine. We'd like some *desi daru*. The good stuff."

Karem's brow rose. "A kitty party, eh?"

"No, no." Saloni laughed. "We'll be giving it to the men."

Karem nodded. He presented two of the same glass bottles Geeta had seen when she bought *tharra* for Samir. Saloni asked him to add it to her husband's tab. Karem obliged, marking a note in his ledger. "I'm still waiting for that 'vine,' Karembhai."

He grinned. "Oi madam, how will I keep it from spoiling? Not all of us have fridges." He winked at Geeta, who immediately looked away. None of it escaped Saloni; Geeta knew this as surely as she knew her own name.

"How are you, Geetaben?"

"I am well." It was so stilted it was suspicious. She tried to fix it with a "Thank you," which was, of course, even more formal. Saloni's smile was wider than India. She put the bottles in her jute bag with a telltale tinkle.

"Oh my god," Saloni said as they left. "You like Karem."

"What! No—I—that's madness. I do not."

"Yes, you do!" Saloni bumped her shoulder into Geeta's. "You *like*-like him! You're blushing!"

Geeta batted Saloni away. "I am *not*. I can't blush. I'm brown. And you're inappropriate."

"Fine, but you would be if you could. Because you *like*-like him."

"Even if I did," Geeta started, and when Saloni clapped in delight, she raised her voice: "And I'm not saying I do, but even if I did, what would be the point? Nothing can come of it."

"Why not? One minute, I forgot my keys." She gave the bag to Geeta and hustled back to the shop. When she returned, hitching the clip to her sari, she asked, "Why not? It'd be a bit of happiness. Ram knows you deserve some."

"How would it even work? He's a Muslim widower with four kids."

"And you're a 'Hindu widow' with none. We could sell the movie rights."

"Things like that don't happen in our villages. City people can mingle, not us."

"Who says you're marrying the guy? Have some fun. *Chakkar chal*."

"Fun? Everyone is up everyone's butt here. If you fart in one corner of town, they smell what you had for dinner in the other."

Saloni's nose wrinkled. "My, what an elegant metaphor, Geeta. Take a right. They're usually near the water tower."

The village's water tower was to inebriated men what the water pumps were to the women. Every so often, they'd congregate, pour a few pegs and tease each other about their low capacities for booze. At times, they stumbled up the stairs, hoping to catch a breeze and a view, but neither were readily available in their village. There were few trees here and the men's voices carried easily. A burst of raucous laughter guided Geeta and Saloni.

The men sat on a blanket covered in snacks and liquor bottles in various stages of depletion. Someone squatted near a makeshift fire, roasting papadam. When he shakily stood, Geeta recognized Saloni's husband, Saurabh, and he was properly drunk. Saurabh handed the crisp papadam to Zubin, who sprinkled diced onions and lime juice on it before chomping down. Brittle flecks flew onto his shirt.

"Ahhh," Saurabh greeted his wife. "Mother of Arhaan, I salute you." He namasted his hands near his forehead and bowed low in deference. He dipped too far and lost his balance.

Saloni laughed. "Father of Arhaan, drink some water."

"Pssh!" he said, flapping his hand. "Water. How was dinner?" Saurabh asked but was then distracted by the rustling of someone opening a Haldiram's snack bag.

"Boring, *yaar*." Saloni yawned and said, very nonchalantly, "We left right after you, Zubin. One of the kids had a nightmare and blah blah."

A man Geeta didn't know was splayed on the blanket, propped on shaky elbows. "You invited the *churel* into your house? Watch yourself, Zubin, you'll wake up a shriveled old man." He chortled himself flat.

Geeta burned, but no one else joined the laughter. Saloni said with a frown, "We went to Karembhai and have gifts. *Lo!*"

"What's the need?" Saurabh said to his wife as the men happily relieved Geeta of the two bottles. "I could get intoxicated from your eyes alone."

"*Hutt!*" Saloni said, tenderly slapping his cheek.

Saurabh looked at Geeta. "*Arre!* You two are friends again? *Sha-bash!* You know, Geetaben, my wife talks about your childhood days all the time. The mischief you stirred!"

"She does?"

"I do no such thing, you drunk duffer." Saloni told Geeta, "I do not."

"Yes, you do. After two pegs, you always say that you miss her and that Ramesh was the lowest fool ever birthed."

"I also say I wish to be married to you for a thousand lifetimes. See how well I lie, *gadheda*? Pah! *Chal*, Geeta, let's go."

As the women left the water tower, they were quiet. Due to Saloni's obvious embarrassment, Geeta didn't mention Saurabh's revelation, which now occupied more of her mind than Darshan. Instead, she said, "How are you so . . . *fine*? With everything that just happened, I mean?"

Saloni's shrug was honest. "I really don't know. I just know what guilt feels like, and I know I don't feel any now." She hesitated, then continued. "After Runi killed herself, I . . . I was in a bad way." Pain pinched her eyes and Geeta felt her heart budge. "I thought the same as you: that I killed her. Everyone heard the things I said to her. I wanted her to wake up, see her son for the viper he was and stop being such a gullible fool. But afterward, I went back alone and told her I'd lend her the money. For the loan sharks. I said once we got them off her back, we'd figure it out. We'd get her boy clean. Lock him in a room if we had to. I've been over it ten thousand times. If she knew there was a solution with the money, then she killed herself because she was ashamed. Because *I* shamed her."

Manners dictated that Geeta protest but integrity kept her mute. "Where's her son now?"

Saloni sighed. "I have no idea. He disappeared. Didn't even show up to light Runi's pyre, the selfish *chut*. Better barren than a son like that." She looked at Geeta. "Sorry."

Geeta did not correct her. "So then, who paid for her last rites? You?"

Saloni nodded. "It didn't make up for anything, but it was the right thing to do." She almost smiled. "What did your mother always say? 'After eating nine hundred rats, the cat goes on a pilgrimage.'"

Geeta did not mention that the same proverb had occurred to her a few days back. "Yeah."

"I really miss that woman."

"Me, too." But the ache of her lost mother was a bit lightened in sharing her memory. Geeta wasn't the only one who remembered, and that made her mother feel less far away. Geeta said, "She loved you so much. She'd have been really happy to see you and Saurabh so happy."

Saloni snorted. "Sure, he's happy now. Wait 'til he wakes up tomorrow." She cleared her throat. "But yeah. We are. All things considered. I thank the One Above that he doesn't have a temper."

"Can you imagine? There's room for only one firecracker per relationship."

"Shut up. But he's always been modern. Like with the drinking, he likes it when I join him. How many husbands would allow that? And he's good about not always taking his mother's side over mine. He had to break that gargoyle down to not demand a dowry from my parents. Can you imagine? I mean, they had nothing. But we're from the same caste, and that was apparently more important than money. Well, that and I was fair-skinned. Oh, and my eyes. Did I tell you? When the kids were born, she fasted for two weeks, praying their eyes would turn green. What a bitch."

Geeta did not say that Saloni had not told her because they'd not been speaking for the past sixteen years. Instead, she nodded. "The previous generation's always more about *sanskaar* and all that. Ramesh had the same battle, but he convinced his family not to take a dowry. Which I'll always be grateful for, however much of a monster he turned out to be. My parents didn't have a son to live with, so they really needed their savings." She paused. "Not that they had any. I still can't believe my father left so much debt. I know he didn't mean to, but it's just surprising because I thought I knew him better than that."

"Right." Saloni coughed. "Listen, Geeta, I—"

"Oi, what's he doing here!"

"Oh! I forgot."

"What's going on?" Geeta asked Karem, who was playing fetch with Bandit near her door. Upon their approach, Bandit sniffed Saloni's ankles and then mounted her calf. Saloni shook him off and moved to the other side of Geeta. Bandit followed.

"Saloniben asked me to drop another one off for you." Karem pulled a bottle from a cloth bag.

Saloni tittered, still shooing Bandit. "Oh yes, my gift to you, Geeta. I'm tired of coming over and you only having water. Oi, can you please tell your dog that I'm a married woman?"

"When did you—" Oh. The keys she'd allegedly forgotten. "Never mind. Fine. Do you want to come in? Bandit! Leave it!"

"No," Saloni said as Karem said, "Yes." He began stammering. "Oh shit, I—my mistake."

Saloni's grin was mortifying. "Karembhai, I'd promised Geeta some company but now I must be off. Will you stay and have a chat?"

"Sure." When Karem bent to pet Bandit, Geeta pinched Saloni's elbow and hissed, "What are you doing?"

"What are *you* doing? You need an alibi! Let him stay!"

"We already set our alibis."

Before she left, Saloni waggled her brows in a way Geeta could only describe as obscene. "Let him stay anyway."

Geeta unlocked her door but did not go inside. "You don't have to. She—she's just messing around. I'm sure you need to be with the kids."

"They're okay. I'd like to talk to you, if that's all right?"

She nodded. "Bring in Bandit, too. He must be hungry."

Karem surveyed her home much like she had his. His focus landed on her desk while she took the bottle and went to the outside stove to boil some water. "Why don't you drink?" she asked. "Is it for religious reasons?"

He pressed a light finger to her radio. "I've tried it, I just never cared for it. Was always more about tobacco. My daughter's made me promise to quit, though, and I'm down to one *beedi* a night."

"Saloni wants me to try it with her."

"I didn't know you and Saloniben were so close."

"We used to be. Maybe we are again. I dunno. It's all very new."

"New can be good."

"Karem, I feel I should say: that night, what we did, I . . ."

"Yes?"

"I had a nice time." Here she tried to roll her eyes at herself—to let him know the joke was on her and she knew it—but it fell flat and ugly. "Before I ruined it, I mean."

"You didn't ruin anything." At her doubt, he laughed. "We both ruined it. It was a mutual failing. And I also had a nice time. You're a straightforward woman, and I respect that."

Geeta cringed, but he must've been too preoccupied with his next words to notice, because he continued: "So I'll also be straightforward. I said we're friends, Geeta, which is true, but we're adults, too; and it's obvious I have motives that go beyond friendship. It'd be childish to deny it, not to mention a waste of time, and I have so little of that as it is. But nothing *has* to go beyond friendship—I just like your company."

Geeta swallowed. People didn't play games in these matters because it was fun, she realized, they did it because the alternative was to fling open your arms to rejection and say *do with me what you will.* The water was roiling. As she added a bowl of rinsed lentils, she said, "I like yours, too. You're correct: we're adults and my . . . motives also go beyond friendship."

"Yes, I suspected."

She smiled with a self-deprecation that emerged from this new security. "What gave it away? When I nearly ate your face off?"

His laugh was sharp but not unkind. "That was one clue, yes. See? Straightforward."

"So you're okay with . . . keeping this between us?"

"It should be between us anyway. It's not anyone else's business."

"Yeah, okay, good." She nodded. And kept nodding. "So, um, what does this mean, exactly?"

"I think it means we see each other when we want and can. And we can eat each other's faces off if we want, too."

"And . . . the rest? The other stuff?"

"Ah. Um. We'll just figure that out as we go? How does that sound?"

"Nice. It sounds nice."

She vacillated between relief that she was able to smile and guilt for the same. It was a nauseating pendulum.

"I'll just feed Bandit." She drained the lentils and cooled them. They walked inside, where Bandit immediately abandoned his lizard nemesis for food. At the moment, she could not imagine ever eating again.

A gamut of dread awaited in the days ahead. A month prior, a quiet life had yawned before her. Now she was plagued by the realization that what she had done would stain her for all her lonely days. But tonight, tonight she couldn't quite summon anxiety or dread or guilt, she could only manage numbness. The relief of it! She knew it was not sustainable. This reprieve was a boon she had not expected. Even her gratitude for this gift was distant and academic, such was her numbness. She should send Karem away—it wasn't decent to drag him into her damage—but the prospect of being alone with memories of the night ("trauma" was a word she felt dramatic using despite its applicability) was enough to make her ask, "Will you sit with me? I—I don't think I'm ready for more right now, but would you mind sitting with me?"

If he was surprised by the request, he did not reveal it. "Of course." He left the plastic chair for her cot. He held her hand in his lap. It was warm and dry. Their skin rasped together. Solace journeyed through her, relaxing the painfully taut space between her shoulder blades. She felt, with the indigenous instinct born from occupying a body for decades, that if she were to lie down with the comforting weight of his hand on her forehead, she would sleep well. But if she realized this on an inhale, by the accompanying exhale she knew it couldn't happen.

"Tell me something about her."

"Who?" But he knew. "Sarita?"

"Yeah. I saw her in school, but she was a couple of years ahead so we didn't talk much." When he was quiet, she added, "Sorry. Is it weird I asked?"

"No, it's not. I like talking about her, especially with the kids. It's painful for me to remember, but it'll be more painful for them to forget. Let's see." He thought. "She was obsessed with politics. Very much wanted to be a politician."

Geeta scooted until her back was against the wall, her legs hanging over the bed. "Really?" Karem shifted as well.

"Really. Jewelry-making, she hated—likely why it's so god-awful. But she was fantastic with people, so charming. I think she could've done it, if the cancer hadn't . . . you know."

"That's a shame. She could've joined the council. When they started their quota seat."

"Well, I'm not sure how the *panchayat* would've felt about a Muslim woman on the council. That, too, a Dalit woman."

Her head turned. "What?"

Karem cleared his throat. "Sarita's parents converted to Islam before she was born, they thought it'd help their status. But it didn't change a thing until they moved here from a different village and passed as upper-caste Muslims."

She recalled Farah's words. "Islam doesn't have caste, though."

Karem laughed. "*Ji.* But India does."

Something else occurred to her. "Girls either marry someone local or leave town. But not only were you an outsider, you moved *here* for her. Did you know beforehand? About her being Dalit?"

"Yeah, I knew. And it didn't matter to me. No, you're looking at me like I was noble or selfless. Let me be clear. I didn't care because I had nothing—no family left, no job, no proper home—and her parents offered me all of that in exchange for some safety and credibility. It sounds crude, but it was a deal of sorts. I guess most marriages are. After we married, our friendship happened quickly enough, then affection, and then came a time when I couldn't remember not loving her."

Geeta had little time to reflect on this before he continued, "She made me promise to never tell the kids. She said she regretted her parents telling her, that she was always looking over her shoulder, waiting for someone to call her an imposter. But I think I must tell them. I don't want them to be afraid, but I also don't want them to be ashamed, or think they're better than others. But I don't want to break my promise to her either."

"That's a hard one. But you'll make the right decision. You're raising pretty great kids." After a long moment, Geeta asked, "How did Sarita feel about your business?"

"She worried. We both did. I still do. But it provided for us, plus I got to be home with her and the kids so . . ." He lifted his shoulders.

"Were you happy?"

"Hm, what a question." He rubbed his stubble with his free hand as he thought. "There were far more good days than bad days. Maybe that's what happiness is?"

"Did you fight?"

"Of course." But he knew Geeta's mind, he must have, because he added, "Never physical, though."

"Don't you all hit once in a while? It's not beating, not really."

Karem paused. "Yes, it is. Don't get me wrong, Sarita and I —it wasn't perfect, nothing is. And there were times we hurt each other plenty with words, but no, Geeta, no. I don't hit."

"Not even your kids?"

"No. Sometimes I wonder about that. I wasn't beaten as a kid, but I was spanked, and I think that fear helped me turn out okay. They—those little tyrants are fearless. I think you can be a good parent and spank. But Sarita said never, so I promised and I meant it."

"I remember my mother slapped me once or twice when I disobeyed. But my father never did. He hit her a couple times, though. But it didn't make me love him any less. I wonder if it should've."

Lately, each night a new memory landed upon Geeta. "Landed" was the wrong word. It wasn't a sudden memory, startling her with its new presence. No. Each memory's gentle unearthing was met with mild recognition: the one and only time she'd ever tried chicken, with

Ramesh, the taste not bad but the forbidden secret tying them together better. The elusive name of the Dalit girl from school, the one with the high marks whom they'd all branded a cheater—Payal. Saloni and Geeta attempting to remove their pubic hair with expired Veet cream they'd found, and incorrectly reading the instructions to boot, nearly burning off their clitorises (plus she'd itched something awful when the hair grew back). Her father bringing her a chocolate on her birthday, massaging her legs when she fell ill, slapping her mother for a domestic trifle that was more about his mood than her failing. Was it really so much easier to be a decent father than a decent husband?

Geeta closed her eyes, suddenly exhausted. The remainder of her adrenaline was subsiding. Karem's voice rumbled near her, a balm: "I think when we're kids, we just accept things. We don't think to question until later, sometimes not even then."

Her head rested against the wall, and she let it tip sideways until it met Karem's shoulder. Her defenses were lowered just enough for the images of Darshan's spite-ridden face to loom. *You're so starved for a fuck that you invited yourself into my house . . . to throw yourself at me.* Her body jerked, her head whipping up.

"Geeta," Karem began, squeezing her hand once, twice. He didn't continue speaking until she looked at him. "Are you all right?"

"Yes," she lied.

"Okay. But you'd tell me if you needed my help, right? Like with what happened to your neck, for instance?"

Geeta's free hand flew to span her clavicle. Across the room, in the armoire mirror, she saw the darkening skin. "If I thought you could help, yes, I'd tell you."

"So, no, then." His laugh was humorless.

"You're helping me now," she said, letting her head return to the shelter of his shoulder.

TWENTY

F arah stood, gourd in hand. Geeta stared, unsure of whether this was merely another febrile dream. After Karem had left late last night, Geeta slept fitfully, waking every ninety minutes or so, her clothes damp, cramps crawling in her belly. Sometimes she collapsed back into sleep, the scent of Karem either on her bedsheets or conjured by her hyper brain. Other times, she felt like she'd drown in bile if she remained horizontal, so she stepped over Bandit's sleeping form into the kitchen. She drew water from her clay pot and parsed through her dreams.

They usually began with her and Karem on her bed, echoing what they'd shared before he'd left. But invariably the face she kissed would morph. Or she'd look down and it'd be Darshan's head between her thighs. When she'd try to kick him away, he'd only laugh and tell her to be a good girl.

Her other nightmares began with the reverse: Darshan, his vile hands clawing. She'd grip the statue, cold as salve, and crash it into Karem's unsuspecting head. She'd realize her mistake a fraction too late, and see stunned betrayal occupy his eyes before death did.

Her hands had performed an act her mind couldn't yet accept. Geeta looked at them, distorted with fading orange henna. In the moonlight, the patterns looked like the faint breath of a dragon.

She did not regret her actions, but Darshan's. She resented being put in a position where those were her choices: violence or violation. She didn't want to be built to endure, a long-suffering saint tossed by the whims of men. She wanted, for once, not to be handed the short end of the stick by a system that expected gratitude in return.

As she sipped water in her moon-drenched kitchen, all quiet but the crickets, she submitted to the slow conclusion that, at least for her near future, there would be a difference between her waking and unconscious. The former had walls, mantras she could stack to protect her from her culpability; as Saloni had said: *Darshan killed himself. He broke the contract first. When someone threatens your body, you have every right to protect yourself.* He had hurt her, he had hurt others, and he would've hurt more.

Nonetheless, when she slept, her guilt roamed free, sans warden, loosed prisoners bent on havoc. They'd terrorize her, but she knew it wouldn't be permanent. She'd survived other awful things; this, too, would pass. Morning would come and with it, the safety of her mantras, but for the time being, Geeta felt small and naked, trembling in her kitchen nook, stomach and heart roiling. She was bathed in a light she felt unfit to accept. Her traitorous lungs trapped air, she gripped the lip of a shelf and kneeled. *"Kabaddi, kabaddi, kabaddi,"* she exhaled until the knot unraveled. Bandit was awake, keening his concern. She couldn't release the ledge to pet him. She looked at him as she breathed. *"Kabaddi, kabaddi, kabaddi."* Her distress was his; he roamed for a way to help her, as restless and impotent as she was.

When next she awoke, it was at Bandit's behest. He whined his need until she stumbled to the door in the early morning hours, bleary-eyed, to let him outside to *su-su*. The two temples played competing *bhajan*s to rouse the villagers. The morning air was cool, untouched by the day's inevitable wet heat. It felt delicious to her hot skin. She fell back into a kind of sleep that was more escape than rest, until Farah disturbed her by knocking, looking as fresh as Geeta did fuzzy.

From the doorstep, Farah absorbed Geeta's tangled hair and house gown. "You're still sleeping? It's ten," she said with the tacit superiority early risers felt toward night owls. "Did you hear about Darshan? The whole village is buzzing."

"What?" Geeta's tongue was thick, her mouth sour. Punitive sunlight stabbed her eyes and she gestured Farah inside so she could shut the door.

"Darshan's dead! His wife killed him!"

"No," she corrected automatically before catching herself. "That's, uh, unbelievable."

"The police came. Took everyone to Kohra."

"Insane."

"I know. Lately we've seen more action here than Delhi even— *Arre*, what happened to your throat?" Farah pointed to the necklace of bruises that had stained Geeta's skin deeper overnight.

"What? Nothing, don't worry about it."

"O-kay," Farah said, offering Geeta the gourd. "So, actually, the thing is . . . I can't give you more time, unfortunately. I need the money sooner than I thought."

As Geeta poured herself some water, she grew livid. To be oppressed by men was one matter, to allow a woman to also sit on her chest was another. Her power was meager, sure, but it was time to wield it. Matching Farah's apologetic tone, Geeta said, "Actually the thing is . . . I can't give you more money, unfortunately. You're on your own."

"Gee*ta*!" It was a mixture of wheedling and shock. "Don't make me go to the cops."

"Go. I'll tell them you killed him yourself."

"It was *your* idea. If *I'd* wanted to kill him, it would've looked like a simple heart attack. I have access to all the pong pong in the world— only a total moron would go for a mosquito coil. Seriously, Geetaben, if I actually wanted you dead—you'd be dead. I wouldn't have bothered with mosquito coil samosas. But, like I said, you're of no use to me dead."

Geeta's heart quickened, anger thrumming in her ears. "This was your plan all along? Trick me into helping you and then blackmail me?"

"Not at first, but then you flipped on me and— It doesn't matter." Farah waved a dismissive hand. "You know you loved it. You loved feeling all useful and helpful."

"You," Geeta said, "are no bonobo."

Farah blinked before saying slowly, "I don't know what that means."

"They're primates whose females band together against male aggression. They're allies, unlike you."

"Am I supposed to be hurt that you *don't* think I'm a monkey?"

"Ape."

"Whatever."

"I wouldn't be so confident, Farah. You had Samir's body burned. Very suspicious, don't you think?"

"Nope. The police think the Dom fucked up."

"Either way, there's no evidence tying me to Samir."

Farah's eyes widened in faux innocence. "Except that conversation I overheard between you two."

"What are you talking about?"

"You don't remember? The one where he said he'd take your money, and you said that you'd kill him."

Geeta played along. "Then why didn't you come forward sooner, since you suspected me after Samir died?"

"Of course I delayed. Geeta, you threatened me and my children next. I mean, what *could* I do?"

"Are you serious?"

Farah smiled, her teeth gleaming. She winked. "As murder."

What, Geeta thought, would Saloni do? *People like that don't understand words, only kicks.*

So Geeta asked, incredibly pleasantly, "Is it lonely, Farah?"

"Is what?"

"Not being like anyone else here." She continued, her posture taller with defensive dignity. "I don't just mean because you're Muslim, that's too obvious."

Confusion marred Farah's features. "It is?"

Geeta felt a brief thrill. A petty part of her now understood what had motivated Saloni all those years ago to not only be a queen bee but a bully. Did people ever completely shed playground politics?

"Sure. You know how it is, people like people who are similar to them. They trust people who look like them, talk like them, act like them. It's just . . . more comfortable. But you—I mean, the women tolerate you, but they don't really *like* you, do they?"

"They do. I mean, some do. I think." The falter in Farah was like fuel.

"Nah," Geeta said, shaking her head and smiling. "They really, really don't. Which is why you came to me for help in the first place, correct? Because you knew they didn't like you, and you thought they didn't like me, so you figured I was your best shot. And there's actually nothing wrong with that. But. *But.* You weren't seeking solidarity, or a friend, you were preying on me. And that makes you just as bad as Samir."

"What! No, I—"

"Maybe even worse. You told me the other day I'm not the Bandit Queen; you're probably right. But neither are you." Geeta did not wait for Farah's response. "You're Kusuma."

"Who?"

Geeta's smile turned genuine as she snapped her fingers. "Exactly. Why would you know of her? She's not really worth remembering; didn't make the cut in most of the books or films. Kind of a poor man's Phoolan. Kusuma named herself *dasyu sundari,* 'beautiful bandit queen.' Isn't that so fucking catty—she just *had* to one-up Phoolan, twist that knife. And of *course* it'd be about looks, right? Low-hanging fruit of the jealous.

"Anyway, Kusuma was also part of the gang—well, more of a shared concubine-mistress than a proper dacoit. But she was extremely jealous of Phoolan. So much so, in fact, that when the upper castes killed Phoolan's husband—Vikram, you remember him—and began abusing Phoolan, Kusuma helped the attackers. She tore Phoolan's clothes. She took her jewelry, helped the men tie her up, and as Phoolan was being raped, Kusuma told her she deserved it."

"I—"

"You could never be a real friend to any woman, Farah, because you're too fucking broken. You can try to lie to the village and the police, but I doubt anyone's going to believe you. You lied about the Dom messing up and cremating Samir—"

Farah's eyes flared with brief triumph. "But see? The cop *did* believe me."

"Sure, over a Dalit. That's the shitty hierarchy I'm talking about. Which is why the cop wouldn't believe a Muslim over four Hindus."

"F-four?"

Geeta ticked her fingers. "Saloni, Preity, Priya. Me."

"But they're not with you. You said so yourself, that you and Saloni were—"

"Sure they are. Saloni and I made up. I went to her party." She presented her henna as evidence. "See, you really are removed from things around here, aren't you? And the twins are my new best friends. We had dinner together last night. I did them a 'small favor,' as everyone here likes to call it, so they'll say anything I need them to."

"Small favor? What small favor?" Farah's eyebrows knitted and then rose with realization even as Geeta said: "I removed her nose ring. Just like I did yours."

"*You* killed Darshan?"

It was Geeta's turn to bare her teeth in a smile. Her menace was chipper. "I have a way of making problems go away. You should know that better than anyone. Do you see why I'm not an enemy you want to make, Farah?" Geeta casually assessed the gourd, testing the skin with her thumb. "I've been patient with you. Too patient for your own good. It's given you bad habits. So, I won't be patient any longer, Farah, because unlike how you feel about me, you're of zero use to me alive. Do you follow?"

She nodded.

"Are you sure? I know you're a little slow at times."

Farah's voice was curt, each word a thread snipped. "I understand perfectly."

"Oh, that's fantastic. They say you're slow, tubelight like, but I don't think that's true. You just count on people to underestimate you. Which is pretty smart in its own way."

"Thanks."

"You're very, very welcome," Geeta said warmly. "Now, I have a big day ahead of me, so kindly get the hell out of my house."

She escorted a shell-shocked Farah to the door. But when Geeta opened it, there stood Arhaan, hazel eyes wide. He did not immediately inquire about snacks, which indicated that something was amiss even more than his solemn expression.

"What's the matter?"

"The police called my house. They want you and Mummy to go to Kohra now."

This, of course, lent further credibility to what she'd told Farah. But Geeta couldn't appreciate Farah's face because her own was slack with dread. Sweat blossomed on the skin between her breasts.

"Why?" she squeaked.

"So they can arrest you."

TWENTY-ONE

The state of the Kohra police station should have eased her hummingbird heart. It was a station in name only: three men in khaki uniforms lounged in the courtyard on plastic lawn chairs, ankles crossed over knees, blowing on stout glasses of chai. Neither their beige berets nor their spirits wilted in the heat. Despite the relaxed tableau, as Geeta dismounted from the scooter's pillion, she felt as though she were trudging toward her hanging.

Saloni parked her husband's scooter, her sandal missing the kickstand on the first attempt. They approached together. The pathways to the entrance as well as the courtyard were lined with bricks, all angled like fallen dominoes. Geeta heard laughter. An office boy collected the officers' empty glasses. The joke must have been his because he was beaming while the men chuckled. The eldest, the one with the most decorated sleeves and epaulettes, clapped the boy's back in approval. Music floated in from an unseen radio, possibly from one of the neighboring businesses. Golden oldies rather than recent pop hits.

It would have been an idyllic scene, were it not for the two officers in a holding cell driving their *lathi*s into a weeping man. Geeta winced as a stick hit the back of the man's knees and he crumpled. The officers each took one of his elbows to right him. Once his balance was restored, the three resumed their striking and sobbing. Things could go either way, Geeta realized, absorbing the dichotomy. On one hand, if this truly was a routine formality—and Arhaan was a dramatic duffer, as Saloni had insisted—they'd soon be sipping tea. Alternatively, in fifteen minutes' time she could replace that man making the ghastly noises. At the thought, Geeta's fingers worried her earlobe until Saloni smacked her hand down.

"Stop that! I swear, you should never play poker." She whispered last-minute instructions to Geeta: "Just remember: Follow my lead. Act casual. You know *nothing* about how he died, okay? That's how they nab the perp on *C.I.D.;* he always knows some detail that he shouldn't." She adjusted Geeta's scarf higher. "And keep your neck covered."

Nab? Perp? Geeta was about to question just how many episodes Saloni had watched, but there was no time.

The senior officer did not look up when the women approached. Nor did he when Saloni said they'd been summoned regarding the recent expiration of a Mr. Darshan Varesh. He merely slurped his fresh glass of chai, mustache dampening, and angled his head toward a table manned by, well, a woman of all things. She sat just outside the yellow entrance, under the awning, her desk positioned between two open doors.

At the sight of the female officer, Geeta's hope ballooned. After Phoolan Devi enacted her Valentine's Day revenge massacre, she was imprisoned. As a celebrity, she was treated far better than most inmates, and she formed a friendship with the prison director, Kiran Bedi, who helped Phoolan enter that last bastion of criminals: politics. In jail, Phoolan waited for a trial that the authorities ensured would never take place. But then, all forty-eight charges were dropped and she was, suddenly, finally, abruptly, at last, free. After eleven years in prison, she was released and elected a member of parliament . . . until her assassination at the age of thirty-seven—but Geeta did not want to dwell on that part of the story. Instead, she focused on creating an ally, her own Kiran Bedi.

"Uh, namaskar," Geeta greeted, palms together. "We were called to give a statement? We're from the same village as Mr. Darshan . . . ?"

"Varesh. Yes. Sit. We'll start shortly."

Saloni and Geeta sat on two flimsy lawn chairs, purses on their laps. The woman's face was severe; her dark hair scrapped back into a low bun to accommodate her beret. She was young—Geeta would've guessed twenty-six or so—and investing great pains in hiding her beauty. She wore no eyeliner or *bindi;* her lips were as bereft as her fingers. Just like the men, she wore a black name tag over one breast pocket and a pin of the Indian flag on the other.

Sushma Sinha, ASP, wrote many notes into a red folder. Her assigned desk—really a foldout table, Geeta observed while they waited—was piled with many similar folders, all neatly quartered by twine. ASP Sushma Sinha's pen was tied to her folder with identical twine. She paused her writing to drink from her purple water bottle. She did not touch her mouth to the rim, nor did she spill a single drop.

Competent, Geeta thought, her hope souring to dread, this woman was very competent. Sushma Sinha, ASP, looked as though she, too, was About the Work. Under different circumstances, this might've pleased Geeta. When Sushma Sinha, ASP, resumed writing, without a word or glance to her reluctant guests, Saloni and Geeta looked at each other. Saloni shrugged, but Geeta could no longer abide the uncertainty.

"Er, Officer Sinha, ma'am?"

Sushma Sinha, ASP, held up one unpainted finger. "Just a moment."

From the left, each blow to the unseen man was a preview of Geeta's bleak future. And didn't cops do even worse things to female prisoners?

Murderess though she was, she'd never survive this dreadful place, subject to beatings and Ram knew what else, all to the tune of golden oldies. No, Geeta would simply have to follow Samir and Darshan, and shuffle off this mortal coil. Surely, by now, she was an expert and could arrange for the same punishment she'd been meting out to everyone like temple *prasad*. She'd gnaw on a mosquito coil, bake a pong pong dessert or—

The beaten man released another bleat of pain. Geeta said, "Excu—"

"Just a moment, ma'am," Sushma Sinha, ASP, repeated with hostile courtesy.

So they stewed in the midday heat, Saloni inspecting the state of her regenerating arm hair, Geeta devising her suicide, until Sushma Sinha, ASP, said, at long last: "Where were you yesterday evening?"

"For you!" Geeta burst out, removing Farah's gourd from her purse and thrusting it across the table.

ASP Sushma Sinha glared at it. "What will I do with that?"

Saloni tittered: "Makes excellent *subji*. Much better than the market here—they're so hard, na? You can use this one tonight. Feel."

"No. Yesterday evening?"

Geeta set the rejected gourd back on her lap as Saloni answered, "We had dinner at the twins' home."

"Yes, the twins. Preity Varesh and Priya Bhati."

"*Ji*. We had dinner and—"

"Vegetable curry!" Geeta blurted again, her voice far too loud.

"What?"

Saloni ground her sandal into Geeta's toes. "That's what we ate for dinner. This one's just wild about veggie curry."

ASP Sushma Sinha's brows furrowed; she was unamused. Her scowl added years, which Geeta gathered was strategic. "When did you leave their home?"

"Right after dinner."

"When was that?"

"Oh, hmm. Maybe nine? We would've stayed longer, but she had to take care of her kid. Nightmare, you know."

"Who's 'she'?"

"Preity," Saloni said as Geeta, distracted by the prisoner's flogging, answered, "Priya."

Shit. Which one had she said? Which one should she have said?

Sushma Sinha, ASP, finally smiled, but it provided little relief to her two suspects.

"Could we move somewhere more private?" Geeta asked, thinking quickly. "It's difficult to hear your questions."

"It'll be far too hot inside. None of the fans are working," ASP Sushma Sinha said. "We can manage, go on."

Geeta twisted in her seat toward the sound of the beating. "That man—he—uh—he says he didn't do it."

"They all say that. He just needs a little convincing to remember that he stole the television."

"I mean," Geeta said as the man's howls pitched higher, "he seems pretty sure he didn't."

"Did you see Mr. Varesh when you left his home?"

"Yes," Saloni said.

"And he was alive," Geeta offered helpfully.

Saloni's eyes closed in a prayer for patience.

"I see. What did you do after you left the twins' home?"

"We went to Karembhai's store to get—er—snacks for my husband and his friends."

"Yes, but he says that you didn't show up to buy 'snacks' until ten. Yet you say you left at nine. What did you do in the meanwhile?"

"You talked to Karem?" Geeta squeaked. She'd already ensured his Kohra business was taken—if she got him arrested to boot, it'd be worse, karmically speaking, than either of the murders on her head. His children! Who'd take care of the kids if he was jailed and she killed herself? What if—

"Yes, I did. Is that a problem?"

"No, ma'am." Geeta's fingers fluttered up toward her ear, but at Saloni's glower, she sat on her hand instead.

ASP Sushma Sinha regarded them with the same contempt she'd

shown their gourd. "We've spoken to many. It's our job. So. Your husband and his friends say you arrived with the 'snacks' at fifteen past,
but where were you from nine to ten?"

"Nowhere." Saloni offered her hands in apology. "I didn't look at
the clock when we left. It could have been later."

"Hmm, *but* you said that you left when one of the kids had a nightmare, correct?"

"Correct."

"But the kids say they—"

"You talked to the *kids?*" Geeta asked. All throughout India, citi-
zens complained they couldn't get government authorities to do their
jobs, and here was Sushma Sinha, ASP, of Kohra, managing a month's
work in the span of hours.

Sushma Sinha, ASP, set down her pen in exasperation. "Yes. Did
I need your permission?"

"No, no," Geeta said. "You can speak to whomever you wish."

"Dhanyavad." Sushma Sinha, ASP, thanked her with such scorn
that Geeta, duly castigated, looked down at her spurned gourd. It was
becoming increasingly apparent that Sushma Sinha, ASP, would be
no Kiran Bedi. "Now, the children said they never sleep until well
after ten. Nor do they remember anyone having a nightmare last
night."

"Did you talk to Sonny?" Saloni asked, waving a hand in the air.
"I tell you, that boy gets so high, I doubt he can find his own nose
much less tell time. At the Raval wedding—"

But ASP Sushma Sinha was not interested in the Raval wedding;
she whipped up a hand and Saloni shut her mouth so quickly, her
teeth clicked.

"Children forget things in sleep, na?" Geeta said.

ASP Sushma Sinha's eyes pinned Geeta. "Do you have
children?"

"I—er—no, I don't."

"Why not?"

Saloni said, "She's doing her part to help population control. Do you?"

ASP Sushma Sinha did not appreciate that, despite—or possibly due to—Saloni's aggressively friendly mien. Sinha turned to Geeta, all but snarling, "It's not because your husband mysteriously disappeared five years ago?"

Good god, Geeta thought, dazed. Sushma Sinha, ASP, clearly did not believe in hobbies or drinking chai in the courtyard. "How—"

Saloni laughed before Geeta could finish. "You know, my eldest once sleepwalked to the kitchen, ate some chips and fell asleep right there! Didn't remember a thing in the morning. He's obsessed with snacks, I tell you. Won't eat a meal, but he'll snack all day. The joys of motherhood, know what I mean? *Do* you know what I mean? Are you a mother?"

"Not that it's any of your business, but I'm currently focusing on my career." The words fell out easily, in the same order and cadence as a recited address. Clearly Sushma Sinha, ASP, had said them many times over. "There's plenty of time for kids. I'm young."

"Yes," Saloni said, nodding. "You are. Careers are important. Especially for women. You know, we are also working women. We have—"

"Yes, a microloan, I know. What do you know about Samir Vora?"

Geeta's eyes widened, but she bit the inside of her cheek and managed, she thought, to look the appropriate cocktail of confused and innocent. "Samir? Well, he was a drinker, you know."

Saloni sighed. "And alas, the drink killed him."

Geeta looked at Saloni while the ASP made a long, damning note. "'Alas'?" Geeta mouthed.

"Samir Vora's death was allegedly due to alcohol poisoning. Last night, during the second death, many members of your village were also inebriated with, how did you say, 'snacks.'" She said the English word with an exaggerated Gujarati accent—which Geeta found a tad offensive—and it sounded more like "snakes."

She tried to sit still but couldn't get comfortable in the chair. Her

clothes slid on the plastic and she kept sinking under the ASP's interrogation, shoulders hunching in what was sure to be construed as
guilt. How was Saloni still upright?

"I'm wondering how all these 'snacks' are magically appearing in
a state that specifically bans such 'snacks.'"

Even Saloni, so dependably voluble, was mute then, her lips rolled
inward. Geeta tried for a nonchalant shrug, thinking of how to best
protect Karem. "Well, from what I hear, they come from here."

The tortured man's insistence of his innocence and ignorance,
which had blended into the background, now grew louder. Sushma
Sinha, ASP, had to lean forward to hear. "What?" Behind her, the
office boy walked by with a tray of Thums Up bottles. Sushma Sinha,
ASP, called out for one, but he blithely continued toward the holding
cell. Saloni masked her sputter of amusement with a cough.

"I hear there's a don in Kohra. He goes by Bada-Bhai—"

"Yeah, I'm familiar with Chintu. We've got our eye on him. He's
slippery, though, butters the right *roti*s."

It likely wouldn't do to point out that those *roti*s belonged to this
very department.

"Well, if you can't catch him on that, can you at least punish him
for the dogs?"

Again, they had to raise their voices. "Eh?"

"Dogs. The dogs."

"What?"

At that specific moment, the abusive officers took their soda break
and their victim quieted, while Geeta hollered, *"Kutte!"*

Everyone looked.

It was unfortunate, of course, that while the literal word for dogs
was *kutte*, it was also the colloquial term for "bastards." For all the station to hear, Geeta had just cursed Sushma Sinha, ASP, and her fellow
officers to her face.

"Not you! Not her," she reassured the skeptical courtyard. "Actual
dogs." She lowered a hand a half-meter from the ground to indicate
as such. "Puppies."

"What about them?"

"He's abusing them. He's cutting his supply with methanol and then testing it on the dogs, some are going blind."

"Really? Well," Sushma Sinha, ASP, said with a shrug, "we'll need more than that to nab him. Animal cruelty is a ten-rupee fine." She stopped. "I mean, unless it's a cow of course. And just how do you know all this?"

"I was—I found out by accident and he threatened me. That," Geeta rushed on, "is why I didn't come forward before. I was scared."

"Yeah," ASP Sushma Sinha said, devoid of concern. "You two seem real scared. Now, back to the deceased. Darshan Varesh."

"*Ji,*" Saloni said. "What about him?"

"It's interesting that no one seems torn up about it. Especially his wife. Or his sister-in-law. Sure, they've been crying all day, but they keep whispering about a pair of dumb earrings and some Sikh boy."

"But it's not exactly a tragedy, is it?" Geeta said. "I mean, he did attack Priya."

"How do *you* know about that?" ASP Sushma Sinha asked, her voice like a sharp stick.

"I didn't—*you* said—I mean I assumed—or I overheard . . ."

"What is this, multiple choice?" ASP Sushma Sinha's eyes gleamed with triumph as she stood. "One minute."

"Shit," Saloni hissed when they were alone. "What'd I say, Geeta? Never reveal too much. Dammit!"

"Fuck," Geeta whispered. "Fuck, fuck fuck." When her head still felt light, she switched to: "*Kabaddi, kabaddi, kabaddi.*"

ASP Sushma Sinha, floating on importance, went straight to her senior officer, who watched her approach much like the women did when a child nagged them with a demand they had no time to entertain. She spoke. He shook his head in refusal. She insisted. He turned from annoyed to angry.

"What's the need for all that? Just do it here, na?"

"Sir, I'd like to separate them and collect their statements."

"*Bey yaar,* this again? Isn't it enough that you're so bored, you harassed those other two ladies all night? Asking them the same questions over and over again—" Saloni and Geeta exchanged a look, which Sushma Sinha, ASP easily caught. Her eyes darted between her superior and the women sitting behind him.

"Sir—" She held up a finger to politely quiet him, but he spoke over her. He walked to the table and she scampered behind.

"Meanwhile, the drunk fool of a husband is still inside snoring away."

Which, Geeta realized, was why she didn't allow them indoors. ASP Sushma Sinha's face twisted in the loss of possibility, as though someone had just ruined the ending to an enjoyable book. "Sir, we should speak to every witness alone to verify the events. They just now mentioned that the victim attacked his sister-in-law prior to his death."

The senior officer, whose name tag read M. D. Trivedi, sighed. "He did. She said so. Over and over."

"But how did *they*—"

"Oi, ASP madam!" Trivedi thundered pitilessly. "Didn't anyone teach you that there's a difference between talking to a witness and interrogating a suspect? What, will you interrogate me next?"

"But, sir, this is the second incident in the same small village. Something's black in the lentils. They knew about the attempted rape. They *just now* mentioned it!"

Trivedi expelled a generous sigh. He asked Geeta and Saloni: "How did you come to know of the attack?"

Geeta raised a meek hand. "I actually didn't know, sir, until just now. But I'm not much of a gossip."

Saloni nodded. "It's true." She whispered to Trivedi, "Not enough people like her. So . . ." She put an elbow on the table and leaned forward with prurient interest. "What's this about a rape? Don't tell me Darshan . . ." She clapped a hand over her mouth. "*O baap re.* Shame, shame."

ASP Sushma Sinha looked like she might stamp her foot. "Lies! That one just now said that Darshan attacked Priya!"

Geeta blinked. She arranged her face into a suitable expression of benign confusion. "No . . . oh, I see how you're confused. *Preity*. He threw acid on *Preity* many years back. You must have that in your notes?" Geeta flipped the red folder over to review notes in English she could not decipher. Still, she pretended, sharing the book with Saloni as they both hummed in feigned scrutiny.

"Get away from those!" ASP Sushma Sinha screeched like an injured monkey, yanking the book back. "That is official police business."

Saloni carried on, stage-whispering to Geeta: "Poor Preity, na? Hasn't she suffered enough? Wait 'til the group hears—"

"Not Preity! *Priya*! He attacked *Priya* and *she* killed him!"

"Oh?" Saloni perked with curiosity. "Really?"

"Very good, Sinha," Trivedi said caustically. "Why don't you just take out an ad in the paper?"

"Sir, these two are definitely up to some *hera pheri*. I just need a room—"

"We don't have the extra space for you to play cop, Kali Maa. Maybe one day you'll have an entire police department for your hysterical conspiracies." His hairline had crept behind his ears, occupying the liminal space between more bald than not. His eyes went to the women, then stayed on Saloni. Geeta could always pinpoint the exact moment someone—man, woman or child—noticed Saloni's green eyes. Split seconds of denial, confirmation and appreciation, all in neat succession.

Flicking both hands, he shooed away ASP Sushma Sinha and sat down. "I'll take these ladies' statements myself."

"Sir—"

"You're dismissed, ASP."

She sighed, deflated. "Yes, sir."

Geeta almost felt sorry for her. Didn't she know too well how it felt to be dismissed? Underestimated and shelved? Saloni had been right, they might get away with this after all.

Trivedi rolled his eyes at Saloni, inviting her into a private joke. "Quotas, you know? 'Hire a woman,' they said. 'Hire a scheduled caste,' they said. 'We need diversity,' they said. Blah blah blah." He smiled at Saloni. "Did she even offer you water or tea?"

"Er—no."

He shouted for the office boy, the call like a very long belch, but no one came.

Saloni said, "No matter. It's really very simple. We went for dinner—"

"No, no." He extracted his mobile. Shortly after dialing, he began screaming. "Where? Huh? Again? Every time I call you, you're either shitting or eating. *Bey yaar*. Get here quick. Shit on your own time. Bring tea and biscuits."

Geeta grimaced. Saloni raised a finger and said, "Not necessary," but was ignored.

"What's that?" he asked, nodding toward Geeta's lap.

"Oh, for you!" Saloni said and Geeta extended the gourd. "It's just the right amount of soft. Your wife should make it tonight only, tomorrow it might be too mushy."

He assessed it. "Nice."

"It's rude to come empty-handed, na?" Saloni continued. "And our village has the best gourds."

"As I always say, 'The future of India is in its villages.' "

"Wasn't that Gandhi—" Geeta started but Saloni was giggling, and eyelashes that were usually reserved for Varun the loan officer were now working overtime.

"*You* came up with that? So clever, na?"

Trivedi beamed. "Where was I?"

"Um, last night we went to have dinner at the twins' place."

"Twins? Which twins?"

"Preity and Priya."

"They're twins?" He squinted at ASP Sushma Sinha's notes. "They have different surnames."

Saloni did not laugh as Geeta nearly did, but instead patiently said, "They're married, sir."

"Oh, right, yes, I knew that, of course. And after dinner?"

"After dinner, we went to a local shop for snacks, and then I brought them to my husband by the water tank. He and his friends were there . . . socializing."

"Yes, I know. I'm not here for petty things like bootleg booze. Victimless crime."

That solved the mystery of whose *roti*s were being buttered by Bada-Bhai. Geeta snuck a look at ASP Sushma Sinha, who was down the corridor, gesticulating wildly and berating the office boy.

"Right. And then we each went home." Saloni looked at Geeta.

"Correct." Geeta nodded. "Straight home."

"And you stayed there all night? Can anyone corroborate that?"

It was such a sharp turn of professionalism that Saloni blinked. "Er, yes, my children saw me. And my helpers."

"And you?"

"No, I—I live alone, but—" Geeta was about to offer Karem as an alibi, but Trivedi did not appear interested.

"Alone? That's unfortunate. You know what they say about women living alone—they're like unlocked treasure chests, just inviting looting."

"Er—"

"Now, it's true you're no longer in the height of your *jawani*, but you can't be too careful. Even in your diminishing years, men can be dangerous creatures."

Geeta sputtered, but Saloni put a quelling hand over hers. "Thank you, sir. We look after each other. We're very close; it is the way of our village."

"Not all men, of course," he said, puffing. "Some of us support M.A.R.D., you know?"

"*Ji,*" they said, though they did not.

He recited in painstaking, flawed English: "'Men Against Rape and Domestic violins.' A film star founded it, so you know it's credible. He's a Muslim, but still."

"*Ji.*"

"Some men don't need to rape. Some get plenty of offers."

"Che," Geeta muttered.

"What was that?"

"I said *'ji.'*"

"So you were not in the house when Darshan attacked Preity? Or when she attacked him?"

"Um, sir, do you mean Priya?"

"What? Er, yes, whichever isn't"—he gestured vaguely to his face—"you know."

"No, sir, we'd left. We would have done something if we'd been there, na?"

He shook his head. "If only Zubin had not left to 'socialize.' He could have protected his wife."

Geeta couldn't help but say, "I think she managed to defend herself pretty well. He's dead."

"Yes, but it took many weak blows to do what would've taken a man one."

Geeta narrowed her eyes. "It seems to me that she did a satisfactory job."

"Now, now, Geeta," Saloni chided. "'A single blow of a blacksmith is equal to a hundred blows of a goldsmith.'"

"That's good," Trivedi said, smoothing the corners of his mustache. "Very good. You came up with that?"

"Me? No, no!" She laughed. "How could I, sir? My father used to say it."

"Yes, that makes more sense." He cleared his throat. "Where is that damn boy with the chai? I bet you he's shitting again."

"Don't mind, sir, no need for you to take the trouble. You must have very important work waiting. And you finished here anyhow, much faster than ASP madam."

"I did?" He looked down at the folder where he'd written no notes. "Yes, I did."

TWENTY-TWO

"Since we're here," Saloni said as they left the station, "can we stop by the salon? I need to get my arms done." She presented her forearm, where fine roots of hair disturbed the skin.

"Sure."

Outside the station, a voice gave Geeta pause. Not because it called to her, but because it was familiar. She turned to see Khushi speaking into her mobile phone. With her free hand, she let her sandals fall to the ground. One landed upside down and she toed it upright before stepping into them. Geeta moved toward her in greeting, but a uniformed man reached Khushi first. He shook his head, pointing at her *chappal*s and then at the road. Khushi nodded absently, bent to collect them and walked past Geeta and Saloni.

"Khushiben?"

"Ji?" She hung up. "Namaste." Now officially out of the station's ambit, she donned her shoes. Geeta saw she looked weary, the skin beneath her blue-clouded eyes puckered with fatigue.

"What are you doing here?"

"Ay-ya." Khushi's sigh was taxed. "There was a mix-up with a body I collected. I cremated him, but turns out he's Muslim, so obviously I made a mistake. Which they just love to rub in."

Geeta balked at the thought of the fallout crashing on Khushi's head instead of Farah's. "Samir Vora?"

"*Ji*. If this place had a proper funeral home, I wouldn't even deal with Muslim last rites, but where else are they gonna go?"

"We know his wife, er, widow. Let's go back inside and sort this."

"I'm not allowed inside," Khushi said. "I was fine with waiting outside, but that damn lady cop was all, 'Article 15 this, Article 15 that.' Then the fat cop kicked me out. Why do *I* need to be in their drama? But forget it, na? It's sorted now. I just wanted to pay them and be done, but that damn lady cop was all, 'bribes are offensive to the badge.' Going on about how I destroyed evidence in a murder investigation. Bah! What murder? The drunk choked on his own vomit. Smelled worse than a dry latrine, and I would know."

Saloni aimed to lighten the mood: "One honest cop in all of India and she's in Kohra. What're the odds?"

Geeta didn't laugh. "How is it sorted?"

"Oh, the fat cop was happy to take the bribe." The left corner of Khushi's mouth twisted up in a deprecating smile. "I guess my money's not polluted."

"Do you need a ride back?"

Saloni coughed. "Shit, but I only have a two-wheeler." A valid point, but Geeta realized she didn't know how Saloni, a Brahmin, regarded caste.

Khushi wagged her mobile. "My eldest is on his way. He took the scooter today for his tuitions. He goes to school nearby."

"Why doesn't he go to the school at home?" Saloni asked.

Khushi shook her head. "He did once, long time back, but the teacher just had him cleaning toilets. I mean, I sent him to school so he *doesn't* have to clean toilets. Ay-ya, I should've charged the school for the labor, but he was five—didn't do a great job. Anyway, let it be. This school is much better—he's studying to be a dissectionist. A lot fancier than 'corpse collector,' na?"

Geeta felt Saloni's incredulity matching her own. This woman had enough money to buy officers, better teachers and a scooter. Khushi must have known their minds because she smiled. "I meant what I said, about my house being bigger than yours, Geetaben. When you do the 'dirty work' no one else wants to, you get to charge whatever the hell you want." She continued, "Don't get me wrong. If someone is poor, I only charge what they can afford. Everyone deserves last rites. But others . . ." She shrugged. "Well, I never forget a face. Even when they're dead, I can recognize someone straightaway. And when pyre time comes for that fat cop's mother . . ." Khushi trailed off, simply rubbing two fingers against her thumb in a universal semiotic indicating *paise*.

Saloni snorted so loudly, Geeta pinched her. "What?" Saloni whined, rubbing her elbow. "She's funny." To Khushi she said, "He deserves it. Gouge the pig, I say."

A scooter pulled up. Khushi's son's feet patted the ground as he slowed. "Mom," he said.

Khushi rolled her eyes at the women. "'Mom,'" she aped, her face distorted. "Before he studied here, it used to be 'Ma.'"

"Joys of motherhood, am I right?" Saloni said.

"Yeah. Rewarding."

"Mom." Khushi's son was more embarrassed than impatient, but as Khushi hefted herself onto the pillion, she said: "I'm coming, I'm coming, give your old mother a break. You didn't exactly arrive in five minutes either, you know."

They left in a plume of dust. Saloni backed up her husband's scooter, curving it out into the road. While Geeta mounted as Khushi had, Saloni pulled on long gloves and wound a scarf across the lower half of her face and over her head like a dacoit.

"Ready?" she asked, her voice muffled.

"Ready," Geeta said into her friend's ear. They could talk while driving so long as Geeta kept her head close to Saloni's and they both shouted.

"Did that happen when we were in school? I don't remember Dalit kids cleaning toilets. I remember Payal, though."

"Who?" Saloni turned her head so her words weren't snatched by the wind. "I remember them in class—they always sat in the back. On those gunny bags, though, not at the desks."

"Shitty."

"We weren't as bad as other places, you know, with the beatings and the shit-eating and stuff. They kept to themselves; we kept to ourselves."

Grit from the road hit Geeta's eyes and she closed them as they watered. Wind whisked the moisture away. "That's our best defense? That we're 'not that bad'?"

"Listen, I'm Brahmin and I grew up with way less than Khushi's sons. And my duffer brothers were so proud. They could've died of starvation, but at least they'd have died 'unpolluted Brahmins.' Never mind that we ate whatever we could get our hands on, meat, too. 'Unpolluted' my left tit! Forget caste, Geeta, *money* is power. And Khushi has it."

"They kept her outside the police station, shoeless; how is that power?"

Saloni's staticky groan was aggrieved, as though Geeta was pouring the fault on her head alone. "What can we do? We can't even get them to update the census data in our town, and you wanna change two thousand years of 'tradition'? Obviously, abusing them is wrong. That's why it's just easier to, you know, keep quiet, understand and accept it."

Saloni tried to park near a passport photo shop, under a faded red Airtel sign. A guard in a blue uniform waved her away. She dismissed him with a comparable hand motion. He pulled a face but returned to his chair in the shade. Saloni peeled her arms and head bare, then locked the cloths in the storage space beneath the pillion.

Geeta said, "Like how husbands will hit us and we should keep quiet, understand and accept it? Is that also 'tradition'?"

"Geeta . . ." They walked up the chipped steps toward the salon. Saloni gave her name and indicated Geeta should also sit with her behind a curtain.

"Wait, let me finish. I've been thinking about this since this whole mess began. If Ramesh hit you, that would be unacceptable. But he hit me, so it's marriage. Darshan tried to rape me, so I was justified in attacking him. But if he'd tried to rape Preity, that would've also just been marriage. Khushi is Dalit, so she can't sit with us or eat with us, and she can only do one job; her sons can get a degree, but they, too, can only do one job. And—"

Geeta quieted when a girl in a *kurta* top ducked into their side of the drawn curtain. She wore those skinny jeans Geeta often saw on the youths, but they were a misnomer here, baggy and voluminous around the girl's twig thighs. White buds plugged her ears, twin wires draping down her front and disappearing to her pocket, which housed her mobile phone. Thin strains of a recent rap song filled their cordoned world. Geeta heard on repeat: *"Lungi dance, lungi dance, lungi dance."* Without so much as a hello, the girl took Saloni's arm and began smearing wax with the apathetic practice of a medical professional.

Saloni peered around the girl down to Geeta, who perched on a stool so low that she might as well have sat on the tile. "Where is this *andolan* coming from, *yaar*?"

"I don't know," Geeta confessed. She supposed she *was* agitated. Karem's words floated to her, about kids not questioning injustices. But what about when adults didn't either? If the women were able to help each other commit murder because they felt it was morally right, then why couldn't they help others being wronged, too?

When Geeta was young, well before the *panchayat* voted to build a separate but equal water tank on the south part of the village, the Dalits would come to the well to fill their steel and clay pots. They weren't allowed to draw, of course, but Geeta watched as her mother, or another woman, pulled water for them—the "Harijans," as that generation condescendingly called them—pouring from a prophylactic height, careful not to bump the pail against their pots. Their village spotted caste on sight like it was gender and behaved accordingly. Her mother hadn't shown malice, hadn't abused anyone, but by following the rules, she'd accepted them, taught Geeta the same. But now, all the shibboleths that Geeta had been conditioned to regard as level were revealing themselves to be crooked.

Geeta was no rebel; she'd never be one to bring the world to its knees. Phoolan Devi hadn't either, but she'd brought some men to theirs, and her story had resonated with countless other women, including Geeta. She'd always regarded Phoolan's life as delineated by gender: one woman against scores of men who constantly used her womanhood to dehumanize her, to grind her, literally, into the dirt. But Geeta now saw that caste had marked Phoolan's story as much as, if not more than, gender had.

She'd been born Phoolan Mallah, a Dalit and a woman, therefore twice-trodden. Even in a gang with no regard for civilization or law, caste reigned. Her husband, Vikram, was slaughtered over caste, she was gang-raped because of her caste. She killed twenty-two upper-caste men in revenge. And only then did she cease being a woman and become a legend; the country dropped her caste-marked surname "Mallah," and made her a Devi instead.

But Geeta had few words to express this to Saloni, whose face was patient but expectant, peering at Geeta behind the teenager. So Geeta tried again.

"I've been fine keeping to myself for years, you know that. But . . . the best I can describe it is like this. Sometimes when I'm with Bandit in the house for too long, I get used to his smell. Then I leave for water or a loan meeting or whatever, and I come back and I smell him and realize he's dirty, he stinks, he needs washing."

Saloni didn't wince when the girl ripped off the cloth, re-pressed and once again ripped.

"I think I've been nose-blind all my life and now I can smell. It's dirty, Saloni. It stinks and it needs washing."

"Legs?" the girl said so loudly that Geeta jumped.

Saloni shook her head no.

The girl left them. Saloni examined her arms, which bore tacky bits of residual wax.

"But, Geeta, think about it: if we invited Khushi over for dinner or had her draw from our pump instead of theirs, you'd feel good about yourself, but they'd go after *her*, not you. They'd burn *her* house down, beat *her* up.

"A few years back, a local girl married some doctor from Ahmedabad, right? The wedding was a few villages away, and they invited a Dalit family since the bride was the girl's best friend from childhood. Right after, some upper castes beat their spines into their ribs for eating with everyone. They tied gasoline rags around the man's hands and burned them right off. They raped the woman and their daughter." Saloni swallowed with difficulty. "It's not right; I know it, you know it. It shouldn't be this way. But regardless of your intentions, there are consequences to your ideas that don't land on your head."

As Saloni paid, it took longer than Geeta would've liked to scrabble up from the stool. Her knees cricked in a way that was more embarrassing than painful. Once they were back on the road toward home, Geeta said, "But why can't we try for new rules? I mean, you're on the *panchayat*!"

Saloni rolled her eyes. "They *had* to have a woman; it was compulsory. My father-in-law made sure I won so he'd have another vote in his corner. Half the time, they don't even tell me about council meetings."

"You have more pull than you realize. I remember two years ago, you weren't even on the council yet, but when they were all voting on that girl's honor killing, you convinced the *panchayat* to just settle for a fine."

Saloni's snort was derisive. "Yeah, and the family went bankrupt trying to pay it. I hardly helped anyone. Plus, they had the marriage dissolved, so really, what was it all for?"

"That girl's *alive* because of you! And remember what you said about Preity? How if people stop her from trying to do things just because she's a widow, they'll have to answer to you? *That's* power, too, Saloni. And we should use it."

After they exited the highway, the ground grew bumpier and their teeth jarred. "How?"

Saloni parked in front of her home. Geeta dismounted first, and as Saloni balanced the kickstand, inspiration struck. Geeta snapped her fingers.

"We could marry your daughter to Khushi's son!"

As Saloni once again freed her face from her scarf, Geeta saw she was glaring. "Aparna's five, Geeta. You're not gonna fix untouchability with child brides. And shouldn't we first resolve our more immediate problems? Like you-know-what? Then we can 'be the change we want to see in the world,' Gandhi."

Geeta smiled. "Are you sure Trivedi didn't invent that saying, too?"

Saloni barked out a genuine laugh. "What a butt boil. And people think *I'm* conceited. God."

"When's the next council meeting?"

She shrugged. "I dunno, but I'll ask Saurabh."

"Good. I think I have an idea. If we can get Khushi on the council, then—"

"Geeta, don't get your hopes up, okay? This system is as old as India and we're women, in case you've forgotten."

"What happened to being 'facilitators of karma'? You're underestimating what villages can do. Like, every time they have those riots in the cities, Hindus and Muslims all killing each other, nothing ever happens here, na? If we can do that, we can do this."

Saloni waggled her hips suggestively. "Ohhhh," she sang. "*Now* I see why you're banging this equality *bhajan*. We want peace so no one blinks when you and Karem . . ." She puckered her lips and kissed the air three times in rapid succession.

"*Che!* Don't be gross."

"Gross? Are *you* five, too? It's not gross. It's sexy," she said, the English word sounding so pornographic that Geeta's head swiveled to ensure no one had overheard.

"Okay, I'm going."

"To Kar-eeem's?"

"Shut up."

"It was a joke."

" 'I don't like jokes.' "

" 'I don't like *you*.' "

This dialogue was some of the only English Geeta knew, still famous years after the movie's release. Before her wedding, Geeta had seen *Kuch Kuch Hota Hai* with Saloni over Ramesh's protests. Things had been very tense between them and a film seemed like a stalemate; they couldn't bicker in the curated peace of the movie hall. They'd enjoyed the movie—much of India had—and by tacit agreement neither of them had mentioned the wedding or Ramesh. They'd argued about films on the way home, however, something about the realism (or lack thereof) of a former lover returning just as the protagonist has moved on. After their squabble, they separated, mumbling something about "next time," though there never was.

But now, she and Saloni had found each other again. Saloni and Karem were modest bolt-holes in a shitstorm of murder and mayhem and blackmail, and Geeta sank into that refuge with relief, if not happiness. Over the years, loneliness had become a dead arm, useless and heavy but nonetheless hers, so she'd lugged it around, her other appendages pumping harder to compensate for the burden. Now it was as though that arm was working in tandem, finally helping rather than hindering. She didn't realize she was whistling until she stopped, her feet hiccuping as she saw the visitor on her doorstep.

He'd never been particularly handsome and now, as Ramesh stood up to greet her, Geeta found that though much else had changed in five years, this fact had not.

TWENTY-THREE

Ramesh smiled at her. His focus was off, a touch too far to the left, but he said, "Geeta? I knew it was you. It's like that song you used to like: 'Even if my eyes close, I'd still recognize your footsteps.'"

They were butchered lyrics, but she was too busy denying what her very open eyes were seeing to correct him.

"You can't be here."

"No, it's really me. In the flesh." His arms rose at his sides, presenting himself as a dubious prize. He held a white cane in his right hand. He was, she realized as she cautiously approached her front door, blind.

"No," she said. "I mean you *can't* be here." If word got to Farah that Ramesh was alive, that Geeta hadn't removed her own nose ring, it would turn Geeta's threats thinner than water. Meanwhile Geeta's lofty aspirations for Bandit as a watchdog were clearly dead. Where was that mutt? "How long have you been here? Did anyone see you?"

He gestured to his cane with a rueful smile. "How would I know?"

But she had bigger concerns than his lack of sight. "Get inside!" she hissed.

He didn't move. "Help me?" he asked, his voice so small and pathetic that Geeta's palm itched to slap him. Still, she maneuvered him, her touch unkind, and shut the door behind them.

"Why are you here?"

"May I have a glass of water? It's so very hot out," he asked in the same meek manner. Geeta obliged with a grunt as deep as her reluctance. After a moment of him grasping and failing, she impatiently wrapped his hand around the steel cup.

She'd imagined this moment many times, especially in the first year of Ramesh's absence. That he'd return, brimming with apologies and explanations, was consistent in each fantasy. The variable was her reaction, which changed as time passed. They'd fall into each other's arms, crying; he'd give up the drink and she'd get pregnant. Or she'd initially refuse, make him suffer, and he'd slog for her trust like a film hero. Or she'd deliver a long, emotionally charged speech (which she rehearsed while washing her hair) about how she'd survived all by herself and no longer needed him so he might as well stay gone.

After drinking, Ramesh wiped his lips and she demanded again: "Why are you here?"

"You're my wife."

She couldn't help her hyena guffaw.

His voice grew peeved. "What? You are."

"Yeah, the one you abandoned five years ago. So why're you really here?"

Perhaps he'd intuited she'd found another, moved on, and swooped back to stamp her as his. Not out of love or even desire, but simply as a landlord marks their property from encroachers. But that was paranoia; there was no possible way he knew about Karem. This was just life unfolding how it desired and, once again, completely and totally fucking her.

"I've missed you."

Geeta stared at him. His eyes were open but unfocused. He tapped his cane to get a sense of her furniture. These were the words, in some form, from her fantasy. She wanted to ask how he'd become blind, but didn't want to give him the impression that she cared. It was peculiar, but his diminished condition diluted her memories of terror. Or perhaps it was that he'd aged, or she'd aged and had faced problems more fearsome than him. Perhaps she was just too flabbergasted to be afraid. Whatever the reason, the result was that, at the moment, she was more annoyed than threatened.

"So you want money, then."

"No! Listen, I know I fucked it all up. But I want to make it up to you. Please, let me."

"Impossible."

"Let me try."

"You need to leave. But not now—at night when no one can see you."

He tried to move toward her but didn't check for clearance with his cane first, and tripped over a plastic chair. It clattered on its side, and Geeta lunged forward to steady him before she could remind herself that it didn't matter to her if he fell and split his skull open. "Geeta, please. I have nowhere else to go. Look at me. It took me weeks just to find my way here."

"And it took me five years to find my way here."

"But I'm *blind*." He wheedled, Geeta thought, just as Farah did.

"Easier to be a blind man than a dropped woman. You can't just show up and ruin everything I've worked for."

"I don't want to ruin it."

"But you *will*, that's just what you do."

"But I'm your *husband*."

It was a long time before she was finished laughing. "You'd think it'd be less funny the second time," she said, "but no."

His voice was sour. "I get your point. But I meant what I said: I want to make it up to you. Let me, Geeta." After a long pause, he asked, "What're you thinking?"

"I'm thinking I liked it better when I was a widow."

Except she wasn't a widow. She was a murderess and—now her thoughts turned to Karem and their time together—technically an adulteress to boot.

Voices filled the room. Through the bars of her open window, Geeta saw people, mostly in white, walking toward Darshan's house, where a professional mourner already sat, beating her chest and encouraging Preity to wail her sorrow. Meanwhile, though they didn't know it, the girls in the south part of the village were safer than they'd been in a long while. After the priest led everyone in prayers, Khushi and her sons would take the body for cremation and Darshan's son would light the pyre.

"What's going on?" Ramesh asked, head cocking.

"They're getting ready for last rites."

"Whose?"

"Geeta?" someone called from outside her door.

"Shh!" Geeta hissed at Ramesh, though he hadn't said anything. She recognized Farah's voice. "Hide."

"Huh?"

"I said shh! You need to hide. She can't know you're alive."

"Why?" he whispered because she had.

"Because my life depends on her thinking you're dead and that I killed you."

"Come again?"

"Go out the back. No, wait, others might see you. Get in the armoire."

"Geeta? I know you're home, the padlock isn't on."

"One minute," she called. "Armoire. Go."

"But—"

She made her face spectacularly ferocious, though the effort was wasted. "You say you want to make it up to me? Get in."

He felt his way inside, folding his body against her saris. She shoved his cane into his gut and shut the double doors on his *oomph.* She exhaled into the mirror, then turned to open the front door with a barked "What?"

Farah stood in pale clothing. "Charming. Aren't you supposed to be in jail? Anyway, are you coming to Darshan's? I can't tell if it's ruder if you attend or don't, considering. They don't really have an etiquette book on mur—"

"Why are you here?" Geeta interrupted, acutely aware of Ramesh, who could hear everything through the cotton swaddling him.

"Because your mutt is jumping everywhere. Some of us are trying to *mourn,* you know. Not *you,* obviously, but—"

"Bandit, come." He bounded up the steps and licked her proffered hand. He froze then, immediately losing interest as he ran to yip at the armoire.

"What the hell?"

"He, uh, does that sometimes," Geeta said. "I'll see you at next week's meeting."

"Wait, what happened at the station—"

She shut the door on Farah's question.

"Bandit, quiet!" Even as she reached for the armoire door handle, she hesitated. It would be far easier if she could just keep Ramesh tucked away and out of her hair. Or if fiction turned to fact and Bandit extended her the ultimate favor by eating her husband.

"Geeta?" he called. "Is there, like, a dog in here?"

Ever the clever one, this man. She sighed, maneuvering Bandit out the back before releasing Ramesh, who spilled out of the closet, cane in hand.

"Did I hear right? Darshan's dead?" Ramesh sighed. "*O baap re.* I used to drink with him."

Geeta scowled. "You used to drink with everyone, *gadheda.*" She never would've dared speak to him this way before and pride swelled in her.

He took no offense. "That's true. I'm dry now, though. Haven't touched the stuff since . . ." He raised his arm to wave his hand in front of his eyes, and Geeta's entire body panicked. Suddenly she was twenty-two again, curled on the kitchen floor, Ramesh's foot burrowed in her gut, her back. She flinched, fumbling backward with a gasp, before she registered his movement as benign.

But it was too late. It was as though a switch had been flipped. She tumbled from secure in her power to having absolutely none. An awful fist squeezed her chest; she couldn't speak. Looking at him was too troubling, so she did not, focusing instead on her trembling hands, how her left pinky wavered at an unnatural angle. She tried to breathe and found no air. Her only consolation was that he couldn't see her sudden, volatile reaction.

"How?" She managed to push out the word without wavering.

"*Tharra.* Got a bad batch. Mixed with some poison or something."

She didn't have the will to mention Bandit or Bada-Bhai's methanol. She limped to her desk and sat down, staring at the photograph of the Bandit Queen, trying to unknot the anxiety behind her sternum. There was no need to fear; she had a life and friends here, Ramesh didn't. Even as she told herself that he couldn't touch her anymore, she found she didn't believe it.

"Why'd you leave?"

"I was shit to you, I know that. I was a coward: the loan sharks were coming for my head. They would've killed me. But I knew they wouldn't hurt you—they knew you didn't have anything valuable."

He inspired about as much faith as a blind pilot. "*You* hurt me plenty."

"Never again, Geeta. And I'm blind, yes, but I promise I'm no burden. I know how to live like this. There was this NGO in Ahmedabad—"

"So you've been in Ahmedabad for the past five years?"

"Not all that time. I was begging on the street for a while before the NGO found me. They taught me to work like this. I can still fix bicycles and cane chairs. I'm still good with my hands."

"What about your parents? Your brother said they couldn't find you."

"I was too ashamed to see them, and I didn't want to be a burden on my brother either—he already has to take care of our parents. I couldn't bear their disappointment."

He could be lying, but what was paramount, she knew, was making certain that Ramesh didn't hear her fear. She kept her voice light as she said, "Well, at least you wouldn't have to see it."

He smiled. "Funny. You were always funny." His brows knitted. "They really didn't reach out to you? All these years?"

"Everyone thought I did something to you. Made you disappear."

"Oh, Geeta."

She cleared her throat. "It's done. And so are we. Please leave."

"At least let me stay through Diwali," he said.

"That's over two weeks! No!"

"But I haven't been home in so long. Look, I'll save up some money for my cane and if by then you still don't want me around, I'll go." He pinched the skin of his throat. "Promise."

"What cane?"

His face was animated. "There's this new SmartCane. Some students in Delhi came up with it. It's amazing. I dunno how, but it senses things around you and vibrates to warn you."

"Like sonar?"

He frowned. "Huh?"

"Like with bats."

"Huh?"

"Never mind. How much is this cane?"

"Twenty thousand."

"If I give you the money, will you leave?" Evidently, it didn't matter how much time had passed; if her reaction to the man was this visceral, she needed him gone no matter the cost. Like with Farah, she needed to start protecting herself instead of just reacting.

"I couldn't ask you to—"

"It's a yes or no question." But she was already moving toward the armoire. She'd never reveal her box to another, but Ramesh couldn't see its contents. She extracted her *mangalsutra*. "Your family paid for this," she said, pooling it in his hand. "So you might as well have it. Leave and sell it for your cane."

His fingertips read the beads. "Is this your . . ."

She nodded but then realized her mistake. "Yes."

"Oh, Geeta . . ."

"No, stop. I don't want your gratitude or filmy bullshit. Just take it and go."

His face, divoted with deep smallpox scars, was sheepish. "It's not that. God, this is so awkward. I can't believe—I should've made it right earlier, but honestly, I kinda forgot and then it hardly mattered and . . . God, this is embarrassing. That's the thing about being sober— you remember all the selfish shit you've pulled."

"What are you saying?"

"The *mangalsutra*'s fake. I—I used the money my parents gave me for it to repay someone. And I bought a costume one."

It wasn't shocking. Still, she said, "You what?"

"I was going to replace it! I swear, once I got some money, but . . ."

"Who did you repay?" She needn't have bothered asking. "Of course booze. You"—to her complete relief, she emerged from the tunnel of fear and rounded upon a very familiar corner of rage—"are a shit nugget."

"I know," he moaned. "I know I am. That's why I want to make it up to you. I'll get a job, I'll earn some money. I'll buy a *mangalsutra* and a cane."

"Forget it," she snapped. "What am I going to do with a fucking marriage necklace from you, Ramesh?" She was livid with herself and her stupid, futile gesture of kindness—no, weakness. At least she hadn't tried to sell it; she'd have been laughed out of the shop. "God Above, I forgot what an ingrown hair you are."

"Forgive me," he said. "Please forgive me. I'll find a way to make this up to you, I swear." The necklace was in his hand between them. It dangled as he asked timidly, "Do you, like, want this back or . . ."

Geeta yanked it from him. "I should shove this up your piss hole."

He blinked. "Were you always this vulgar?"

———

She didn't attend Darshan's mourning. Saloni did, however, so Geeta waited on her porch. When Geeta had left her own home, Ramesh had attempted to inquire about her plans, which she quickly quashed, informing him with false bravado that she had no interest in returning to a life where he had any say over her. Bandit had walked with her and was now in a losing battle with a new lithesome lizard.

"Bandit!" Arhaan shouted when he arrived with his family. In mourning Darshan, they'd all worn white and now resembled an advertisement for Nirma washing powder.

"Hey," Saloni said. "Are you okay?"

"Not really."

Arhaan and his sister led Bandit to play in the street. After nodding a greeting at Geeta, Saurabh went inside. Geeta explained how Ramesh had returned, broke and broken.

"Are you serious? Why?"

"He says he wants to try again, but I'm not sure."

Panic flooded Saloni's usually confident face as she balked. "Not sure! You cannot take him back, Geeta! Not after all he's—"

"No, no, I mean I'm not sure what he's actually up to. I offered him money and that didn't work."

"The only thing you should be offering that *chutiya* is two tight slaps. He's stolen enough from you."

"What?"

Saloni shook her head, faltering for only a second before her words were fluid once again. "You know what I mean. Like your time. Love. Your salt."

Geeta felt close to tears. "It was awful seeing him again, Saloni. I can't even tell you. I felt— it felt like no time had gone by, even though everything's changed. When I think about Ramesh, I hate him so much I could tear his limbs off, but then . . . when I saw him today, it wasn't that. It was . . ."

"What?"

"Terrifying," she whispered. "I wasn't angry, I was just scared. I can't have him here."

Saloni hesitated. "Should we, like, 'get rid' of him?"

Geeta smacked her forehead. "Why is that always everyone's go-to? I just want to 'regular' get rid of him, not *get rid* of him."

"I dunno, I mean everyone already thinks he's dead. We could just . . . you know. You said he's blind, right? So it's gotta be easier than the others."

"Or, hear me out, the *panchayat* could decide that he's no longer my husband so I don't owe him anything and he has to leave."

Saloni's mouth pulled down in doubt. "You want to take this to the council? What if they rule against you?"

"Well, I have your vote, correct? And you and Saurabh can convince your father-in-law. Whichever way he leans, the others will follow."

"It's still a big risk."

Geeta looked down the street, where the kids were tugging a stick clenched between Bandit's teeth. "I've been thinking about Khushi."

"O Ram." Saloni sighed. "You have a monsoon of shit pouring on your head and distracting yourself isn't gonna clean it, Geeta."

"If Khushi gets a *panchayat* seat, she would also vote against Ramesh. Plus, she could help herself and other Dalits. It's a win-win."

"*Assuming* you win. They'd never allow two women on the council."

"They may have to—there's a reserved seat for a scheduled caste, just like for a woman."

"So what? Hasn't been enforced thus far."

"Right, but I have a feeling that ASP Sushma Sinha *would* enforce it."

"We barely got that woman out of our lives, why would we invite her back in?"

"I'm not asking her to move here, just demand that the *panchayat* abide by the law. You heard Khushi, Sinha's all about Article 15."

Saloni shook her head, her tone wry. "Your house is on fire and you're just giving away water?"

"If I have the votes, I'll be rid of Ramesh for good."

"There's another way to be rid of him for good." At Geeta's exasperation, Saloni said slyly, "I'm just sayin'."

"I meant," Geeta said, trying for a smile and failing, "a way that doesn't ensure I reincarnate as a cockroach. I'm going to talk to Khushi."

"Now?"

Geeta remembered her fright when Ramesh had idly moved his arm. "I—I can't go back home right now."

———

As advertised, Khushi's house was indeed much larger than Geeta's. Two looming stories plus a terrace with a garden. Once she'd reached the south portion of the village, following the drain water down, her way had been easy. Everyone knew where the wealthy Khushiben lived. Each person Geeta asked pointed her closer.

She knocked on the green double doors. A barefoot girl answered and when Geeta inquired after Khushi, the girl looked behind her but said nothing.

"I got it, Amali," Khushi said. "You make more tea."

The girl left with the same subservience she'd shown answering the door. Khushi's frame, generous and soft, swallowed the lacunae of the open doors. She didn't smile, per se, but her tone was light as she said by way of greeting: "I hope your dog didn't die."

"What? Oh." Geeta laughed. "No, touch wood. I wanted to speak with you." Her last sentence lingered between them, a scent souring as Khushi continued to not invite Geeta inside.

"I have company," Khushi said.

They were of Khushi's ilk, was the unspoken information tracking beneath her words like subtitles, and Geeta's caste would necessitate uncomfortable adjustments. They wouldn't be able to sit on furniture in her presence, instead standing in deference before moving to the ground.

"Oh, right, I see. Um, I can come by another time?"

"No, no, tell me."

Translation: *Make it quick.*

"Right, okay. So, uh, I was thinking of how much you've achieved and how impressive you are—as a businesswoman and as a woman—and I thought, well, you should be on the *panchayat,* 'cause with that kind of platform and power, you could bring the same kind of achievement to others that you have to yourself—others meaning Dalits, definitely, but also other women. Anyway, I think you'd have a real chance at winning, especially if your running means Dalits actually vote this time around because, you know, most don't because they think it doesn't matter, not that they're not justified in feeling that way, 'cause nothing ever really changes, so why bother? But if *your* name was on the ballot, it *could* mean change and they *would* vote, which—"

"Breathe," Khushi instructed.

Geeta obeyed, gulping air like it was water. She smiled. "Will you run?"

"No."

Geeta deflated. "No?"

"No, thank you," Khushi amended.

"But—"

A voice from inside interrupted: "Khushiben? Is everything all right? I need to be home by nine and we still have to— Oh, hello, Geetaben. Welcome," Farah said, drinking tea from Khushi's courtyard like it was her own.

TWENTY-FOUR

Portions of Khushi's home were erected with mud carefully lined to look like brick, but the majority was cement. The more recent additions, such as the toilet and two sitting rooms Geeta saw as she was led through the courtyard, were discernible by the brighter paint and lack of water stains. Not a little gobsmacked, she sat in a large sitting room on a divan next to Farah, who slurped her tea dregs until the girl returned with a tray of fresh glasses. Geeta was about to reach for one when Khushi spoke:

"You'll not take tea, of course," she said mildly from her separate divan.

"Oh, I—"

But the girl, Amali, had already heeded her mistress's words, walking to where Khushi reclined against a bolster pillow, smoking hookah with the relaxed power of a sultan surveying a courtesan. Silver toe rings adorned each foot. Above her hung a framed black-and-white portrait of Dr. B. R. Ambedkar. Khushi selected a folded *paan* from Amali's tray and tucked the entire leaf into her mouth. Amali balanced the tray with one hand while rearranging the hookah coals with a pair of tongs. As Khushi inhaled, the water gurgled.

"Ah, Amali," Farah said warmly, relishing her fresh cup. "You always remember that I like more sugar."

Geeta blinked at the familiarity; her tongue itched to ask about Farah's relationship with Khushi, but Geeta refused to give Farah the satisfaction of admitting any curiosity. After a slight bow of acknowledgment, Amali opened the room's four doors to circulate the air and then left.

"They offered it to me years ago, you know. When the quota first began." Khushi spoke around the *paan*.

"Huh?" Geeta said.

"The *panchayat*. They even said they'd pay all the expenses for me to run. It makes sense. A woman *and* a scheduled caste—fills both reservations but only one seat, one vote."

"But you said no?"

Khushi's snort was derisive. "Why would I say yes? So I can drag my ass to the office once a year to pose for a photo while they do whatever the hell they want the other days of the year? If anything, it'd be worse, because then everyone here would think I'm actually a part of the shit they decide. I've worked too hard for too long to let them spoil my reputation. And all for a false crown? Ay-ya!"

"But it doesn't have to be false! You could make real change." She'd planned on explaining her Ramesh problem, but Farah's presence complicated matters.

"Listen, er, what was your name again?"

"Geeta," Farah supplied helpfully. Her glee radiated like heat from asphalt.

"Right. Geetaben." Khushi released a generous plume of smoke. "I have very little use for your guilt."

"No, I—"

"I don't feel particularly honored that you 'lowered' yourself by coming here, entering my home. You let my kids touch your dog, so what? I'm not gonna fall over in gratitude."

"I didn't think you would, I just—"

"Yes, you did." Khushi's smile was indulgent but knowing. And now, finally, Geeta registered Khushi's titanic anger, initially blanketed by a close-lipped smile and a livid civility that had since fallen like a veil. A little spit collected in the corner of Khushi's mouth as her voice crescendoed.

"You thought that you'd run here to the bad part of town offering to save me so you could feel like you did something of consequence with your little life making . . . jewelry, was it?"

"*Mangalsutra*s," Farah answered before Geeta could. "But it's still 'art,' right, Geetaben?"

Geeta glared at Farah, whose smile was all teeth. Not for the first time, Geeta marveled at the vast emotional gamut of women. Here sat Farah, repurposing her tenderness toward Amali and Khushi as a further foil for her savagery against Geeta. Geeta wasn't offended so much as impressed. And it wasn't just Farah, it was all of them: Saloni, the twins, Geeta herself. Their ranges, as women, were extreme. Men gravitated toward one side or the other and remained; Ramesh certainly had. Women splayed the far corners, their cruelty and kindness equally capacious.

"I just wanted to help," Geeta said quietly, unable to look at either woman. She omitted that she also desperately needed help. "I didn't mean anything bad by it. He," she continued, pointing to Ambedkar's photograph above Khushi's head, "wanted separate seats for Dalits in government. Because he knew you couldn't expect the 'touchables' to look out for others. It didn't happen, but I thought it could here, at least."

Khushi's face softened a fraction. "Dr. Ambedkar also thought it'd be better for us to live separately from caste Hindus. To him, untouchables only existed where the idea of 'touchability' does—it's parasitic. But his reasoning doesn't work. Because it follows us. Do you see her?" Khushi pointed to Amali, who was outside in the courtyard. Geeta looked as Amali tossed a bucket of water on the ground and squatted with a *jhadu* broom. Her scarf bisected her torso, the two loose ends tied in a knot at her hip while she worked, ambling on her haunches as she swept.

"Amali got a job cooking meals at the school, but when they found out she was Dalit, they fired her and threw out all the food she'd touched. So I offered her work here, and her parents refused. Why? Because she's of the Dhobi caste and I'm a Dom, and working here would pollute her.

"Her parents died last year, starved to death. They would rather she die than pollute them, can you imagine? Of course you can—it's not exactly a special story. My point is: we don't need you caste Hindus to tell us we're untouchable, not when we're too busy keeping each other down."

"But Amali's here now."

"Yes." Khushi nodded. "She eats from my vessels and lives here, too. She values her belly before her karma."

"Or maybe she just doesn't believe in this bullshit either."

Khushi laughed then and Geeta felt the relief like a cool breeze. She wanted Khushi's approval with the same eager desperation that likely hindered it. Knowledge of this, however, did not equal the power to alter or mask her thirst. Though Geeta had gotten her answer, and knew she wasn't exactly welcome, she sought to avoid being shown the door. All that awaited her was Ramesh. She procrastinated:

"So, how long have you two been friends?"

"'Friends'?" Khushi said the word like she was trying on an outfit she didn't find immediately flattering. "Would we say 'friends'?"

"Sure, friends," Farah said. "But more business partners."

Khushi nodded but corrected her. "Not even partners, more like we made a necessary arrangement." Khushi inhaled from her hookah wand while Geeta tried to determine what a dressmaker and a corpse burner needed from each other. It read like the very odd premise of a riddle.

"What arrangement?"

"Khushiben here burned Samir's body before the police could even think to ask for it. She did all the paperwork for me and paid off the cops." At Khushi's alarm, Farah explained. "It's fine, Geeta already knows about Samir. She's the one who 'helped' me."

"This is mosquito coil-*wali*?" When Farah nodded, Khushi

released a bawdy laugh at Geeta's expense. "Don't mind, na? It was very cute. Wouldn't have been my first choice, but sometimes people like to take the tougher road. Builds character."

"Forgive me." Geeta sulked. "I wasn't exactly experienced."

"Untrue—what about Ramesh?"

With the idiot insisting on sticking around, there was no sense in secrecy. Not in a village where your neighbor's sister-in-law's second cousin knew about your hemorrhoids before you did.

"I didn't kill him," Geeta said through gritted teeth. "He left me. But he's back now."

Farah did not seem upset. "Of course," she crowed, clapping one hand on her thigh. "Well, that makes far more sense. You're definitely not cut out for murder."

Which should've been a compliment, though it was very much not. Geeta scowled at her while addressing Khushi. "That's why I came here; I need your help."

"And here I thought you wanted to help me?" Khushi asked, feigning surprise.

"I figured we could help each other. If you're on the *panchayat*, you could vote that my marriage to Ramesh is null and he'd have to leave."

"Why don't you want him back?" Khushi asked, before waving her hand. "Never mind, stupid question. Still, that's a lot of ifs. If I run, if I win, if I vote in your favor."

"I don't know what other option I have. He's not leaving willingly."

Farah shrugged. "Kill him."

"Why?" Geeta snapped. "So you have more dirt to blackmail me with?"

Geeta looked at Khushi for a reaction, but she seemed neither surprised nor dismayed, and Geeta belatedly realized that she'd been hoping to plummet Farah in Khushi's esteem, like a friendless school-girl striving to be teacher's pet.

Farah scoffed. "You tried to threaten me, too, okay?"

"Only after you tried to extort me for money and—oh yeah—poison my food!"

Farah rolled her eyes. "Haven't you let that go yet? I keep telling you it wasn't *personal*."

Geeta ignored her, addressing Khushi instead. "Will you at least think about running?"

"No. Any other questions?"

She'd have to find another way to scour Ramesh from her life. Still, she could not bear going home and seeing him again. "Just one. You did Farah a huge favor. Why?"

Khushi smiled and reached for another *paan*. "You're saying I don't seem like the generous sort?"

Geeta held Khushi's gaze. "You don't seem like the stupid sort. You cremated a Muslim man, lied to and bribed the cops. You wouldn't take on that kind of risk unless you benefited."

Khushi shed her coyness. "Of course I benefited. She got rid of Samir. Which means he can't assault my girls. I owed her a favor back."

Geeta's head whirred with multiple, conflicting questions. "I thought you only had sons."

"I do, thank the One Above. Girls are impossible to protect. Any daughter is a burden, but a Dalit one? Forget it. Your upper-caste men think our shadows pollute them, but they see no problem with invading our cunts."

At the word, the muscles in Geeta's low abdomen tightened as she thought of Darshan.

"The one time we wouldn't mind being untouchable." Khushi jerked her chin toward the door, though Amali, done sweeping the courtyard, had left for another chore. "Like I said, Amali's of a higher subcaste, but she's also the help, so she wouldn't use our toilet. One morning a couple of months back, she went to the fields and as soon as she undid her pants, some man started choking her. He tried to force himself on her and would have succeeded, too, if a group of other girls hadn't passed by and scared him off. Now she uses our toilet—when she *can*, that is—my son hogs it day and night. Dairy doesn't agree with him but he'd die before giving up Amul cheese, ay-ya!"

"Do you have a refrigerator?" Geeta asked.

Khushi blinked at the non sequitur. "Er—no. We were going to, but with all the power holidays, why bother?"

How, Geeta thought, had that not occurred to her?

"I'll continue? So we complained. And what did the *panchayat* say?"

"Fuck all," Geeta said fiercely. "That's why I wanted you on it—to do things differently!"

Khushi waved away her hookah smoke and Geeta's objections. "Well, we did it differently anyway. He's dead, isn't he?"

Which prompted another question. "But the attacker wasn't Samir—"

Farah interrupted, "Yes, it was. Sometimes he'd stay out all night, wouldn't come home until after dawn. And two of those nights were when girls here had been attacked. Plus, Khushiben says there haven't been any attacks since he died."

Still, Geeta pressed. "What about Darshan?"

"What about him—my boys are cremating him now." Khushi checked the time on her mobile. "They'll be back soon."

"Darshan was the attacker—"

Her sons entered the courtyard, and with them the odor of charred flesh and smoke from wood, tobacco and something sweeter. Drugs, though Geeta wasn't sure which kind. The stench was so overwhelming, she breathed through her mouth as the boys greeted their mother.

"How'd it go?" Khushi palmed her son's head when he touched her feet in deference. "Have you been drinking?"

The boy rolled his eyes. "It's the only way to handle the smell, Mom."

"You need all the brain cells you can get for school—and if you ever let your brother, I'll . . ."

"Yeah, yeah." He pointed to the hookah stand. "And this?"

Khushi gave him an affectionate slap. "Vices are for the old." When they left to bathe, Khushi asked the women, "Where were we?" She pointed the wand at Geeta. "Are you sure about Darshan?"

"Fairly." Geeta paused. She'd already bragged about killing him to Farah and, if she were honest, she wanted Khushi's admiration, too. "Before I killed him—"

"Oh, like you 'killed' Ramesh?"

"Screw you, Farah. Before I killed him, he choked me." She gestured to her wounded neck. Farah quieted, turning on the divan to give Geeta her full attention. "I figured that he'd been the one. Same M.O."

Wonderful, she was starting to sound like Saloni mid-*C.I.D.* marathon. Farah's tittering indicated she, too, found Geeta's parlance laughable. Geeta elbowed her. Farah elbowed back.

Khushi tuned out their bickering. As she rubbed the hookah tip against her lips, she mused aloud, "It could've been both of them, Ram knows there's no shortage of rapists in the world."

"And the way I see it, I killed two of them. So you don't owe Farah a favor so much as you owe me one."

Khushi's eyes sharpened on Geeta with what the latter recognized as respect. Geeta glowed. "Interesting opinion. You really killed Darshan, eh? I think I can guess, but why?"

"I doubt—" Farah started, but Geeta spoke over her.

"Because they might see no problem with 'invading our cunts,' but I do."

"Amali," Khushi called without looking away from Geeta. "Bring our guest some tea. Now, Geetaben, let's negotiate."

TWENTY-FIVE

Worm that he was, Ramesh quickly re-ingratiated himself with the locals and landed a few odd jobs. Equal parts charm and industry, he repaired bicycles and rewove chairs, served tea and wrapped *paan* for various vendors, all by feel. He accepted only single notes, but could distinguish coins easily.

Karem had not visited since word of Ramesh (*He's alive! I guess she's not a churel, after all!*) permeated through the village like a flu. Geeta wondered if Karem was upset, given the intimacy they'd enjoyed before Ramesh returned. Regardless, she was upset with Karem. She'd spent the last few nights revisiting their shared moments (to the tune of Ramesh's snoring) and now had her own grouses: he'd twice let Ramesh's blind state slip—how had he known? Still, she hoped he didn't think any *chakkar* was going on. If he was privy to the gossip, he'd know that the worm slept outside Geeta's door (on a donated charpoy) in hyperbolic public penance. Prodigal husband returns, humbled, to woo his estranged wife.

It was, to the village, a love song of apology.

It was, to Geeta, a bottomless well of annoyance.

She had yet to request a formal ruling from the *panchayat;* it wouldn't do any good currently, not with the town regarding him as a profile in courage, a testament to resilience and adaptability. She had to wait for two things: for Khushi to find a suitable Dalit candidate to run for the council as she'd promised a few days prior, and for Ramesh's social currency to drop. As it was now, people remarked at her good fortune; it was easy to fall in the dirt, nearly impossible to lift out of it. Ramesh was legally her husband, his name was still on the deed to their old home; he had a place in the village and it was with Geeta. She had no standing to refuse him.

At least she had an ally in Bandit, whose continued hostility toward Ramesh was satisfying, if peculiar. He wasn't simply suspicious as he'd been with Farah or Saloni while vetting them. With Ramesh, Bandit's antagonism was unyielding—he growled each time the man neared, and the feeling was mutual, which suited Geeta just fine. Bandit's fixed post under her bed dissuaded Ramesh from seeking entry in it. While he hadn't been so bold as to touch her yet— indeed Geeta ensured a wide berth between them in case a random movement triggered her anxiety again—his intentions of eventually rekindling their domesticity were clear. Geeta wasn't swayed by his words, but with his continued sobriety, she flinched around him less and less.

Roasting papadam aside, he couldn't cook—a defect owed to his upbringing, not his eyesight—but he prepared tea in the mornings. He stood on a chair and tightened her ceiling fan. He drew water even though it was well-established women's work. To her alarm, she'd even once found him squatting over the *sigri* stove flipping papadam for her.

"How can you tell when it's done?" she asked when he removed it from the flame. She waited for it to cool.

He grinned and tapped his nose. "I can smell as good as your dog now, I bet."

So. Could suffering turn a rotten man good? Unlikely. But could it turn him less rotten? Evidently. While Geeta didn't find herself *liking* Ramesh, she did find less to loathe about him, which, considering where they'd left off, was a minor miracle. But then: "I have to admit . . . the papad is not entirely free—I do have a favor to ask."

Of course. "What?" she said flatly.

"Do you think I could start bathing inside?" He'd been washing at the circle near the well where men often lathered in their underwear and rinsed. "It's just hard to figure out a time when no one's around. And I keep losing the soap."

She cracked the papadam in half and crunched loudly. Crumbs floated to her chest like ash. "Fine."

A concession that led to him sitting on the floor cross-legged, drying his hair while he listened to the second half of her radio program with her. (*Who knew killer whales were such mama's boys? I bet they're Indian.*) Which in turn morphed into a shared meal one night when none of his bosses—one of whom usually provided food—had leftovers. (*Are you sure there's enough? I don't want you to go hungry.*) But offering food did not mean breaking bread; Geeta had him eat outside and rinse his utensils afterward. (*Barely need to wash anything, Geeta. That was so delicious, I licked the* thali *clean.*) The following afternoon Ramesh bought vegetables from the market. (*A tiny thank-you for your feast last night.*) Geeta found chopping a bit extra took little time, cooking a bit extra took none, and company afterward wasn't painful, even if it was Ramesh's. (*Wanna know a secret? I actually don't think I lost much. I was drunk, which is its own form of blindness. I'm sober now, which is its own form of sight.*) Thus, they found themselves knee-deep in ersatz domesticity: Ramesh pleased with each minor victory, Geeta reassuring herself that she was not losing ground because she was in control of the privileges she'd extended and could withdraw them at any time. As she could with Karem, whose store she walked to one morning under the guise of due diligence.

"Hi," she said. He looked well.

"Hey."

"How're the kids?"

"Rowdy. How've you been?"

On her exhale, she said, "Ramesh is back."

"I heard."

"Has he come to see you—to buy from you?"

Karem shook his head. "Nope."

"I guess he really is sober, then," she said.

"I wouldn't be sure about that."

She squinted. "Meaning?"

"I don't trust him, Geeta."

"But I should trust you?"

It was his turn to narrow his eyes. "Meaning?"

It wasn't a simple matter of her transferring her faith in Karem into Ramesh. She didn't trust either of them. But his light implication that she was being fooled or was capable of being fooled—hell, that she *was* a fool—smarted. That, coupled with the knowledge that Karem had kept secrets from her, made her feel doubly duped.

"You knew Ramesh was blind, you said as much—I just didn't think anything of it then. Plus, you've always talked about him in the present tense; everyone else said 'hato' or 'tha.' Which means you knew he was alive. You knew where he was all this time and never said one word to me."

From the other side of the counter, Karem sighed, his shoulders sinking, and she was forced to release her pocketed hope that she'd gotten it wrong.

"No. Geeta, I swear. Okay? I saw him once in Kohra, over a year ago. Bada-Bhai called all his men over because he thought Lakha— you remember the Rabari woman?" Geeta nodded; she doubted she'd ever forget seeing the woman be slapped in Bada-Bhai's kitchen. "Well, she and their son had gone missing. We went looking for her and I saw Ramesh at the house."

Which finally explained Bandit's immediate and unequivocal distaste for Ramesh; he'd met him before.

Geeta asked, "Did she say why she ran away?"

Karem was surprised but answered readily, keen to return to her good graces. "Lakha? Bada-Bhai's wife abused her. She said she wasn't running, just hiding. Geeta, listen. I didn't talk to Ramesh or anything, I just saw him and Bada-Bhai mentioned he'd gone blind. And then he was gone again, and didn't say anything because Bada-Bhai's pretty adamant about his workers keeping their mouths shut. And I swear, this was way before . . . us."

Geeta shook her head at Karem. "Qualify it however you'd like, but you know you should've told me. Otherwise you wouldn't need qualifiers in the first place."

His sigh was heavy but he nodded. She noticed he wore his earring again. "Fair enough. Don't trust me. Not until I've earned it back. But don't trust Ramesh either, okay? He's far from having earned it."

What Karem and others—even Saloni—didn't know was that she wasn't a discarded wife tricked into forgiving her louse husband. She was just waiting for the right moment to play her hand. If she was civil to Ramesh in the meantime, it was only because, whatever else, she admired the discipline sobriety required.

"I don't trust him," she told Karem. "But it's not like he can get up to much; he's blind."

"Isn't that offensive? Having lower expectations for the blind?"

She glared at him. "We're not back to jokey just yet."

"Sorry," he said, as subdued as a castigated Bandit. "I still want us to be friends."

"Me, too, I just need some time to sort things out."

"Like how you feel about Ramesh?"

Geeta was quick to correct him. "No, but I need to be careful. I can't legally kick him out, and everyone here feels sorry for him."

Karem shrugged. "Not everyone."

"Most of them do. I mean, the guy's *blind*, Karem. You said yourself, that's rock bottom."

"But he's *been* blind. And still, he stayed away. Why come back now?"

It was not, Geeta thought as she walked back home, an unfair question. Which was why she pulled the bottle of clear rum—the one Saloni had impelled Karem to deliver—from the forgotten back corner of her provisions and tucked it near the canister of loose tea Ramesh reached for every morning. Was there a difference between a test and a trap? Maybe just what one hoped the outcome was.

Whether it was overkill or insurance, Geeta adjusted furniture akimbo, watching Ramesh as he tripped over the chair left here, the bucket placed there. He walked with the authority of someone who'd memorized and depended upon a layout, and each time Geeta saw him stumble, shame shrouded her. But the most despicable she felt was the night Ramesh asked, over their plates of potato curry, "I never expected you to trust me overnight, Geeta. And you're due a bit of revenge. So move all the chairs and buckets you want. I deserve it. But sabotaging me?"

"What?"

"I found the bottle. Like you meant me to."

"Oh. I . . ." Though she was scrambled about her motivations for her test-cum-trap, she was also mildly triumphant. "Wait, how did you even see it? You—"

He tapped his nose.

She deflated. "Oh."

"But why?"

"I—I'm not sure what I was trying to prove. That you haven't changed, maybe."

"I said I don't drink anymore, not that I'm not tempted to. That's how addiction works. I try to keep myself away from temptation because I accept that I'm powerless. So what you did . . ." Ramesh shook his head. "It wasn't kind."

"You're right."

"I understand you're angry with me. And that doesn't just go away because I've changed. I hurt you so much for so many years." His unfocused eyes swam with tears. "Sometimes I'm grateful I'm blind just so I don't have to actually face you. Cowardly, huh?"

"I—"

"I came here to make amends. But I don't think you're ready."

Surely she was a better person than this? Confusion writhed fiercely inside her and her guts felt like a wrung dishrag. She didn't want to live with him, but that didn't mean she had to ruin him, turn him back into the monster he'd been. "I—I'll get rid of it. It was wrong of me."

"Thank you, but that's not necessary. I'll move tomorrow."

His words were so sad, so surprising, so lacking in censure that it prompted more self-loathing. Instead of basking in the relief of freedom, she found herself blurting, "Why?"

"Geeta, I can't risk my sobriety by being around someone who wants me to fail."

"I don't—"

He held up a hand. "I can be blind, deaf and dumb, but I can't drink again. My sobriety is everything to me. Without it, I'm nothing."

"I'm sorry."

He gave her a rueful half smile. "It's just disappointing, is all. I was finally discovering how wonderful you are, finally able to appreciate you as a person. This past week with you has been great. It made me believe what they told us: when you stop drinking, things start falling into place."

Geeta couldn't face him. It was a pathetic day when she was a viler human than Ramesh. People changed, she knew that, they grew. She had, Saloni had. She didn't have to open her arms for Ramesh, but neither did she have to be as malicious as he'd once been. "And I shat all over it."

"I didn't say that."

"You didn't need to. I risked something precious to you, and for what? To convince myself that you're the same? More like I *wanted* you to be the same. Because then I wouldn't have to wrap my mind around forgiving you, which is something I never thought I'd have to consider."

"You don't have to. But forgiveness is a gift you give yourself. Which is why *I'm* forgiving *you* for your little trick, whether or not you ask for it."

Despite his words, a question, a request, a demand bloomed in the space between them. She felt certain about the words that fell, but as an automaton, blank and mechanical. She was performing a memorized task, one born of survival, buried upon freedom, resurrected now: "You're right. I'm wrong. I'm sorry."

TWENTY-SIX

The women were arguing. The loan officer was due to arrive in a few hours, but they were still missing two hundred rupees. Rather, Geeta and her two hundred rupees were missing. The other four women of their group had convened at Saloni's, as they did every Tuesday, to aggregate their respective funds.

"Where is she?" Saloni asked.

The others looked at her blankly.

"Well, when was the last time anyone saw her?"

No answer. Priya scratched a scab on her left elbow while Preity hunted for a strand of shed hair that was tickling the valley between her breasts.

Even Saloni's plosive sound of irritation, which signaled her displeasure and usually triggered at least minor amounts of sycophancy, did little to gain their attention. Complacent. When had they all gotten so complacent? She pointed at Farah. "You."

"What." Farah's voice was bored.

"You're always lurking around, trying to squeeze money out of her. Where is she?"

Farah shrugged. "I dunno, I've been super busy. It's nearly Diwali. I've been up to my tits in measurements and—surprise, surprise—turns out Irem stitches like she's as drunk as her dead father. The joys of motherhood."

Priya offered, "I think I saw her about a week ago."

"Where?"

"Here."

Saloni closed her eyes and tried to summon patience. "So at our last meeting, then? Where we *all* saw her?"

"Yeah."

"Thank you, Priya. As helpful as ever. Anyone seen her *since* then?"

"I mean," Preity whined the last word. "We have *lives,* you know. I'm a widow now, remember? And it's not just sitting around crying all day, okay? I've had to find ways to boost sales since Darshan's savings won't last long. It's hard work!"

"Like, *so* hard," Priya said. "Anyway, why assume something's black in the lentils? Geeta's never been social."

Preity nodded in support. "She's probably just busy with Ramesh. I hear he's been trying to win her back. Blind and still working so hard. It's romantic."

"Like, *so* romantic."

Saloni glared at Preity. "And when people thought Darshan was reformed, trying to *prayashchit* his way back into your panties? To you, he was still the same *chut,* correct?" Preity squirmed, silent, but Saloni hadn't been planning on letting her answer anyhow. "Correct. Because a *chut* is a *chut* is a *chut.*"

Farah squinted. "So then why don't *you* know where she is?"

Self-censure hadn't escaped Saloni. She, too, had not registered Geeta's absence. Habits weren't altered easily, and Saloni had long ago grown accustomed to not seeing Geeta. Their reunion had been an anomaly in an otherwise hectic rotation of housework, pottery, mothering and daughter-in-lawing. Recently added to her lazy Susan of duties was Geeta's righteous voice banging on about how to abolish casteism. After their trip to the Kohra police station, Saloni had been subtly hinting to her father-in-law that they may want a Dalit on the village council, as per the quota.

Meanwhile, as preparations escalated for her annual Diwali-cum–New Year's party, she went about town, squandering her best eat-shit-and-die glares on that *chut* Ramesh wherever she saw him working—not that he was aware of her venom. But Geeta . . . well, excuses and assholes being common to all, at the end of the day, Saloni had known The Chut was sniffing around and still she'd failed to check in on her friend.

It'd been many years since she'd thought of her personal sobriquet for Ramesh, longer since she'd had to use it. Early on, The Chut had revealed himself as a Baniya—though, now that Geeta had planted the scourge of casteism in Saloni's mind, she figured stereotypes were also harmful. Fine. Early on, The Chut had revealed himself as a greedy, money-salivating miser, with the looks and morals of a male bedbug (a breed Saloni now unfortunately knew, courtesy of Geeta and her blasted radio program, was prone to something called *traumatic insemination,* an adjective Saloni also felt after image-searching on Arhaan's computer).

At first, when Ramesh's interest in Geeta had proved exclusive and absolute, Saloni had been pleased; her friend deserved a man with steadfast eyeballs. It seemed Ramesh wasn't invested in looks, and Saloni's pretty head (it wasn't vain if it was *true*) hadn't budged his. But, while The Chut's crotch wasn't greedy, his pockets sure as hell were. Geeta's allure wasn't in being a kind, funny, intelligent young woman, it was her status as the only daughter of a family with some material possessions and no male heir.

No sooner had Geeta's parents sent out the wedding invitations than The Chut & Co. (as Saloni dubbed him and his avaricious family of like-minded bedbugs) surged their dowry demands. The Chut swore his devotion to Geeta, lying about refusing a dowry; the Co. meanwhile gouged her parents for a scooter, gold jewelry, furniture, kitchen appliances, a television and an actual silver platter of cash to be presented by Geeta's father. Their side was to be served first at every function, with food and drink of better quality than the bride's side. Prostrated over a barrel of dishonor, Geeta's parents relented on each demand—moving money, calling in debts and favors, signing over their house, taking on outrageous loans. They had no choice; the invitations had already been delivered. If the wedding was canceled, Geeta's name would be mixed with dirt. And, as she was to spend a lifetime with The Chut & Co., Geeta's parents swore Saloni to secrecy. There was no sense, they said, in Geeta entering her marital home with resentment. This is what parents did for their children, Geeta's mother assured Saloni as she removed her own wedding jewelry to be weighed and pawned. And they did it gladly. It wasn't sacrifice, not when it was your child.

*Bull*shit, Saloni had seethed. Bull*shit*. Parents' dreams were too myopic—they clasped their hands and prayed to get through their daughter's wedding. *If we can just get her married, everything will be all right.* No one bothered with the question Saloni found frantically obvious: if they were a pack of shameless extortionists pre-wedding, what kind of in-laws would they be afterward? Try naming a village that hadn't seen a new bride burned alive when retroactive dowry demands weren't met. No, Geeta would never be safe in that household.

So Saloni had tried, without breaking the promise she'd made to the people whose salt she'd eaten most of her life, to guide Geeta toward seeing The Chut & Co. for what they were: the bowels of outdated Indian society, terrorizing others by wielding the two penises that The Chut's mother had happened to expel from her smug womb, all under the guise of tradition. But one fucking papadam had Geeta in rosy horse blinkers. As blind as The Chut was now.

An unwelcome thought: what if history was repeating itself?

"Oh, fuck no," Saloni announced aloud to the befuddled loan group. "Farah, come with me."

"Where? Why?"

"We're gonna check on Geeta."

"But I don't *care* about Geeta," Farah whined. "Take one of them." She pointed to the twins.

"Need I remind you how much Geeta has done for you? For *all* of you? The least you can do is come with me."

Farah walked, Saloni stomped. Despite having far less heft, Farah struggled to keep pace. Saloni's face, fair enough to flush, was thunderous, brooking no patience for pleasantries, but she was still a well-known village figure: the daughter-in-law of the *sarpanch* and a member of the council herself. "Ram Ram," every passerby greeted her. And to each passerby, Saloni muttered a hurried "Ram Ram."

Huffing as they neared, a thought occurred to Farah. "We can't show up empty-handed! Should we get a gourd?"

"Now is not the time for a fucking gourd."

"Oof, fine. You really don't like him, huh?"

"He's a terrible, terrible man."

Farah scoffed. "He's got some competition in this village."

Saloni shook her head. "No, I mean it. He's—he's . . . I don't have the words."

"Are you okay?"

Saloni knocked on Geeta's door, noting grimly that the charpoy The Chut had been heroically sleeping on was no longer outside. "I dunno. Ask me in two minutes."

Geeta answered quickly, to Saloni's surprise. Though what had she expected, Geeta bound and gagged?

"Oh, shit! Is it Tuesday?" She appeared hale, if alarmed. No visible bruises, Saloni catalogued. No marks on her arms or face, or hidden by hair that was combed but loose, not in her typical severe bun. That material difference impelled Saloni to notice others.

"What," Saloni said, "the fuck are you wearing?"

Geeta looked down at her orange sari. "Ramesh got it for me."

"Not that. This." Saloni tapped her own nose ring.

"Oh." Geeta's hand fluttered to cover her nostril. Ramesh

appeared behind her, cane in hand. A wave of loathing swept over Saloni, leaving her breathless. Dizziness pixelated her vision and her chest felt like a very fat man was squatting on it. When her eyes finally cleared, Farah was giving her a curious look.

"Geeta? Who is it?"

"Namaskar, goat fucker," Saloni greeted pleasantly.

Ramesh scowled. "Saloni. Geeta, I thought you said you weren't friends anymore."

"Oh," Geeta faltered with a timid deference Saloni ironically wanted to slap off of her. "I—we—it—"

"We *weren't*, an oversight we recently fixed. And I see you've made changes, too," Saloni said. "Orange still isn't her color, duffer, not that I'd expect blindness to improve your fuck-all taste."

Ramesh narrowed his eyes, his gaze unfocused but nonetheless hostile. "I wish I could say I've missed you, Saloni. But I'm no liar."

"Since when?" Saloni snorted. "Why are you here? Other than to ruin Geeta all over again."

"Ruin her? How, by giving her jewelry? Why shouldn't she wear it? She's not a widow, she doesn't have to dress like a martyr."

"You have to admit," Farah whispered, "she does look way better." She drew closer to Geeta and squinted. "Did you *exfoliate*?"

"Shut up," Saloni told Farah without tearing her eyes away from Geeta. "I need to talk to you. Alone."

"Anything you can say to her, you can say to me."

"Geeta?" Saloni implored. "Please?"

Geeta's voice was calm as she told Ramesh, "It's almost noon, you need to go to the tea stand anyway. I'll be fine." Saloni's fear intensified. Geeta didn't harbor actual tenderness for The Prodigal Chut, did she?

Ramesh left with a sigh, cane tapping.

Saloni sang after him, "*Aavjo*, goat fucker."

"*Aavjo*, you fat shrew."

Still on the doorstep, Saloni then noticed the quiet. "Where's your dog?"

Geeta fiddled with her earlobe. "Oh, he . . . Well, Bandit and Ramesh don't get along, so I only let him in when Ramesh is away."

Saloni's hand gestured from Geeta's head to her feet. "All this for a blind asshole?"

"It's for *me*. What, I'm not allowed to look nice? You and the twins were the ones who said I was a disaster."

Saloni craned her neck to peer inside. Geeta's desk was gone, replaced by the charpoy. "Is that jackass sleeping in here? With you?"

"Only since it's gotten colder."

"Where's your desk?"

"Everything is fine. It's different this time, trust me," Geeta said, still standing in the doorway. "Listen, sorry I missed the meeting. I'll give you the money, but I may as well tell you now: I don't need to be in the loan group anymore. Ramesh is working and he said he'd like to support my business. He's trying to make amends so . . ."

"So . . . *what?*" Saloni echoed nastily.

"I'll pay what I owe, and then I'll be leaving the loan group."

Farah asked, "Without the loans, how will you grow your business?"

"Ramesh will invest in the business, interest free. It makes far more sense than a loan."

"Tell me you see it," Saloni demanded. "He's doing it again."

Geeta's denial was swift and adamant. Her hair swung as she shook her head. "Not true. He hasn't touched me once. I didn't want to believe it either, but I think he's changed. He's trying to make amends for what he did. And honestly, don't I deserve to let him after what he did? I deserve his money, his apologies, all of it."

Saloni ticked her fingers. "He's isolating you again. He's taking away your independence again. No meetings, no loans, no friends."

"We don't need the loan group to be friends! Hold on, let me get you the money."

After she shut the door for privacy, Farah turned to Saloni. "See? We should've brought a gourd."

Saloni tapped her foot in barely leashed anger. She vented at

Farah rather than to her. "God, that *chut* works fast. I can't believe he's already got his hooks back in her. Now she's leaving the loan group? It's worse than I thought."

Farah's shoulders drew near her ears. "She seems happy?"

"*Che!* How can she just forgive him?"

"I mean, she forgave you."

"Excuse me?"

"Well, you were friends and then you weren't, but she gave you another chance. Why *not* him? What, you're the only one worthy?"

It was an unwelcome aperçu. "Shut *up*."

"Oi! Did you drag me here just to abuse me? I have better things to do, you know."

"Your ugly-ass dresses can wait. We're on a rescue mission here."

Farah growled, "What's your problem?"

Ramesh, herself. "You! *You* are my problem. You're a loyal-less bitch and you picked on Geeta, trapping and blackmailing her."

"I was just trying to protect myself. I made some bad choices, but I backed off, didn't I?"

"And now she's in deep fucking trouble and you're too self-absorbed to help."

"*I'm* self-absorbed? Ha! You're mental, you know that? You ostracize Geeta for years, then the minute it looks like she might be moving on—making a new friend, reuniting with Ramesh—you get all crazy possessive."

"Listen, I've known that woman longer than I've known myself. *I'm* allowed," Saloni said, stabbing her own chest. With the same finger, she jabbed Farah. "And you're not her friend. You're not a bonobo."

Farah swatted Saloni's hand away. "Why is everyone so obsessed with monkeys lately?" She exhaled vehemently, her nostrils bullish as she strove for calm. "*Kabaddi, kabaddi, kabaddi . . .*"

Saloni rolled her eyes. "Oh, shut—"

"If you tell me to shut up one more time, I'll sew your lips shut. Maybe then you'd lose some weight."

"You—"

Like children, they immediately quieted when Geeta opened the door, jewelry box in hand. "Get in here before you two draw blood."

They stood in the middle of the room, between Geeta's bed and Ramesh's charpoy. Saloni wanted to ask if Geeta had slept with him. But for Farah's presence, Geeta likely would've answered. Why had she thought bringing Farah was a good idea?

"I know you don't understand why," Geeta said, sitting on her cot as she opened the box. "But it's my choice. We're not back together or anything, I'm just letting him make amends. I'd've thought you'd be all for second chances." Saloni ignored Farah's smug smirk. "And, if I change my mind, I can always go to the *panchayat*."

"Seriously?" Saloni stopped when she saw Geeta's bemused expression. "What?"

"There was more—I thought—where . . ."

"What? What is it?"

"I had about nineteen thousand rupees in here. Now there's less than seven."

"Oh, that son of a fat bitch." Saloni punched the air in ire. Yet, if this was what it took to awaken Geeta, then she was glad Ramesh was too stupid to cover his tracks.

"He wouldn't, though," Geeta said. "Maybe I miscounted?"

To Saloni's surprise, Farah spoke up. "Okay, I was fine with you being on a dumb journey to rekindle some two-cent romance. But this? This is too much. You threatened to kill me for *asking* for money— okay sure, 'blackmailing,' if you wanna get all *technical*—but still just asking. This fucker stole from you. He's gotta go."

"How did he know?"

"Please," Saloni spat, pacing the length of the room. She kicked The Chut's charpoy leg. Her big toe stung. "A jewelry box is your big hiding spot? Any moron could find that. Any moron *did*. Ramesh has been a greedy prick from day one. And I should've told you. I promised your parents, but I should've broken that promise. They wouldn't have wanted this life for you."

"What are you talking about?"

Saloni rolled her shoulders back. "If we're gonna do this, I need a drink. Where's that bottle Karem brought over?"

"Cupboard," Geeta said, gesturing vaguely. "Maybe he took it for his new cane?"

"Yes, and maybe I'll get thin by Diwali." Saloni pointed at Farah. "You in?"

Farah refused primly, with ample judgment. "I don't drink. Plus, we have to meet Varunbhai soon, na?"

"It's not *tharra*, it's actual rum."

"Ooh." Farah perked up. "Okay then."

Saloni wasted no time with glasses. She twisted off the cap and sipped before choking. "This," she announced with distaste, "is water."

"What?" Geeta held out her hand. She gave a delicate sniff. "Shit."

Farah scoffed. "Oldest trick in the book. Plain lazy, actually."

Geeta stuttered, her hands suspended in the air near her head. "Hold on, this doesn't make any sense. I've seen him; he's sober. When he found the bottle, he said—"

"Wake up, Geeta!" Farah snapped, smacking the back of one hand against her other palm in rapid succession. "He's a drunk and a thief. Just like Samir. The only question here is what you're gonna do about it."

Saloni surveyed Farah with begrudging respect; perhaps bringing her along hadn't been a misstep after all.

"I'll confront him about the money. We don't know the whole story yet."

"Whole story?" Saloni asked. "Okay. Fine."

Geeta sat very still, frozen and pallid under her brown skin, as Saloni spoke of the dowry. At one point, Farah, noticing Geeta's gooseflesh, opened the door and whistled. No further invitation was necessary. Like an actor in a prompt corner waiting for his cue, Bandit burst through the doorway, heading straight for Geeta's lap. She finally moved then, a small shift to hold him. She tolerated his eager tongue and damp nose, but her lack of enthusiasm was contagious

and he soon settled on her lap, paws kneading her orange sari in comfort. Saloni continued speaking, unsure whether any of her words
were penetrating. She looked at Farah, whose shoulders rose and fell,
her face a matching question mark.

"A refrigerator?" Geeta repeated, her voice so clear and cogent, it
startled the other two women.

"Huh?"

"They demanded a refrigerator, you said."

"Yes," Saloni said cautiously, puzzled. "Among other things."

"And my parents gave it?"

"Yes."

"Son of a fat bitch."

Saloni's arms rose in victorious relief. "There she is!"

Geeta's words rushed out, anger driving them louder and higher.
"He said, he *said,* so many times, that my father left us—*me*—with all
these debts. That he'd pretended to be good with money, that he'd
tricked Ramesh's family into marrying me. He bad-mouthed my
father to everyone in the village. He told me I was 'lucky' to find someone who didn't demand a dowry. I actually felt *gratitude* toward him,
do you believe that? God*damn* him! I'm such an idiot!"

Farah patted Geeta's back, the comfort genuine but still awkward
between bodies unaccustomed to proximity. "Breathe. Remember?"

Geeta nodded. She rocked with Bandit in her lap. *"Kabaddi,
kabaddi, kabaddi."* But it brought no relief. She hiccuped.

"And now that *chut* has the balls to come back for more," Saloni
said.

"I want my money back."

"We'll get it back."

As the ramifications of what Saloni had confessed landed, Geeta's
mien of rage crumbled. She buried her face into Bandit and wept.
"What's the point? My parents gave up everything for me, just to die
with nothing. And it's all my fault." When a man had a baby girl put
in his arms, he saw his name and legacy disappear, to be swallowed by
another man. His grandchildren would have to strain to recall his

family name, a name that his great-grandchildren would never know. And she had cost her father much more than that in agreeing to marry Ramesh.

Geeta looked up, her damp face bleak. "This is why people want sons."

Farah angled away. "That's not true."

"Isn't it? Is it any different than what Khushi told us about daughters?" She didn't await a reply. "All we are are liabilities. After everything my parents did for me, they died poor and hungry."

Bandit whined his concern, lapped Geeta's tears like they were sustenance.

"Geeta, it wasn't that bad," Saloni said. "I promise you. As soon as I married Saurabh, we helped them. By that time, they'd already taken on too much debt—like Runi—but they didn't go hungry. I swear." She pinched the skin of her throat.

"So you . . . ?"

"Of course. I ate their salt for two decades. It was an honor to help them."

"How did *I* not notice, though?"

"They didn't want you to worry about them. That's why they took on all those loans in the first place, to keep up appearances. And they didn't want to come between you and Ramesh. They begged me not to tell you. I shouldn't have listened. I'm so sorry."

Geeta dismissed the apology. "Thank you," she said, "for taking care of them. God, I'm such a fool. How the hell did I end up here again?"

Saloni's exhale was sympathetic. "It's not your fault. You believe the best in people. That's not a bad thing. But sometimes we go back to who we used to be around someone. We don't even realize it, it just . . . happens. He had a hold over you."

"Can I ask . . . why?" Farah said. When Saloni shushed her, Farah grew defensive. "What? Like you've never wondered the same thing? He's no Akshay Kumar." Under her breath, she added, "*Kishore* Kumar, maybe."

Saloni said, "I'll talk to my father-in-law. I think we have enough evidence to banish Ramesh, maybe even get it in writing that you're no longer married and he has no right—"

Geeta interrupted, abruptly announcing with the same dull frankness of requiring a toilet, "I want to kill him."

"Of course you do."

"No. I mean, I am going to kill him."

"Oh." Farah coughed. "Er, that's a little more—"

Saloni bent, hands on knees until Geeta met her eyes. "Okay," she said, nodding.

Farah leapt to her feet. "Excuse me?"

"She helped you remove your nose ring, time to return the favor."

Farah sputtered. "Samir was a drunk and a predator. Darshan, too. Ramesh is a total maggot, agreed, but that's not, like, a killable offense. We can't just knock off everyone we don't like. This isn't *Indian Idol.*"

"The rationale for all of them is the same: he's going to keep ruining her life until we end his, so why not?"

"Because," Farah said, agitated. "There are rules to these types of things." She floated one hand level with her forehead and the other near her chin. "Alcoholic child molester definitely trumps alcoholic blind thief."

"So you want us to wait for him to molest a child?"

"*Bey yaar!* That's not what I'm saying and you know it. You and the *panchayat* can boot him from town, but we can't kill him. You think the police are going to be okay with yet *another* dead guy in one village?"

"Weren't you the one who said that they don't get to make all the choices," Geeta told Farah, "that we get to make some, too?"

"We'll be smart about it," Saloni said, resuming her pacing. "He's blind, he's drunk. An accident waiting to happen. Maybe he 'falls' off the water tower."

Farah's head plummeted into her hands. "Ya'Allah," she groaned. "This always happens. Killers get cocky and then they get caught."

Saloni swung around, her face blooming into a smile. "You watch *C.I.D.*?"

"Religiously."

"Did you see the 'Cursed Haveli' episode?"

"Ooh, that was a good one. I love it when he says, *'Daya,—'*"

Saloni chimed in: *"Darwaza tod do!"* She laughed with Farah. "So, you in?"

Farah scoffed. "No! I have, like, seventy dresses to make; I don't have time to kill another man. But, if you want my advice, you should wait until after Diwali. That'll give everyone time to cool their brains and, you know, *reevaluate.*" Over Geeta's bent head, Farah gave Saloni a pointed look, her eyebrows soaring to her hairline.

"I won't change my mind," Geeta said into Bandit's fur.

Saloni cleared her throat. "After Diwali is better for me, too. All this party planning is killing me."

"Ooh, ooh! Are you gonna have those little cutlet things again? With the cute teeny chutney boats? Those were first-class."

Saloni nodded. "Yeah, they're *paneer,* you know."

"*Paneer?* Wow. I'd love that recipe."

"I'll give it to you . . . if you help us."

"Absolutely not."

Saloni sighed. "Worth a shot. Geeta? Are you going to be okay?"

"Not until he's dead."

"You can do this. You just have to play along for a few days, pretend nothing's changed. Then we'll figure something out. But we can't tip him off. Do you think you can do that?"

"I don't know." Geeta rubbed her face, felt her nose ring and growled. She stood to study her reflection in the armoire's mirror. Her nostril stretched as she undid the pin inside. "I forgot how much I hated this thing." After it was removed, she sneezed once, twice, then said to the waiting women, "I'll manage."

TWENTY-SEVEN

Winter caught hold and while the village's denizens, aglow with Diwali celebrations, didn't much notice, the cattle did. The November days still offered warmth, but the nights bore a desert chill. The nomadic herders came from Rajasthan, as they did every winter, sheep and goats in slow tow, and negotiated their annual contract with the *panchayat* to use the grounds on the village outskirts.

Geeta walked to their camp, dispatched by Ramesh to buy milk for the busy tea stand. He was working alone over the holiday while the owner celebrated with relatives in Ahmedabad. At the camp, the Rabari men had taken the cattle grazing, but the women remained, tending a fire and organizing the manure they'd collected that morning into cow pies for sale. When they saw Geeta approach, one stood from her squatting position and wiped her hands on her skirt. Stacks of thick white bangles decorated her upper arms, forming a funnel: the top bangles wider, tapering smaller and smaller as they neared her slim elbows. Her neck and hands were tattooed with neat rows of tiny, repeated symbols: a circle, a "Y," a star, an arrow, a diamond. At the base of her throat, a dark green ॐ was nestled between her clavicles.

Rabari women began *godna*—burying the needle—at a young age, starting with their hands and feet. Geeta idly wondered when Lakha had begun, and whether her tattoos now were a source of happy memories, or just an unwelcome reminder of what she'd lost.

As a child, Geeta had heard classmates saying the Rabari tattooed their women to make them unappealing and therefore safe from other, preying tribes and castes. When she'd asked her mother for verification, her mother had said the Rabari had no permanent home to store possessions; everything they valued or needed, they carried as they traveled. Tattoos were weightless jewelry that could never be left behind or stolen or misplaced. Geeta still did not know if either, both or neither of the explanations were true, but now the idea of certain jewelry—like a wedding necklace—being indelible disturbed her.

When Geeta greeted, "Ram Ram," the woman nodded. Geeta requested milk and the woman asked which kind. "Goat? Camel?" Ramesh had not specified and Geeta did not care.

"Whichever," she said.

Each corner of the woman's eyes housed a tiny chevron tattoo. They wrinkled as the woman smiled, and Geeta got the feeling that she was being lightly mocked. And why shouldn't she be? She was an idiot who'd learned little in the five years she'd spent scrabbling a life together. Even before Ramesh had left, her existence was a travesty: latched to a man who not only gobbled her birthright and beat her (the side effects of most marriages), but who'd dressed his theft as love, worn the skin of a somewhat principled man. For so long she had categorized Ramesh's love as ragged and defective, too late she realized it was no kind of love at all.

As the woman poured milk into a steel container, Geeta watched her strong, decorated hands work. The words flew from Geeta's mouth like trapped birds: "Do you know a Lakha, by chance? She's about our age, lives with her son in Kohra."

The woman did not stop pouring, though her brows lifted. "Family name?"

"Er—" Geeta hazarded a guess. "Rabari?"

Taking no umbrage, the woman nodded. "Not sure, but I'll ask around."

After thanking her, Geeta left with a promise to return the vessel shortly.

To say Geeta was moving through these five days of Diwali on autopilot would not be strictly true. For the past week, bouts of rage toward Ramesh or regret over her parents' sacrifices seized her at inopportune times. While Ramesh couldn't see her hostility, he could certainly hear it in her voice. His puzzled response was to be unctuously kind, which only exacerbated Geeta's fury. Then she'd check herself with a reminder that she was meant to feign ignorance, lest Ramesh get suspicious about their plan (what the plan was exactly, Geeta did not know; that was within Saloni's purview). So she'd overcorrect, dousing Ramesh in abrupt sugar-kindness as he reeled from her labile mood. The result was that they were risibly generous with each other, dividing chores (*No no, let me, I insist.*) and sharing food (*No no, you, please, I couldn't possibly.*) with a solicitousness that bordered on maniacal. Desperate for a reprieve, she suggested he visit his family; Diwali was, after all, a time to release resentment and forgive wrongs. Ramesh demurred, citing her forgiveness as an embarrassment of undeserved riches already.

The amount of bullshit that fell from that fucker's mouth could fertilize half of India.

He was, she observed, comfortable. In his position in the community and in her home. So comfortable that now he was angling for a position in her bed. He'd made a few tentative comments about intimacy and being closer to her, which Geeta deflected. Last night, however, he'd grown frustrated, grumbling from his charpoy, "I'm getting tired of begging here."

Soon, Geeta'd soothed herself, curling her body into a comma away from him. Soon this odious imbecile would be plucked from her life like a wiry chin hair.

Soon, she reminded herself now as she carried the container of milk. Soon she'd burn his charpoy and his clothes and cane. Soon

Bandit would return indoors. Today was the second day of the festival. Tomorrow would be Diwali and the following night, Saloni's annual New Year's party. Then, they'd set to work disposing of Ramesh.

Perhaps Geeta should have studied the change in herself, marveled at how she went from protesting to promulgating murder, compared the woman who'd agonized over Darshan's blood to the woman who now salivated for Ramesh's. Perhaps she should have been, if not censorious, then at least *curious* as to the shift on her sliding morality scale. But instead, it simply felt long overdue.

Though Phoolan Devi stabbed her first husband, the one who'd raped her as a child bride, she hadn't killed him. But at some point, her attitude changed and she began executing her rapists, others' rapists. With each man Phoolan killed, the bounty for her head increased. As her crimes piled, so did her lore, until she was revered and reviled in equal measure. Previously Geeta had equated Phoolan's lack of regret with stalwart courage. But now Geeta saw that her theories were based upon corrupt data. If Phoolan Devi didn't feel regret for her crimes, perhaps it was because, to her, they weren't crimes at all, simply justice.

In the village, marigolds and bunting again decorated homes, as they had for Karva Chauth, but now twinkle lights in assorted colors also latticed overhead. Many girls sat outside their front doors, outlining festive shapes in white chalk before filling them in with colored powder, to form *rangoli*s. While walking, Geeta counted several floral patterns, a few Ganesh renderings, a lopsided dancing woman holding a *dandiya* stick in each hand, and one especially wonderful peacock.

Karem's shop sold seasonal firecrackers and Geeta was positive his shelves were barren by now. The next two nights would be alive with smoke and noise pollution. Families would unfurl long strips of clay-colored firecrackers that, once lit, would fissure and sizzle for forty seconds or longer, each timed by giddy video recordings on mobile phones. Sky lanterns were also popular, though the following day the local papers were abuzz with fire incidents wherever the things landed, scorching yards and shanties and sleeping animals' tails.

Geeta paused to switch arms, the milk more cumbersome now than when she'd left the Rabari camp. Children in costumes shrieked, chasing each other. Hanuman was always a popular choice with the boys because of his extraordinary strength. Some of them donned ape masks and wielded blunt maces wrapped in cheap gold paper. She waited until they ran past her, limp tails dragging in the dust. She didn't realize she was checking to see if any of them were Raees until she knew none were. A man hopped off his ladder and nodded at her. "Ram Ram," he said.

"Ram Ram." Ever since Ramesh's return, Geeta was no longer mixed with dirt, and the number of times she now had to say the greeting rivaled Saloni. It was, she found, tiresome.

As she neared the festooned tea stall, she paused, allowing herself a moment before she once again had to pretend that she did not wish to flense Ramesh's face like halal meat on a spit.

Ramesh bustled with a confident economy of movement. He'd situated the stand to his liking, knew the tea, sugar and glasses would be exactly where he'd left them previously. He'd installed small statues of Ganesh and Lakshmi, offering them all the money he accepted from customers for blessings. By now Geeta knew that he sometimes held court, telling customers stories and explaining how he managed without sight. Two Dalit men, barefoot, approached for tea. Ramesh set to work immediately, pulling apart two plastic cups and pouring the tea. He fingered their coins, counting, while they squatted away from the unoccupied plastic chairs and sipped.

Geeta had not spoken to Khushi since that evening at her home over two weeks ago. Saloni had reported that she was making progress on convincing the council to give a seat to a member of the Dalit community, which pleased Geeta, even if she no longer required the *panchayat*'s vote, as Ramesh would be dead soon enough.

"Milk," Geeta told him. She guided the handle into his grasp.

"Geeta! Just in time!" He announced to the stall, "I tell you, not since Ram's Sita has such a wife existed!"

Geeta looked around the vacant area. The two men were laughing at a shared joke, their attention unwavering. "Yeah, there's no one here."

"Oh."

"I should return the pail."

"Okay, I'll see you at home? Our own *choti*-Diwali celebration?"

A gaggle of older men with thick ear hair and thin calves arrived for tea, sparing Geeta from having to answer with any affection. Something was amiss, itching her brain like an old name buried under new information. She concentrated but no epiphany struck, just the lingering gnaw of a missed opportunity. Frustrated, she tried to release the question as she began the return journey to the Rabari camp. Lately, all of Ramesh's words irritated her like cheap polyester. Yes, describing Sita as belonging to Ram was irksome, but Geeta's objection there was more academic than personal.

Really, comparing her to Sita was pink salt in the wounds Ramesh had reopened. Before the first domino of this entire mess tipped, before she'd helped Farah kill her husband, Karem had jokingly referred to Geeta as *adarsh nari*. The Ideal Indian Woman was, everyone from politicians to cowherds knew, Sita. But Karem's jest hadn't driven up her hackles, not like Ramesh's saccharine praise now did.

The story of *Ramayana* was especially popular during Diwali, when children dressed up as its various characters. Geeta recalled one classmate who'd refused to change out of his pungent Hanuman costume for the entire two-week school holiday. Boys had their choice of heroes: Ram, Lakshman, Hanuman, even Ravana and his ten heads. Their list was ample, but the only option for girls—lecherous vamps and old crones aside—was Sita. Beautiful, patient, silent, long-suffering Sita. A stick used to beat other women, their heads hanging in shame when they dared express *un*ideal emotions, like indignance or self-respect.

On paper, the holiday marked the end of the battle between Ram and Ravana, the triumph of good over evil. The Festival of Lights, some dubbed it, because when Ram and Sita returned to their kingdom, villagers lit *diya* lamps to welcome home their prince. But that fire was not the only fire, just as Diwali was not a happy ending, merely a happy pause. The stories we tell ourselves, Geeta realized, empty pail clanging, the stories we tell each other, are dangerous.

The *Ramayana* began when Ram was about to be crowned king but was instead banished from his kingdom for fourteen years at his stepmother's behest. His faithful wife, Sita, chose to accompany him, trading her plush palace life for an ascetic one in the forest. While the couple was ostracized, Ravana (king of Lanka) kidnapped Sita to avenge his sister, whom, Geeta thought it was worth noting, Ram had bullied and maimed. Ravana then fell deeply in love with Sita but wanted her love in kind (meaning he did not rape her). Geeta supposed it was a dark day in this world when a man received kudos for not raping, but Ravana acted with honor. Though Diwali celebrated light banishing darkness, Ravana was not a flat villain. And Ram was not an infallible hero.

Ram (with a lot of simian help from Hanuman) ultimately rescued Sita, but to her chagrin, he rebuffed her affection with icy apathy. Apparently, Ram had some trouble believing his wife had remained "pure," what with her "living" with another man for so long. The roots of slut-shaming, Geeta surmised, ran deep. Only, back in 7292 BCE, it'd been called "dharma."

While Sita was displeased at such inimical treatment, she loved Ram and wished to go home. Though she was a mere woman, she had the benefit of being privileged and wellborn, which Geeta likened to being the best player on a losing team (akin to how Khushi was the richest of the poor Dalits). Sita proved her purity by surviving a sacrificial fire. And lo! Ram's pesky, chauvinistic doubts were assuaged! Their lauded homecoming in Ayodhya then gave rise to Diwali. But evil wasn't vanquished in the battle. Evil came home with them. And the fairy tale soured.

Ram's subjects considered him a cuckold. His authority severely compromised, he exiled the by-then heavily pregnant Sita back into the woods. To his credit, he was pretty crestfallen over his own deci-sion, didactically babbling about how he'd suffer too, pampered and forlorn, ruling the people from his giant, lonely palace.

Meanwhile, destitute in a hut, Sita delivered and reared twin boys. When they matured, they reunited with Ram, who then extended Sita a mealy-mouthed invitation to return, so long as she could once again prove her purity by surviving fire. Sita, for some silly, hysterical reason (probably dignity), declined Ram's magnanimous offer and instead asked Mother Earth to swallow her. The goddess Bhumi, aware of her daughter's unhappy lot in life and her son-in-law's trifling love, promptly obliged. Behold Sita! The *Adarsh Bhartiya Nari*: the Ideal Indian Woman. Truly, Geeta thought, Sita had every reason to come back as a *churel*.

What odd damage, Geeta wondered with sudden alarm as she watched costumed children play throughout the village, were they perpetuating with these stories? Sita was admittedly a top-notch lady: levelheaded, bright, kind and loyal. But in idealizing her suffering, people justified Ram's punitiveness. An apology, for fuck's sake, would have gone a long way. But from the get-go, they trained boys not to apologize and women to not expect it of them, to instead mutate pain into an art form. It was—

"Geeta!"

She started with a yawp, nearly dropping the steel pail.

Saloni stood, fanning the heat on her cheeks. "I've been calling you. Didn't you hear me?"

"No, I was just thinking— Hey, is Aparna dressing up as Sita this year?"

Saloni looked puzzled. "*That's* what you were—never mind. Yeah, in the school play. She grew, though, so we had to stitch a whole other outfit. And Farah wasn't lying. She has no time to die, she's so slammed."

"Yeah, but *should* she?"

"Why not? It's good money."

"No, I mean Aparna. Why glorify the sexism in—"

Saloni groaned and clapped her palms over her ears. "Are you kidding me with this? For weeks, I've been chewing my own brains trying to not only convince my father-in-law to give a council seat to Khushiben, but also to convince him that it's *his* idea. *Then* I chewed the sad leftovers of my brains to figure out how to do you-know-what to you-know-who. And now you wanna boycott Sita mid-Diwali? I swear, Geeta, you have more causes than I have pubic hairs."

Geeta was too excited to remind her that Khushi wanted no part of the council. "You figured it out?" She gripped Saloni's hand in gratitude. "That's incredible! What's your plan?"

"Oh no," Saloni said, shaking her head. "I remember you at the police station; you're a terrible liar. The less you know, the better."

Geeta frowned, mildly offended. "Did you tell Farah?"

"No, she still refuses to get involved. It's fine; we don't need her. I know we said we'd wait until after the distraction of Diwali, but I just realized: *use* the distraction! Most of the town will be at my party. Firecrackers will be going on all night. It's the perfect time to strike."

"Won't Ramesh also be at your party?"

"Yes, that's why I was looking for you. At the party, you need to send him back to your place for something you forgot. I'll be waiting there—"

"Wait, but if you're not at your own party, people will notice."

"Nah, there's so much work, I'm never *at* the party. Saurabh floats around and people just think they see us both."

"Really?"

Saloni's pointed look was softened by her smile. "You would know, if you ever came."

"I didn't think you wanted me there."

"I did and I didn't. I don't know. Hard to explain, and no time anyhow. Anyway, it's the perfect alibi for me. I'm usually so busy coordinating that I barely eat, much less mingle. *You*, on the other hand, have to make yourself seen by everyone, got it? Shit, that reminds me, I have to pick up the *kaju katli*—argh! There's never enough *time*!"

"Saloni. If this party is so stressful, why do it?"

Saloni cocked her head, mouth parted in wonder. "Huh," she finally said. "It never occurred to me to *not* do it." She shrugged. "Where're you off to?"

Geeta held up the milk container and Saloni nodded. "Tell Meenaben I say hi."

"Who?"

Saloni pointed to the empty vessel. "The woman who sold you that."

When Geeta relayed the message at the Rabari's camp, Meena's lined face broke into a smile at the mention of Saloni. "She convinced the *panchayat* to agree to a better barter this year."

"She can be very persuasive." Geeta handed Meena the container.

"And she pays attention. I like that. I asked around about your Lakha, by the way."

"Oh?"

"She's from Kutch, correct? She and her family had plans to meet last Diwali, but she never showed. They couldn't get a hold of her after that."

Geeta's laugh was incredulous. "How did you find all this out so quickly?"

Meena waggled a Nokia mobile phone, her white bangles clacking.

"I can talk to her if that'd help? Next time I'm in Kohra, I mean." Geeta wasn't exactly sure how she'd manage it, but she'd concoct a plan, perhaps loiter around Bada-Bhai's house until Lakha left for an errand. "Or I can get you her address. My friend Karem knows where she's staying."

Meena thought for a moment before saying, "Take my number, Geetaben. If she wants to see her family, we can help."

"Sure, I— Hey, how do you know my name?"

Meena's smile widened. "I pay attention, too."

TWENTY-EIGHT

Farah's "art," which even Geeta begrudgingly conceded was stunning, was showcased throughout Saloni's New Year's party. Nearly every woman in attendance swirled in a new sari or *lengha* stitched by Farah's now-swollen hands. The neon trend had filtered in from the cities, and the women were swathed in glowing, fluorescent patches. Embroidered sequins and beads winked as guests circulated from Saloni's sitting room to her porch. The designer herself, however, was half asleep, propped in a corner next to a Styrofoam plate piled with untouched snacks. All of Farah's fingers were wrapped in white tape. She slumped on a wicker stool shaped like an hourglass, her head leaning against the wall. Unlike her vibrant art, she looked like death.

"Hey," Geeta said. "You look like death."

Farah blinked, too weary for a row. "I'd take dead over how I feel."

"Why don't you go home and rest?"

"No," she said drowsily, arcing a bandaged hand around the party. "I want to see my creations."

"Good god," Geeta muttered. Pinching two fingers, she extracted a hunk of Farah's hair from her *lassi* cup.

"Oh," Farah said with little interest. "Whoops. By the way, I'm glad you're not leaving the loan group. Samir was just like Ramesh, you know, he didn't want me to join either."

"Yeah?"

"Yeah. I think he was scared. We're pretty much the only Muslims here and he didn't think we belonged. And I think he wanted me to be scared, too. So I'd stay home. So my world wouldn't get any bigger."

"What made him change his mind?"

"Booze was more important than fear, I guess. Turns out, he didn't need to worry. It's not like my world got any bigger with our loan group anyhow."

Geeta nodded her sympathy. "They didn't like me either."

Despite her state, Farah's snort of disagreement was energetic. "It's totally different. You and Saloni had your thing—whatever it was—and the group revolved around your bickering. At least you were seen. Hated, but seen. I was just invisible."

This measure of honesty was, Geeta assumed, owed to Farah's exhaustion. Or perhaps the recent intervention at Geeta's home had diluted their acrimony. "Is that why you blackmailed me?"

She shrugged. "If I was gonna be excluded, I might as well profit."

Because then it turned circumstance into choice. Geeta knew a thing or two about recharacterizing events through the lens of pride. She asked Farah, "Have you talked to Saloni recently?"

"No, and I don't want to know any details. But I promise not to tell anyone. Afterward, I mean."

"Thanks." Geeta was about to leave her, but she paused. Bending, she established eye contact with Farah, whose lids were ponderous. "You'll remember this, right?"

"Remember what?"

"Seeing me here. That we talked. At"—Geeta checked the wall—"eight-thirty."

"Yeah," Farah yawned. "Got it."

Though the night was cool—Geeta had walked here in a shawl she'd since misplaced—there were enough guests to warm the air. All the doors of Saloni's home were propped wide open. Saurabh was dewy with the intoxication of being a successful host and, Geeta guessed, a few nips of the imported stuff. She'd given him a robust greeting and casually referenced seeing his wife working hard in the kitchen.

When Preity and some of the men had begun playing cards, Geeta sent Ramesh back home under the guise of coitus. It was more difficult than she'd anticipated to conjure a faux but feasible task for a blind man. First, she'd asked him to refill Bandit's water bowl. *Wouldn't it be faster if you went?* he'd not unreasonably asked. So she'd suggested meeting him there for an—ahem—private celebration. And off he scampered with his cane. Often the promise of sex was far more potent than intercourse itself.

Since he'd traipsed off on his fool's errand, Geeta occupied herself with mingling as per Saloni's instructions. She'd joined and lost a few rounds of *teen patti*. Now, upon leaving the somnolent Farah, she wandered near a snack table, searching for fresh guests to engage. *Diya* lamps and flowers decorated various plates of sweets. She pretended to survey them before wandering near the *pani puri* station, where Karem touched her elbow. He wore a black *kurta* and had shaved, which made him look younger despite the grey shot through his hair. "Geeta, can I speak with you?"

She wanted to oblige; he was a reprieve from the exhausting social rounds. She'd talked to more people tonight than she had in the last five years. But Geeta had already chatted with Karem earlier, asked after his kids. Then he'd tried to settle in for a more serious discussion, she could tell by the way his voice lowered with gravitas and his head bent toward hers. Like most of the other guests, a red *tilak* with a few grains of stuck rice decorated his forehead from when he'd been greeted.

Far more palavering was in order; Geeta had to showcase her attendance. "Umm . . ." she hedged, looking up at him. The rice had fallen from his now-dried vermillion.

Past Karem's shoulder, she saw Preity and Priya approaching, their plates empty. Priya's laughter abruptly died when she saw who was standing near the *pani puri*, and she elbowed her sister twice with urgency, whispering something. Preity's eyes widened and they executed neat, identical hairpin turns. Geeta was too confused to be offended. She'd already spoken to them, made the necessary eye contact, and checked them off her list, but she'd been hoping to parlay them into a reason to dodge Karem.

"It's important," he stressed.

Geeta laughed far too loudly, purposefully drawing attention from those nearby. She explained, dividing a millisecond of fixed eye contact between all those who looked her way: "He's just too funny! Talk about making memories, am I right? Happy New Year! Saal Mubarak!" she barked at bewildered guests as he led her outside.

A puzzled Karem waited until they were on the porch before saying, "Listen, it's about Bada-Bhai. I've been trying to talk to you all night, but you've been . . . busy."

"Busy making memories!"

"Right," he said doubtfully. "Are you feeling okay?"

"What do you mean?"

"You keep staring everyone down, demanding that they remember you." He widened his eyes and looked at her, unblinking, following her whenever she twisted her head away in discomfort. "Happy New Year!" he cawed with manic merriment. *"Saal Mubarak!"*

"I'm not that bad!"

"Then why is everyone talking about the crazy lady with the bug eyes?"

"Okay," she said, still laughing. "Maybe I'm more nervous about returning to the social scene than I realized."

"Well, it's just a party. Try to have a good time. You know, eat, drink. Maybe blink once in a while."

"I think I forgot that I miss talking to you."

He smiled. "Me, too. You look nice, by the way."

She wore a silk sari in red and green that Ramesh had presented as another gift, the funds undoubtedly coming from her dwindling jewelry box savings. Thanking him had nearly given her an ulcer, but she'd managed by imagining him dead. She'd begun to regret allowing Saloni to handle the matter alone; Ramesh would never know that Geeta had conspired in his demise. But hubris tripped lesser murderesses, Geeta reminded herself. The Bandit Queen had pride, surely, but she also had brains.

Karem's compliment left her more embarrassed than flattered. She gave her bun a self-conscious pat. Before leaving her home with Ramesh, she'd speared in an old costume pin, the two sharp prongs buried in the coil. Most women tonight, however, had lined their buns with fresh jasmine.

"You do, too. What were you saying about Bada-Bhai?"

Karem sobered. "I was in Kohra, trying to see if I could drum up some new business, and I overheard one of his goons at a *chaat* stand. He was on the phone, saying something about clearing someone's chit."

"Okay," Geeta said, frowning. "What does that—"

"Have to do with you? Well, he also said it was in exchange for getting revenge on the 'bitch who took the dogs.'"

A hot fist of dread squeezed her chest. "What?"

Karem nodded. "Exactly." It was clear he'd connected the pieces just as she was doing now: a forgiven debt for revenge on Geeta, mixed with Ramesh's sudden and inconvenient arrival. "Geeta, I'm not trying to overstep here. And I know your relationship with Ramesh is between you and Ramesh, but . . ."

"You think Ramesh came back because Bada-Bhai wants revenge on me in exchange for Ramesh's debt."

"I'm sure it sounds farfetched because Ramesh has been dry, but—"

"No," she said, chewing the dry skin off her lip. "It's not farfetched. Ramesh is still drinking. On the sly."

"Oh." Karem took a step back. "That's . . ."

"Not at all surprising?" she supplied. "I know."

Her mind chirred. If Bada-Bhai came looking for her, perhaps she could reason with him, offer him what little money she had remaining. Geeta was not too keen on the idea of having a confrontation with an aspiring don, but somehow she felt more equipped to handle him now than she would have three weeks prior. Should she get a gun? No, no, that was lunacy. Well, maybe a little one with—

Beyond Saloni's porch, a *lassi* station had been set up next to a *jalebi* maker's huge caldron. The confectioner wielded a cone of batter that he swirled in tight concentric circles. Once fried, they were dipped in sugar syrup. The result was bright orange, shiny wheels. Shaped, Geeta thought idly, like mosquito coils. Her mouth watered, which was odd as she didn't care for sweets the way Saloni did.

"Okay, okay," Geeta said, convincing herself. "It'll be fine, I'll be fine. I'll figure something out."

"Geeta," Karem said, her name a warning.

"What? You said so yourself that he's not an actual *don*, how dangerous can Chintu be?"

"Listen, if I had to guess, I'd say he's more upset about being bested by a 'housewife' than your freeing the dogs. But I'm worried that he'll use you as an example to, I don't know, make a name for himself."

For if you kill twenty, your fame will spread; if you kill only one, they will hang you as a murderess.

"Maybe we could use the police to scare him."

Karem sighed. "The same ones he bribes?"

"There's one who isn't in his pocket. ASP Sinha."

"Should we call him?"

Geeta was too aghast to correct him. "God no! She won't believe anything I say. But Bada-Bhai doesn't know that."

The *lassi* maker poured milk from a steel cup into a glass. Then back into the steel. Back into the cup. The distance between the two vessels grew and grew as he created a long foaming fountain, but he never spilled. He kept pouring, fomenting, and his dance was oddly hypnotizing. She felt soothed in a strange way, relaxed but awake, as though someone was scratching her head with long fingernails. A stressed slice of her mind clicked off, allowing a dormant portion to wake and suddenly she knew what had been itching her brain two days ago when she'd delivered milk to Ramesh.

"Fuck," she whispered, her voice nearly reverent as she set down her disposable plate.

"What's wrong?"

"Fuck, fuck."

"*Arre,* what?" Karem's forehead pleated.

"I have to go. I . . . forgot to feed Bandit. Poor guy. I'll be back."

"I can come with you. With Bada-Bhai looking for you, you shouldn't be wandering alone at night, right?"

"No, I'll take Ramesh," she lied. It was true Karem might be able to help the situation she now realized she'd spectacularly misread, but he had already helped her plenty. And she didn't want to repay him by dragging him further into danger. "Don't worry. I'll see you later, okay? And thanks—for everything."

She sprinted home, or tried to. Her party sari was stiff silk rather than her usual cotton, and it impeded her until she hefted her skirts. How had it taken her so long, especially in light of all the other lies? He'd recognized her footsteps, he'd identified the alcohol, he hadn't burned the papadam—Geeta had heard that upon losing sight, other senses heightened. Fine. But he'd known to use plastic cups with the two Dalit men at the tea stand before they'd even said a word.

"Fuck, fuck, fuck," she chanted as she ran. She passed a family unrolling firecrackers. "Ram Ram!" she greeted before resuming her "fuck, fuck, fuck" mantra. Couldn't *one* damn thing go correctly? How was it that everyone's husband was killable except hers?

She raced past some skittish cattle. Firecrackers boomed behind her. Many villagers were at Saloni's, but a few others hosted their own card parties or preferred to celebrate with immediate family. Now, after dinner, they all took to their yards or clear fields to unfurl and light the leftover *pataka*s that hadn't been used the night before. Geeta's bun loosened in its jeweled net, the decorative pin she'd placed earlier sagged. The powder she'd patted under her arms forfeited, and her sweat prickled. The winter chill had teeth but was no match for this level of exertion. Her mouth was dry and she felt queasy. She'd been so busy assaulting everyone with unwanted eye contact, she hadn't eaten. Finally, she saw her home, the overhead bulb shining inside. She sprinted up the two steps and burst through her front door shouting, "He's not blind!"

"Yeah," Saloni mumbled around the gag peeling back the corners of her mouth. "I kinda figured that out."

TWENTY-NINE

The provenance of a *churel* is a woman wronged. A pregnant woman's demise. Death at the hands of vicious in-laws or a violent husband. Dying during childbirth or within the twelve-day period of impurity afterward. Whenever a woman died grossly unfulfilled, she'd return as a *churel*. Those surviving her could attempt to stymie her transformation: bury rather than burn her, weigh her down with stones, dress her grave with thorns, set her in the ground facedown so as to disorient her. Were that she'd been given such healthy regard in life, rendering such measures moot. Nevertheless, if her revenge-lust was potent enough, she'd find her way home and so it would begin.

Men were to fear her, but their stories varied. She'd lure them to a hillside lair where her fangs drained them of all bodily fluid, semen included. She'd hold them prisoner, demanding repeated coitus until they withered. Some died, some stumbled home, grey and wrinkled, suffering a strange and sudden dotage.

A witch. A banshee. A succubus. Men who'd survived an encounter with her shared consistent details as to her appearance. On this point, the stories no longer varied: her true form was always hideous.

Long black tongue, sagging breasts leading to a potbelly, matted hair—both of head and pubic variety—and feet twisted backward.

Seeing as how this image was not conducive to sirening prey, the *churel* disguised herself. She could transform into a young and comely woman, but was unable to hide her deformed feet, the telltale mark of a virago.

Geeta and Saloni had always assumed this was a cautionary tale written by men for men. Only a man would imagine retribution wrapped in lust rather than just painful death. Only a man would morph a wounded woman into a hideous monster. Only a man would then, for the sake of phallic pride, attribute her with shape-shifting powers, so that the creature he'd lain down with over and over again was deceptively gorgeous.

But what if, Geeta thought as she stood frozen near her front door, desperately trying to think of a plan, the *churel* was a cautionary tale created by women for women? If the natural world afforded them no protection, then a supernatural story might. A way of terrifying men into considering a woman's well-being from time to time.

Geeta looked around her home: Saloni, muted and bound to a plastic chair, green eyes dark with fear; Bada-Bhai leaning in the doorway of her kitchen alcove; Ramesh lurking in another corner. Geeta would've held some hope of talking their way out of this, if not for the gun in Bada-Bhai's hand. Geeta lifted her hands in surrender, training her eyes on the revolver rather than Ramesh. She knew he must be salivating for a chance to gloat about outmaneuvering her. Idiots always expected a parade when they finally managed to be clever.

Whatever the *churel* tale's source, the bitter point was that the story simply didn't work. It hadn't stayed Ramesh's hand, nor Samir's, nor Bada-Bhai's. Men could wield the *churel* label to rob a woman of her femininity, and they could dismiss it to rob her of power. But, like everything else, it was *their* choice.

"Welcome, Geeta of Geeta's Designs," Bada-Bhai said with cold congeniality. "We've been waiting. Sit." He signaled to Ramesh, who sifted through Geeta's armoire and withdrew a sari—the orange one he'd given her. He set to work winding the nine yards around Geeta's torso and her spare chair. He walked four circles around her—like wedding *pheras*—before knotting the two free ends so tightly, Geeta and the chair jerked with each tie. Three knots to tie her to the chair now, three knots when he'd tied her wedding necklace all those years ago: the first knot representing her obedience to her husband, the second signifying her commitment to her in-laws, and the third— Well, the third escaped her distracted mind at the moment.

"No." Bada-Bhai stopped Ramesh when he moved to gag Geeta with a sari blouse as he had Saloni. "I wanna talk to her."

Geeta looked at Bada-Bhai, who was conspicuous in not having dressed for the holiday, wearing only a simple polo and jeans. He leaned against her wall in an affected air of nonchalance, arms crossed above his rice belly, one hand holding the revolver. Though his arms and legs were slim, he had the abdomen of a man who hadn't yet learned to recalibrate his diet with age. He was still in his sandals— they all were—a rare event in an Indian home. It was as alien as the rest of this interaction.

"Are you okay?" Geeta asked Saloni. A stupid question, but Saloni nodded. To Bada-Bhai, she asked, "What do you want? Money?"

"I doubt you have any. Look at this place, you don't even have a TV. Is that a *radio*? God." Bada-Bhai's mustached mouth pulled down in a sneer. "These villages are so backward. How do you people live like this?"

"Oi, I hab two TBs, okay?" Saloni said around her gag. "We aren't so behind. We eben habe sober thighs."

"What?"

"Solar lights," Geeta translated.

"Listen, you *halkat randi*, you screwed me. You took my best *tharra* supplier. You stole my dogs, my testers. And worst of all, you made a fool out of me."

"Then take the damn dog and go," Saloni garbled, spittle darkening the blouse.

"No!" Geeta shouted.

"Forget the dog. I can't have people thinking Bada-Bhai doesn't get revenge when he's been wronged. You can't be a don if you're soft," Bada-Bhai said, extracting two pouches of liquid. "So *you* two can be my new testers."

"Oh," Saloni said, perking up. "Is it vine? I vanna try vine! I'll do it if it's vine."

"He said 'testers,' not 'tasters.'" Geeta shook her head. A rabid buffoonery pervaded the situation: Ramesh picked his nose in boredom, Bada-Bhai vacillated between waggling his gun with menace and completely forgetting what it was and using the barrel to scratch his chin or tap his temple. His carelessness was almost more terrifying than if he'd been competent. "It's *tharra*. With methanol."

Saloni's nose wrinkled in distaste above her gag. "Oh. No thank you, then. Don't want."

"Oi!" Bada-Bhai set down the liquor bags and thumped his free hand against the wall. The women flinched. He shook his gun for emphasis. "This isn't a four-star hotel, you *halkat randi*s. This is revenge. You stole from me, Geeta. You screwed me. You wanna save all the dogs in India? Well, *you* can go blind instead."

"Is that really want you want, Chintu?" Ramesh asked, eyeing the moonshine. His desire was unconcealed. A true addict, unable to forgo even tainted alcohol. "A don's revenge should be quick and terrible, na?"

Bada-Bhai frowned. "So what, then?"

"Just cut off a finger or a toe to send a message—isn't that what dons do?"

"Bery nice," Saloni mumbled. Her spit had sogged the gag, further distorting her words. "Vat a hero. Some vay to treat your vife."

Ramesh told Bada-Bhai, "She needs to be reminded of her place. Look at her. In ten years, she wasn't able to give me a single fucking child." He moved from disgusted to defensive. "And you said you'd get those dons in Baroda and Surat and Rajkot off my back if I got you Geeta, *plus* give me booze. And none of that cheap *tharra* shit, got it? Imported stuff only."

Bada-Bhai squinted at him. "Listen, I generally try to avoid saying this to my customers, bad for repeat business and all, but I think you might have a problem."

Saloni snorted. *"Might?"*

"Shut up, you over-smart bitch," Ramesh hissed. "That one we can kill, BB. But I need Geeta alive. Her stupid little hobby is actually profitable, and since what's hers is mine . . ."

Geeta balked. Her priority since walking into her home had only been survival; she'd assumed if she and Saloni managed to emerge alive, Ramesh would take off again, find another city to start another tab. But surviving this only to live under Ramesh was no victory.

Bada-Bhai considered the two women. "I don't have a problem with the fat one. It's Geeta who screwed me. I vaccinated those dogs, trained them, neutered them. None of that's free, you know. And then she just let them all go. Would you believe, not even one came back?"

Geeta said, "Shocking."

Bada-Bhai loomed over her. "You button your lip, woman. Look around, you don't exactly have the upper hand here."

"Speaking of," Saloni asked, "vat's the plan here, Chintu? May I call you Chintu?"

"I prefer Bada-Bhai or BB."

Saloni's brows knitted. "As in . . . lady?"

From Bada-Bhai's erumpent irritation, it was clear he'd suffered identical misunderstandings on prior occasions. "No, not *bibi*. The letters: 'B-B.' For Bada-Bhai? Ramesh said it wasn't confus— Whatever, look, it's not carved in stone, okay? It's a work in progress."

"Understood, er—do you mind?"

"Huh? Oh yes." He unknotted the makeshift gag, which fell around her neck.

"Do you think I could go *su-su*? I drank, like, three . . ." At his glower, she coughed. "Never mind, then. Okay, what's got you so upset?"

BB pointed the revolver at Geeta, whose eyes closed instinctively. "This *halkat randi* stole from me, she took my dogs. She scr—"

Saloni nodded impatiently. "Yes, yes, Chintu, she's a ruthless whore who screwed you. So you said. But what're you gonna do with her—us—now?"

Bada-Bhai hesitated. "Well, the plan was to make her drink the *tharra,* but now . . . I dunno. Some other revenge-type stuff, I guess."

"Sure, naturally, but what *kind* of revenge? You want money? New dogs?"

Bada-Bhai tapped his gun to his chin as he reflected. "No," he said. "I don't think so."

"I see. Then you just want her to suffer, is it?"

"Saloni!"

"Quiet, Geeta, this doesn't concern you."

"Yes," BB mused. "Yes, suffering would be nice."

"Done." Ramesh grinned. A cold sheet of fear enveloped Geeta. "Let's take a toe. Her hands make me money, so a finger won't do. Unless it's a pinky."

"Hmm," Saloni said, revealing none of the terror Geeta felt. She spoke solely to BB: "So, here's what you don't know. I'm kind of a celebrity around here. I'm on the village *panchayat* and I throw a big New Year's party every year. My husband and guests are probably looking for me right now. Something *he* should've warned you about." She jerked her chin toward Ramesh, who scoffed.

Uncertainty troubled BB's brow. "You were never supposed to be here. Ramesh promised me Geeta would come home alone." He cocked his hip and head. "Why *are* you here?"

"To poison me," Ramesh said, grinning. "She thought I was blind, so she put rat poison in my liquor while I was outside calling you." He turned his smirk toward Saloni. "You were ridiculous, tiptoeing around."

Saloni ignored him. "The point is: a search party will show up any second."

"She's lying."

"I dunno. She's dressed up for a party. Come to think of it, you all are. *Saal Mubarak* everyone!"

"Happy New Year," the other three echoed mechanically.

"If you let me go right now," Saloni said, "I won't tell anyone anything. Ramesh gets a toe, you get revenge, I get to *su-su*. Everyone wins."

BB looked more judgmental than tempted. "You're just gonna abandon her, too?"

Saloni shrugged within the confines of her constraints. "Eh, we're not that close."

BB turned to Geeta, brows slanting in unexpected empathy. "First your husband, now your friend. Your life is really shit, isn't it?"

Geeta closed her eyes. "You have no idea."

"So?" Saloni pressed. "Not to rush you, but I, like, really need to *su-su*—"

"Don't do it," Ramesh said. "She's a slippery bitch. She'll run straight to the police. If you let them go, Chintu, I'm done. I owe you money, not my life. What's it gonna be?"

BB's hands, gun included, clapped near his ears in tortured irritation. "Everyone just shut up and let me think for one damn second." His mobile rang. He answered with a barked "What? Not right now. I'll sort you two out when I get home." He hung up, his breathing like heavy static. "Goddammit! Can't get any peace at home, can't get any here."

"Lakha and your wife fighting again?" Geeta asked.

Ramesh twisted Geeta's ear. The back of her earring bit into her soft flesh. "He told you to shut up."

"Who's Lakha?" Saloni asked.

Geeta answered, "The unwed mother of his only son."

BB was more curious than suspicious. "How did you . . ."

Geeta affected nonchalance. "I pay attention."

"Whatever." His surprise dissolved into exasperation. "My mistress and my wife fight all the time. About everything! Food, clothes, the children, money, money, money. And my mother just makes it worse. The doctor says she's going through 'menopause' and then I made the mistake of looking it up . . ." He trailed off with a shudder.

Ramesh sucked his teeth. "I keep telling you a few tight slaps will solve all your problems."

Bada-Bhai glared at him. "I'll just smack my mother around, is it? So that in the next life, I come back as an untouchable? Useless man." He turned to Saloni. "It's getting so bad, I hide in the toilet for quiet. They now think I have problems." He gave his stomach a vague wave. "You know, with the digestion."

Saloni, who'd clucked her commiseration while BB had spoken, said, "Excuse my saying so, but you should protect your wife over your mistress."

"On the other hand," Geeta said, "you have to protect your son from your wife."

Ramesh released an aggravated roar. "What the fuck is this? *Koffee with Karan*? BB, let me cut them and be done with it already!"

From outside Geeta's door came a clang and a bark, followed by muffled curses and continuous barking.

"Who is it?" Bada-Bhai called. From his expression, he realized his words were far too tentative and said, louder and gruffer: "Who the hell's there?" Despite the danger, Geeta rolled her eyes. Dying at the hands of this fool after killing two men and evading the police would be like the Bandit Queen being felled by a mosquito bite.

The clanging must have been a pot or other metal object—Geeta thought of Bandit's water bowl. All four of them watched the still door. Distant fireworks burst intermittently, disturbing the staid song of the crickets. It occurred to Geeta that BB and Ramesh had likely had the same idea as Saloni, to use the clamor of New Year's as a distraction.

When no one announced themselves, BB crept toward the door, moved to open it, but then must have thought better of it. He jerked his head toward Ramesh, who issued a silent refusal. But BB's bulging eyes brooked no further protest and Ramesh obliged.

"Farah!" Geeta said as the door opened.

Farah filled the doorway, puzzled and bleary-eyed, Bandit's water bowl in her hand. Bandit shook himself, a welter of droplets flying onto

Farah's sari. "I accidentally kicked this onto the dog." Then, noticing BB for the first time, she yawned and asked, "Who the fuck're you?"

"Who the fuck am *I*? Who the fuck are *you*? Never mind, I don't care. Get in here before someone sees you."

Farah finally registered the bound women and the gun and grew alert. "Er—no, that's okay. You lot carry on. Happy New Year."

Bada-Bhai pointed the gun at her. "It was not a dinner invitation. Get in here or I'll have him drag you in here."

Farah complied, hands awkwardly rising to shoulder level in the manner television taught civilians. Ramesh relieved her of the water bowl and closed the door, but not before a damp Bandit ran into the crowded room, skidding when he recognized his former master.

"You!" BB said to Bandit, who generously apportioned his snarls between Ramesh and BB. "You kept him?"

Geeta nodded. "He's a good dog."

"I dunno. He always seemed like the dumb one of the group."

"Oh! Like Farah!" Saloni said.

"Well, fuck you, too," Farah sulked.

"Tie her up. Ram Above, we're out of chairs." BB glared at Saloni and Geeta. "Did you two invite anyone else?"

Ramesh fished through the meager armoire, this time selecting a yellow sari with a faded diamond pattern. Once Farah was seated on his charpoy, he trussed her in similar fashion, tying her wrists and ankles.

"Why are you here?" Geeta asked.

"It hit me that Ramesh might not be blind. And I figured I should warn you." Her eyes tracked the revolver, which moved back and forth across the room as BB anxiously paced. "A choice I now deeply regret."

"How did you know?" Ramesh asked, his curiosity genuine. "I was pretty convincing."

"Well, I was at the party and I fell asleep. Right on the sweets table. When I woke up, I realized that the other day, when we were here for Geeta, he called Saloni fat."

"So what?" BB said. "She is. No offense."

"I prefer voluptuous, but whatever."

Farah shook her head. "But how did *he* know? The last time he saw you, you were—"

Saloni sniffed in self-satisfaction. "Devastatingly gorgeous."

Farah's eyes rolled. "Sure, fine. I was gonna say 'skinnier.' And, sure, someone might've just told him Saloni was fat—sorry, 'voluptuous,' but I had a bad feeling so . . ."

"So you came to help us?" Geeta asked.

Saloni cocked her head. "Why?"

"I was trying to be a bonobo, okay?" Farah squirmed on the charpoy, her range of motion hampered.

Geeta's lips tugged up, but Saloni simply sighed. "Well, a weapon or something would've been useful. It's like you've learned nothing from *C.I.D.*."

"Well, hindsight is almost a bigger bitch than you."

Saloni sputter-laughed. "*I'm* the bitch? You tried to blackmail Geeta, not to mention you threatened to kill her."

Farah growled. "Ya'Allah, how long are you gonna bang that drum? I'm *here*, aren't I? Let it go already."

"Enough! *Halkat randis!* I get enough of this headache at home." BB rubbed his temples. "Wait. You were at this party, too?" When Farah nodded, BB frowned, the valleys between his brows deepening. "But you're Muslim, na?" Farah nodded. "So why're you celebrating Diwali?"

"Because she's our friend," Geeta said, and saw Farah's faint smile.

BB shook his head. "Villages. I swear, if a Muslim came to *my* Diwali party, it'd start a riot."

"You worked with Karem; he's Muslim."

"That's business. Money has no religion. Now, if he wanted to marry my sister, we'd have a problem."

"And, uh, who are you again?" Farah asked.

"BB," he said.

She was bewildered. "Woman?"

"No! Goddammit." He turned to Ramesh, who shrugged. "I told you it'd be too confusing."

"'B-B,'" Geeta spelled. "Bada-Bhai. It's not carved in stone, though."

"It's a work in progress," Saloni supplied helpfully. "He's here to get revenge on Geeta."

"Because I screwed him."

Farah's eyes widened with naked, prurient interest. "Really? You two? When?"

Geeta's noises of disgust mirrored Bada-Bhai's, who dope-slapped her, umbrage pitching his voice higher. "I know why *I'm* saying *'che, che,'* but why are *you* saying *'che, che'*?"

Geeta burned, not from the insult, but the mortification of being struck like a foolish child in need of reprimanding.

Bandit loudly sniffed out his lizard nemesis, who skittered up the wall and panted, resting out of reach. He barked at the wall, ears canted back. His tail thumped so orgiastically, it was a wonder he didn't levitate. Geeta closed her eyes in parental shame. Two menacing men, one of whom wielded a gun, and her dog's prioritized threat was a reptile.

"What's its problem?" BB asked, jerking his chin toward Bandit.

"Just shoot it," Ramesh said.

"No!" Geeta shouted. "Don't you dare."

But she needn't have worried because BB looked equally appalled. "Are your brains scrambled?" he demanded of Ramesh. "I'm not shooting a *dog*."

"What's the big deal?"

"Shooting people makes me a don; killing dogs just makes me a psychopath."

"Wow," Saloni drawled. "Even the criminal holding three women hostage thinks *your* moral compass is fucked. Let that sink in for a second."

Ramesh scowled. "Fat bitch. Did you actually birth children, or just eat them?"

They launched into respective invectives, each tirade drowning the other out. Saloni's face reddened. Ramesh was so livid, his mustache nearly vibrated in tandem with Bandit's tail.

"Listen, *chutiya*," Saloni said, stamping her joined feet on the floor. "You don't know! Everything changes after a baby, okay? You don't even recognize your own body." She calmed, her voice lowering as she addressed the room. "Did you know, when my son came out, he stretched everything so much, I now *su-su* a little each time I sneeze? And that brat can't even be bothered to eat a vegetable for me."

"What!" BB recoiled. *"Che, che."*

At his vehemence, Farah nodded and joined in. "Me, too. But only after my second. I also pooped on him during birth."

"O Ram," Ramesh said, his face contorting into a dry retch.

Farah piled on. "And what about nursing? My kids just *ruined* my breasts. Like, absolute *barbaad*."

"I don't wanna hear this shit!" Ramesh threw his hands up, seeking an exit. But there was no corner of the small room where he couldn't hear. Besides which, each time he shifted, Bandit— temporarily torn from the lizard—was at his ankles.

Geeta watched as the lizard, granted a reprieve from the dog, darted diagonally toward the ceiling. It moved above her head, then Saloni's, and hovered over a rapt BB.

Saloni said, "Right? I remember back when my nipples pointed in the same direction." Out of the corner of her eye, she studied BB's reaction.

He did not disappoint. His wince was deep as he said, *"Offo."*

Geeta blinked, no longer concerned with the lizard's migration. "Wait, wait. They don't just . . . go back to normal after you're done?"

Farah chuckled, but Saloni's laugh was a honking bray. She abruptly stopped. "Shit. I just peed a little."

"No, Geeta," Farah said with exaggerated patience. "Hardly

anything goes back to normal. It's all saggy boobs and sneeze-peeing and ungrateful children."

BB was gobsmacked. "But what about the rewards? The joys of motherhood?"

Farah raised one shoulder before letting it fall. "Meh."

"What! But it—it's the best thing you could do with your life, correct?" He divided a look between them, his tone increasingly uncertain. "Being . . . a . . . mother?"

Saloni and Farah both shrugged. "Meh."

BB's voice dimmed. In fact, everything about him seemed to shrink. His face was woeful as he inquired: "So . . . you don't love your kids?"

"Tauba tauba!"

Saloni's vehemence was identical to Farah's. "You shut your damn mouth, Chintu. My kids are my favorite fucking things in the world."

"I'd *kill* for them. Happily." Farah blinked. "Oh. I guess I already did."

"But. But. You just said—"

Saloni gave him a look of reproach. "Things can be more than one thing, you know."

"So what do you think I—"

Ramesh thumped the heel of his palm against his forehead. "BB, they're manipulating you, *yaar*. Let me cut these *bhosdas*!"

Farah's eyes saucered. "Hold on, cut?" She turned to Geeta and Saloni for clarification. "Cut? Cut what?"

"But there's so many of them now," BB whined. "What use do I have for three fingers?"

"Fingers!" Farah gasped. "But I make art!"

"Listen," BB told Ramesh. "I can bribe the police to ignore the moonshine, but maiming half the village? I don't have that kind of money. How about we scar the *halkat randis*, on their faces. A reminder, so they don't mess with me. A message to others not to mess with me. That's small enough to pay the cops off. I think."

"Fine," Ramesh said. "Do I just slash them?"

As the men conversed, Farah cried quietly, her chin wobbling. Saloni shushed Farah, but her panic was not only self-sustaining, it was contagious. Bandit grew increasingly hyper, alternating between jumping and humping furniture, which Geeta had thought she'd trained out of him. As Ramesh and BB workshopped various messages to carve onto the women's faces, they raised their voices to be heard over both Bandit's yips and Farah's moans. "Ya'Allah," she chanted, rocking back and forth on the charpoy.

"Farah! Shut *up!*" Saloni hissed.

"Why? Don't you understand? Things are never going to be okay because for every Samir we handle, there are fifty others waiting. There's no point in clawing forward a centimeter when they can blow us back ten kilometers anytime they want."

"Farah, we *are* going to be okay," Geeta lied. "Breathe. *Kabaddi,* remember?"

Farah nodded, whispering the mantra while she rocked.

" 'BB'?" Bada-Bhai suggested loudly. "Like one on each cheek?"

Ramesh kicked Bandit away as he counseled BB, "I dunno if that has the power you want—considering how everyone misunderstands it."

On this point even Saloni agreed with him. "It isn't carved in stone and it shouldn't be carved on our faces."

"The name was *your* fucking idea!" BB screeched. "God, you're an imbecile."

"Kabaddi, kabaddi, kabaddi . . ."

Bandit—agitated by the mantra he'd heard often from a distressed Geeta, long weary of barking rather than biting, and still smarting from the lizard's evasive tactics—focused instead on less adroit prey. His teeth sank into Ramesh's ankle with a relish usually reserved for leftovers. Ramesh, who'd never held much capacity for pain, yawped in a cocktail of injury and terror, and shook his hijacked leg, hopping on the other for balance. But Bandit held fast, his eyes manic in a way Geeta had never witnessed, the black lining of his jaw glistening in the dim light. Ramesh tried to escape, stumbling until the far wall caught

his back with a reverberating thump. There he slid to the floor, breath
escaping his chest like a startled bat. The double impact dislodged the
lizard perched on the ceiling. As it soared down, it neither flailed nor
spasmed, as though serene in its prospects, confident the universe
would provide a new home. And provide it did. Rather than tumbling
the full eight feet from the ceiling, it instead found a soft respite mid-
way through the pilgrimage, a *dharamshala* in the form of Bada-Bhai's
left shoulder.

BB's squeal of disgusted shock rivaled Saloni's, whose revulsion
was vicarious as she watched from her chair, mouth agape. He jerked
and wheeled, shaking the creature to the ground, where Bandit eagerly
awaited, but not before BB's right hand seized, at long last pulling the
trigger he'd been nervously caressing since this night began.

The gunshot was, at least to Geeta's ears, deafening. Surely someone would hear the ruckus and burst in. But even as she allowed herself hope, several other resonate cracks interrupted the night, and she
knew the celebratory fireworks were still going full tilt.

Everyone froze, shocked and silent. The women's eyes darted
between each other, sharing variant expressions of the same panicked
fuck. Farah stopped crying. Bada-Bhai stared at his hand as though
someone had presented him with a disgusting delicacy and he wasn't
sure how to extract himself from the situation diplomatically. Ramesh
remained on the floor, sweating and moaning from Bandit's bite as
though he'd been amputated. Geeta's loathing for him amplified,
even as she conceded that there was an awful lot of blood pooling
near him. But Bandit had lost his puppy teeth; his bite wasn't as fierce
as all that. It wasn't until Farah gasped and Saloni cackled her joy that
Geeta realized that BB's errant bullet had found its way into Ramesh's
calf.

"You shot me," Ramesh said. Rather than accusatory, he sounded
dazed. "Why did you shoot me?"

But BB was far too consumed with his own recent trauma to
indulge Ramesh's. "Where did it go?" he demanded of the women,
who shook their heads. It was a question of utmost importance to

Bandit as well, who had taken to sniffing the floor and air with the sudden disciplined investment of a security dog. "I *hate* lizards! But at least they're good luck." He extracted the gold ॐ pendant from under his collar to kiss it. "Where were—"

Someone thumped on the front door so hard, it shuddered. "Geeta, you sneaky little bitch! I know you're in there. Come out now!"

"Oh, what the fuck now?" BB groaned. "Someone answer it." Upon realizing he was the most mobile, BB huffed his annoyance and walked to the door, gun behind this back.

"I know what you did, Geeta! A guest at my party congratulated me on the ballots. Did you think I'd just go along with it? We had a deal, you—oh." Khushi balked as the door opened. Bandit ran outside. "Who are you?"

"Who are *you*? Never mind, I don't care. Get inside."

Khushi faltered at the threshold, holding a box of sweets in one hand and a ballot paper in the other. She displayed more ornamentation than Geeta had ever seen her wear: bangles and *jhumka*s and a large red *bindi*. If Geeta had to guess, Khushi was also wearing a Farah design. The taut energy, as discernible as a foul odor, set her at unease. "Er—no, I can't. If I could just speak with Geetaben?"

"Geeta's indisposed at the moment. And now, so are you." BB brandished his gun with one hand and reached for Khushi's forearm with the other. She tried to avoid his touch, but he yanked her inside and locked the door behind them. "No, no," he told her. "Forget your shoes. It's fine."

Khushi removed them anyway.

"Tie her up," he instructed Ramesh, who rolled up his pant leg. From her chair, Geeta saw that it was a flesh wound, the bullet wasn't even in his calf. Ramesh rolled his eyes. "Fuck you."

"Fuck me? Fuck *you*! You said she was a sad spinster with no friends. That no one would miss her. Look at this—it's a goddamn kitty party!"

"You *shot* me!"

"It was," BB said by way of apology, "a regrettable mistarget."

"Look on the bright side," Saloni taunted Ramesh. "At least you already have a cane."

"Listen," Khushi said slowly, standing in the middle of the room with her hands up. Geeta tried to make eye contact, but Khushi was absorbed by the revolver. "I don't want any trouble. I just came over because I was upset with Geeta—"

"Get in line. Hey, are those sweets?"

"Er—yes, but—"

BB relieved her of the box before she could finish. "Are they homemade? Never mind, I don't care. I'm too damn hungry." He pushed a large sphered sweet in his mouth and gestured to Geeta's bed. "Sit down," he mumbled.

Khushi made to sit on the floor, but Geeta shook her head while BB reached for another yellow *boondi ladoo*. "On my cot," she whispered.

"But—"

"Trust me!"

Khushi lowered herself slowly to the cot, buttocks tense, as if it might bite. She sat facing Farah, Saloni and Geeta flanking either side of the cot.

"Don't be mad at Geeta," Saloni whispered. "The ballots were my fault."

Khushi's teeth were clenched. "Not really my highest concern anymore."

"These are good," BB said, crumbs spraying. "Better than Mummy's even, but don't tell her."

"I won't," Khushi promised slowly. "Er—who are you?"

"This is Chintu," Saloni said. "He's here to get revenge on Geeta."

"And the rest of us?" Khushi asked.

Farah's sigh was morose. "We are what is known on *C.I.D.* as 'collateral damage.' Basically, we're fucked."

Rather than rejuvenating BB, the sugar made him anxious. He paced, pausing to kick the leg of the charpoy. Farah flinched. "Shit! I never should've come here. I only wanted Geeta and now I have an entire cricket team of aunties. Not fucking worth it." He tamed his mustache with his thumb and forefinger. More crumbs fell to his shirt.

"So let us go," Geeta said. "Before anyone else comes looking for us."

"Who?" BB shouted, his voice caustic and furious. "Who else could possibly come when the entire goddamn village is already here?"

Geeta sighed, prevaricating as though grappling with an embarrassing confession, while her mind raced. She needed insurance without dragging Karem into this chaos. "My . . . boyfriend may come over to check on me. I was with him at Saloni's party and since I never returned, he'll be worried."

"He'll definitely come," Saloni quickly added. "They're, like, together-together."

"What!" Ramesh turned, imbalanced by his injured leg. "What's she talking about?"

"Boyfriend? Really?" Farah muttered to herself. "I guess Geeta-ben really *is* a *halkat randi*."

"If I release you, you'll run to the police and then I'll be really screwed." BB walked to where Khushi sat on Geeta's bed and, with a desultory wave of his hand, barked, "Side!" She complied, scooting, and he sat down, resting his head in his hands. The women tried to appear as though they were not watching the gun, which had been set down on the mattress between BB and Khushi. Even Farah stopped slumping.

"We won't," Geeta said. "We promise. Look around: you have all the power here. Why would we cross you ever again?"

"This—right here—is why you have no peace at home, BB," Ramesh said. Rather than restrain Khushi as instructed, he sat on the floor to staunch his bleeding calf with a petticoat from Geeta's armoire. "You let women walk all over you. Your mother, your wife, your mistress, even three random bitches. Be a *mard* for once."

Khushi's pinky had crept toward the gun, but she froze when BB's spine straightened with umbrage. His face twisted with what Geeta recognized as fomented temper. She wished Ramesh would shut up. "Who the fuck do you think you are, talking to me like that?" he demanded of Ramesh. "I'm twice the man you are."

"I know that," Ramesh said. "I'm not trying to disrespect you. I'm trying to help you."

Khushi's steady hand was six inches from the gun.

"Help me?" BB said, his voice cold. His body had grown very still. After all his fumbling and indecision, this purposeful transition spilled dread down Geeta's neck. Questioned masculinity, she'd learned, was a dangerous gauntlet. And the resulting destruction was usually borne by her kind, not theirs. "You're nothing but a useless drunk."

"See? You've been getting angry with me all night, instead of with the bitches manipulating you. They're just like your mistress and wife. You *let* them fuck with your head and instead of doing what a man would do, you hide in the toilet."

Four inches.

BB's eyes glittered as he narrowed them at Ramesh. Menace hardened his features. Geeta heard his rapid breathing, an animal poised for attack. She willed Khushi to hurry. "No one fucks with Bada-Bhai."

"They have." Ramesh jerked his chin toward the women. "Remind them you're a man."

Two inches. Geeta was sweating so profusely she didn't think she'd ever need to urinate again. Her thighs were slick under her petticoat and she could smell her own underarms. BB's chest heaved with a fury that threatened to erupt.

"Cut them and—"

"Oi!" BB leapt to his feet, snatching the gun from Khushi's fingertips. The women wilted. Farah moaned aloud. "Traitorous bitches," he seethed. When he crashed the butt of his gun against Khushi's temple, she splayed across the bed so quickly, Geeta thought she'd simply fainted. Then the blood dripped through the springs, the soft plops the only sound in the room.

THIRTY

"Is she dead?" BB's breathing was labored as he stood over Khushi's still body. Her cheek was pressed against the cot; blood continued to pool.

Farah was crying again, her sniffles wet. Saloni had paled, her eyes trained on Khushi's blood.

"You better pray not," Geeta told him, feigning bravado. The muscles in her thighs trembled, she hoped it was not obvious. Self-loathing joined her fear. This was her mess alone, but she'd dragged three others down with her, including Khushi, whose life she'd naïvely prattled on about improving. Instead, she might've left Khushi's boys orphaned. Saloni had been right: *there are consequences to your ideas that don't land on your head.*

"Meaning?"

As her pulse hammered, Geeta aimed for nonchalance. "It's inauspicious to kill a woman during Diwali because she'll return as—"

"A *churel*," Bada-Bhai finished with a shudder. Geeta imagined a lightbulb dinging above his head. He surveyed Khushi in horror.

"That's only for women who die pregnant," Ramesh said. He'd bled through another cloth and tossed it aside with a curse.

"It's for any woman who dies of unnatural means. And *that*," Geeta said, looking at the revolver, "is definitely not natural."

Bada-Bhai waved his gun between the three of them. "Any of you pregnant?"

"She can't be," Ramesh said, pointing to Geeta. "Though Ram knows I've tried."

"How would you know?"

"Because, we haven't—oi!" His face twisted into outrage. Despite his leg, he lunged toward her and struck her hard with the back of his hand. Her head flung to the right. It had been years since Geeta had been slapped and, while the pain was certainly not negligible, what she'd forgotten was how deeply humiliating it was. Her eyes watered, she tasted her blood. As soon as her head corrected, Ramesh drove his fist into her stomach. She saw white. Her chair scrapped backward against the floor. Air fled her; she gasped for oxygen and failed. Her organs cramped and she felt dizzy.

Saloni gasped. "You asshole," she whispered.

"None of that—" Geeta started and then broke off with a wheeze. Though her side ached terribly, she could breathe again. "None of that changes the fact that you might've just killed a low-caste woman during Diwali." She jerked her chin toward Khushi's body. "She could already be a *churel*."

"Low-caste?" BB echoed, his neck swiveling. "Who said anything about low-caste? What's her name?"

"Khushi Balmiki."

Ramesh cursed.

BB gaped. "She's a Harijan? She doesn't look it!"

"Dalit, yes," Farah said.

BB looked at his hands, much as he had when he'd inadvertently fired the gun at Ramesh. He turned to Saloni, enraged. "But she came inside! She's right there, polluting everything!"

"You didn't really give her a choice."

"I touched her!"

"And the *ladoo*s," Saloni added. "You ate all of her *ladoo*s."

Bada-Bhai slapped Saloni with a movement so economical, it took a long moment for Geeta to register what had occurred. Then Saloni's cheek bloomed red with his print, her lips parted in shock. She, Geeta figured, hadn't been struck since she was a child.

Bada-Bhai grabbed a fistful of Geeta's loosened bun and yanked hard. Geeta's face jerked up. "You didn't tell me about her on purpose, didn't you? To fool me again."

"I—I didn't," she lied. "I swear. I was scared; I—I wasn't thinking straight. Please."

He released her with a growl. Dismay pooled in her belly. This man had an appetite for violence she foolishly hadn't taken into account. His temper was now titanic, mutating his face until she had trouble recognizing his formerly soft jowls. "Each one of you miserable bitches has made my life impossible tonight. With your constant yammering and your tricks and your goddamn lies. And he's right, I've let you, but no more. You think this is a fucking joke?" When Geeta was silent, he slapped her, shouting, "Answer me!"

Though it stung little compared to Ramesh's hand, it was far stronger than the patronizing slap to the back of her head that BB had meted out earlier, and fear roiled through her. She was afraid of dying, certainly, but it was a distant fear. Her more urgent fear was of pain. She'd gone a long while without being subjected to this sort of physical suffering and its return shook her. She wanted to be impervious, to be enraged, but instead only felt cowed and scared.

All those years with Ramesh flooded her, pulling her under, snatching her air. She remembered her marriage too clearly. That trip to Ahmedabad where Ramesh hadn't let her use the toilet all day. That night she'd woken to find his hands around her throat. How when they went places together, he made her walk behind him and look at the ground. When he'd locked her out in the middle of a monsoon and she'd slept on the wet concrete outside their door. How there was always just enough affection to keep her hoping for more, how it'd been easier to obey than fight, how angry she'd been with herself; if she could just behave, he wouldn't need anger. Ramesh had waited until everyone who ever loved her was gone before dismantling her. When he was done, he showed her how he saw her: small, worthless, stupid, unloved, unlovable.

"No," Geeta whispered to BB, her eyes filling. "I don't think this is a joke. Please." If this ended as badly as she feared, she hoped Saloni wouldn't blame herself as she had with Runi. She hoped Saloni would know and remember them as they'd been as girls: not only on the same team, but as the same player.

"I'm polluted!" he shouted into her face, spit landing on her cheek. This close, she saw a tic pulsing below his left eye. Like a clock, it measured the time she had left. "On New Year's, of all days. You clearly don't give a damn about your karma, you invite Muslims and *chuhra*s into your house. But some of us are decent fucking Hindus." BB snapped his fingers twice. "Do you think I'm stupid? All the *churel* legend means is that I can't kill you. It doesn't say I can't make you wish you were dead."

He nodded at Ramesh, who limped to the kitchen, favoring his wounded leg, and returned with a knife. He walked to Geeta.

"Stop it!" Saloni shouted, struggling to her feet, the lawn chair strapped to her backside. She tried to hop forward. Her eyes were wild with distress. "Stop it right now. BB! Make him stop!"

"Shut up!" BB thundered. He pushed Saloni, who staggered a few steps toward Geeta's cot, but remained standing. "You'll get your turn next. You all will."

Ramesh left Geeta to stalk toward Saloni, but Geeta knew no relief. She could read that gait. He threaded his knife tip through Saloni's nose ring. Saloni sucked in a thin breath. Geeta pulled at her restraints. Farah shook her head back and forth as though denying she was there. The blood left Saloni's cheeks. Ramesh flicked his wrist to pull the gold hoop, her nostril stretching grossly. She mewled, leaning closer to Ramesh's hand to mitigate the damage. "I'm going to pull this right out."

Geeta looked at her pinned photograph of the Bandit Queen; she'd moved her desk for Ramesh's bed but hadn't taken down the clip. It was from an eighties' newspaper: Phoolan surrendering with her gang, forehead wrapped in a cherry-red bandana. She was short, made even smaller by all the men surrounding her. Though her gaze was down, she did not look defeated. It was hard to be certain, but based on her lips and jutting cheekbones, she appeared to be smirking. Geeta inhaled.

"Bada-Bhai, there's still time to fix this. You're right: the cops are in your pocket. But our *panchayat* isn't. And you already killed one member."

"Who?"

"Khushiben. If you harm us, the council will demand justice and then the cops won't be able to look away, no matter what you pay them. Saloni's husband isn't like Ramesh. He'll never stop going after you, and he won't take any bribe. And her father-in-law? He's the head of the *panchayat*! Face it: if you hurt us, it's over for you."

"I—" BB's mobile rang. He checked the caller and sucked his teeth. He answered with a clipped "Speak. So? I'll just pay him the usual, na? What do you mean, 'she'? Shit. That ASP Sinha bitch is bloody relentless."

At the familiar name, Saloni's watery eyes met Geeta's. Ramesh lowered his knife to listen.

BB continued angrily, "Of course, only Sinha has nothing better to do during Diwali. But how the fuck does she even know I'm here?" His face darkened. "Did *you* tell— Oh, I see. I should've known. I'll phone her boss right now; he'll handle her. I appreciate the tip. I won't forget this." BB hung up. "Fuck!"

It must have been Karem. Of course. He was far too careful to actually involve the cops—not after what Geeta had told him—but he was certainly clever enough to lie to BB to ensure his departure. And he was certainly kind enough to go out of his way to protect Geeta.

"I need to make some calls and get Sinha off my nuts. Don't do anything, Ramesh. Just watch them until I've sorted this out."

As soon as BB left through the kitchen exit, Ramesh moved toward the *tharra* and ripped open a packet with his teeth. Rather than clean his leg wound, he drank.

Saloni lowered her chair to the floor, this time with the chair's back to Khushi, partially obscuring the cot from view. Her nostril was red from Ramesh's abuse.

"Where's your head, Ramesh?" Geeta asked. "How long do you think you can keep us here? You heard BB—the cops are coming."

Rather than answer, he took another pull of *tharra* and winced. "Ah, that's better. You know, BB had the right idea, putting his name on you. I think I'll add mine, too." He pulled one of Geeta's arms from the constraints and twisted it so her palm faced the ceiling. The *tharra* packet was empty; he turned it inside out to suck the plastic before tossing it.

"BB told you not to do anything. You want to piss him off further?" Saloni asked. "Besides, you touch her and you won't be able to stay. Everyone will turn on you."

He didn't look at her. "They didn't before."

On the other side of the room, past Ramesh's falcate back, Saloni's arms were free. Geeta blinked to be sure. Khushi must've quietly come to and untied them; Geeta could only see her legs, her upper body was blocked by Saloni's chair. Saloni rolled her lips inward, carefully removing her gold bangles without a sound. She bent to free her ankles. Geeta gave a small shake of her head; between Saloni's shoes and heavy dress, she wouldn't be able to move without alerting Ramesh.

Saloni said, "It's different now."

When Ramesh made to turn, Geeta squirmed, drawing his attention back to her.

"Is it?" Farah exhaled through her nose in a laugh that was not a laugh. "He's right. Nothing's changed, Saloni. Look at us. We only got the microloans because the men think the female empowerment *bhajan* is cute. Harmless. Don't you get it? We were never actually advancing; we were just being tolerated."

Ramesh stroked Geeta's arm with the knife's cold teeth. "Listen to your friend. Geeta's my wife, I own her. You, all of you bitches, are nothing but a headache. This town used to be semi-decent, everyone understood their place. What, a couple of two-bit charity loans for your hobbies and suddenly you think you're something? You only have what *we* allow, understood? If tomorrow we were to say 'no more loans,' what would you idiots do then, huh? You've fooled yourselves into thinking you don't need us.

"You are nothing without me," Ramesh emphasized loudly. He thumped Geeta's temple with his fingers in a gesture that was meant to demean and did. "Haven't you figured that out by now? After I left, you were lower than dirt. If I hadn't come back, you would've stayed that way. And once BB leaves, I'm going to teach you a lesson you'll never forget."

Geeta closed her eyes. The other women's biggest threat was Bada-Bhai, but she knew that even if BB left them unscathed, Ramesh would stay and spend his life ruining hers. He was her husband and she wouldn't be free of him until one of them died.

"Ramesh," she said, "you might as well kill me now."

Saloni gestured for Farah to come closer; Farah refused, her chin jerking toward Ramesh's back. Saloni's face twisted ferociously. Farah scooted on Ramesh's charpoy and extended her bound arms silently; as a widow, she wore no jewelry and only a thin, simple sari. Saloni leaned over to free Farah's bare wrists. While the women moved, Geeta tried to capture Ramesh's full attention. Nausea made her mouth water.

"Does a farmer kill his best-producing hen?"

"He does if the hen pecks his eyes out."

Ramesh appeared amused. "Oh? Is that what you'll do, my little hen?"

"I asked Saloni to kill you; that was my mistake. I'll do it myself. And I won't stop trying until I watch your body burn."

"You barely ever had brains, much less balls."

"I've killed before. And I didn't even hate them. Imagine what I'll do to you."

Ramesh scoffed. "Who? Who'd you kill?"

"Samir was first," Farah said behind Ramesh. She'd abandoned her sandals and, like a specter, moved toward him. He whirled, wielding the knife. The moonshine had made him sloppy; Farah sidestepped easily.

"How'd you get free?" Ramesh demanded. "Sit back down. Right now."

"No," Saloni said, jumping to her feet. He turned again, swinging the knife between the two women. "It's your turn to fucking take a seat."

"I'll cut you."

Saloni pretended to consider that. "You're going to cut *all* of us? Even if you could manage, think it through. BB will be furious with you. The council will banish you, and then how will you suck Geeta's blood?"

"The *panchayat*? You mean four men and a token bitch?" Ramesh laughed. No longer taken off guard, his confidence returned. "I'll take my chances."

"Two token bitches," Khushi corrected, carefully rising from the cot. Ramesh started. With blood staining the right half of her face, her hair in disarray, she looked every bit a *churel*. "And we don't need the council to handle you."

"You think I'm afraid of you, *chuhra*? Try it and see what happens. I'll break her legs first." He stroked Geeta's split lip with his thumb before smudging the blood into her hairline like vermillion, the mark of a married woman. "But not her hands of course."

"Where was this concern when you broke my fingers?"

"I did?" He seemed surprised. "When?"

She didn't answer, stunned. Pain had defined her time with Ramesh, it had been her moon, her seasons. That he should regard her suffering as inconsequential was hardly news, but that he was capable of entirely forgetting baffled her.

"Do you know what happens when a man dies, Ramesh?" Saloni asked. All three women stepped closer, the circle tightening. "He pisses himself."

"You'd be amazed how many shit themselves, too," Khushi said.

Farah added, "Samir did. He also begged me to help him. I thought it would be difficult to watch him die, that I'd want to leave and not come back until it was done. But I stayed for every minute. Geeta will, too."

"You're bluffing," Ramesh said, his back hitting the wall. His panic was a balm to Geeta. "BB! Chintu, get in here!"

"She's not bluffing," Khushi said, nodding toward Geeta. "We all killed Samir."

"And Geeta killed Darshan all on her own," Saloni said. She moved to untie Geeta. Ramesh, sweating and too confounded by the piling revelations, did not stop her. Once free, Geeta stood by Saloni.

"Darshan?" He reared back. His balance was unsteady.

"Yes," Geeta said. "I beat his brains in. I wish they'd been yours."

"Bitch!" He lunged forward sloppily, but forgot his leg, which gave out, and Geeta evaded his grip easily. With a flattened foot, she shoved his wound. As he fell, he yawped, half in pain, half in fury.

"He's not answering," BB said as he returned from the back door. "That Sinha bitch will probably be here in half an—" He halted upon surveying the tableau. "Are you fucking kidding me, Ramesh? Three tied, one half dead, and you *still* managed to fuck up?"

Ramesh was on the floor, cradling his injury. Between Geeta aggravating the wound and the alcohol thinning his blood, a fresh torrent quickly stained through the petticoat he'd tied as a tourniquet. "It's not my fault! These bitches are murderers, BB."

"Then maybe I should hire them instead!" BB hollered, lifting his gun. The women instinctively raised their hands. "You go on about being a man when you're a quarter of a *mard*. Fuck! Look at them: they're just women, not murderers."

"Actually we are," Geeta said. "It's become sort of a side business. Wives who'd prefer to be widows."

"You couldn't," he scoffed. "How would you even? You're a bunch of housewives, not dons."

His words roused her temper. "Exactly, we're a bunch of house-wives. We make your food, we watch your children, we hear your business. We know your lives well enough to ruin them. So I'd be careful."

"My wife would never—"

"Would Lakha?"

BB's face slackened. Geeta spoke over his sputtering. "I told you: I pay attention. You keep calling her your mistress, but she's not, is she? More like your prisoner. Remember when she nearly ran away? No, no—don't worry about how I know that. Worry about if she decides to take a different approach. You don't think her life would be better without you and your shrew wife? You don't think she wishes you were dead so she and her son could be free?"

"Are you threatening me?"

Geeta shook her head. "I don't need to threaten you; there are four of us, BB. You can't shoot us all. And despite what you think, I'm not your enemy."

Saloni said, "None of us is. So be smart enough to listen when I say I know how to help you."

BB snorted. "You think I trust you?"

"Geeta!" Ramesh ordered. "Come here."

"The police are coming," Saloni said. "You don't have much of a choice."

When BB's face contorted, she added, "Listen, Chintu, you're thinking one step ahead instead of ten. What if, by the time the cops come, it's like you were never here in the first place?"

BB looked tempted, but he gestured to the room's blood and disarray. "How?"

"If you leave, we'll say this was a domestic dispute. You were home the entire night; your family will vouch for you. Ramesh hurt Geeta, we tried to stop him."

BB frowned, still dubious, but he listened. "How will you explain how he got shot?"

"It's just a flesh wound; we'll say the dog bit him or whatever. But to be safe, we need to find the bullet. On *C.I.D.* they always trace it back to the gun."

"Geeta!" Ramesh thundered. He clapped his hands twice for attention. "If you don't get over here right now, I swear to Ram I'll break your damn head."

"But if we lie for you," Geeta said, looking only at BB, "this is all over, Bada-Bhai. Swear on your son's head: no more revenge, no more threats, no more. Otherwise, we'll make your life hell. We'll get Sinha crawling all over your business. We'll help Lakha take your son. You think you have no peace now? Just wait."

"What happened to not being my enemy?"

"Make the deal and I won't be."

BB appraised the women. After all that had transpired, she couldn't believe she had the ability to hope, but there it was, beating like a wing behind her chest. *Let this work,* she begged all available gods. *Let us get out of this.* The tic under BB's eye throbbed as he weighed his anger and pride against his neck. "How do I know all four of you can get a story straight with the police?"

Farah said, "We've had plenty of practice."

BB said, "If you *halkat randi*s fuck this up and that Sinha bitch comes to my house, I will find you. And I'll bring better goons than him." He pointed to Ramesh.

Since she knew in her gut that there were likely no cops en route, Geeta's calm was real when she said: "Then we're very motivated to not fuck it up, aren't we?"

Saloni lowered her eyes with calculated shyness, her voice very quiet as she said, "You have all the power here, Bada-Bhai. Just say the word and we'll obey."

BB did not look happy, but he gave a terse nod. "Help me find the damn bullet and we have a deal."

Ramesh slapped the ground. He hissed like a spurned goose, "You can act all high and mighty with your bitch friends around, Geeta, but the minute they leave, I'll make you pay for this."

Geeta finally looked down at his pathetic form. "Does your thick head really not understand, Ramesh? I will never, ever live with you again. You will never, ever steal from me again. I'd say I'd kill myself before letting it happen, but that'd be a lie. I'll see you dead first. Do you understand? If you stay in this village, I will make sure you die."

Khushi nodded. "We all will."

"We're happy to be accessories. Like jewelry, but way more dangerous," Saloni said, her lips peeling back in a feral grin. She grabbed Geeta's broom.

"Is that supposed to scare me?" Ramesh was propped up in a corner, his leg extended. Sweat stippled his forehead as he gripped his knife tighter.

"Yes," Farah said encouragingly, as though he were a student who'd finally recited the correct answer.

"BB, give me the gun," he snarled. But BB was across the room near Geeta, bent at the waist as he searched.

"I should mention there's more of us," Saloni said casually, sweeping the floor for the bullet. "Preity and Priya will be happy to help."

"The twins?"

"Who do you think wanted Darshan dead?"

"O Ram," BB muttered as he looked. "No man is safe in this village."

"You're all insane." Ramesh studied Geeta, hunting for a weakness to rip wider. She kept her face placid.

"Hardly," Farah said, kneeling to check under Geeta's cot. "We never killed anyone who didn't deserve it."

"Why did they deserve it?" Ramesh demanded, the jut of his chin belligerent. "Just because you thought so?"

"They were molesting children," Khushi said. "They deserved far worse than death."

Ramesh quieted. "Still?"

"You knew?" Geeta blinked, stunned. Her ears roared. "And you never said anything?"

Ramesh tried to shrug. "I mean, yeah, it's kinda fucked up, they're little girls—but what, I'm gonna tattle on my *friends*? No way. There's a code to these things you'll never understand. Besides, it's not like *I* touch little girls."

"So you're not a pervert, just a coward?"

Ramesh's face twitched in rage at the insult and he launched himself off the wall toward her, knife poised.

When Geeta pulled the gun from BB's waistband and shot Ramesh in the face, she was not reacting impulsively. Later, when the women would tell the twins the story, they'd fill in what they assumed: Geeta's instincts overcame her. She would not correct them, she would not try to explain how in that moment time was generously slow, allowing the far-reaching dendrites of her mind to leap several places as she first squeezed the trigger and then squeezed harder when she met resistance. She thought of the hanging tree on the village's edge, those young girls strange fruit. She thought of Darshan's hands on her, Ramesh's hands on her. She thought of entitlement and vulnerability, shame and lechery, justice and inequity, and she thought of how only half of these were available to her gender. She thought of how much she hated male cowardice and the way they all protected each other and got away with it every time. So, no, then. Geeta did not react.

She *decided*.

Ramesh's head jerked to the side as though he'd been slapped. The sound cracked through the room and ricocheted, vibrating off the walls and through their bodies. After a suspended moment, Ramesh slumped to the floor.

"Oh my God! Geeta!"

BB's jaw hung loose. "What the fuck!"

Geeta offered his gun back. He warded her off.

"Oh no. I am done with this fuckery. I'm outta here."

"I mean, you did shoot him first," Farah pointed out.

"By *accident*. She did it on *purpose*! Bitch is already a *churel*!"

Ramesh lay supine, legs splayed out, head turned away from them. Blood spread around his head in a dark corona. It would be, Geeta knew, a bear to clean.

"Is he, like, dead?" Farah asked, looking to Khushi.

"We should check," Khushi agreed, looking to Geeta.

Geeta looked to Saloni, who conceded with a growl. As she

squatted near Ramesh, her fingers on his neck, she muttered, "I don't like how this is just my job by default now. His pulse is slow but, yeah, he's still alive."

A mixture of relief and disappointment extinguished Geeta's adrenaline. She felt exhausted as Saloni continued, "God, Geeta, you, like, blew his jaw off. Well, not *off*-off. It's just . . . hanging there."

"Mandibular fracture?" Farah asked with mild interest.

"Yeah," Saloni said. "He won't be talking anytime soon."

"*C.I.D.?*" BB guessed and the women nodded. "I should really start watching that show." He checked his watch. "Okay. Fuck the bullet, keep the gun. No way I'm getting caught in this mess."

"Not so fast," Geeta said, the revolver warm in her hand. She was willing to push her luck if it meant freedom from Ramesh. "The price for our silence just went up."

He eyed her. "Are you seriously stupid enough to keep threatening me?"

"That's blackmail actually," Farah said.

"Extortion," Saloni corrected. "I think."

"You," Geeta said carefully, "are a businessman. We are businesswomen. I think we can come to an arrangement that satisfies everyone." She looked at Ramesh's body. "And screws him."

"Why should I bother?" He looked at the gun, however, and stayed.

"Because we can help you finally get that don reputation you want so much. We won't tell the cops anything, but you can take full credit for shooting him. Twice. People won't mess with Bada-Bhai then."

BB rubbed his jaw. "That, I like. But I could just tell people that anyway. I'm a man, who's gonna believe a loan group of women?"

Geeta nodded in earnest. "Exactly. No one's gonna believe we're murderers. But you know we are. You've seen what I'm capable of." Men like him would always look at her and see the things they were glad they weren't: weak, small, timid, powerless. Let them. She'd expended so much energy vying for a broken seat at an uneven table. Fuck it, she'd make her own damn table. "But don't look so stressed.

You're going to get your number one *tharra* supplier back. Because you're not going to test on dogs anymore. Not now that you have a very willing human subject."

BB glanced at Ramesh's slack form with doubt. "He doesn't look like he'll be testing anything anytime soon."

"You'd be surprised. Monsters don't die so easily." Geeta pulled in a shaky breath. "But in exchange, you take him and make sure he never comes back here. You get our silence, your freedom, your reputation and your *tharra* business. But Ramesh never bothers me again. Have your men threaten him or cage him or whatever it takes, I don't care, but you keep him away from me. Forever. Understood?"

BB evaluated her and, for an agonizing moment, Geeta thought he'd dismiss her. That he'd leave and all their leverage would disappear with him. But then he nodded. "All right, Geeta of Geeta's Designs. I'm in so long as Sinha stays out." He stuck out his hand. "We're even?"

Geeta squinted, remembering the impotent degradation of being tied to the chair as he'd smacked the back of her head. Quick as thought, one hand darted out to dope-slap him with the humbling censure she'd seen the women use on their children. He was so surprised, his hand remained extended, frozen. She pumped it twice before he could renege on their deal. "*Now* we're even."

EPILOGUE

Geeta stood in front of the refrigerator. It was old. It would have to be; seventeen years had passed. Her in-laws could surely afford a newer model but, as it still functioned, there was little point. So it seemed her parents had chosen well all those years ago for the dowry she'd never known they paid. Geeta extended a hand to touch it and then changed her mind. Such sentimentality was, while not outright absurd, not particularly useful today.

"He's ready for you," her mother-in-law said. "Well, as ready as he'll ever be, I guess."

Geeta turned away from the refrigerator. "I won't be long," she said, hiking her purse strap higher. In it, she carried an envelope of papers as well as the day's purchases thus far: treats for Bandit, sequins Farah needed and Raees's requested uninflated balloons, which she'd give him when he and his father joined her for dinner that night.

"Of course not," her mother-in-law said snidely. "Why should such a thing take longer than a minute?"

"It's taken six years," Geeta corrected. "*He* left *me* six years ago." Her mother-in-law had aged, but then again, so had Geeta. Rancor furrowed the woman's mouth more than wrinkles. It must be difficult,

Geeta thought. To birth a son with a sigh of relief because now you had someone to carry you in your dotage, only to have that son collapse on your stooped back instead.

"You made a vow. You never gave him children, the least you could do is look after him."

A fizzle of quick anger flared in Geeta. "What, and deny you the joys of motherhood? It's a privilege, I hear."

Her expression further soured. "'Forgiveness is the attribute of the strong.'"

"I have forgiven him. In that I expect and want nothing from him," Geeta said. It was true; Phoolan Devi had spent her truncated life vacillating between terror and rage, understandably, but Geeta now knew she didn't want to live that way. "But forgiveness doesn't mean I'm right back where I started."

Geeta walked down the hall without waiting for a reply. She knocked lightly and listened for a grunt of permission. She then entered, closing the door behind her. Angled toward the bed was a wooden chair, its back ornately carved. She sat, purse on lap, and pulled out the manila envelope so as not to crumple its papers. "You're looking better," she lied.

The onus was, naturally, on her to speak first. Her bullet had shattered Ramesh's jaw and drilled a hole in his tongue, leaving him unable to speak or chew properly. The veterinarian Bada-Bhai initially took him to may have done more harm than good, but subsequent doctors predicted that, after a few years, Ramesh's range of motion might increase. The imposed liquid diet, Geeta noted as she observed the glass bottle and cup near his bedside, did not seem to inconvenience him. He'd lost teeth; she'd seen them on her floor, but the gaps were not apparent because he couldn't part his lips more than an inch.

"Bada-Bhai says hi." When he glared in her direction, she amended, "Okay, not 'hi' exactly, but he sent you a new batch. He finally dropped the 'BB,' you know, said it was too confusing." She set a few baggies on the table near the bottle. "By the way, we got approved for higher loans. Plus, Chintu introduced Farah and me to a whole new clientele. I don't *love* that they're mostly goons, but Farah says money is money, and I guess she's right. And at least no one's going blind from his *tharra* anymore. You did that. Something to feel good about, na?

"Oh, don't pout. Let's see, what else? Hey! You remember Bandit, my dog? He's a *she*! This whole time, well, I never checked. I still call him—*her*—'good boy.' It'll take some getting used to. But look at me, going on." She coughed. "How're you?"

He smacked the bedsheets for his paper pad. He was more jaundiced than the last time she'd seen him. "'Still blind,'" she read aloud from his pad.

"It could be temporary, you know," she said, shaking the bottle so he could hear her meaning. "If you tried to stop."

She read: "'Not worth it.'" She sighed. "Chintu says he tweaks the formula based upon when you can see again, but you just keep drinking it. You know it's killing you."

"'Not fast enough.' Okay then, your choice. I wouldn't mind being a widow, as you know. But you're wearing out your mother. She looks exhausted. I assume she still thinks some goons shot you because you were behind on your tab?"

He remained immobile. A puckered scar on his cheek marked where her bullet had exited, and his jaw and chin did not align properly, like a shirt buttoned incorrectly. There were, of course, times when Geeta wondered if she regretted shooting him, if she felt remorse at causing another human being such pain, especially one she'd once loved. She loved him no longer, it was true, but often the memory of love was more powerful than the love itself. For a short while that had felt like a long while, he'd been her world. But her world was bigger now. So the ruing, she decided, should be his alone. For her, regret was like sifting water; besides, she had plenty of other regrets higher on her list, such as the time she and Saloni had lost.

Perhaps there was a version of her who had the grace not to shoot, but Geeta had been forged in fire and fire shaped her mettle. This was the version of her who had survived and there was no sense in apologizing for being a survivor.

She pulled the papers from the envelope. "I do appreciate this. The advocate says that mutual consent divorces take half as long as contested ones."

He pointed at her and then brushed his thumb near his hairline.

She laughed. "No, I'm not getting remarried."

Palm up, he spread his fingers in a fan. *Then why?*

"Because our lives aren't tied together anymore, Ramesh. I've been living as a single woman for years, and I want that to be official. For me. I don't want your name."

He was motionless, and Geeta feared he'd changed his mind. If he did, she had avenues, options, but didn't relish resorting to them. They'd leave her feeling as exhausted as his mother looked. Finally, he jerked his hand in a writing motion.

"Yes." She guided his hand over the page. "Little to the left, lower, yes, now. Perfect."

Ramesh thrust one taut word through his immobile jaw. "Done?"

"Not quite. This is just the first motion for our joint petition. Later, we'll have to appear in court. Will you be up for that?"

He shrugged, but it was petulant, a child wielding his silence like a sword. She knew he could, and likely would, turn on her during the multistep process. He'd forget her capabilities and she'd have to remind him: she could always remove her own nose ring for free, rather than pay for a cumbersome divorce. The latter was a gift to him, prolonging his minor existence, allowing him to reach for the drink a bit longer, before the cirrhosis finally prevailed.

"You know," she said, stretching out her legs and wiggling her toes. "When you think about it, you got everything you ever wanted."

His brow lifted.

"You get to drink like it's your job, which it is. Your family won't buy you any, but Chintu gives it to you for free. I don't expect thanks, but wasn't that your dream?"

His eyes scowled when his jaw wouldn't cooperate.

"You never did understand irony."

He dismissed her with a flick of his wrist. *Go.*

"Before I do," Geeta said with cheer, "I'll tell you what I suspect you've already figured out: you're a rotten person, Ramesh, and nearly dying didn't change that. You were rotten for marrying me, for lying about Saloni, for letting those girls be abused, for letting your parents rob mine. Leaving me was bad, but not worse than staying. Thank you for that. I know you did it to hurt me, but I still thank you.

"I think if I were you, I wouldn't want to be sober either. It's a lot easier to tolerate yourself if you're just perpetually a few drinks in, right? Speaking of . . ." Geeta poured a peg and a half into the glass and wrapped his fingers around it.

"I know why you tried to ruin me and Saloni, by the way."

"Oh?" he slurred, more from his defective tongue than the drink. He took a draught. Liquid dribbled down one corner of his mouth, his finger caught it and brought it to his lips.

"It was the weakest I'd ever be, without her. With her around, you didn't stand a chance at making me feel small. Your failures are not my fault, but all you did was blame me for them.

"You know, everyone told me I had to work at marriage. They all said, 'You've attached your life to his, you're together now, there's no alternative, you must forgive and make it work.' An argument or a fight—or a fist—isn't the end because it can't be, not in marriage."

At Ramesh's "so what" expression, Geeta smiled.

"But I should've had the same rule with Saloni. Why didn't anyone say, 'You've attached your life to hers, you must forgive and make it work,' and all that? I'd known you for a minute and her my whole life. But still, it didn't occur to me that it was just as important to not let a fight with her ruin our friendship. Why was I so busy protecting the copper I had with you, that I destroyed the gold I had with her?

"I know, I know. 'Why are you dumping all this on me and not her?' Don't worry. I've told her, too." She dusted her hands as though having just completed a chore. "Well, I'll take your leave, then. And, Ramesh?"

When he angled his head toward where she stood near the door, she said: "You're wrong, I'm right, and I'm definitely not sorry."

Her mother-in-law was not in the common room, and Geeta let herself out without any further goodbyes. Saloni would be waiting with her scooter at the end of the alley; they'd decided to do some shopping while in the city, maybe see a film or finally track down some wine, and Geeta had kept her long enough. As she shut the door behind her, she caught another glimpse of the old, mint-green refrigerator.

Hers was much nicer.

AUTHOR'S NOTE

Though Phoolan Devi (born Phoolan Mallah) was a real person, she lived a life flooded with extremes beyond credulity, such that her legend adopts a cinematic, fictional patina. This aura of epic mythos is certainly furthered by the various adaptions of her life, some made with her consent and cooperation, others not.

Phoolan began life with a myriad of disadvantages: born poor, born low caste, born a woman. Nonetheless, at a young age, it was exasperatingly clear to her parents that Phoolan would neither be silenced nor quelled. This is likely why they married a very young, headstrong Phoolan to a man thrice her age, with disastrous results. After joining a gang of dacoits, she both committed and was subjected to a series of crimes. She eventually surrendered to the police and was imprisoned for eleven years. Upon her release, she became a member of Parliament and an activist until 2001 when she was assassinated at the age of thirty-seven.

As with any flesh and blood person, there are inconsistencies and contradictions in what was seen, what was heard, what was done. I've attempted to adhere to her autobiography and researched accounts, but there are some events that Phoolan was understandably reticent to discuss. In fact, I'm grateful she shared as much as she did with us in her autobiography, *I, Phoolan Devi: The Autobiography of India's Bandit Queen*. I was also fortunate to access sources such as *India's Bandit Queen: The True Story of Phoolan Devi* by Mala Sen and the beautifully rendered graphic novel *Phoolan Devi Rebel Queen* by Claire Fauvel. That said, any mistakes made are mine alone.

I invoke Phoolan's name and story many times throughout this novel, and while writing and rewriting those passages, I asked myself: Is this honoring Phoolan or exploiting her? The former was my intent, the latter my nightmare. I strove to draw readers' curiosity to the remarkable person Phoolan was, not use her as a one-dimensional tool to further my agency while robbing hers. She's lionized by the novel's protagonists; however, in paying homage, I was cognizant of the fact that none of us are inspired by a person's *entire* story. Phoolan is an example of an unlikely alternative, an inspiration to any woman seeking to make her own choices in a world where she is told—and her circumstances consistently confirm—that men will make her choices for her. In this way, she is a source of inspiration to this novel's characters, a group of women making their own choices.

The characters of Geeta and Farah bloomed in my mind a decade ago, when I was visiting my father and brother in India and we drove to Samadra, Gujarat, to attend a meeting of a microloan group my father was involved in financing. The women's stories of empowerment and financial agency were, of course, heartening. But I kept wondering what, in a rural area of a patriarchal country, could stop any of their husbands should they choose to exert their dominance? Loans alone did not, *could* not eradicate female vulnerability. Which led me to an uncomfortable observation: These women were mobile, but only within ambits delineated by men. Thus, this book began, but as a short story with no murder, no mayhem, and minimal mystery.

During 2020's quarantine, I returned to its brief pages and a larger world unfolded, and Saloni, Preity, and Priya joined this ragtag cadre of vengeful women. As I buried myself in fiction, I found myself craving what countless others also craved during the pandemic: joy. I found humor, albeit dark humor, creeping into the pages. While I sought to respectfully and accurately address the scourges of domestic abuse, gender/religious/caste ostracization, and patriarchy, I believed humor could act as a bolster and prevent the book from collapsing under the weight of these timely and troubling topics. What made such gallows humor possible, I think, was the resilience of women and the power of sisterhood.

The unfortunate status quo is that it is tough for women *everywhere,* and female friendships are what will carry us through the darkness and absurdity of life. Such connections, however, are not always easily forged in a world keen to divide, mark, and label as "other." I sought to address the pernicious construct of caste with the irrepressible character of Khushi. Given the book's running motif of Phoolan Devi, exploring the ramifications of being a Dalit woman in rural India felt not only organic, but fated.

Though the details and nuances differ, there are centuries of oppression and abuse in every society. Not enough is written about these struggles and deaths, and it was and is my fervent hope that this book sparks a curiosity that draws readers to narratives of the historically marginalized and creates a clamoring for more.

For me, fiction is when research meets compassion; I believe this is often why facts don't change people's minds, but stories do.

ACKNOWLEDGMENTS

I am grateful to and for:

My mother, Anjana Shroff; my father, Pratul K. Shroff; my brother, Advait P. Shroff; and the rest of my wonderful, wild family, who let me constantly pester them with "just one more question." Thank you, all.

Téa Obreht, whose love keeps lifting me higher.

My wonderful champion of an agent, Samantha Shea, and my brilliant editors, Hilary Rubin Teeman and Caroline Weishuhn; Rahul Soni at HarperCollins India; and Kate Ballard at Allen & Unwin: each of you made this journey fabulous and this book better.

My friends and teachers spread near and far, for being generous with their time, support, laughter, and insight: Elizabeth McCracken, Scott Guild, Cassandra Powers, Lucas Schaefer, Christine Vines, Teresa DiGiorgio, Dan Sheehan, Roxane de Rouen, Freya Parekh, Aashni Shah, Muskan Srivastava, Mohan Kachgal, Sara Ferrier, Ren Geisick, Serena W. Lin, Alex Chee, and Mark S. Edwards. You are all my bonobos.

The various art residencies that were kind enough to give me the gift of time and space: The MacDowell Colony, Djerassi, Jentel, The Studios of Key West, Kimmel Harding Nelson Center for Arts, and Sangam House. And the women of Samadra, Gujarat, who let this interloper observe.

Arthur T. Javier, first and best reader, dear friend and kindred spirit. This book belongs to us both.

And Devin, who had faith to spare when I couldn't manage any.